EXILE

BOOK #2 OF FLATLINE FREQUENCY

K.D. BUSTER

Flume
Creek
Press

CHAPTER ONE

"Have you received my package and proposal?"
"The large book labelled May 2027 Global Scheduled Depopulation Agenda?"

"Yes, Mustafa."

"I have the package, Abby."

"Thoughts?"

"My secretary added 475 million, how should I say, accelerated entries."

Vice-President Abby Walker paused. "Did you propose any special commutations or decelerations?"

Mustafa Muscat spilled out a bucket of range balls at the Dubai Creek Yacht and Golf Club. "About ten."

"Ten million names?"

"No, Abby." Mustafa laughed. "I'm not *that* generous. Only ten names."

"So, we're ready?"

"What about your obstacle?"

"I'm mitigating it."

"Expect a seat on The Syndicate after a successful operation."

"But ten Syndicate seats are already filled, Mustafa."

"One of my accelerated entries is Syndicate Seat Number Seven."

"Understood." Vice-President Walker clicked her ballpoint pen and admired the Cherry Blossoms outside her Washington DC window. "Then we're ready to begin."

Mustafa Muscat silently donned his soft leather golf gloves in the hot Dubai sun.

"Mustafa, I need a green light."

"Commence Operation CHAOS."

Click!

CHAPTER TWO

"Gracie, get out of Peaksville."

I carried Mom from her bedroom to our living room. "Hush, Mom."

"You're twenty-five."

"Don't be silly." I gently set Mom down on her favorite couch.

"Go live with Gloria."

"Chinese food gives me indigestion." I fluffed a pillow, lifted Mom's head, and made her comfortable.

"Go live with Gigi."

"You want me to eat raw fish?" I flipped on Mom's favorite television show. "You really are trying to get rid of me."

"Go live with the Kernan girls."

"I get nose bleeds above ten thousand feet." I brought Mom a glass of water and lined up her pills in her preferred order.

We sat on the couch and waited for the show to begin. "Mom?"

My mother smiled. "Oh, no."

What?"

"This is the part when you ask me if I miss Dad."

I wiped her forehead with a damp cloth.

"Do you?"

"This is the part when I tell you my answer."

"What's your answer?"

"Every day." Mom smiled.

"Mom, I think I'm ready to love again."

Mom's thin right arm raised to wipe my tears.

"It's been seven years, today. Hasn't it? I didn't want to remind you, I noticed the date earlier."

"Mom, why did Marcus have to let go on the waterfall?"

"Because Ryan wasn't going to let go, Gracie."

"Maybe Ryan wouldn't have slid off the rocks. Maybe Ryan was going to save Marcus. Maybe Marcus didn't have to die."

Mom wept. "Now you're going to make me cry. Don't make an old woman cry."

"You're not old."

"Well, I feel old, Gracie. Look at me. Go out with Charlotte."

I crossed my arms and leaned back on the couch. "Mom, this is our television night."

"Gracie, this is *my* television night. I'm fine. You fluffed my pillow. You turned on my TV show. You even lined up my pills. Go hang out with Charlotte."

"What if you need something?"

"Gracie." Mom smiled. "Please go out."

"Good morning Cathay Pacific 925, this is Hong Kong Departure, squawk one-niner-eight-four."

"Cathay 925, squawking one-niner-eight-four."

"925, Hong Kong, radar contact. We see you passing six thousand feet. Climb and maintain Flight Level two-eight-zero, expect higher in ten minutes. When able, turn right and proceed direct Singapore Changi Airport."

"Hong Kong Departure, Cathay 925 —"

The local controller transmitted his call with a mild Chinese accent. "Cathay 925, you were stepped on. Please read back instructions."

No reply.

"Cathay 925, Hong Kong."

No reply.

"Transmitting on Emergency Guard Frequency one-two-one point five, Cathay 925 we show you picking up a descent. Maintain level flight and current heading."

No reply.

A nearby pilot interrupted in a Texas accent. "Hong Kong Departure, United Two-three-three, I've got a visual on Cathay 925 in a descending left turn towards Lamma Island."

"United 233, copy. Maintain visual separation."

The Texan watched the NORDO, off-course Airbus. "Cathay 925, this is United 233. Level your wings and pull nose up."

The local controller reattempted. "Cathay 925, Hong Kong Departure, Radio check."

"I love your accent, dear."

Ruby Kyle smiled. "Thank you, Ma'am."

The elderly Australian couple proceeded through the Café Opera's *Land and Sea* lunch buffet line. "Canada?"

Ruby replenished the lobster tails. "Close. United States. One hour south of Canada in Idaho state."

The woman slid her tray towards the roast beef cutting station. "We hear Idaho is beautiful."

The Australian gentleman read Ruby's name tag. "What brings you to Sydney, Ruby?"

"My boyfriend, I guess."

The woman smiled. "How romantic."

"Well, actually he's a boy... That's a friend."

"Aussie?"

"No, we grew up together in Idaho."

"Crikey! That *is* romantic, Ruby."

Ruby blushed. "Are you both enjoying the InterContinental Hotel Sydney?"

The elderly woman leaned over, reached into her purse and whispered. "My 'Bruce' is treating me to an 'evo' at Opera House tonight. Here are two extra tickets for you, dear."

Ruby beamed with excitement. "You shouldn't."

"You take your boy that's a friend."

Ruby smiled. "You're an angel."

"Mr. President, good day, Sir."

President Voigt leaned back his leather chair behind the Resolute Desk. "Dr. Moriarty, you look tired."

The Surgeon General agreed. "Sir, Charity Ferguson and I have been working round-the-clock to wrap our arms around the enigmatic global health epidemic."

President Voigt unleashed his wisdom and wit. "Don't work too hard, I wouldn't want it to hurt your marriages."

Dr. Moriarty flinched. "Oh, okay, Sir. Anyhow, the Peaksville Institutes of Health is leading a cooperative meeting of the minds."

"Explain."

"The PIH has organized a tiger team of experts from Harvard, Yale, Fort

5

Dietrich Bioweapons, Peaksville State University, Walter Reed Military Hospital, and Stanford to ascertain the cause of the epidemic."

"And what have your experts come up with?"

"So far, Mr. President, we believe the global heart attacks may manifest psychosomatically responding to the first actual heart attack. The first medical episode triggers a social chain reaction of fear, emotion, and panic, resulting in multiple heart attacks."

President Voigt sighed and spun his chair around and looked outside the Oval Office.

Surgeon General Moriarty waited thirty seconds to speak. "Sir?"

President Voigt spun back around to address Dr. Moriarty. "Your experts believe that the millions of heart attacks this week are manufactured in the person's mind from watching other heart attack sufferers."

"More or less, Sir."

"Is this chain reaction theory *settled science*?"

"Our experts are exploring other possibilities."

"Explore other possibilities and get back to me."

W*ham! Wham!*
        Nineteen-year-old Jack Kernan gripped his hand pads as his Dragon Muay Thai Camp student alternated left and right punches.

"Okay great, Ricky! Let's work on some kicks."

Wham! Wham!

The twenty-three-year old tourist from New Zealand, barefoot in his white kickboxing rental gear, wailed on young Jack's hand pads with his feet.

Jack smiled. "Nice!"

Wham! Wham!

"Just like that, Ricky."

The Kiwi yelled with each kick. "Muay Thai! Muay Thai!"

"Two more," Jack instructed.

Wham! Wham!

"How did that feel?" Jack asked.

"Better than yesterday."

Jack Kernan checked his watch. "Three-hundred and sixty-five more days until the 2028 Olympics."

"Ha! I wish!"

"What part of New Zealand are you from?"

"Christchurch," Ricky said. "I'm on military leave. Up here on holiday."

"South Island. Right?"

Ricky nodded. "Right on!"

"Army?"

"Right on, again! Infantry. You're quite young to be an instructor in Phuket, Thailand. Are you from America?"

Jack nodded and handed Ricky his head-gear. "Ready for some light sparring with a nineteen-year-old ankle-biter?"

Ricky held his heart. "Give me five minutes, mate."

"You okay?" Jack asked.

"Must be the Pad Thai noodles I ate for lunch."

"Sit down here, Ricky. I'll get water."

"Dambuster 303, Atsugi Departure. Radar contact. Contact Tokyo Departure on one-two-two point nine."

The young, female F/A-18E Super Hornet quickly poked through the rancid incinerator smoke plume south of the U.S. Navy air base. "Three zero three, switching one-two-two point nine, Good day."

"Tokyo Departure, Dambuster —" The pilot prematurely unclicked her mic.

"Dambuster 303, Ah. This is Tokyo Departure. Cleared direct Okinawa NAHA VORTAC, crimb and maintain FL220."

No reply.

"Dambuster 303, Tokyo Departure, how copy?"

The Japanese controller keyed his mic, hesitated, made a sucking-through-teeth sound, then called a nearby U.S. military airplane. "Basher 5, Tokyo on 122.9, do you have a visual on a single-ship Rhino tracking one-eight-zero into the Sagami Bay?"

"Basher 5, Standby." The USAF F-35 Lightning II pilot referenced his TCAS and tactical Multi-Function Display then scanned below. "This is Basher 5, visual on Dambuster, request descent to eight thousand."

"Maintain visual separation. Descend and maintain eight thousand."

"Leaving one-two thousand for eight thousand.

The northbound, single-ship F-35 attempted to get a closer look as the southbound F/A-18E passed underneath with six hundred knots of closure.

Zoom!

"Dambuster 303, Tokyo Departure, we show you in a gradual descent."

No reply.

"Tokyo, Basher 5, cancel IFR, request VFR. Proceeding visually in pursuit of southbound Rhino. Declaring an emergency on behalf of Navy 303."

The Japanese controller keyed the mic, sucked through his teeth and replied. "Ah, Cancel IFR, proceed VFR. Maintain visual separation."

The USAF F-35 pilot from Yokota AB pulled into a vertical Immelman and rapidly reversed course in full afterburner. He joined the southbound, descending Navy F-18 from Atsugi NAB by stabilizing in loose cruise.

"Dambuster 303, Basher 5, on guard frequency, how copy?"

No reply.

"Navy Airwing FIVE Badman Base, this is USAF Basher 5 from Yokota, declaring an emergency. Dambuster 303 is NORDO and appears to be experiencing a P.E."

"Basher 5, Badman Base, copy Physiological Episode with 303, say position."

"We just passed Oshima Island heading 195 at five-thousand. Currently in parade formation. Dambuster pilot slouched forward, NORDO and gradually descending out to sea."

"Copy all, Sir."

The CVW-5 duty officer instinctively called an airborne Navy Commander. "Dambuster One, this is Badman Base on Badman frequency. You copy the previous transmissions, Sir?"

"A-firm." The VFA-195 Commanding Officer transmitted from the southern training area. "Dambuster One is inbound. Supersonic."

G loria yelled up to the flybridge. "Ryan, look!"
Ryan quickly surveyed his Hong Kong-based fishing charter boat Ben Gunn, his fifteen customers and one local deck hand. "What's wrong?"

Gloria pointed at a descending airliner. "Up there! Is that normal?"

Ryan studied the Airbus flight profile.

"Too steep?"

"Not good." Ryan nodded. "He's coming down."

"Towards us?"

Ryan rang the bell. "Li Jie. Fishing lines up!"

Li Jie quickly complied. "Lines up!"

The Airbus 320 continued its descent towards the West Lamma Channel ten miles south of downtown Hong Kong.

Li Jie and Gloria helped the passengers quickly reel in their lines and stow their rods.

Ryan started his engine and retracted the anchor.

"Lines are up, Captain Flynn!" Li Jie exclaimed with a 'thumbs up' as the A320 got closer.

Gloria ushered the passengers into the cabin.

Crash!

The Airbus impacted the choppy water, skipped past the Ben Gunn, broke into two sections, and settled one mile west of Lamma Island.

The fishing customers screamed in horror.

Ryan applied maximum throttle, aimed his eighty-foot boat towards the airliner's forward fuselage section, and broadcasted on the 1MC. "Sorry for the inconvenience, folks. Attempting to render assistance."

Gloria went to the refrigerator to hand out complimentary cold drinks. "Sit tight, everyone. We're safe and trying to help."

Li Jie translated English into Chinese on the 1MC for the local customers.

"Mayday! Mayday! This is the Ben Gunn declaring an emergency. Airliner down one mile west of Lamma Island. Repeat. Airliner down. Possible Cathay Pacific. One mile west of Lamma Island."

Gloria climbed onto the flybridge with Ryan. "Survivable?"

"Unlikely."

Gloria scratched Ryan's back. "Maybe?"

Ryan lost his baseball cap in the forward breeze. "We'll find out."

"Good morning, Mr. President."

President Voigt shuffled binders, folders, and papers then set them aside on the Resolute Desk. "Good morning, Secretary Light."

"Bud, do you have anything interesting to report from the TSC this morning?"

"What topic would you be specifically interested in, Mr. President?"

"Oh, I don't know. Maybe the weather. Maybe the Nationals' bullpen arm injuries. Maybe the beauty of Cherry Blossom Season in Washington DC. Or maybe —"

Mr. Light waited ten seconds and then spoke. "Maybe what, Sir?"

"Maybe the urgent global health crisis that is causing millions of worldwide fatal heart attacks on air, land and sea."

"Sir, I'm no medical expert. Isn't this a question for Surgeon General Moriarty?"

"Possibly."

Mr. Light interrupted the uncomfortable silence in the Oval Office. "What would you like The Safety Corps to do, Sir?"

President Voigt keyed his intercom. "Please hold my calls."

"Yes, Mr. President," the White House secretary replied.

"Bud."

"Mr. President."

"Where were we?"

"Sir, you were saying how the TSC could help Surgeon General Moriarty with the global medical epidemic?"

"Bud, I have intelligence that the heart attacks are the result of a rogue government or faction."

Mr. Light nervously stuttered. "Which rogue government?"

President Voigt shrugged.

Mr. Light paused. "Source?"

President Voigt shook his head. "Protected."

"Credible?"

President Voigt shrugged.

Mr. Light whispered. "You're implying a well-funded, massive, worldwide killing operation."

President Voigt nodded.

"Indiscriminate or targeted?"

President Voigt shrugged.

"You'd like me to investigate."

"You're the Secretary of The Safety Corps."

"Give me a few days, Sir."

CHAPTER THREE

I opened the Peaksville Bread Company dinner menu and set it down and laughed.

Charlotte smiled. "Why are you laughing, Gracie?"

"Because I'm not sure why I even looked at the menu. You'd think forty hours-per-week working here would be enough to memorize it."

Charlotte studied the menu. "What's good?"

I winked. "Can't go wrong with *any* soup and sandwich combo."

We ordered and sat near a window overlooking Schweitzer Mountain.

"Thanks for going out with me on short notice, Charlie."

Charlotte smiled. "I had to cancel a dinner reservation with my Scottish highland cattle."

I laughed.

"It's okay. The Hay & Water Combo is the only recommended item on the *Epley* Bread Company menu."

"What are we going to do, Charlie?"

"Eat dinner?"

"No, with our lives? I've already achieved Manager here. I'm no longer upwardly-mobile at age twenty-five."

Charlotte squeezed a lemon into her sweet tea. "Come work full-time on the farm. I'll make your title General Manager of Livestock. I'll put five goats, five horses and one hundred chickens directly under you."

"We have college degrees, Charlie. When are things going to start happening to us?"

Charlotte whispered. "Things already *did* happen to us. Remember, Gracie?"

"Good things!"

Charlotte sipped her tea and shrugged.

I sighed. "So, what now?"

A well-dressed gentleman on a neighboring table leaned and whispered. "Peaksville Institutes of Health is hiring."

The man was in his mid-fifties and definitely overdressed for a rural mountain town. "Excuse me?"

"PIH," he smiled. "We're hiring young ladies like yourselves with college degrees. The medical biotech industry is booming right now. Have you ever been inside the Peaksville Institutes of Health?"

I nudged Charlotte under the table. "I heard it's nice."

Charlotte flashed the most ridiculous look at me as we both non-verbally reminisced about my senior year PIH ventilation ducting adventures.

I laughed out loud.

"What's so funny?"

I semi-privately scolded Charlotte with my eyes then looked at the man. "We're a little slap-happy tonight, sorry."

He looked at Charlotte and me. "College degrees?"

We nodded.

"My name is Dr. Gunnison." He leaned towards our table and handed us two business cards.

"I'm Charlotte."

I studied his card then looked back at Dr. Gunnison.

Dr. Raymond "Raygun" Gunnison
Colonel, USAF, (Ret.)
Chief Executive Officer
Peaksville Institutes of Health (PIH)

"I'm Grace, Dr. Gunnison."

Charlotte shrugged. "Our degrees are not in the medical field."

"Most Medical Equipment Operators have zero experience in the medical field. It's a growing field. Starting pay is good."

Charlotte couldn't resist. "How good?"

"Ten-thousand dollars per month."

I dropped my spoon on the floor as Charlotte coughed.

"Is that a lot?" The man asked.

We nodded.

"What does a Medical Equipment Operator do?"

Dr. Gunnison "As a Medical Equipment Operator, we assign you ten local patients."

Charlotte tapped my leg. "And?"

"And you simply help their ailments through advanced electronic therapies. We use cutting-edge invisible blue-light technologies. State of the art. And it's non-invasive."

I looked at Charlotte. "Thanks for the business card, Sir."

Dr. Gunnison smiled. "I was just finishing dinner. Sorry to intrude. I'll leave you both alone. Hope to hear from you."

Chloe Epley slowed her Thai horse, Yul Brynner, to chat with her Phuket Equestrian Tour customers riding on the beach with her. "Aussies or New Zealanders?"

The twenty-five-year-old beach-riders smiled and trotted alongside young Chloe.

"Aussies," Grant said.

"We live on RAAF Base Pierce. Near Perth!" Jake said.

Chloe expertly controlled the pace of the ten Phuket Equestrian Tour horses on the beach. "Ah! Military men!"

"Just finished an exercise at U-Tapao Airbase near Phattaya Beach," Grant said.

"We went on holiday in Phuket before going home."

Chloe led the equestrian tour south under the high equatorial noon sun on the white Phuket beach. "What do you do in the military?"

"We're Pilatus PC-9 instructor pilots. It's the prototype for your T-6 Texan II used to train *your* military pilots."

Chloe smiled. "Ooh! Pilots."

"American, right?" Grant asked.

"Yes."

"Long way from home," Grant said.

"Thailand is home." Chloe scratched Yul Brynner's neck. "Now."

"Parents took you here?" Grant asked.

Chloe noticed that Jake was slumped forward on his horse. "You getting tired, Jake?"

No response.

"Sit up straight, buddy," Chloe said.

No response.

Chloe called her fellow tour guide. "Mr. Bali!"

"Whoa!" Chloe calmly halted her horse while holding Jake's horse and jumped down from her trusty steed.

"Grant, gently dismount on your left and come help me lower Jake. Very slowly and calmly."

Grant helped Chloe as Mr. Bali arrived to help.

Mr. Bali called for an ambulance on her cell phone in his local language.

"Jake, we're going to get you down, mate." Chloe said.

Jake nodded affirmatively.

Grant and Chloe lowered Jake and carried him thirty meters to a nearby lounge chair close to the Phuket Le Meridien Resort Hotel.

Jake held his chest. "My heart."

Chloe wiped the sweat from his brow with a cold cloth. "Hang in there, Jake."

A thirty-year-old man experiencing a medical episode ran into the Café Opera from the InterContinental Hotel Sydney lobby and collapsed as Ruby worked the hostess station.

Slam!

Ruby quickly knelt at his side. "Are you okay?"

The man looked Ruby in the eyes and clumsily grabbed her apron.

"Sir, do you want me to call an ambulance?"

The man held his heart and replied with an American accent. "Opera House."

Ruby remained calm as customers became interested. "Nicole, can you call for an ambulance?"

"Got it." Nicole picked up the restaurant phone and dialed.

Suddenly, a second military-aged, muscular man wearing Oakley sunglasses, tactical gray pants, a black Under Armor t-shirt and a black tactical backpack ran into the Café Opera.

Ruby looked up at the mysterious man. "May I help you?"

The second man quickly exited the InterContinental Hotel as fast as he entered.

The man on the floor winced in pain and held his heart.

"Your heart hurts?" Ruby asked.

He nodded.

Ruby looked at her manager. "Ambulance coming, Nicole?"

Nicole knelt with Ruby. "Just called, dear."

"Are you hurting badly?" Nicole asked.

The man lay on his back, nodded and held his heart.

"Heart attack?"

"Not sure. Heart hurts. Bad."

Ruby Kyle wiped his forehead with a cool, clean, damp cloth. "Help is coming. Just relax."

Nicole measured his pulse and looked at Ruby. "Erratic. I'll go flag down the ambulance."

The man grabbed Ruby's apron, pulled her close and whispered. "Don't go to the Sydney Opera House tonight."

A my keyed her SkiArena Andermatt-issued walkie-talkie and spoke into the microphone fastened to her left shoulder. "Kernan Two, this is Kernan One."

"Ha!" Emma laughed and keyed her walkie-talkie mic. *"This* is Kernan One!"

"Where are you?"

"Got nine noobs halfway-through Basic Snowboard Two! I'm on the training slope. Where are you?" Emma asked.

"I have a private in ten minutes. Intermediate Four. Sven from Sweden again. Jealous much?"

Emma keyed her mic and laughed. "Don't forget to teach."

Amy laughed. "Don't worry."

"Teach *skiing*, Weirdo."

"Sven's going to learn some things, trust me."

Emma smiled, double-clicked and started to speak to her students.

Amy donned her dark visor and looked into the sky. "Swiss Life Flight is too active. Anything happening?"

Emma answered the call. "Just the heart attack at nine o'clock."

"Did they rule it a heart attack?" Amy asked.

Emma nodded. "Affirmative. I have to go teach."

Amy watched the Swiss Life Flight helicopter orbiting. "He was younger than us."

"I know, babe. Gotta go, BSB-2 noobs are waiting."

"Careful, Emma."

"B en Gunn base, this is Ben Gunn," Ryan transmitted.

"Got you loud and clear, good buddy!" Madison Goodwell replied from the Flynn Brothers Fishing Charter Office in the Hong Kong Star Ferry Terminal.

"Maddie, there's been an airliner crash west of Lamma Island in the channel. Attempting to render assistance."

Madison Goodwell keyed the base radio microphone. "They just talked about it on CNH News! Be careful!"

Gloria took the mic as Ryan navigated through the debris. "Approaching the wreckage, Maddie. It doesn't look good."

"Copy all! Be safe, Lovebirds!"

Gloria Flynn laughed. "Ben Gunn, out!"

"Secretary Michaels, President Voigt will see you now."

"Hello, Mr. President!"

"Good morning. Thanks for your *All Education is Local* campaign report. How much did that Department of Education program end up costing Uncle Sam?"

"Sir, I believe the initial grant was $665 million. Then we got an augment after a few months for another $300 million. Total was $965 million. We wanted to be cost effective and keep it under a billion."

"Very thrifty, Secretary Michaels."

"There was left-over 2026 money. So technically, it didn't cost taxpayers a dime. Creative accounting, Sir."

President Voigt disguised his instinctive face-palm with a cough.

"Sir, I want make the United States a world leader in STEM, Fine Arts, Literature, Music by 2028!"

"How is that coming? Seems like we've been falling."

"The Department of Education is ensuring inclusiveness of other cultures to help bridge the gaps and reverse our global ranking slide in education."

President Voigt quipped. "It's important for native-born American children to be nice to people who they will later work for."

Secretary Michaels paused. "Sir?"

"Listen, what is the Department of Education doing to combat the global health epidemic?"

"Sir, we're educating millions of children in primary, secondary, and undergraduate educational institutions paralleling the latest Surgeon General campaign."

"What campaign is that?"

"The Department of Education's $3 billion advertisement campaign has reached every school in the nation."

President Voigt braced himself. "The theme, please."

"The settled-science theme. That heart attacks are psychosomatic and can be avoided."

"Avoided how?"

"By crouching under a school desk at the first indication of a heart attack nearby."

"Like a tornado drill?"

"Similar. But —"

"But what?"

"The *Heart Attack Avoidance Procedure*, or HAAP, requires eyes and ears to be closed."

"Really."

"Sir, the training videos and posters in every American school teaches children a slogan."

"Let's hear it."

"*Crouch, Close, Cover*."

President Voigt looked out the Oval Office window onto Pennsylvania Avenue and sighed. "Close eyes and ears and shelter in place for a healthy heart."

"For a healthy heart. I like that. Can I use that, Sir?"

President Voigt sighed. "Secretary Michaels, you've given me a lot to think about."

"Thank you, Mr. President."

"Dambuster One, Basher 5, we're now descending past three thousand."

The VFA-195 Commanding Officer advanced his power levers to afterburner and manipulated his Multi-Function Display. "I'm coming out of twenty-five thousand. Fifteen miles per minute. Forty miles south of your position. I have you on radar."

The F-35 pilot studied his gauges. "We're in a 5000 feet-per-minute rate-of-descent, Sir."

The VFA-195 Commanding Officer "She'll impact the ocean in forty seconds?"

"A-firm, Sir."

"Call her again!"

"303! This is Basher 5! Level off! Pull up! Do you copy?"

"Basher 5, this is Dambuster One. Thump her!"

The F-35 pilot maintained parade position abeam the doomed F-18 pilot. "Sir?"

"Jet wash. Thump her."

The twenty-five-year-old USAF pilot saw the Super Hornet's head slouching forward in her ejection seat. "Basher 5, WILCO!"

The F-35 initiated a cross under, applied afterburner from below her fuselage, accelerated until his exhaust stacks were forward of her F-18 nose cone, then pulled nose up through her flight path.

Whoosh!

The F/A-18E shuddered and buffeted in the F-35's hot, turbulent fuel-air mixture.

The F-35 pilot glanced at the whitecaps of the dark blue Pacific Ocean below. "Passing nine hundred feet! Didn't work, Sir!"

The VFA-195 Commanding Officer zorched inbound. "I'm supersonic, got a visual. Thump her again!"

The USAF F-35 repositioned under the Navy F-18E and checked his altimeter. "Last chance, Sir."

"Please send in the Secretary of Child Trafficking, Experimentation and Abuse."

Secretary Ferguson knocked and entered the Oval Office. "Good morning, Mr. President."

"Good morning, Charity." President Voigt kindly gestured to a chair or couch. "Please, sit. How's the family?"

"Great, Sir."

"How's your husband?"

"Couldn't be better."

"Skylar seems to be doing well on CNH News."

Charity smiled. "My daughter is a piece of work."

"Her reporting is very —"

"Very what, Sir?"

"Is Skylar a Democrat or Republican?"

"Good question. I've never asked her."

President Voigt paused. "She seems to be very critical of my Administration."

"Skylar has always been painfully honest." Charity slunk in her seat after realizing her unfortunate verbiage.

President Voigt removed the verbal spear from his chest and got down to business. "Secretary Ferguson, tell me about the Department of Child Trafficking, Experimentation and Abuse."

Charity sat up straight. "Things are going very well, Sir."

"Let's start with Child Trafficking."

"Okay Mr. President. Child Trafficking is holding steady."

"Holding steady? Say again."

"We are attempting to limit new rogue governments or world leaders from participating in any new, unsanctioned child trafficking."

"That's good, Charity."

"Yes."

President Voigt paused. "How do you catch rogue actors who are dealing in the importation or exportation of children?"

"Mr. President, our Department works in conjunction with the TSC to trap rogue actors wishing to import our children from different parts of the world."

"Okay. So, the TSC uses adults as bait, acting as children to lure importations of impoverished children."

"We use real children as bait, Sir."

"You bait them with real children?"

"Modern rogue governments and traffickers are far too advanced and savvy to succumb to deception."

"Then you arrest the traffickers."

"Eventually. After a lengthy, multi-year investigation, Mr. President."

"And then you get the children back."

"Sometimes."

President Voigt gently face-palmed. "How many of these children used as bait do you recover?"

Charity paused and looked around the Oval Office in deep thought. "Sir, I would say we recover thirty percent of the children, who will then be used again in future TSC law enforcement operations. Usually on a different continent. Unless they age-out."

President Voigt rubbed his eyes.

"We only use children who are *already* victims of trafficking, Sir."

"You recycle."

Charity smiled. "Yes, Sir."

President Voigt stood up. "Charity, your operations are very informative about you as both a professional and person."

Charity Ferguson looked at the flag and beamed with pride. "Thank you, Mr. President."

President Voigt ushered her to the door. "We'll save child experimentation and abuse discussions for another day. You've given me plenty to consider."

"Very well, Sir."

CHAPTER FOUR

I grabbed another alfalfa-timothy-mix bale of hay and deadlifted it onto my shoulder. I walked fifteen feet from the trailer to the Epley barn, bent my legs, and power-lifted it up to the high stack. "Eighty pounds, Charlie?"

Charlotte followed me with a bale over her right shoulder. "Only seventy-five dry. Luckily, this first-cutting just missed getting rained-on in the swath."

I caught my breath and put my hands on my knees to slouch and joke. "Good! I thought it was eighty. Only seventy-five. This is a cakewalk."

Charlotte and I returned to the hay trailer for more.

I saw some large machinery and pointed. "Don't those combine-looking tractor thingies work?"

Charlotte heaved a bale over her right shoulder and shook her head negatively. "Broken."

I lifted a bale with the two red bands of twine. I sidestepped it into the barn as it bumped against my right knee. "Can you fix them?"

"Ugh!" Charlotte power-lifted her bale up to the eight-foot high stack. "Too expensive. And Dad was the only grease-monkey in the family."

I exhaustedly set the hay down on the ground in the barn.

"Gracie, just set it right there. We'll start a new row."

I accidentally inhaled then immediately tried to spit the hay dust from my mouth and lungs. "How many more?"

Charlotte already had another bale from the trailer on her shoulder. "You can quit, Gracie. You helped a lot."

I stubbornly walked to the trailer and lifted another. "How many more?"

Charlotte stacked her bale, exited the barn, and counted with her index finger. "About sixty more bales... Twenty-six bales per ton... Just a couple more tons."

"Oh. Okay. Just a couple tons." I continued to spit out the hay dust. "So not a *ton* of tons, just a couple tons."

Charlotte helped me with my bale. "Let's rest."

We plopped our tired rear-ends down onto a bale.

"Gracie?"

"Yeah, Charlie?"

"Do you think Luke and Ruby are engaged?"

I shrugged. "They both live in Sydney."

"I miss him."

"You miss his dancing?"

"Okay, so he can't dance. But I just can't stop thinking about him."

"You should visit, Charlie."

"I don't want to intrude on their lives. Plus, Mom is getting old and can't take care of the farm by herself."

"How long are you going to do this farm thing, Charlie?"

Charlotte shrugged. "This is our life."

"This was your *parent's* life."

"My mom is scared, Gracie."

"Same with my mom."

"We can't blame them for being scared," Charlotte said.

I sighed and looked at our makeshift bench. "My mom weighs less than this bale of hay."

Charlotte put her arm around me. "Grace?"

I tried to smile.

"Some days I work for hours in the barn or pasture, just hoping."

"Hoping what, Charlie?"

Charlotte pointed into the pasture beyond the pond. "Right there."

"What's right there?"

"That's where my Dad will walk home. Over that hill. Wearing a red plaid shirt, blue jean overalls and his dirty *North40* baseball cap. Cradling a fuzzy, little newborn heifer tenderly in his arms."

"Charlie, you're going to make me cry."

Charlotte displayed her dusty hands and wrists as she wept. "Don't wipe your eyes, Gracie. You'll regret it."

We leaned on each other in the Peaksville sun with fresh tears streaming down our dirty faces.

. . .

"**M**r. Speaker, President Voigt is here to see you."

Speaker of the House Tex Bonner stood up, smiled and stepped around his desk to greet him. "Send him right in, Betsy. Thanks!"

President Voigt entered and smiled. "Tex Bonner! How the hell are you?"

"Mr. President, I'm fine. I'm glad you stopped by."

Speaker Bonner walked to the lounge area of his Congressional office. "Please, have a seat. What's on your mind, Mr. President?"

"Tex, I am saddened to hear about the seven Congressmen that recently passed away in their sleep."

"Mr. President, we are speechless. Thank you for your support this week."

President Voigt sighed. "Flags at half-mast just doesn't seem like enough."

Tex whispered. "Seven Reps and four Senators in one week. President Voigt, if you knew something, you would tell me, wouldn't you?"

President Voigt paused. "Tex, I have been calling my Cabinet into the Oval Office one by one. I'm like a mushroom, I'm kept in the dark and fed crap. So far, they're all telling me it's psychosomatic."

"Psychosomatic heart attacks?"

"It's ludicrous, Tex. I know."

Speaker Bonner leaned back. "Mr. President, in my district, we've had ten-thousand fatal heart attacks this week. The average age of our cardiac arrest victim has been twenty-nine."

President Voigt nodded. "Thirty million Americans have died. That's ten percent. Do you want to hear something interesting?"

"What's that?"

President Voigt whispered and held up his index finger. "Washington DC has only lost *one* percent."

The gentlemen diverted their attention to breaking news on the television.

"We interrupt scheduled programing with breaking news. I'm Skylar Ferguson, CNH News Military Correspondent in New York. We have just confirmed that a Cathay Pacific Airbus 320 has crashed after departure ten miles south of Hong Kong International. We will provide more details as they become available."

President Voigt watched the screen. "Damn. Another airliner down."

Speaker Bonner paused. "Find out what's going on, Mr. President."

"I will."

The two political leaders stood, walked towards the door and shook hands.

"I'll find out, Tex." President Voigt whispered. "Even if it's the last thing I ever do."

.   .   .

Ruby saw Nicole directing the ambulance crew to the Café Opera restaurant inside InterContinental Hotel Sydney then whispered to the man having chest pains as she comforted him. "Is there danger at the Opera House?"

The man nodded and squeezed her apron as the paramedic team entered. "Danger."

Ruby wiped his forehead one last time. "I believe you."

A female paramedic smiled at Ruby. "Thanks, we got it from here."

The male paramedic performed an assessment. "We hear you're having a problem with your ticker, mate?"

The man nodded.

"We'll get you fixed up in a jiffy." The paramedics carefully lifted the ailing man and wheeled him away on a stretcher.

"Nicole?"

"Yes, Ruby."

"The man said there is danger at the Sydney Opera House tonight."

"What kind of danger?"

Ruby shrugged. "Didn't say."

"He was probably delirious."

"You think?"

Nicole nodded then held up two Sydney Opera House tickets. "I'm taking my mother for her birthday tonight."

"But he —"

Nicole interrupted Ruby. "Mother hasn't seen the Orchestra in ten years."

Ruby paused. "Maybe you shouldn't go?"

Nicole condescendingly and confidently smiled.

"What if he knew something?"

Nicole smiled again. "Ruby, he stumbled into the restaurant with a bum ticker. Not carrying a crystal ball."

Mr. Murdstone answered his satellite phone on the Sharjah Blue yacht as it loitered fifty miles south of Yokosuka, homeport of the USS Abraham Lincoln. "Hello?"

"Nuke?"

Mr. Murdstone rapidly sat up straight in his bow deck chair. "Mr. President!"

President Voigt exchanged pleasantries with the forward-deployed TSC Officer. "How are you?"

"Fine, Sir."

"You sound like you're out on the water. Is that wind?"

"I'm in Tokyo, Sir. It's merely windy. Investigating the global crisis as you instructed."

"Any leads?"

"I'm exploring every angle. Not just medical. If it's *not* medical, and it *is* a rogue government or criminal network, I'll be the first to let you know."

"You're my TSC Senior Intelligence Officer, aren't you?"

"Yes, Sir."

"Well, keep up the great work. I'm not convinced that this is medical."

"Same here, Mr. President."

"Excellent. Great minds think alike."

Mr. Murdstone covered his phone and whispered to Dr. Braun on the Sharjah Blue deck. "It's the President."

"You there, Nuke?"

"Yes, I'm here."

"Very well."

"I'll report back to you soon, Mr. President."

"Keep up the great work."

Click!

Dr. Braun sat next to Mr. Murdstone as they steamed southeast of Mount Fuji in the Sagami Wan (*Sagami Bay*).

Mr. Murdstone stowed his satellite phone.

"Does Voigt suspect PsytoSCOPE or Peaksville Defense and Space MEDWEAPS?" Dr. Braun asked.

"Perhaps, but he doesn't verbalize it."

"Does he suspect that you are double-dipping as the Sharjah Blue Weapons Officer?"

"Voigt doesn't even know the Sharjah Blue exists."

Dr. Braun smiled. "Good."

The young USAF F-35 Lightning pilot tucked twenty feet under the fuselage of the USN F/A-18E Rhino and slammed his PCL into afterburner.

Whoosh!

The F-35 pilot pulled nose up only five hundred feet over the unforgiving blue sea forty miles south of Tokyo.

The F-35's hot, turbulent jet exhaust buffeted and shook the F-18 the second time.

The young F-18 Super Hornet pilot continued her slow, unconscious descent into the Pacific passing two hundred feet with her Navy Skipper on her right wing and a young USAF pilot on her left wing.

The Navy Skipper yelled into his mic. "Dambuster 303! Pull your nose up, Tater! Pull up, Tater!"

The F-35 pilot repeatedly screamed into his microphone inside his oxygen mask. "Dambuster 303! Pull up!"

The VFA-195 Skipper from Atsugi Naval Air Base mentored the Good Samaritan F-35 pilot from Yokota AB. "Too late, Basher. I don't want you to splash. You tried. Back away from the frag pattern. The impact will be violent and dangerous. Back off, Son."

"I got this, Sir!" The USAF F-35 pilot quickly tucked under the low F-18 into the Pacific sea spray and thumped her for the third time with jetwash barely over the crashing whitecaps.

Whoosh!

E mma Kernan visited the SkiBrief platform between sessons. "You must be Amy's private. Are you Sven from Sweden in Switzerland?"

Sven smiled and raised his visor. "I think I'm seeing double."

Emma shook Sven's hand. "I'm Emma. Amy and I are twins. But I'm the smart one."

Amy corrected Emma. "We adopted Emma from a third world country. Her name was a series of tongue clicks. At Emma's request, my family got her got facial reconstruction surgery to look like me. Unfortunately, most of Emma's body parts don't work. It's a sad story. But we still love her."

Emma and Sven laughed at Amy's nonsense.

The Swiss Life Flight helicopter performed another low pass overhead.

Amy lowered her visor. "Emma, don't you have nine-year-old noobs to teach? Grown-ups are working, here. Scram."

Emma walked five feet and turned around. "Hey Sven!"

"Yes?"

"Call me when you're ready for Advanced."

Amy whacked Emma in the rear with a ski pole. "Scram!"

Sven laughed.

Amy inspected her student's gear. "Questions?"

Sven smiled. "I'll try to impress you."

Amy yelled over the helicopter noise. "You impressed me at *hello*!"

Sven blushed in the Alpine Mountain sunlight.

"Ready, Sven?"

"Born ready, Amy!"

. . .

J ack quickly returned from the Dragon Muay Thai Camp instructor shack with a complimentary water bottle. "Here you go, Ricky. Are you okay?"

Ricky slumped back in his chair and held his heart.

"Ricky?"

"Jack, my heart. I think I'm done for the day."

"How bad?"

Ricky convulsed in pain and slid down onto the floor. "Not good, Jack."

Jack helped Ricky get comfortable on the floor and ran to the instructor shack. "Mr. Bo! Call an ambulance. Possible heart attack."

Mr. Bo ran to Ricky with his cell phone and called for an ambulance in Thai.

Other kickboxing students and instructors gathered around.

Mr. Bo performed crowd control. "Step back so Ricky can breathe."

Jack folded a clean towel and placed it under Ricky's head. "They're on their way. Do you have a bad heart?"

Ricky shook his head negatively and winced in pain.

"No worries, Ricky. You'll be fine. Here they come."

The Phuket Ambulance crew arrived under an orbiting helicopter, assessed Ricky and spoke to Mr. Bo in their native language.

Jack watched the ambulance speed away with Ricky. "Damn."

Mr. Bo stood with Jack. "How old?"

"Twenty-three."

Mr. Bo gasped. "Heart attack? Twenty-three? Too young."

Jack agreed and studied the departing helicopter.

L uke Bartholomew smiled and hugged Ruby Kyle. "I thought you were working the dinner buffet tonight in the Intercontinental?"

Ruby shook her head. "Nicole gave me the evening off."

"Hold on while I deliver a Roo Burger and Schnitzel to Table Number Seven."

Ruby sat in the lobby of The Australian Heritage restaurant looking at the two Sydney Opera House tickets.

"Okay, sorry about that. How was work?"

"Good. Actually, something happened."

"Something good?"

"Something bad. Some man stumbled inside and had a heart attack."

Luke gasped. "That's terrible."

"He was being chased."

"By whom?"

"A man in tactical gear with a giant backpack was twenty seconds in trail. He looked inside and quickly left."

Luke sat closer to Ruby. "Are you okay?"

Ruby nodded affirmatively.

"The young man having the heart attack whispered something to me."

"What?"

"He whispered 'don't go to the Sydney Opera House tonight due to danger.'"

"Well, we can't afford tickets anyway."

Ruby held up two tickets. "These were given to me this morning by an elderly Australian couple at the buffet."

Luke held the tickets and smiled. "Wow."

CHAPTER FIVE

General Marsh smiled as he answered his phone. "Love it when you call, Bud. Just like old times."

"I miss Peaksville. Wish I was there with you, Swamp."

"I *don't* miss Washington DC."

Mr. Light sighed.

"You called to reminisce?"

"Yes," Mr. Light said.

General Marsh chuckled in his Peaksville Defense and Space Chief Executive Office. "Then go to the Washington DC National Zoo, jump into the spider monkey exhibit and reminisce with *them*."

"Seriously," Mr. Light said. "Life was simple in North Idaho."

"And then you crashed."

"Things are getting complicated here, Swamp."

"How?"

"President Voigt has changed a lot since his days running CABESA."

"I heard."

"He doesn't like me anymore," Mr. Light said.

"Bud, President Voigt already fired you in Peaksville in 2020. What's he going to do, fire you again?"

"Maybe."

General Marsh shrugged. "Burn that bridge when you come to it."

"Thanks, Swamp."

"No monkey business, Bud."

Mr. Light sighed.
Click.

"Help!"
    Gloria listened and watched from the Ben Gunn bow to Cathay Pacific 925. "Ryan, cut the engine. Someone is alive down there in the wreckage."

Ryan reduced power, idled closer and jockeyed reverse.

Bang! Bang! Bang!

Li Jie pointed towards the Airbus 320 cockpit. "Noise, Boss!"

Bang! Bang!

"Boss, person alive! Person alive!"

Ryan secured the engine and yelled from the flybridge. "Ahoy! Make a noise if you hear us!"

Bang!

"Help!"

"Mr. Flynn! Li Jie request permission to swim to person!"

Gloria looked at Ryan. "I'm scared, Ryan."

The forward fifty feet of the broken fuselage was rapidly sinking with only the nosecone and right cockpit window visible.

Ryan hesitated. "Li Jie, it's not safe."

The deck hand leaned over the bow railing. "Captain Flynn, Li Jie see pilot in window! Alive! Li Jie try to save pilot!"

"I got this, Li Jie." Ryan dropped anchor, shot a flare into the sky, jumped down from the flybridge, donned a life vest and grabbed a large, red axe. "Gloria, make another mayday call!"

Gloria gasped. "Ryan! Don't!"

"It's okay." Ryan kissed Gloria and leapt onto the sinking Airbus 320 nosecone.

President Voigt stuck his head in the Vice-President's office. "Abby, do you have a minute?"

Vice-President Walker stood and smiled. "Mr. President! Come in. Can I get you a drink?"

"No thanks. Actually, yes. Could I get a water bottle?"

"Secretary, please bring Mr. President a water bottle."

President Voigt sat with Vice-President Walker.

"It's so nice to see you, Sir."

President Voigt opened his water. "Abby, tell me what you know about the global cardiac arrests."

Vice-President Walker whispered. "I'm not buying the psychosomatic angle."

"You're not, Abby?"

"It has to be some sort of plague or disease. The government and media decide on settled-science though."

"Can we 'unsettle the science' blaming psychosomatic causes?"

Vice-President Walker shrugged. "Once the media claims settled-science, it's statistically and historically irreversible."

"Maybe so, Abby. On a related issue, I'm not very happy with Secretary Light and The Safety Corps."

Vice-President Walker laughed. "What's new?"

"I don't feel like he's investigating the criminal angle of the epidemic."

"Criminal angle?"

President Voigt paused. "You know, Abby. Remember Peaksville?"

"That was all sanctioned, CABESA medical testing benefitting American children. You're not suggesting that these heart attacks are man-made. Oh, come on, Mr. President."

President Voigt stood up. "I just wanted to check with you."

Vice-President Walker walked him to the door. "I'll have the medical professionals visit the disease, plague or contaminated food source angle."

"Take care, Abby. Thanks."

I was halfway through my day manager shift at the Peaksville Bread Company when Dr. Gunnison from the PIH entered. He ordered the usual. Turkey, Avocado and Swiss.

I smiled. "Hello Dr. Gunnison."

He whispered. "Grace, have you and Charlotte thought about employment at PIH?"

My unfortunate life experiences were both a gift and a curse. I knew better. "We're still thinking about it. How are you doing, today?"

"Can't complain." Dr. Gunnison paid and took his iced tea. "Because nobody will listen."

I worked the register for five more customers then did a sweep of the Peaksville Bread Company for cleanliness.

Dr. Gunnison was obviously a military veteran. I knew this because he was a loud phone talker, and my dad was a loud phone talker.

His *USAF (Retired)* business card was my other clue.

"The Sydney Opera house performance is going to be a real heart-stopping performance, Swamp."

Then laughter.

What did I just hear? I moved in closer to wipe tables around 'Dr. Loud-Talker.'

"The chess pieces are moving into position in the next few hours."

Okay, that was cryptic but not revealing.

"Couple hundred."

I kept wiping the nearby tables.

"Voigt or Walker?"

Did he just mention the President and Vice-President's names?

"Yeah, he's a problem."

Dr. Gunnison laughed at the cellphone reply.

"Soon. Very soon."

I wiped the table behind 'Dr. Loud-Talker.' Over. And over. And over.

"A storm is coming Down Under."

Click!

He set his iPhone down and looked at me. "Grace, the restaurant is always cleanest when you manage. Please consider making the leap over to PIH. We're sending fifty Medical Equipment Operators to Australia today for training. Ever been to Australia?"

I shook my head negatively.

"You'd like it. Great travel opportunities."

"Sounds great."

"Think it over."

Thomas Stallworth sat on the top steps of the Lincoln Memorial. "Aaron Webster!"

"Tommy Boy!"

The Peaksville Class of 2020 graduates shook hands.

"I haven't seen you in months, Web."

"I heard you just passed the bar exam, Tommy Boy."

Thomas nodded. "First attempt. Georgetown University prepared me well apparently."

Aaron sat next to Thomas overlooking the National Mall. "Congrats."

"Thanks."

"What now?" Aaron asked.

"Time to get a real job."

"In Washington DC?"

Thomas shrugged. "Not sure."

"Do you miss Peaksville?"

"I miss our Peaksville friends." Thomas sighed. "Not the town."

"Same."

Thomas looked around and whispered. "What do you think of the global epidemic?"

Aaron whispered. "It's getting worse."

"Are you still in the Speaker's office?"

Aaron nodded.

"Does he know what's going on?"

"Tommy Boy, Congressman Bonner knows less than you and me."

"How? Didn't he sponsor the CABESA Initiative in 2013?"

"He didn't grow up in Peaksville."

Thomas watched several small airplanes and helicopters navigate around the Washington DC airspace in no apparent hurry. "Peaksville stole our innocence. It sucks knowing too much."

Aaron agreed. "I wish we were naïve and gullible."

Thomas laughed. "Like I used to be."

"You were the most gullible of all." Aaron nodded and smiled. "Can't go back in time, can we?"

"Nope. We can't 'unlearn' what we learned in Peaksville."

Aaron looked around and whispered. "The Speaker has chest pains this week."

"It's happening?"

Aaron nodded, checked his watch and stood up. "I have to get back to the Capitol Building. Be safe, Tommy Boy."

The VFA-195 Commanding Officer leveled off with Basher 5 at one hundred feet. "Dambuster 303, this is Dambuster One. Brace for impact, Tater. Fair winds and following seas, Shipmate."

"Damn." The F-35 pilot raised his visor to wipe his tears as he took a ten-degree cut away from the distressed F-18.

Suddenly, only thirty feet above the Pacific, the F-18E Super Hornet's empennage squatted down, vapors formed on the upper wings, and two afterburner fireballs roared from the twin-engine fighter into the Pacific.

Whoosh!

The young F-18 pilot yanked full backstick until the rapid onset of g's knocked her out again.

The F-35 pilot screamed into his mic on Badman base. "Woohoo!"

"Dambuster 303, this is Skipper. Easy with it, Tater. Level your wings. Click your mic if you hear me."

"Click. Click." The F-18 pilot double-clicked.

"We're climbing at twenty degrees nose up. Hold that pitch. When you're ready, gently roll into a shallow right turn towards land."

The young F-18 slowly complied and eventually rolled wings level at a 340 heading. "Skipper?"

"Just fly, Tater."

"What happened, Sir?"

"You had a physiological episode. Basher 5 and I will lead you to Atsugi. Can you fly loose cruise on the Lightning II?"

The F-18 pilot saw the F-35 and double-clicked.

"Atsugi Tower, Dambuster One, flight of three, twenty miles south, three thousand feet, declaring an emergency, confirm Runway 36 short field arresting gear rigged."

"Affirmative, short field and long field gear is rigged."

"Atsugi Tower, request permission to land for Dambuster 303. Full stop. Anticipating short field arrested landing."

"Dambuster 303 is cleared to land on 36 or 18. Winds calm."

Clunk!

The F-18 pilot popped her gear handle down, set her flaps, lowered her hook and extended her speed brakes.

"Okay, Tater. Basher 5 and I are breaking off. Take runway 36. We see your wheels down and locked. Your hook is down. No power in the wires like at the boat. Just retard the power levers to idle after touch down. If you miss the short field cable, roll into the long field at idle. Easy on those binders. Don't blow your main tires."

303 double-clicked.

The Rhino engaged the Atsugi runway 36 arresting gear cable, pulled it out like a fishing line, and safely came to a stop.

Crash and Rescue quickly arrived.

"Basher 5, Dambuster One."

The F-35 pilot was already headed home to Yokota Air Base. "Yes, Sir?"

"What's your name?"

"Skid."

"Tater, Skid saved your life. Thank him."

Still hooked to the cable, Tater shut her engines down, double-clicked her radio then passed out.

. . .

"Swamp how is that $210 billion for fiscal year 2027 working out so far at PDS?"

General Marsh smiled. "I think we're going to make it to September 30 just fine, Mr. President."

President Voigt looked out the Oval Office window. "I'm glad that I could help get you that CEO position at Peaksville Defense and Space."

General Marsh kicked his feet up on the desk in his CEO Office overlooking the MEDWEAP production line. "Maybe when you leave Washington, you could get me the Presidency."

Laughter.

"How are PDS sales?"

"Mr. President, we can't fill orders fast enough. The TSC is growing worldwide at ten percent, the military is arming all vessels in the air, land and sea, and the domestic medical profession is growing. We are surpassing all projected sales estimates every quarter."

"That's wonderful."

"Our 2027 MEDWEAP technology is phenomenal. Mr. President, we've come a long way since you and I were burning holes in the sky in the USAF with barely enough power to cause a tummy ache."

"Understood. Hey, Swamp, I have a question."

"Yes, Mr. President?"

"How do you ensure that PDS MEDWEAP's don't end up in the wrong hands?"

"What do you mean, Sir?"

"I'm trying to tackle this global health epidemic. There have been upwards of 233 million world-wide heart attacks in one week. How do you know that some of those health-related deaths are not extra-judicial killings?"

"Mr. President, that's a great question. We have controls, checks and balances that are locked down tighter than Tom Thumb's ass."

"Explain."

"You want to learn more about Tom Thumb's ass?"

President Voigt looked at his watch. "Swamp!"

General Marsh smiled at his own joke. "Just kidding. The PDS produces the MEDWEAP. The Peaksville Institutes of Health distributes MEDWEAP's only to The Safety Corps, the U.S. Military, and Medical personnel with 2027 MWOP Qualifications."

"Is there a weak link in the chain?"

"Mr. President, Dr. Gunnison has reformed and modernized the PIH since the unfortunate passing of Dr. Hertz in 2020."

"Thanks, Swamp. So, all MEDWEAP's pass through Raygun. Even the ones destined for the military?"

"More or less."

"Swamp?"

"Yes, Mr. President?"

"I need your loyalty during this global crisis."

"Copy, Sir," General Marsh said.

President Voigt paused. "Can I expect your loyalty, Swamp?"

"You can count on me, Sir."

CHAPTER SIX

L uke called Ruby from his wait staff employment in Sydney's historical
district known as The Rocks.

"Ruby, it's me."

"Hey babe."

"I'm off at five o'clock."

Ruby smiled. "Same here."

"We'll go to the Opera House and forget all about the guy with the heart
attack."

Ruby laughed nervously. "Did you hear what I said earlier, Luke?"

"Two tickets. I heard it."

"Someone who was being chased with a failing heart told me to avoid the
Opera House tonight. I saw the guy chasing him. He was scary, in a tactical way."

Luke shrugged. "He was having a heart attack. People say things during heart
attacks."

"They do?"

"I don't know. I assume so."

Ruby looked at the Orchestra tickets. "What if he was right?"

Luke shrugged. "We'll just be careful."

"We'll talk over dinner."

C hloe tended to the Australian RAAF pilot on Lounge Chair #5 on Phuket Le
Meridien Resort Hotel's luxury beach in the hot, equatorial sunlight.

Mr. Bali tied the horses to a light post.

Jake held his heart in pain. "Where's Grant?"

"He ran through the hotel lobby to guide the ambulance crew."

"It hurts, Chloe."

Chloe Epley removed her Camelback and tried to cool him down.

Jake began to cry in pain. "Am I dying, Chloe?"

Chloe smiled and gently wiped the sweat from his brow. "You're too young, Jake. Besides, it's probably just heartburn or dehydration. Whatever it is, you'll be fine."

Jake nodded as the Ambulance crew arrived with Grant. "I hope."

Chloe and Grant helped the two Thai medics carry Jake's stretcher from the beach to onto terra firma.

The senior paramedic bowed to Chloe. "Thank you."

Chloe looked at Grant and yelled over the low, orbiting helicopter. "What do you want to do? I can return both horses to the barn."

Grant agreed and climbed into the vehicle. "I'll go in the ambulance."

"Good choice." Chloe comforted Jake. "You'll be fine, buddy!"

R yan stood on the sinking Airbus 320 and struck the co-pilot side-window with his axe.

Crack!

Ryan tried again. This time harder.

Crack!

The window broke.

Ryan kicked out the residual broken glass and reached inside. "Give me your hand!"

The Cathay Pacific co-pilot grabbed Ryan's hand as saltwater from the South China Sea flooded the doomed Airbus 320.

"Ugh!" Ryan screamed as he pulled the two-hundred-pound crewman through the small window.

Li Jie lowered a rope ladder and helped the injured co-pilot board the Ben Gunn.

The co-pilot in the wet Cathy Pacific uniform saw the aircraft sinking. "My pilot!"

"What?" Ryan yelled from below as the nose cone submerged under his feet.

"My pilot. He's alive."

Ryan immediately dove underwater.

Gloria screamed. "Ryan, no!"

Li Jie watched and waited at the rope ladder. "He okay, Mrs. Flynn."

Gloria checked her G-Shock watch. "It's been thirty seconds."

Li Jie yelled into the water. "Boss?"

No response.

"Fifty seconds."

Gloria panicked. "Li Jie, please help!"

The deck hand jumped into the Lamma Channel to find Ryan.

Two other Hong Kong fishing boats arrived on scene to observe.

Within seconds, three heads popped out of the water.

Gloria jumped for joy. "Ryan!"

"Emma! Help me! Sven's down!"

Emma stood in the SkiArena Andermatt sandwich shop and keyed her mic. "Say position, Amy!"

"We're two-thirds of the way down the slope. Sven held his heart. He said it hurt. He's not conscious! Send Life Flight!"

Emma hurried to the dispatch office. "Franz! Did you copy the last transmission?"

Franz held his landline phone in his hand. "Copy all, Emma. Scrambling Swiss Life Flight."

Emma removed the defibrillator from the wall, grabbed her snowboard and hurried down the slope. "Thanks, Franz!"

"What's Life Flight doing?" Amy yelled from Sven's side as Emma arrived. "It passed by twice and didn't stop."

Emma keyed the emergency frequency. "Franz, this Emma, did you call Life Flight?"

"Yes, Emma. Five minutes ago."

The helicopter pilot interrupted. "Got you in sight, ground crew. Be there in thirty seconds."

Swiss Life Flight hovered and lowered a rescue medic with a stokes litter. "We got it from here!"

Amy discontinued aid and whispered in Sven's ear in the rotor wash's man-made snowstorm. "You'll be okay, Sven!"

Sven flashed the Kernan twins a 'thumbs up' as he was hoisted into the red helicopter with white cross.

"Dr. Hands, thanks for visiting on such short notice."

Dr. Hands entered the Oval Office. "My title is Advisor to the President. I'm here to advise as you see fit, Mr. President."

"Have a seat."

"Thanks."

"Your firm is international, now."

"Yes, Sir. Peaksville KidCare *Global* Counseling Services."

"Perfect, I wanted to make sure that we're reaching out to the children. 233 million heart attacks in a week. We probably have one billion sons and daughters grieving."

"Yes, Sir."

"In addition to grievance counseling, we're trying to tackle the fear aspect. Many children have seen schoolmates die from heart attacks. They're scared."

"What are your solutions?"

"Based on the Surgeon General's study revealing that the heart attacks are psychosomatic, we are advising the children to not stick around and help when heart attacks happen. The psychosomatic heart attacks occur in clusters. Fear seems to be the primary contributing factor."

President Voigt sighed. "You're saying that one kid goes into cardiac arrest. Then the second kid goes into cardiac arrest from fear."

Dr. Hands smiled and agreed. "And third, and fourth —"

"Like dominoes."

"Correct." Dr. Hands nodded. "It's settled science because there are billion-dollar government advertisement and Public Service Announcements being launched."

President Voigt leaned back. "You said that the billions of dollars spent on PSA's make it settled science."

"It's only logical." Dr. Hands nodded and shrugged. "The government wouldn't spend the money if it was *not* settled science."

President Voigt face-palmed. "Please continue, Dr. Hands."

"We are simply piggy-backing on what experts, doctors, and scientists from the leading medical institutions of America are saying. Our goal at Peaksville KidCare Global Counseling Services, therefore, is to educate children about techniques to mitigate fear."

"This prevents heart attacks."

"Yes, Mr. President. We have observed a twenty-five percent reduction in heart attacks."

"So instead of 233 million global heart attacks in a week, you purport that you saved about 60 million lives."

Dr. Hands smiled. "Yes, Sir."

President Voigt cupped his hands together. "Your words and level of medical expertise are truly breathtaking. I have heard some very thought-provoking things lately. Your statements and assertions are toward the top of the list. Thanks for sharing your gems of wisdom and knowledge."

Dr. Hands smiled and exited the Oval Office. "Good day, Mr. President."

President Voigt sighed as the door closed. "Why me?"

"Hello?"

"Nuke, this is Abby."

"One second, Ma'am." Mr. Murdstone walked towards the starboard hull inside the Sharjah Blue Officer's Mess to improve satellite phone reception.

"You there?"

"Okay, that's better. Yes, Ma'am."

"How was your travel to the United Arab Emirates?"

Mr. Murdstone looked at Mount Fuji through a porthole northwest of the massive, luxury yacht. "Fine, Ma'am. Thank you for arranging this position with The Syndicate."

"You're welcome."

"We steamed to Tokyo on the Sharjah Blue. Mr. Muscat closed several petroleum contracts in Tokyo and Yokohama."

Vice-President Walker clicked her ballpoint pen. "I realize that, Nuke. I brokered the contracts."

"Yes, Ma'am."

"You spoke with the President."

"How do you know, Ma'am?"

No response.

"Yes, Ma'am. I spoke with President Voigt."

"What did he say?"

"The President definitely doesn't buy the health or epidemic angle to the heart attacks."

"What did you say?"

"I told him what he wanted to hear. I said the deaths seem suspicious."

"Then what," Vice-President Walker said.

"He told me to investigate."

"Then what?"

"I told the President that I would investigate."

"That's all?"

"That's all."

Vice-President Walker instructed her foot soldier at sea. "Keep that dialogue with the President going, Nuke. Let him think that you're a trusted agent and on his side. False sense of hope and security. Send him down different roads."

"Different roads that all lead to dead ends?"

"Exactly, Nuke."

Mr. Murdstone smiled. "I'll dangle a fresh carrot every time I speak with the President."

Vice-President Walker smiled. "Atta boy."

"Tell me about the Sharjah Blue."

"I'm still learning. This ship is like a Caribbean cruise liner with more fire power than the entire Seventh Fleet in Yokosuka."

C harity Ferguson grabbed a handful of pretzels in the Washington DC Ritz Carlton lounge. "CNH News is flying my daughter, Skylar, to Sydney."

Dr. Moriarty spoke with potato chips in his mouth. "Sydney didn't happen yet."

Charity shrugged. "They know it's going to be big news. Nothing wrong with planning ahead."

"What will people think about the news crew prep?"

Charity laughed. "All of the news channels are sending someone in advance. What's the big deal?"

Dr. Moriarty poured himself another beer from the pitcher.

Charity played with the umbrella in her Whiskey Sour. "Do you think Vice-President Walker brokered talking head positions for our daughters to reward us for hard work? Or does she —"

Dr. Moriarty dribbled beer on his chin. "Or does she what?"

"Does Abby want our daughters to be her media-narrative slaves?"

"Probably the latter," Dr. Moriarty said. "Does it really matter?"

Charity slid towards Dr. Moriarty in the Washington DC Ritz Carlton booth. "I want to be *your* slave."

"I don't think my wife would approve."

"Aren't you taking care of that situation?"

"She's in Peaksville for the summer." Dr. Moriarty chugged his beer then set it down. "And let's just say it's going to be a hot summer in Peaksville."

"M urdstone."

"Speaking."

"Nuke?"

"Sorry, Ma'am, I didn't realize it was you, again."

Vice-President Walker paused. "You should be more careful."

"Yes, Ma'am."

"Nuke, as Weapons Officer on the Sharjah Blue, are you required to actually *identify* targets before firing upon them or terminating them?"

"Yes, Ma'am."

"Do you have a copy of the May 2027 Global Scheduled Depopulation Agenda MEDWEAP Operators Manual?"

"Yes, Ma'am."

"Who was inside the Super Hornet over the Sagami-Wan when the Sharjah Blue opened fire on the pilot?"

"I presume a Navy pilot."

"You presume."

"Was the Navy pilot important, Ma'am?"

"Yes. Very important to me." Vice-President Walker paused. "I don't care if it's a single seater, a jumbo jet or a gyrocopter. From now on, I need a manifest of passengers and crew prior to any attack. In advance, Nuke."

"WILCO, Ma'am."

Click!

Soaking wet, Ryan Flynn debriefed his fifteen fishing charter customers after the rescue. "Please excuse the inconvenience." He was interrupted with thunderous applause.

The two Cathay Pacific surviving crewmen shook Ryan's hand and entered the Ben Gunn customer cabin to warm up.

Gloria smiled. "You did good, Ryan."

Li Jie hoisted the anchor and stowed the rope ladder. "Boss! We ready! We go home with pilots!"

Ryan advanced the throttle and raced home into the Hong Kong harbor from the West Lamma Channel. "Mayday! Mayday! This this is the Ben Gunn returning to Star Ferry Terminal with two *very wet* Cathay Pacific pilots."

"Copy that, Ben Gunn. This is the Hong Kong Star Ferry TSC. We'll see you when you get here."

Gloria rewarded the cold, wet aviators with cups of hot oolong tea as the Ben Gunn steamed northbound. "What happened up there?"

"We got dizzy. We passed out."

"Hypoxia?" Gloria asked.

The pilots shook their heads. "That only happens over ten thousand feet. We never cleared six thousand. Plenty of oxygen down at six."

"Both of you passed out?"

The pilots looked at each other and nodded.

Gloria flashed her beautiful smile. "You're safe now."

. . .

J ack arrived home on a baht bus as Chloe arrived on her small, red Honda Spree scooter.

"Jack!"

"Hi Chloe!"

"Good day at Muay Thai?"

Jack shook his head negatively in the hot, equatorial evening sun.

"Same here. Tell me about it inside."

Chloe opened the door to their bed and breakfast and found Chanatara weeping. "What's wrong, Chana?"

Chanatara wiped her eyes. "Sister. She call Chana. Brothers in Bangkok had heart attack. Under forty years old."

Jack heard 'brothers' in broken English but tried to clarify. "You said brothers. You mean brother? One brother?"

Chanatara held up two fingers. "Two brothers, Jack. Two brothers die. Chana sad."

Chloe sat and comforted her. "I'm so sorry, Chana. We're sad with you."

"Chana go cry now." Chanatara kissed Jack and Chloe on the forehead. "Thank you."

Jack and Chloe walked to the patio overlooking the home's Thai garden.

"How sad," Chloe said.

Jack sat pensively and quietly.

"Jack?"

No response.

Chloe leaned on Jack. "Something happened at work."

"Heart attack?"

Chloe gasped. "How did you know?"

"Because my army kickboxing student from New Zealand had a heart attack."

"Same, my military horse rider was a RAAF pilot. Only twenty-five."

Jack faded away into deep thought.

"What's happening, Jack? Are we safe here?"

Jack shrugged.

"H ello, Raygun. This is President Voigt calling from the Oval Office."

"Good morning, Sir."

"First, I just want you to know that I am considering you for a cabinet position."

Dr. Gunnison stood up and closed the door of the Peaksville Institutes of Health CEO Office. "Wow! Thanks, Mr. President."

"Second, I realize you run the PIH, but I had some military hardware questions for you."

Dr. Gunnison took it off speaker phone. "Go ahead, Sir."

President Voigt leaned forward on the Resolute Desk. "Swamp told me that you control all MEDWEAP distribution from the PDS production line."

Dr. Gunnison nodded. "Swamp is correct. The PIH acts as a gateway since the weapons are medical in nature. Our 2027 MEDWEAP Operator Master List is updated hourly. Only trusted agents are allowed to possess or operate them."

President Voigt rubbed his eyes. "Trusted agents?"

"You know what I mean."

President Voigt rubbed his forehead and looked out the Oval Office window. "Raygun, is there any way that a rogue government or group could get their hands on a MEDWEAP?"

Dr. Gunnison paused. "Absolutely not, Sir."

"Thanks for your honesty, Raygun."

"You can't be too careful during times like these, Mr. President."

President Voigt paused. "I just need a pledge of loyalty from you."

"Absolutely. I got your back, Mr. President."

CHAPTER SEVEN

R uby Kyle approached The Australian Heritage Hotel restaurant at five
o'clock."

Luke Bartholomew smiled, neatly hung up his wait staff apron and exited the
restaurant. "Perfect timing!"

Ruby hugged Luke and kissed his cheek. "What are you in the mood for,
Luke?"

"I've been having 'Kebab-withdrawals' all week!"

Ruby laughed. "Twist my arm!"

"Hail a cab?"

Ruby extended her hand to Luke and smiled. "Let's walk."

The two Americans selected Luke's favorite local Sydney restaurant, the
Ottoman Grill Kebab restaurant.

Luke received his Beef and Chicken Doner Kebab and took a bite. "Tell me
more about the heart attack guy."

"He may have been some kind of whistleblower."

Luke mowed down his kebab. "Okay."

Ruby continued. "Just like Aaron Webster, Nurse Light or Mr. Goodwell."

"Okay."

Ruby watched Luke eat. "He was trying to help."

Luke kept chewing. "Okay."

"Just like we tried to help the kids of Shady Valley."

Luke took another bite. "That didn't go so well, remember?"

"They didn't want our help."

Luke stopped chewing. "Oh, I see where you're going with this."

Ruby nodded.

Luke took another bite. "I should believe that guy."

Ruby smiled. "Remember when Tommy Boy didn't trust us?"

"Okay fine, we won't go to the Opera House tonight. The tickets were probably expensive. We can sell —"

Ruby smiled, quickly ripped up the two Orchestra tickets and kissed Luke on the cheek. "Let's go dancing."

Luke sighed and continued to eat his kebab. "Yeah, right! You've seen me dance."

Ruby hugged Luke and whispered in his ear. "Amy's not here to make fun of you. Besides, I like your dancing."

Luke looked at the spectacular Sydney sunset. "I miss our Peaksville friends, Ruby."

"Me too, Luke."

"May I speak with Vice-President Walker. This is General Marsh at PDS calling from Idaho."

"Please hold." The secretary pressed buttons.

Vice-President Walker answered her phone. "Swamp?"

"President Voigt called, Ma'am."

"What did you tell him?"

"I told him the millions of TSC, military, and medical critters in America would never misuse the MEDWEAP's and they will only be used for good."

"Critters." Vice-President Walker laughed. "Oh, Swamp. You crack me up."

"Just giving you a heads up."

"Thanks."

General Marsh looked outside his PDS CEO office window overlooking the MEDWEAP production line. "Oh, one last thing, Abby. Web secured a $25 billion with a 'b' purchase from Sharjah Blue Enterprises for ten-thousand Next Generation MEDWEAP's."

"Did he have to twist Mustafa's arm for a contract that large?"

"Web merely had to beat Mustafa last week at the Dubai Creek Yacht and Golf Club."

"I didn't realize Web was a good golfer."

"He's not. Web and Mustafa both shot in triple digits."

Vice-President Walker laughed. "Must have been a real barn-burner. Which reminds me. Get your family and anyone you care about away from Peaksville."

"Bud said he'd warn me in advance, Abby."

"Bud has been known to mix up dates and time zones in the past."

"True." General Marsh laughed. "I'll let you go."

Vice-President Walker looked at the American flag in her office. "Thanks for your loyalty and patriotism, Swamp."

"You can count on me, Ma'am."

A aron Webster visited Speaker of the House Tex Bonner for tasking and other reasons. "There are some books I want to show you, Mr. Speaker."

The senior Congressman stood and greeted Aaron with a hearty, Texan handshake. "My favorite intern. I hope the book has a lot of pictures, Web. I'm not the most 'voracious' reader. Voracious is a word, isn't it?"

Aaron laughed. "It is, Mr. Speaker."

"Good." Congressman Bonner laughed and threw Aaron a water bottle. "Catch!"

"Can I bring them tomorrow, Mr. Speaker?"

"Anytime, Aaron." Congressman Bonner sat down.

"You okay, Sir?"

"My chest has been giving me some trouble this week."

"Hope you feel better, Mr. Speaker."

"W e're crash magnets," Ryan said.

Gloria sipped her Diet Coke inside a Delayney's Irish Pub large wooden booth in Kowloon. "Say again?"

Ryan tilted back his Guinness pint and set it down. "Second airplane that crashed at our feet."

"Don't forget the helicopter." Madison dipped a celery stick into the artichoke dip. "Two airplanes. One helicopter."

Ryan nodded. "Forgot."

Gloria mumbled under her breath. "Dizzy."

Ryan looked at Gloria. "Excuse me?"

Gloria covered her face with her menu. "It's probably nothing. What are you guys going to order?"

Madison lowered Gloria's menu. "Did you say you're dizzy?"

"Not me. The Cathay Pacific pilots. Before we dropped them off at the Star Ferry TSC Office. They said they both got dizzy and passed out. Right before the crash."

"Loss of pressurization?"

Gloria shook her head. "They said they never climbed over six thousand feet, Maddie. They explained that they were too low for hypoxia."

Ryan pointed to the restaurant televisions. "Check it out."

"We interrupt scheduled programing with breaking news. I'm Skylar Ferguson, CNH Military Correspondent with an update on Cathay Pacific 925 that crashed departing Hong Kong International. The Safety Corps and local Hong Kong authorities have discontinued search and rescue operations. They are reporting zero survivors and one-hundred and twenty-three fatalities. Next of kin notification procedures are underway. This is Skylar Ferguson. You're watching CNH News."

"Zero survivors?" Ryan slammed his drink on the table. "That's bullcrap! We saved them."

Gloria placed her right index finger over her lips. "Shhh!"

Madison Goodwell scanned the Hong Kong restaurant.

"We have to tell someone," Ryan said.

Gloria gently caressed Ryan's forearm. "You saved the pilots once. You can't save them twice. Life doesn't work that way. Let it go."

"Bud?"

Mr. Light checked his caller ID while grabbing a quick breakfast in The Safety Corps executive cafeteria. "Yes, Ma'am."

"Tell me about Operation BLINDSIDE," Vice-President Walker said.

"Seventh Fleet will soon deploy from Yokosuka."

"What else?"

"The TSC has registered twenty undercover agents who will board the Lincoln disguised as tech reps. We also have five PDS tech reps on board as well who are aware of the situation."

"What else?"

"Web and Nuke have reported 'all systems go' from The Sharjah Blue."

"Bud?"

Mr. Light opened a blueberry yogurt. "Yes, Ma'am."

"I'm going to give you very specific instructions. There is very precious cargo on the starboard side of the aircraft carrier. I repeat. The starboard side is off limits."

"I'll relay the information, Ma'am."

I lifted Mom from the right seat of my lifted Jeep Wrangler and gently set her down into a wheelchair.

The Peaksville Hospital receiving staff greeted us. "Miss Becker and Mrs. Becker, how are you ladies doing today?"

My frail mom smiled at the attendant. "Wonderfully, thank you."

I locked Mom's rental wheelchair brakes, parked my Jeep into the handicap space, hung the placard, and rushed back to Mom.

"Gracie, you probably have things to do."

"Hush, Mom."

I pushed Mom past Antoine's old room towards the new, high-tech Moriarty Cancer Center.

Mom's favorite nurse greeted Mom and me. "Welcome to the Moriarty Cancer Center, Becker twins."

Mom smiled. "Josie, I like your hair."

"Thanks, Mrs. Becker. You look cute today."

Mom blushed. "Oh please, as if I *had* hair."

Josie smiled. "We have an open booth now. Or if you want to wait a few minutes, it's fine also."

Mom whispered. "Let's get it over with, Josie."

"I think Dr. Chemstrand wanted to speak with you, first."

Josie pushed Mom to the booth, lifted her into the recliner, and turned the television.

Mom smiled and placed her thin hand on Josie's wrist. "You're an angel."

Dr. Chemstrand entered the booth with a chart. "Mrs. Becker, you're looking good. How are we feeling today?"

"*We* feel tired."

"With your permission, I'd like to switch your chemo from INLINE to this other company. We tried the INLINE Pharmaceutical new experimental chemo for three months and your tumor markers shot up from 300 to 750."

"That's why I'm so tired."

"Would you like to switch, Mrs. Becker?"

Mom looked at me.

I nodded affirmatively.

"Yes, please."

"Josie will get you started in five minutes. Do you have any questions for me?"

Mom shook her head negatively and held his hand. "Thanks, Doctor Chemstrand. I like you."

Mom and I sat back. I flipped channels to find a good television program for Mom to watch during the one-hour chemotherapy session.

I saw a *BREAKING NEWS* notification with a Sydney Harbor backdrop.

"We are confirming multiple heart-related fatalities inside the Sydney Opera

House during a packed-house Orchestra performance. Cause unconfirmed. Estimated fatalities number in the hundreds —"

I quickly changed the channel.

"What happened?" Mom said.

I shrugged. "Probably nothing."

Okay, I lied to my mom. It was *not* probably nothing.

"You have friends Down Under."

"Ruby and Luke."

Mom smiled. "Nice kids."

"They're not kids anymore, Mom."

"They'll always be kids to me, Gracie."

I adjusted Mom's pillow again. "Here comes Josie."

V ice-President Walker called the Surgeon General. "Dr. Moriarty?"

"Good morning, Ma'am."

"Are you able to speak?"

Dr. Moriarty drove past the Air and Space Museum with Charity Ferguson in the right seat. "I'm alone in my car, Ma'am."

"What did Voigt want?"

"He asked about the epidemic causes and solutions."

"What did you say?"

"Psychosomatic."

"Did he buy it?"

"Not really. He was the Peaksville Defense and Space CEO. He knows what's happening but won't verbalize it."

"Really?"

"I see his gears turning. Voigt is trapped in our CABESA past, quite honestly."

"He wants out?"

"Yes, Ma'am."

"Life doesn't work that way." Vice-President Walker whispered. "Obfuscate well and you will be rewarded."

Dr. Moriarty parked his Maserati on K Street in Washington DC and set the parking brake. "You can count on me, Ma'am."

Vice-President Walker hung up the phone.

Click!

Charity Ferguson exited the Maserati with Dr. Moriarty. "It's not easy having divided loyalties."

"My loyalties are not divided," Dr. Moriarty said.

Charity laughed. "How's that?"

"My loyalties are with The Syndicate," Dr. Moriarty declared.

"And with me?"

"Yes."

Charity opened the door to the K Street Starbuck's and smiled. "And with your Surgeon General position? And with your wife? And with the Constitution?"

"I have *many* loyalties." Dr. Moriarty smiled at Charity. "But *none* of them are divided."

R uby fastened her apron and Café Opera nametag. "G'Day, Simone!"

Simone cried. "You haven't heard."

"Heard what?"

"Nicole and her mother both had heart attacks at the Sydney Opera House. They both died."

Ruby Kyle gasped. "Oh, God!"

"Apparently hundreds of people died from heart attacks."

"Did they catch the perpetrators?"

"What do you mean, Ruby?"

"Perpetrators."

Simone corrected Ruby as they sadly prepared the InterContinental Hotel Sydney breakfast buffet. "Ruby, they all had *heart attacks*."

"Oh. Sorry." Ruby feigned modern, twenty-first century Western naivety. "Poor, sweet Nicole and her dear mother."

K nock. Knock. Knock.

"Good Morning, Lieutenant Junior Grade Walker, do you have a minute, Ma'am?"

Mercedes Walker lowered her brown leather, steel-toed flight boots from her Division Officer desk and stood up. "I do now!"

Antoine entered her small VFA-195 office in their Atsugi Naval Air Base flightline hangar. "You're the new Powerplants Division Officer, correct?"

"That's what Skipper is telling me."

"I'm Petty Officer Jordan. I'm your Assistant LPO engine mechanic."

Mercedes stood, smiled and shook Antoine's hand. "Nice to meet you. What you got, there?"

"Airman Evaluations for all of the *E-3 & Below* in Powerplants. They're due in six weeks. I'll be working with you to complete them. Can you review my drafts and check my grammar?"

"I can return them by four o'clock. I have a Field-Carrier Landing Practice (FCLP) hop in ten minutes."

Antoine studied her patch and smiled. "Tater?"

Mercedes laughed. "Skipper and Burner had this patch embroidered before I arrived to Japan on the Freedom Flight. Maverick, Goose and Iceman were apparently not options."

"Why the name 'Tater'?"

"I'm from Idaho."

Antoine smiled. "Me too."

"Where?"

"I'm from Peaksville, Ma'am."

"North Idaho neighbors. I'm from Coeur D'Alene."

"I heard about your close call. Glad you're okay."

"Some USAF guy from Yokota saved my rear end. Another Idaho guy, apparently."

"What's his name?"

"Skid. That's all I know. I haven't met him, yet."

Antoine smiled. "I'll let you go. No rush on those evaluations. We can bang them out when we're 'Haze, Gray and Underway' steaming to Hong Kong. By the way, I have a twin brother on the Lincoln named D'Andre. He's ship's company, AKA a black shoe. Navigation Department."

"Well, there's only one of me. Unless, of course, I've been secretly cloned." Mercedes smiled and whispered. "That's a scary thought."

Antoine laughed. "Fly safe, Ma'am."

"Thanks! Nice meeting you, Petty Officer Jordan from Idaho!"

CHAPTER EIGHT

Vice-President Walker pressed her intercom button. "Send the Secretary of Education in here for my two o'clock."

Secretary Michaels opened the door. "Good afternoon, Vice-President Walker."

"Close the door."

Secretary Michaels complied.

"Sit down."

Secretary Michaels carefully chose a seat.

Vice-President Walker reviewed some paperwork.

"How may I help you, Ma'am?"

"I want to learn about Department of Education messaging for our youth."

"Very well. Do you have specific questions?"

"President Voigt gave you some instructions regarding the global epidemic."

"Not exactly, Ma'am."

"Explain," Vice-President Walker said.

"I told him about my $3 billion advertisement campaign."

Vice-President Walker rubbed her hands together and smiled. "Tell me more."

"Well, Surgeon General Moriarty and the medical community decided that heart attacks are triggered psychosomatically."

"Continue."

"The Department of Education, therefore, launched a parallel campaign instructing children in school how to avoid heart attacks."

Vice-President Walker smiled. "I'm very, very eager to hear about this, Secretary Michaels."

"The Department of Education has partnered with Hollywood to create twenty-minute training videos."

"What's in the training?"

Secretary Michaels beamed with pride. "The various IMAX-quality movies instruct children to crouch under their desks during the first indication of cardiac arrest nearby."

"Brilliant."

"Thanks."

"Like a tornado drill?"

"Yes, but eyes closed and ears covered to avoid triggering a psychosomatic response to a neighboring heart attack."

Vice-President Walker laughed. "Oh, that's rich."

"President Voigt seemed to not like the campaign, Ma'am."

"I *really* like it. I'm going to push another $3 billion from emergency funding into this DOE advertisement campaign."

The Secretary of Education became emotional and nearly cried. "Thank you, Ma'am."

Vice-President Walker rubbed his shoulder. "Children should always come first."

"I agree one-hundred percent, Ma'am."

B rianna Jordan refilled her cup with hot tap water and dipped a new green teabag. "How is life in downtown Tokyo, Gigi?"

"It's good."

Brianna selected a sushi plate from the belt and smiled. "Finally. Salmon has arrived!"

Gigi Becker selected a tuna plate. "My favorite."

The Kanagawa Prefecture sushi-go-round restaurant's serpentine belt paraded hundreds of tea-cup-sized sushi plates past fifty booths. Each booth was equipped with a hot water tap, green tea bags, diced ginger roots, wasabi and soy sauce.

Brianna mixed soy sauce and green wasabi in her small dipping dish with her chop sticks. "Tell me about your Tokyo job, Gigi."

"Ginza2Gaijin Modeling Agency hooks me up. They always have a new photo shoot for me daily at Mitskoshi department stores. But —"

Brianna lived vicariously through the nineteen-year-old model's stories. "But what?"

"But my favorite times in Japan are visiting you on Atsugi Naval Air Base. Food courts. Navy guys. American food. Navy guys. Did I mention Navy guys?"

"Oh, Gigi! You crack me up."

"How's your sister?"

"Gracie or Gloria?"

"My classmate." Brianna smiled. "Gracie."

"Kind of lonely. She misses you guys. She takes care of Mom, helps Charlie with the Epley farm, and works at Peaksville Bread Company."

Brianna sighed. "How is Mrs. Becker?"

Gigi shrugged. "They keep switching chemo formulas. Good weeks and bad weeks."

"Your mom's a saint, Gigi. So is Gracie."

"Thanks, Bree."

Gigi looked around the Zama-area sushi-go-round restaurant and whispered. "Bree?"

"Yes."

"Are we safe in Japan?"

"Why, Gigi?"

"The global heart attack thing. Millions are dying. One of our British models just died of a heart attack. She was my friend. Only nineteen, like me. Lots of ambulances in the last few days in Ginza."

"That's horrible."

"Bree, you live on a military base. If you hear something, please warn me."

"I will. You're *always* welcome to visit. The Lincoln deploys soon so I expect regular visits."

Gigi winked and quickly grabbed a plate of crab sushi from the belt. "Cani!" (*pronounced kah-knee*)

"Charity, this is Abby."

Charity turned off her speakerphone. "Mrs. Vice-President, how are you?"

"Oh, cut the crap, Charity. I've known you since high school. Call me Abby."

Charity joked. "Yes, Mrs. Vice-President Abby, Ma'am."

"Give me a break."

Laughter.

"I see your daughter on CNH News more than I see you these days."

"Sorry, I know you're busy with Operation CHAOS."

"The first few days was the most challenging."

"How's that?"

Vice-President Walker whispered. "Convincing a newly-trained MEDWEAP Operator to kill five people is difficult. Convincing that same MEDWEAP Operator to kill the next five thousand people is simple. Corrupting a human being is the challenge. That's why Operation CHAOS had a slow start for thirty-six hours."

"Understood, Abby."

"While we are on the subject of human beings that have been corrupted," Vice-President Walker paused. "Tell me about your meeting with President Voigt."

"I told him about our global TSC child trafficking sting operation using live, young bait."

"You did what, Charity?"

"Think, Abby."

Vice-President Walker paused. "You dirty rat, Charity. You made President Voigt an accomplice by briefing him. You corrupted him."

Charity laughed. "For years, President Voigt has climbed and clawed towards the top of the scary, dark well of corruption to escape his demons."

"And you just pulled him back down into the dark water."

"Splash," Charity joked.

"That's why I like you, Charity."

"Is Skid here?"

Max Burns greeted the tall, blond pilot visiting his Yokota squadron ready room. "I'm Skid."

"Are you the F-35 Skid?"

"Depends. Is the F-35 Skid in trouble?"

"No."

"Does the F-35 Skid owe someone money?"

"No."

"Then, Yes. I'm Skid."

Max's USAF squadron mates studied the attractive Navy pilot's unpolished brown boots, wrinked flightsuit, low flightsuit zipper position, and green NOMEX jacket with Carrier Airwing FIVE patches.

Mercedes Walker smiled and hugged Max. "I'm Tater."

Max squeezed her tightly. "Tater! You were the one. Are you okay?"

Mercedes nodded. "Just got dizzy up there. I wanted to thank you."

"Dehydrated?"

Mercedes shrugged and smiled. "Me just went sleepy. What's your name, Skid?"

"Max."

"I'm Mercedes. Where are you from?"

"Peaksville, Idaho."

"Coeur D'Alene, here. Do you know the Jordan twins?"

"AJ and DJ?"

"Sounds right. Antoine is a Mech in my squadron Powerplants shop. DJ is a shoe on the Lincoln."

"Yeah, I knew the Jordan twins. Amazing guys. Antoine spent some time in a coma. D'Andre spent four years blind."

"Wow. Were you friends?"

Max nodded and faded his speaking volume. "We were friends, Tater. There was a time when we were friends."

"Alright, Flyboy!" Mercedes hugged Max again. "Gotta beat Highway 129 traffic back down to Atsugi."

"Good luck with that, Gaijin. Got your 'yen-gun' loaded for the toll roads?"

Mercedes patted her left flightsuit pocket as Japanese coins jingled. "I keep my laser-guided 'yen-gun' loaded and set to fully-automatic."

Max laughed.

"I still need to pack my skivvies and socks. We're deploying tomorrow."

"On the Lincoln?" Max asked.

Mercedes nodded. "I owe you one. When I return, sushi-go-round is on me, Skid."

"Catch the *three-wire*, Mav!"

Mercedes smiled. "Ha! I'll settle for the *one-wire*, *two-wire*, *ten-wire*, any wire! I still get butterflies in the stomach on final. They say it goes away after logging one-hundred traps."

"Navy talk."

"Sorry, I would talk 'Airforce talk' but I never watched *Iron Eagle*."

Max laughed. "Navy pilots are so stuck in the 1980's. Just like their airplanes."

"Thanks again, Skid!"

"Fly safe, Tater."

"Send in my three o'clock."

The Oval Office door opened. "Good afternoon, Mr. President."

"Dr. Klein, have a seat, please."

President Voigt joined him on the couch.

"Dr. Klein, I realize that you're my Opioid Crisis Special Advisor, but I wanted to ask you about the global heart attack crisis."

"Anything you need, Sir."

"I'll cut to the chase. What do *you* think has caused 233 million world-wide heart attacks in one week?"

Dr. Klein looked around the Oval Office. "May I close the door?"

President Voigt nodded.

Dr. Klein returned and whispered. "Sir, the heart attacks. I shouldn't —"

President Voigt waited ten seconds. "Speak freely."

"Very well. Between 2013 and 2020, we slammed our moral compasses onto the boulders of North Idaho. We shattered them during the CABESA Initiative, Mr. President."

President Voigt sighed. "What about now?"

"I've prayed daily for a replacement moral compass. It's 2027, I live in Washington DC, and I'm still waiting for that package to arrive."

President Voigt fiddled with old USAF coins on the Resolute Desk.

"Unfortunately, I don't think that God ships replacement moral compasses to Washington DC," Dr. Klein said.

President Voigt leaned back and sank into deep thought. "Without a replacement moral compass, you contend there is no reversal to what is happening globally."

Dr. Klein nodded. "No hope."

"I was afraid of that."

Dr. Klein nodded.

"You think this is CABESA-related."

Dr. Klein nodded.

President Voigt rubbed his eyes. "None of us *can* blow the whistle, then."

Dr. Klein nodded.

"You're saying that we're all implicated. You're saying that nobody can or will step forward."

Dr. Klein nodded.

"At least you're honest."

"Too honest, Mr. President?"

President Voigt nodded. "Probably too honest."

"Nuke?"

Mr. Murdstone found a Sharjah Blue deck chair with good satellite phone reception. "Hey, Bud."

Mr. Light sat in the Washington DC beltway traffic. "How's Dubai?"

"I'm on the Sharjah Blue right now. We just left Yokohama."

"Forgot. How was the sushi?"

"Mustafa Muscat's yacht serves sushi daily on the ship."

"Isn't Japan's sushi better?"

"Not really." Mr. Murdstone laughed. "Mustafa cycles the finest chefs from dozens of countries onboard. It's quite luxurious."

"Must be nice."

"Web and I partook in five-star Yakisoba, Shabu shabu, and Kobe beef without walking down the brow."

Mr. Light drove passed the Pentagon in his BMW. "Nuke, the Queen Bee has instructions."

"About what?"

"Operation BLINDSIDE."

"Do I need a pen?"

"It's pretty easy. Left side is off limits. Precious cargo on left."

"Let me write it down." Mr. Murdstone whispered slowly and wrote into his notepad. "*Left side off-limits. Precious cargo on left.*"

"Thanks, Nuke."

"Bud, how's your tightrope act between the President and Vice-President?"

"Exactly like you described it."

"How's that?"

"It's an *act.*"

Mr. Murdstone watched Mount Fuji on the Sharjah Blue's starboard side. "Don't fall from the tightrope, Bud."

"Are you safe in Sydney, Ruby?"

"Gracie." Ruby smiled and whispered in the restaurant lobby. "Thanks for calling."

Charlotte and I sat on the porch swing of her two-story, Peaksville farmhouse. "Tell us you're okay."

"Luke and I are fine."

I whispered to Charlotte. "Charlie, they're okay."

Charlotte gave a sigh of relief.

Ruby stepped outside of the Café Opera into the grand lobby of the InterContinental Hotel Sydney. "Charlie's there?"

I held the phone up to Charlotte. "Hi Ruby! Love you and miss you!"

"Love you, too!" Ruby said.

"Ruby, I'm going to put you on speakerphone, okay?"

"Okay."

Click!

"How's this?"

"Good!"

"We saw the Sydney Opera House news. What happened?"

"Gracie, I don't want to say too much on the phone. Let's just say it was Peaksville Part Two. My friend and manager Nicole died with her mom. Fit as a fiddle. Coroner said heart attack."

"Same stuff?"

"Same stuff."

"Dang."

"But much, much worse. Gracie, that was 2020. Imagine seven years of development."

"Do you know for sure?"

Ruby looked around the InterContinental Hotel lobby and whispered. "I had a veiled warning in advance. It wasn't' even veiled. Someone told me to my face something was happening at the Opera House. Then, he died of cardiac arrest. You want to hear the worst part?"

"What's that?" I asked.

"Nicole personally *heard* the warning and didn't believe it. She went to the Opera House and died with her mom."

"Like Tommy Boy used to be?"

"I couldn't stop her." Ruby cried. "I couldn't *save* her."

"That's terrible. I overheard something in the Peaksville Bread Company before it happened. I think the same North Idaho partners in crime did it."

Ruby whispered. "CABESA is global now."

Charlotte leaned towards my iPhone. "Are you guys actually safe in Sydney? All this stuff is happening around the world. We're worried about you."

Ruby whispered into her phone. "Charlie, Aussies are worried sick after the Opera House event here. Young people are dying around us in The Rocks historical district, movies, restaurants, bars, you name it. Ambulance sirens every fifteen minutes."

"Peaksville doesn't have that problem," I said.

"Hope it stays that way," Ruby said.

Ruby paused. "This is pretty heavy stuff."

Charlotte agreed. "We miss you, Ruby."

"Come stay with us in Sydney."

I sighed. "We have our moms to take care of. And Charlie has the farm."

"Do me a favor, hug Mrs. Becker and Mrs. Epley for me."

"Will do!"

"Gracie, I pray nightly for your mom."

"Love you, Ruby."

"Love you."

Click!

"Send in my next appointment, please."

Dr. Hands entered the Vice-President's office. "Ma'am."

"Have a seat, Doctor."

"Thanks, Ma'am."

"How's the family?"

"Great, Ma'am. Couldn't be happier."

"How is your company? Peaksville KidCare Global Counseling Services, correct?"

"Fantastic. We are hiring one thousand global grievance counselors per day. Our employee morale is outstanding."

"Funding okay?"

"We'll need another $1 billion, soon."

"See my secretary for that accounting data. How's your position as Advisor to the President?"

"It's fine."

"What do you both speak about?"

"Primarily the global health epidemic."

Vice-President Walker sat next to Dr. Hands. "What exactly were the President's concerns?"

Dr. Hands shrugged. "He simply asked about solutions to the epidemic."

"What was your response?"

"I reminded him about the settled science of primary heart attacks triggering secondary psychosomatic heart attacks."

Vice-President Walker accidentally smiled. "Did he buy it?"

"Ma'am?"

"Sorry, Doctor. Did he agree with the settled science?"

"He didn't directly say."

"Did President Voigt ask about rogue actors or exhibit any other suspicions?"

"Rogue actors?" Dr. Hands shook his head. "No, Ma'am. He didn't mention rogue actors. Why?"

Vice-President Walker patted Dr. Hands on the shoulder and led him to the door. "You're a great American. Keep up the great work, Doctor!"

Dr. Hands smiled proudly and exited the office. So proudly, he almost forgot to stop at the secretary's desk for the accounting data approving additional funding.

CHAPTER NINE

"Hello, Nuke are you there?"

Mr. Murdstone fumbled to adjust his satellite phone on a Sharjah Blue deck chair on the bow. "Mr. President, can you hear me now?"

President Voigt leaned back in his leather chair. "I got you *Lima Charlie*, Nuke."

"Same, Sir."

"You sound like you're in a tornado, again."

Mr. Murdstone attempted to shield his satellite phone mic from the aggressive bow wind. "Japan is windy today, Sir. Hey, I found out something that may interest you. An intelligence and security firm operating in Japan is based in China. They may have stolen some of the Peaksville Defense and Space sensitive MEDWEAP technology designed to help children. We're investigating."

President Voigt leaned forward. "Great work, Nuke."

"Thanks."

"What's the name of the firm?"

Mr. Murdstone paused. "Sir?"

"The name of the firm, Nuke."

Mr. Murdstone looked around the deck of the Sharjah Blue. "Lifeboat Enterprises is their pseudonym. I'm working with some contacts to learn more about this mysterious firm which is likely controlled by the Chinese communist government."

"Copy all, Nuke."

"That's all for now, Mr. President."

"Great work."

Click!

Mr. Webster woke up in his lounge chair. "Who was that?"

"Voigt."

"What did he want?"

"Answers."

"Your answer sucked."

"Queen Bee wants me to keep Voigt on daily wild goose chases."

Mr. Webster laughed. "Lifeboat Enterprises, Nuke?"

Mr. Murdstone shrugged and buttered his grilled lobster-tail lunch plate on the Sharjah Blue's bow in the Southeast Asian sunlight near Honshu Island. "Voigt bought it."

Mercedes, flying wing off her skipper, arrived at three-thousand feet over the USS Abraham Lincoln overhead stack, fifty miles south of Atsugi.

The USS Abraham Lincoln Airboss provided instructions for all CVW-5 aircraft hawking the deck for the deployment fly-on. "99, this is Airboss. Hook up first pass."

Skipper checked his wing. "Tighten it up, Tater."

"Copy, Sir." Mercedes concentrated on her skipper's lead Rhino checkpoints and gently made constant elevator and aileron stick corrections. She manipulated her power levers to work her Super Hornet closer in on the bearing line.

"Tater, you good?" Skipper transmitted on Dambuster base frequency.

"A-firm, Sir."

Skipper smiled and tried to put her at ease. "Just a walk in the park, right?"

Mercedes nodded her Navy helmet when he looked back.

"Lookin' good, Tater."

She peeked at the aircraft carrier below with a large white wake, no sea spray and high swells. "Postage stamp is right!"

"Tater, high seas. Ship's making its own wind. Expect a large burble pulling you down and pitching deck. Anticipate the requirement for extra power behind the stern earlier than normal."

Mercedes keyed her mic on the starboard power lever by raising her left thumb. "Copy, Sir."

Mercedes mumbled to herself into her oxygen mask. "Varsity conditions. Great."

"Dambuster 301 and 306, Your signal is *Charlie*."

The skipper smoothly advanced his power levers to avoid spitting Tater out of formation. He adjusted his flight path to intercept a three-mile initial. The O-5 checked the inexperienced O-2 hanging onto his wing and called Airboss. "Boss, 301 and flight, Initial."

Mercedes copped a few sneak peaks at the Lincoln out her front window as her Super Hornet formation leader accelerated for the Navy Overhead Break.

Passing the bow, the skipper kissed her off with a hand signal, broke left and pulled away.

Mercedes looked inside for situational awareness while tracking upwind of the boat. "Okay, Tater, 800 feet, 400 knots, check reciprocal heading, three seconds, four seconds, five seconds. And… break."

She banked left into seventy-five degrees angle of bank, retarded her power levers to idle, popped open her speedbrake and pulled backstick to peg 6 g's.

"Hook-khah! Hook-khah!" Mercedes tightened her sternum muscles to keep her now-heavy blood in her head from falling into her chest to avoid a G-Induced Loss of Consciousness (G-LOC). At 6 g's, her 20-pound head was now a 120-pound head.

She rolled wings level on downwind at her reciprocal heading, popped her landing gear and flaps down, performed shipboard landing checks and mumbled. "Hook up for one. Great."

Mercedes rolled into the groove on final. "306, Hornet ball, fuel state nine-point-five."

"Roger ball, working thirty-one knots of wind, slightly starboard, got you a little high."

Mercedes made corrections to fix her high and mumbled to herself. "Butterflies."

The Landing Signal Officer spoke in a calm voice. "Little power back on."

Mercedes drifted left.

Another calm LSO transmission. "Right for line-up."

Mercedes added too much power while fixing lineup.

The LSO remained calm on Tower Freq. "Easy with it. Attitude."

Slam!

Mercedes hit the carrier flightdeck at 135 knots, threw her power levers forward with her left hand, and immediately lifted off again by pulling backstick with her right hand. She left her wheels down, lowered her tailhook, and intended to fly upwind for a minute.

"That sucked. Need comfort time." She mumbled to herself in her F-18. "Need comfort time upwind."

"306, Airboss, Hook down. Turn downwind. *Now*."

Mercedes rolled left and mumbled to herself. "Dang. Thanks Boss. No comfort time. You can't rush art."

She eventually rolled final again. "306, Hornet ball, fuel state nine-point-zero."

"Roger ball."

Slam!

Her hook engaged the four-wire on the fly and she decelerated from 135 knots to zero in two seconds. Mercedes accidentally keyed the Hornet's mic during her violent, controlled crash. "Ooooh."

The LSO keyed the mic with laughter in the background. "It was good for me too, Tater. You can release your mic, now."

Mercedes accidentally kept her power levers at military power after coming to a complete stop.

The Air Boss transmitted and laughed as the F-18 engines continued to roar. "We got you, 306. Power back."

Mercedes powered down, raised her hook, and taxied her exhaust stacks clear of the landing area five seconds before another Super Hornet trapped.

She gathered her gear and raised her canopy. "Petty Officer Jordan!"

Antoine yelled over the surrounding jet noise. "Looking like a pro!"

Mercedes removed her mask. "Feeling like an amateur!"

Antoine helped her climb down safely.

Mercedes grabbed Antoine's float coat, pulled him close, and yelled over the jet noise into his headset. "I met the Yokota F-35 guy who saved me! It's Max! He knows you guys!"

"Max Burns?"

Mercedes Walker nodded. Thirty knots of flightdeck wind caused her to naturally lean towards the bow. She slapped her helmet bag. "I didn't forget the Powerplant EVAL's! Give me one day! They look good so far, Petty Officer Jordan!"

"Max saved you?"

Mercedes nodded, flashed a 'thumbs up' and nodded. "Jet's up!"

Antoine yelled. "Anything broken?"

"No gripes!" Mercedes walked to the aircraft carrier island to achieve safe passage to her VFA-195 Maintenance Office.

Antoine mumbled as he watched her walk. "Max Burns saved my Division Officer?"

Congressman Bonner quickly paged through the NASDA. "2020 North American Scheduled Depopulation Agenda. What kind of sick, tyrannical horse-puckey this? Where did you get this?"

Aaron shrugged.

Congressman Bonner found his name in the heavy book. "Tex Bonner. 2027. Cardiac Arrest? The PIH printed this in 2020?"

Aaron handed the Speaker of the House the second book. "Here's another, Sir."

"2020 MWOP. MEDWEAP Operator Master List? What's a MEDWEAP, Aaron?"

Aaron paused. "An extension of the 2013 CABESA Initiative."

"CABESA?"

"Mr. Speaker, does your heart still hurt, today?"

Congressman Bonner nodded and paged in disbelief. "I don't understand. I helped get CABESA passed and funded in 2013. I sponsored CABESA."

"Sir, there is no worldwide health epidemic."

"Then what is it, Aaron?"

Aaron pointed at the NASDA and MEDWEAP Operator Master List books. "Murder."

Speaker of the House Tex Bonner leaned back in his leather chair and looked out his window at the Lincoln Memorial. "Land of the free. Home of the brave."

Mr. Murdstone visited CAPT Farsi on the bridge of the nuclear-powered weapon platform disguised as a luxury, 800-foot private yacht owned by Mustafa Muscat of Dubai. "Captain Farsi?"

"Nuke, my friend, staying out of trouble on the Sharjah Blue?"

Mr. Murdstone smiled at the elderly, uniformed Iranian ship driver. "It's like paradise onboard this ship."

"Have you found the bowling alley?"

Mr. Murdstone paused. "No, where is that?"

Captain Farsi smiled at the TSC Intelligence Officer secretly employed as the Sharjah Blue Weapons Officer. "Keep looking, my friend."

"I will."

Captain Farsi smiled at his often-successful bowling alley prank.

"Captain, I got a message from the Queen Bee through Bud."

"For me?"

Mr. Murdstone nodded. "It's concerning Operation BLINDSIDE. Here is the note from my phone conversation with Bud."

"LEFT SIDE OFF-LIMITS. PRECIOUS CARGO ON LEFT."

"Understood, my friend. We will comply. We'll avoid the port side."

"Thanks, Captain. It sounded important."

"My friend, I will follow this instruction from Queen Bee. And now, I would like to invite you for dinner. Tonight's chef hails from Istanbul and prepares Turkish Delight."

Mr. Murdstone smiled. "Sounds delightful."

"Nurse Penang?"

"Yes?"

"Hello, my name is Jack Kernan, this is Chloe Epley."

The Phuket Hospital Emergency Room receiving nurse smiled. "Hello. How may we help you?"

"Two young men, both foreigners, arrived via ambulance yesterday. We would like to visit them."

"Jake from Australia," Chloe said.

"And Ricky from New Zealand," Jack said.

"One moment, please. I will see." The cheerful Thai nurse walked into a small administrative office.

Jack put his arm around Chloe. "Jake and Ricky are probably back in their hotels already."

An elderly Thai doctor exited the office and slowly approached the North Idaho nineteen-year-olds.

The doctor double-checked his charts. "Hello, you came to see the two young men from down under? Mr. Jake and Mr. Ricky."

Jack and Chloe nodded.

"Are you family?"

"Just friends."

"We recently verified notification to their families via Red Cross, so we can pass the news to you. They passed away earlier."

"Oh, no!" Chloe said.

The seventy-year-old Thai doctor gently whispered. "This way, please."

Jack and Chloe followed him into a private wing of the ER lobby.

"What are your names?"

"Jack."

"Chloe."

"Jack and Chloe, I retire next year. I grew up in Phuket and graduated UCLA medical school in 1984. I worked in the Phuket Hospital ER for over 40 years. This week we had several young person cardiac arrests. Ricky was my youngest heart attack fatality in my career. It is a very sad week for me."

"What's going on, Doctor?" Chloe asked.

The doctor shrugged. "I was hoping you could tell me."

. . .

"Mr. President, you called for me?"

President Voigt greeted Vice-President Walker with a hand shake, closed the door, and smiled. "Have a seat, Abby."

"Thank you."

The two CABESA Initiative veterans started their Oval Office meeting with an uncomfortable silence.

"Beautiful day, Sir."

President Voigt nodded. "Cherry blossom season never disappoints."

Vice-President Walker smiled. "Well then."

"How are we doing on the global health epidemic, Abby."

"The TSC is reporting 233 million global fatalities. The United States accounts for thirty million of the deaths."

President Voigt pointed at his Oval Office television set. "I could get a casualty count from CNH or FXH News."

"Then what are you looking for, Mr. President?"

"You said you were going to instruct medical professionals to revisit the disease, plague or contaminated food source angles."

"Oh, yes."

"And?"

"Sir, they're sticking with the psychosomatic studies. 95 percent of medical community and scientists are in unison, which makes it settled science. It's out of my hands. Besides, going against the medical community is politically unwise."

President Voigt stood up and walked to his door.

Vice-President Walker followed.

"Abby, you know damn well what's happening."

Vice-President Walker stood face to face with the President. "And exactly what *is* going on?"

President Voigt looked her in the eyes with parsed lips for ten seconds then opened his Oval Office door.

Vice-President Walker exited, turned around and smiled. "Enjoy cherry blossom season. While you still can, Mr. President."

CHAPTER TEN

"Hotdogs again?"

Antoine set his tray with the embossed CVN-72 logo down. "We're in the Western Pacific Ocean. On a boat, DJ. What do you expect, Turkish Delight?"

D'Andre completed a quick, silent prayer before dinner on the USS Abraham Lincoln Enlisted mess decks. "You wanted to tell me something about one of your VFA pilots?"

"Have you seen Lieutenant Junior Grade Walker?"

"The tall blonde girl who looks like a Kernan twin?"

"Yes."

"She's from Coeur D'Alene."

D'Andre took a bite of his hotdog. "Small world."

"Max saved her life up in Tokyo."

D'Andre stopped chewing. "Who?"

"Max Burns."

"How?"

"She passed out in her Super Hornet. He thumped her with USAF F-35 jetwash until she woke up."

D'Andre became agitated. "Max Burns. Son of the Peaksville TSC Vice-President. Son of CABESA helicopter pilot Mr. Burns."

"Yes."

"The same Max Burns that mustered just enough humanity and ethics to only save Emma in 2020?"

Antoine looked around. "That was seven years ago, DJ."

"His dad experimented on us, and Max didn't care enough to help."

"DJ, his dad died in the helicopter crash."

D'Andre feigned playing a miniature violin on his shoulder. "Our dad was heart attacked in his sleep along with many other dads."

"Anyhow, Max saved my Division Officer."

"Good for her."

The Jordans sat in silence for a few minutes.

"I'm not hungry." D'Andre stood up and dumped his tray in the trash. "And I have to get back up to the bridge."

Charity Ferguson grabbed a handful of pretzels from the basket. "President Voigt is literally trying to solve the 'quote-unquote' global health crisis."

"I noticed." Dr. Moriarty slouched in Ritz Carlton Washington DC hotel lounge.

"Political theater for next year's 2028 Presidential Election?"

"More than that." Dr. Moriarty drank some beer from his mug. "Newly found idealism."

Charity laughed. "Did President Voigt suddenly find religion?"

"Not really. He always faked it in Peaksville."

"True." Charity smirked. "He'd attend church on Sunday before testing Peaksville Defense and Space MEDWEAP's on children all week."

"Thirty years in the military but very naïve."

"How's that?"

Dr. Moriarty poured a new beer from the pitcher. "He thought CABESA experimentation was for freedom."

Charity sipped her beer and smiled. "Voigt made his millions. It's all an act. He knows CABESA buttered his bread for fourteen years."

"I don't think it's an act. He really changed."

Amy and Emma Kernan walked into the Andermatt Hospital Emergency Room.

Amy addressed the receiving nurse. "We're looking for Sven, a Swedish boy who was admitted yesterday."

The Swiss nurse looked at the twins. "Are you family?"

"We're his ski instructors," Amy said. "We called Life Flight."

"One moment, please."

Amy waited for some time in the waiting room then looked at her watch. "It's been ten minutes."

Emma daydreamed and didn't respond.

"Emma, did you hear me?"

"Oh, sorry. I was thinking. The Swiss Life Flight passed over so many times."

Amy interrupted Emma. "Don't say it."

"You considered it?"

"Nonsense, Emma. Switzerland is a free country."

A young ER nurse entered the waiting room. "Girls?"

"Yes?"

"This way."

Amy smiled. "You're taking us to see Sven?"

The nurse stopped walking. "We did everything we could. Sven's heart failed."

"Sven died?" Emma asked.

The nurse nodded affirmatively. "I'm sorry."

Amy cried. "He was twenty-five."

"How?" Emma said.

"2027 has been a peculiar year per our hospital director, Dr. Von Trapp. In his thirty-five-year career, he never tended to a heart attack victim below thirty. This year, after only five months —"

Amy wiped her tears. "This year what?"

The Swiss nurse closed her folder. "I shouldn't say. I'm sorry for your loss."

L uke saw Ruby enter The Australian Heritage restaurant, delivered two Roo Burger and Chip entrees, and walked into the lobby. "I heard about the Opera House."

"The man's warning was real."

Luke whispered to Ruby. "Careful what you eat and drink."

Ruby nodded. "It might be something else."

Luke paused and whispered. "I hope not."

"Nicole and her mom went last night."

"Are they okay?"

Ruby parsed her lips and shook her head negatively.

"I'm sorry, Ruby."

"Nicole was my guardian angel at work. She hired me and trained me."

Luke hugged Ruby and kissed her cheek. "I have to run. Table 12 is signaling. See you tonight, babe. Be careful."

M y iPhone screen alerted me that my sister Gigi was calling from Tokyo. "Mom, it's Gigi calling!" I answered the call. "Gigi!"

"Gracie!"

"How are you? How's Japan?"

"Pretty good, pretty good. Gaijin2Ginza keeps me busy."

"I'll put you on speakerphone! Say hello to Mom."

Click!

"Hi Mom, it's me, Gigi!"

Mom rested in her recliner, recovering from the chemotherapy. "Little Gigi, my love."

"How are you feeling, Mom?"

"I've seen better days, Gigi. I'm getting old, baby."

Gigi paused before answering and started to cry. "I miss you, Mom!"

Mom tried to speak clearly in her groggy state. "Maybe when I get better I'll come to Tokyo and model with you. Do they allow wheelchairs on the runway?"

Gigi laughed and cried. "Oh, Mom."

Mom was too tired to keep speaking.

I changed the subject. "Gigi, tell us about Tokyo."

Gigi paused. "It's been a little weird lately with this whole heart attack thing —"

Click!

I took Gigi off speakerphone and walked outside.

"Gigi, are you safe?"

"I guess so. There are ambulances speeding past my apartment constantly. As long as one doesn't stop for me, I'm good, right?"

What about the Jordan twins and Bree?" I asked.

"The Lincoln deployed so it's just Bree and me. AJ and DJ are underway."

"Hang out with Bree as much as you can. Safety in numbers."

"Okay, Gracie."

"Oh, and Gigi?"

"Yes."

"I'm going to put you back on speakerphone to say goodbye to Mom. Don't mention anything bad happening. I'm trying to shelter her from this global health epidemic news."

"Okay."

Click!

I walked inside.

"Hey Mom, Gigi is going to say goodbye."

"Love you, Mom! You get well soon, okay?"

"I'm surrounded by angels, Gigi. I have an angel in every time zone."

Gigi audibly cried. "Bye, Mom."

. . .

"Web, your TSC H-53 carrying the Tactical Victim Unit is ten miles north of the Sharjah Blue and inbound," Omar Muscat said.

Mr. Webster looked at his watch. "They're early."

"Not early enough!" Omar yelled.

"Copy that, Sir," Mr. Webster replied.

Mr. Murdstone watched Omar leave and whispered to Mr. Webster. "Omar yelled at you."

Mr. Webster shrugged. "Omar *Muscat* is Mustafa *Muscat's* oldest son."

Mr. Murdstone looked around the Sharjah Blue bridge and whispered. "Is Omar senior to Captain Farsi?"

Mr. Webster shrugged as the TSC H-53 set up for landing on the ship landing pad.

"Is Omar senior to Dr. Braun?"

Mr. Webster shrugged. "Dr. Braun has a seat on The Syndicate."

"You didn't answer my question, Web."

Captain Farsi keyed his mic. "Bounty Hunter One, winds zero-three-zero at six, cleared to land."

The TSC H-53 helicopter pilot read back his clearance on Sharjah Blue tower frequency. "Cleared to land."

"Web?"

The one-hundred-foot-long H-53's rotor wash created a small storm of Western Pacific sea spray on the stern of the 800-foot, Dubai-based armed luxury yacht.

Touchdown.

The Sharjah Blue ground crew connected tie-down chains.

"Nuke, here's the deal. Omar Muscat's dad is Mustafa Muscat, the most powerful man in the world. Omar, therefore, *always* thinks he's the senior man in the room. His father pays us a lot of money."

"So, what?"

"So, Nuke. Don't cross Omar."

"Come on in, Bud!" President Voigt exclaimed from the Oval Office.

"Good morning, Mr. President."

"Close the door, please."

Mr. Light walked back to close the door.

"Have a seat, Bud."

"Thank you, Sir."

President Voigt walked around the Resolute Desk to sit on a couch with Bud. "Tell me what you found out."

"Sir?"

"The Global health epidemic."

Mr. Light sat up straight. "Well, I was under the impression that Dr. Moriarty is investigating the causes and remedies for the heart attacks."

"You were?"

"I was waiting for some clarity from the medical side of the Administration before I went chasing down any 'theories' that are not medically supported."

President Voigt leaned forward. "So, Bud's TSC doesn't act until Surgeon General Moriarty figures this out?"

"Not exactly, Sir."

"Oh, really?"

Mr. Light changed his tune. "Well, I tapped a few of my classified contacts around the world to investigate."

"Oh, you have other countries investigating."

"And I am performing an investigation into the cause of the heart attacks."

"You didn't tell me that initially."

"Sorry, Sir."

"We're right back where we started. Tell me what you found out during your investigation."

"It's an ongoing investigation."

President Voigt paused. "Do you think there could be a rogue government that —"

"That what, Sir?"

"Some *things* happened in Peaksville between 2013 and 2020, I have heard."

Mr. Light wiggled in his seat. "I heard that, too."

"These heart attacks. Could they be the result of —"

"Result of what, Sir?"

President Voigt stood up. "Well, it sounds like you don't know."

"Sorry, Mr. President. I guess I'm not following you."

"You're excused, Bud."

J ack and Chloe found a seat at the Pad Thai Shop and checked their menus.

"What's happening over across the street?"

The nineteen-year-olds watched two young tourists being carted away on stretchers into ambulances.

Chloe held Jack's hand. "Are we safe in Thailand, Jack?"

Jack shrugged and pointed at the big screen. "Something happened at the Opera House."

"We interrupt this program with breaking news. The Australian government and TSC officials in New South Wales are confirming multiple heart-related fatalities inside the Sydney Opera House during a packed-house Orchestra performance. Number of heart-related fatalities estimated in the hundreds. I'm Krissy Moriarty, Global Public Health Crisis Correspondent. You're watching FXH News."

"Hundreds?" Chloe asked.

"Heart-related?" Jack asked.

"Ruby and Luke work in The Rocks nearby," Chloe said.

Jack squeezed Chloe's hand tighter. "Something is happening. Something too familiar."

"Keep me safe, Jack."

Jack placed his arm around Chloe and nodded. "I will."

"Promise?"

Jack kissed her forehead. "I promise, Chloe."

I walked into the living room with my iPhone. "Mom, Gloria called from Hong Kong!"

Mom smiled and talked into the phone. "Glory Be."

"How are you feeling?"

Mom struggled to answer. "Like a million bucks, Gloria."

"What's the doctor saying?"

"Oh, Gloria. Dr. Chemstrand is trying. He and Josie are still working in the Moriarty Cancer Center, but they aren't miracle workers."

"I like Josie." Gloria nodded. "What are they saying, though?"

Mom changed the subject. "Gloria, you tell me about Hong Kong. How's that fishing business?"

"It's good."

"Good."

"By the way, Ryan says hi, Mom."

"Tell Ryan I love him. Tell Maddie the same, too."

"Okay, Mom."

Mom got tired. "I love you, Glory Be. I have to go to a tennis lesson."

Gloria cried. "I love you, Mom."

Click!

"Don't hang up, Gloria!" I turned off the speakerphone and rushed outside. "Gloria?"

"Yeah?"

"Okay, I'm outside."

"How is she, Gracie?"

I sat on our Peaksville front porch swing. "Tumor marker shot up to 750. But the doctor is good. It's been over 750 three times in two years. Don't worry. It will come back down."

"I'll keep praying."

"Gloria, you've been watching the news, right."

"Yes." Gloria paused. "Everything old is new again."

"Okay, I wanted to make sure you guys are paying attention."

"Be safe. Love you, Gracie."

"Love you, Gloria."

"Good morning, President Voigt."

"Good morning, Mr. Speaker. What can I do you for?"

"I want to get smart on CABESA," Congressman Bonner said.

"Come on in and sit down, Tex."

The two leaders sat on Oval Office couches after President Voigt closed the door.

"Tex, would you like water? Maybe some tea?"

"No thanks, Sir."

President Voigt began to explain the Cooperative Adolescent Biotech Experimental Science Act of 2013 to the Speaker of the House. "You inquired about CABESA. I know some things about CABESA. I was the Chief Executive Officer of Peaksville Defense and Space between 2013 and 2020."

"The high-tech military weapons manufacturer?"

President Voigt paused. "Yes, Tex."

"Weapons?"

President Voigt uncomfortably nodded.

"I co-sponsored CABESA in 2013."

"I remember, Tex."

"Didn't CABESA have something to do with children and curing cancer, though? It was one of those altruistic *'for the kids'* bills."

"Initially."

"Did it morph into something else?"

"To be honest, Tex, I'm out of the CABESA business. Vice-President Walker has taken the reigns of that program."

"Abby Walker? You trust her?"

President Voigt paused. "Sure, I do, Tex."

CHAPTER ELEVEN

C aptain Farsi utilized his satellite phone from the bridge of the nuclear-powered Sharjah Blue yacht between Taiwan and the Philippine Islands. "We're in position, Mustafa."

Mustafa Muscat lounged near the swimming pool of his 140th floor penthouse atop Sharjah Blue Towers in Dubai, UAE. "Is the area clear?"

"Closest vessel is fifteen miles."

"Commence Operation BLINDSIDE."

Captain Farsi set down his satellite phone and transmitted to the ship's Weapon Control Center. "We have a green light."

An 1100-foot Supertanker named Shanghai Sword steamed towards its Yokohama destination laden with two million barrels of Middle Eastern oil.

The Sharjah Blue flight deck crew removed the tie-down chains from the H-53. Inside the tactical helicopter's cabin, ten members of the TSC Tactical Victim Unit prepared for launch.

Mr. Murdstone watched an older gentleman in tactical gear with multiple weapons run into the black H-53. "Web, who was that?"

"That's Ivan Smirnov!" Mr. Webster yelled over the helicopter noise. "He's one of our shipmates on the Sharjah Blue, but you won't see him much onboard. He's a billionaire Russian oligarch, former KGB, Seat Holder in The Syndicate since its 2001 inception. Ivan is also Mustafa's golfing buddy."

"Why is he flying with the American Tactical Victim Unit?"

Mr. Webster covered his ears as the 5MC system blasted. "One second."

Captain Farsi broadcasted a landing pad warning. "H-53 taking off from Spot One. Stand well clear, stand well clear."

The TSC H-53 pilot lifted off as the Sharjah Blue flight deck crew knelt down and grabbed deck tie-down pad-eyes to avoid being blown overboard.

Mr. Webster continued before his walkie-talkie sounded. "Ivan never misses these missions."

"He looked like he was seventy." Mr. Murdstone said.

Mr. Webster smiled as he fumbled to answer the call. "Ivan's older than he looks."

"Web, ready in the WCC!"

Mr. Webster replied into his Motorola walkie-talkie. "Copy that, Ben. Enroute."

"This way, Nuke."

Mr. Webster led Mr. Murdstone into Sharjah Blue's dimly lit, high-tech, three-thousand square foot Weapon Control Center. "Ben, verbalize your procedures for Nuke. For training, please. Nuke's the new Weapons Officer."

"Copy, Web."

Ben Light, the youngest Officer on the Sharjah Blue at twenty-five, offered Mr. Murdstone a chair and headset. "Okay, Nuke. The nuclear-powered QUAD-Capacitors are at 87% and building. Up there on the Big Board, you can see the Sharjah Blue south of Taiwan." Ben pointed. "Right there."

"Got it," Mr. Murdstone said.

"There is the Shanghai Sword. Right *there*. Tracking zero-four-three at twelve and one-half knots south of Taipei bound for Yokohama."

"Solar Flare, this is Bounty Hunter One on TAC-3 frequency."

"That's the TSC Tactical Victim Unit." Ben tapped his boom mic. "Bounty Hunter One, this is Solar Flare, we got you five-by-five on TAC-3. Say status."

"Up and Ready. We're on your zero-eight-zero at five miles. Fuel state seven point five. Thirteen souls on board. Standing by for tasking."

"Standby, Bounty Hunter One, Solar Flare passing 94%."

"Copy."

Ben pointed at the gauges. "Nuke, here's our nuclear-powered, Third-Generation MEDWEAP passing 95%. Ben switched the Big Board to a high-resolution targeting video."

Mr. Murdstone watched in disbelief. "You can see them through metal on the bridge at ten miles?"

Ben smiled. "Not for long."

Mr. Webster coached his young instructor. "Tell Nuke what you see, Ben."

"Okay. Here you can see these five Chinese people on the ship have had influenza shots laced with Lot-24 or later Imaging Probes from PsytoSCOPE

Nanotech Corporation in Peaksville. Probably old people. I don't see their childhood vaccinations."

Ben Light pointed and instructed. "The other seven people on the ship haven't had a flu shot since 2022. But I'm able to target their Lot-21 Imaging Probes from their childhood vaccinations. That group is probably in their mid-twenties based on the frequencies."

Mr. Murdstone was amazed. "Wow. Through the ship's bulkheads?"

Ben Light interrupted to make a radio call. "Bounty Hunter One, this is Solar Flare on TAC-3. QUAD-Capacitors 98%. All systems go. Confirm up and ready."

"Up and Ready."

Mr. Murdstone watched Ben lift a trigger guard over a large red button.

"Power checked. Traffic checked. H-53 verified and clear. Targets checked. And, *Fire!*" Ben pushed the button and then closed the safety guard. "Any questions, Nuke?"

"All done?"

Ben smiled and pointed to the bridge personnel. "They're all horizontal. All done. The TSC Tactical Victim Unit insertion team has it from here."

"And the crew on the bridge of the Shanghai Sword? Are they dead?"

"Dead." Ben Light smiled. "Or wishing they were dead."

"President Voigt still hates me."

General Marsh flashed his ID to the Peaksville Defense and Space gate guard driving into work. "Tell me something I don't know, Bud."

Mr. Light sat in his BMW, stuck in beltway traffic. "Cheer me up, Swamp."

"Do you want me to make spider monkey noises?"

"On second thought, don't cheer me up."

"Why did he select you for Secretary of The Safety Corps?"

"Maybe he thought he could trust me."

General Marsh paused. "Have you spoken with the Queen Bee?"

"Yes."

"What are you going to do?"

"I guess I'll do what I've always done."

"Go to the zoo and flip off the monkeys?"

Mr. Light laughed. "No, follow orders."

"The Queen Bee's orders?"

"Yes."

"When?"

"Soon."

"Damn."

"Damn is right."

General Marsh paused. "I'll be waterskiing in Peaksville. That's my alibi."

"I'm jealous."

"Hey, Bud?"

"Yeah, Swamp?"

"After this all goes down, I'll deny ever knowing you. Just like Saint Peter, I'll deny you three times before the cock crows."

Mr. Light paused. "That's what friends are for."

General Marsh sighed. "See you, Bud."

C aptain Scott Smart stood next to the Hong Kong Harbor Pilot on the USS Abraham Lincoln bridge. "Petty Officer Jordan, report traffic inside of two miles."

"Captain! Sharjah Blue yacht, Dubai markings, port side, ten thousand feet, five knots! Shanghai Sword Oil Supertanker, Chinese markings, starboard side, three-thousand feet, eight knots!"

The Navigation Officer collapsed.

Captain Smart barked instructions. "Jordan, call DC Central. Gator's down."

"Aye, aye, Captain!"

D'Andre complied.

The Lincoln's internal 1MC blasted. "Medical Emergency, Medical Emergency, Space O9 tack 122 tack 10. Alert the flying squad."

Antoine stood in Mercedes Walker's stateroom as she briefed her corrections on the VFA-195 Airman EVAL's. "O9-122-10! Ma'am, that's my brother's navigation office on the bridge! Can I come back in ten minutes?"

Mercedes smiled in her Navy Liberty Whites with only four ribbons from the Naval Academy and Pensacola flight school. "I'll be here in my state room packing civvies for the Hong Kong port visit."

"Be right back!" Antoine ran towards the starboard ladderwell leading to the aircraft carrier's bridge.

Captain Smart studied the Shanghai Sword and conferred with the local Harbor Pilot ferried to his warship via Navy helicopter. "Is that a typical West Lamma Channel profile?"

The small, Chinese Harbor Pilot shook his head. "Very *abnormal*, Sir. That traffic is pointing our way."

D'Andre provided an update. "Captain! Shanghai Sword, nine knots, two-thousand feet! Converging!"

"Sound the horn!"

Honk! Honk! Honk!

The Hong Kong Harbor pilot collapsed.

"The Shanghai Sword is not responding on any frequency, Captain!"

Three more bridge personnel collapsed, including the OOD.

Captain Smart exclaimed. "Jordan, speed and distance!"

"Ten knots, nine hundred feet!"

Captain Smart's training kicked in. "Call DC Central, Jordan! Initiate General Quarters!"

D'Andre complied.

"Speed and distance!"

"Twelve knots, four hundred feet!"

Another bridge Petty Office collapsed.

Captain Smart keyed the internal 1MC and external 5MC. "All hands, Brace for impact! Brace for impact! Starboard side!"

Antoine was passing the O7 level to check on his brother in the tower.

Crash!

The massive, heavy-laden Shanghai Sword Supertanker T-Boned the USS Abraham Lincoln on the starboard side.

Antoine was knocked down one flight of stairs to the O6 level. (*pronounced "Oh Six"*)

The 1MC blasted in Antoine's ear. "Fire! Fire! Fire! Fire in space O3 tack 110 tack twelve. Alert the flying squad."

"LTJG Walker's stateroom!" Antoine reversed course and slid down the ladderwell like a seasoned fireman from the O6 to O3 level.

Captain Smart collapsed on the Lincoln bridge.

D'Andre screamed. "You gotta wake up, Sir! Captain. The Shanghai Sword is scraping on our starboard side."

Captain Smart groggily climbed into the Captain's chair and immediately ordered course and speed corrections. "Thanks DJ!"

"LTJG Walker!" Antoine ran inside the blazing VFA-195 stateroom. "Tater!"

No response.

Antoine found Mercedes on the floor and turned around to look into the O3 level passageway.

Fire!

Antoine looked at the damaged external bulkhead as the Supertanker slid aft along the aircraft carrier's starboard side.

Scrape! *Crunch*! *Daylight*!

Antoine chose daylight over fire, picked up his Division Officer, and fireman-carried her through the wreckage to analyze the situation.

"Forty-five feet to the water, are you ready, Ma'am?"

No response.

Fire rapidly enveloped her stateroom.

Antoine felt the intense heat. "Wake up Ma'am. We're jumping."

Mercedes nodded her head and wearily whispered. "Jump."

Antoine and Mercedes impacted the cold South China Sea saltwater after the long fall.

Antoine surfaced and looked around. "Lieutenant?"

Mercedes surfaced with her head slumped forward.

Antoine performed a right hand to right wrist water rescue spin then side-stroked her clear of the 95,000-ton American warship's violent wake.

Mercedes remained disoriented for five more minutes in the choppy West Lamma shipping channel leading north to the Hong Kong Harbor.

"Wake up, Mercedes. Don't fade away."

An eighty-foot fishing charter boat appeared on the horizon.

Antoine elevated the downed pilot's chin inside his left elbow and repeatedly whacked downward with his open right hand to create a visible white-water flash. "Over here!"

Antoine heard an American voice.

"Ahoy, swimmers!"

"Hello Nuke? How is your research into the Japanese-Chinese firm named Lifeboat Enterprises?"

"Excuse me?"

President Voigt repeated himself. "Lifeboat Enterprises."

Mr. Murdstone elbowed Mr. Webster on the Sharjah Blue shuffleboard deck. "Oh. Lifeboat. That was unfortunately a dead end, Mr. President."

"The global heart attack rate is accelerating. Do you think you'll be able to crack the code on this crisis, Nuke?"

"Absolutely!"

"What's your next lead?"

Mr. Murdstone hesitated and bumped Mr. Webster again. "What's my next lead, you ask?"

"Yes, what else you got?"

"Okay, this is a little early to speculate on validity, but I'm researching —"

"Nuke, you there?"

Mr. Murdstone covered his satellite phone mic. "Web, help. What's my next lead?"

Mr. Webster set down his bourbon, pointed at his Turkish Delight, shrugged and whispered. "Possible food poisoning by an Eastern European separatist group."

"The Russians?"

Mr. Webster corrected him and quickly whispered. "Eastern European separatists."

Mr. Murdstone spoke into the satellite phone. "Sir, can you hear me now?"

"Got you, Nuke."

"Sir, we're running down leads on possible food poisoning by an Eastern Eurasian separatist group."

Mr. Webster face-palmed, slugged Mr. Murdstone and whispered. "Eastern Eurasian?"

Mr. Murdstone shrugged and waited for the Presidential response.

President Voigt closed out the phonecall. "Okay, sounds like you got your hands full, Nuke. Keep me informed."

Click!

Mr. Webster laughed. "Eastern Eurasian?"

"How would I know?"

"LTJG Walker, a fishing boat!"

Mercedes opened her eyes and spit out salt water. "What happened?"

Antoine held her chin elevated above the West Lamma Channel's surface. "Lincoln got rammed."

"Ahoy, swimmers!"

A rope ladder was thrown down to Antoine and Mercedes by a Chinese deck hand. "Grab line! Grab line!"

Antoine reached. "Got it!"

A large, strong hand reached down. "Give me her arm!"

The hand pulled Mercedes up onto the fishing boat as Antoine pushed from below. "You're next!"

Antoine patiently waited for his turn.

The hand grabbed Antoine's right wrist and yanked him up from the water. "Welcome to the Ben Gunn, Antoine Jordan."

Antoine looked at the young, Irish-looking fisherman's face, laughed and cried tears of joy. "Ryan Flynn!"

Ryan smiled and retracted the rope ladder.

Antoine hugged Ryan. "My brother from another mother!"

Ryan looked at Gloria and Madison. "Look what I caught, Ladies!"

Madison screamed while tending to Mercedes. "AJ!"

"Catch of the day!" Gloria said.

"Antoine, you guys got intentionally T-Boned. I saw the whole thing."

Madison looked at Antoine as Mercedes lay prone. "What's her name?"

"Mercedes. She's a Hornet pilot in my squadron from Coeur D'Alene."

Li Jie, the Chinese deck hand, brought clean, dry towels.

Gloria whispered. "It's okay, Mercedes from North Idaho. You're safe on the Ben Gunn."

Mercedes smiled and coughed.

The grey SH-60 Seahawk from Atsugi-based HS-14 arrived and hovered over the Ben Gunn.

A twenty-year-old Rescue Swimmer lowered himself on a cable and yelled over the helicopter turbine and rotor noise. "My name's Washington. Is Tater okay?"

Antoine yelled. "Starboard side impact knocked her down! Water impact also knocked her silly!"

The HS-14 crewman secured Mercedes inside the stokes litter made of metal bars and chicken wire then hoisted her into the Seahawk.

Washington fitted Antoine with a harness.

Ryan yelled upwards after the winch energized. "Antoine! You got liberty soon?"

Antoine looked at the Lincoln's wrecked starboard side. "Maybe!"

"Flynn Brothers Fishing Charter in Star Ferry Terminal! Come visit! Bring D'Andre!"

Antoine Jordan flashed a 'thumbs up' down to his old Peaksville friends as Petty Officer Washington hoisted him into the Navy helicopter. "Okay!"

CHAPTER TWELVE

"Bree, it's me Gracie."

"Gracie, thanks for calling."

I walked outside to let Mom sleep. "I saw the news about the Lincoln in Hong Kong. Was that the aircraft carrier homeported in Tokyo?"

"Yes, Gracie. That's our boat."

I sat on my porch steps to stop my pacing. "Tell me AJ and DJ are safe."

"They're safe."

"Oh, thank God."

"Bree, you must have been scared to death when you saw the news."

"Actually, I just got a phone call, first."

"From Antoine?"

"Gracie, brace yourself."

I paused. "Okay."

"When was the last time you spoke with your sister, Gloria?"

"Yesterday."

Brianna Jordan sat down in her Atsugi Naval Air Base home on Liberty Lane. "Okay, here it goes. A rogue supertanker T-Bones the Lincoln. The TSC said it was an accident, of course."

"I saw that."

"Lincoln officer stateroom catches fire. Antoine saves female pilot."

"Wow."

"It gets better. Antoine jumps with pilot into Hong Kong harbor to avoid fire. It was about forty feet into the harbor."

"Double wow."

"Wait for it… Guess which fishing charter boat saves AJ and this pilot girl?"

"You're kidding, Bree! They didn't!"

"They did! Gracie, I kid you not. Gloria called from the Ben Gunn to let me know that Antoine was alright. *Before* CNH even broadcasted the news."

"Well, thank God that Antoine and D'Andre didn't get hurt."

"Gracie?"

"Yes, Bree?"

"Now it's my turn to ask you something."

"Okay."

"How's Mrs. Becker?"

I looked and gently made sure the front door was secured and whispered. "Bree, I wish I could say fine."

"Tumor markers?"

"Just jumped up."

"Good doctor?"

"Great doctor, great nurse named Josie."

"Is Mrs. Becker happy?"

"I think so."

"Gracie?"

"Yes?"

"Are *you* happy?"

Tears!

Brianna made me cry. "I wish that I could say yes, Bree."

"Come visit us in Japan. Stay with me on base. Stay with your sister, Gigi."

"Charlie has the farm. I have my mom. I can't."

"It's tough, isn't it?"

"Ask Charlie and me in a couple years. We'll travel the world with you."

Brianna paused. "I love you, Gracie. I'm here for you."

I changed the subject to stop crying. "Gigi told me about the ambulances in Tokyo."

"It's happening on base here, Gracie. It's constant. Two ladies in my Enlisted Wives Club died this week. Both mid-twenties."

I paused a few seconds. "Is it happening-happening?"

Brianna quietly answered. "We've been down this road before. Haven't we?"

"Be safe, Bree."

"Love you, Gracie."

"Love you."

Click!

· · ·

The United States House of Representatives Speaker of the House called the Secretary of The Safety Corps. "Bud?"

"Yes, Sir?"

"Bud, this is Tex."

Secretary Light closed his TSC office door. "Oh, hello Mr. Speaker."

"How are things at The Safety Corps?"

"Very safe, Sir."

Congressman Bonner heartily laughed then continued in his Texan accent. "Very well. But, are you keeping things safe for American citizens? I think that's why we're paying you guys."

"Oh, yes, Mr. Speaker."

"Tell me about Peaksville, Bud."

"Snow skiing. Water skiing. Hunting. Fishing. Great town to raise a family or raise livestock. It's North Idaho. You'll need a four-wheel-drive for the snow. And a rifle for the bears, wolves and cougars."

"Sounds like Texas with snow."

"Yes, Sir. We don't have any Texan wild boars in Idaho, though."

"Sounds nice. But that's not exactly what I meant. Tell me about the 2013 CABESA Initiative in Peaksville. If I remember correctly, and I'm reading my scribble, CABESA stood for Cooperative Adolescent Biotech Experimental Science Act. Does that ring a bell?"

"Sounds about right."

"A little birdie told me there were weapons involved."

"Negative, Sir. Only medical devices, Mr. Speaker. And nothing invasive or harmful."

Congressman Tex Bonner paused. "Well, I'm looking at some vintage CABESA documents, circa 2020, and —"

"Hey, Sir? I've got another call on the line from Vice-President Walker. Could I get back with you?"

"Sure, Bud."

"Thanks!"

Click!

"Who was that?" Charity Ferguson asked.

"Speaker of the House Bonner."

"Problem?"

Secretary Light looked out his TSC office window towards the Capitol Building and checked his watch. "Not for long."

. . .

C harlotte smiled. "Wow, Gracie. Let me get this straight. You said the Ben Gunn rescued Antoine and the female Navy Pilot out of the water after the collision?"

I squeezed a lemon into my Peaksville Bread Company sweet tea at our favorite window seat overlooking Schweitzer Mountain Ski Resort. "Brianna got the whole story from my sister, Gloria, immediately after the rescue."

Charlotte ripped a bread roll and dipped it in her Clam Chowder. "Pretty amazing stuff."

I looked out the window at the same old mountain view. "Nothing ever happens in Peaksville. Anymore at least."

"Maybe that's a good thing," Charlotte said.

I shrugged.

Dr. Gunnison leaned over and whispered. "Excuse me, ladies?"

I smiled. "Dr. Gunnison."

Charlotte smiled, "Hello, Sir."

"I'm interrupting again. I'm very sorry."

Charlotte laughed. "It's perfectly fine. We're just a couple of hens clucking away."

"You're certainly not a couple of hens. You seem like very nice girls."

We blushed.

"I'm going to recommend something to you since you are both so lovely."

I winked at the PIH CEO. "You want to recommend your favorite Turkey Avocado sandwich?"

Dr. Gunnison laughed. "It is very pleasant, Grace. But, no. I would like to say that you both need to take a vacation from Peaksville. Get out and see things. Get into those mountains and explore. Go hiking for a few days."

Charlotte looked at me. "That's a good idea."

Dr. Gunnison continued. "Perhaps you have a favorite hiking trail or camping location. Take a break. Enjoy North Idaho. Then come back and work at the PIH."

I smiled. "I think we'll do that."

"I'm sorry to be nosy. I'm just leaving. You ladies have a nice day. Take that break tomorrow. Just go camping and relax." Dr. Gunnison stood up and walked to the Peaksville Bread Company's entranceway. "Promise me you'll go camping tomorrow, Ladies."

"We promise," Charlotte said.

I smiled. "Why didn't we think of that?"

Charlotte looked around. "Let's go tomorrow morning."

I whispered. "TFZ?"

Charlotte nodded. "You read my mind."

. . .

M r. Light changed lanes passing the Arlington Cemetery and fumbled for his iPhone. "Hello?"

"Bud?"

"Hello, Ma'am."

"Have you seen CNH News?" Vice-President Walker asked.

Mr. Light proudly celebrated. "Operation BLINDSIDE. Mission accomplished with no problems, Ma'am."

"Don't make t-shirts just yet, Bud."

Mr. Light braced for impact. "Ma'am?"

"Have you actually looked at the video and damage on CNH News?"

"Yes, ma'am."

"What side had the precious cargo?"

"Left side, Ma'am."

"What side is 'left side' in *Navy Talk*."

"You mean port or starboard?"

No response.

Mr. Light guessed. "Starboard side is left, Ma'am."

Vice-President Walker paused. "You're Air Force?"

"Yes, Ma'am."

"*Google* port and starboard. I'll wait."

"Right now, Ma'am? I'm driving."

"Right now."

"One second."

Bang! Bang! Thump!

Mr. Light dropped his phone in his BMW.

"Damn."

Vice-President Walker face-palmed and waited sixty seconds.

"I understand now. My apologies, Ma'am."

No response.

"Was the precious cargo damaged?"

No response.

"It won't happen again, Ma'am."

No response.

"I'm hanging up, now, Ma'am."

Vice-President Walker beat Mr. Light to the disconnection.

Click!

.   .   .

Madison responded to the bell of their fishing charter's customer service window inside Star Ferry Terminal. "Welcome to Flynn Brothers. May I help... Antoine! D'Andre!"

Madison ran outside and hugged them as hundreds of Navy sailors shopped in their whites. "Look at you guys, so handsome in those uniforms!"

The Jordan boys beamed with pride.

"Maddie, it's been years! You look great!" D'Andre exclaimed.

"Gloria! Ryan! Get out here! Look what I found!"

Gloria screamed and hugged the young sailors. "Handsome is right. Definitely a very prideful thing to be dressed in those whites. Let me get some pictures."

Click!

Gloria and Madison snapped selfies with the Jordan twins.

Ryan smiled. "Dinner's on me tonight, boys! Delayney's Irish Pub in Kowloon."

D'Andre smiled, stepped back and looked up at Ryan's business signage. "Flynn Brothers Fishing Charter."

Ryan parsed his lips and nodded. "My dad, Marcus, Derrick and I always dreamed of having a —" Ryan couldn't continue and quickly turned away.

"I like it."

"God, I miss your brothers, Ryan!" Antoine said. "I've been thinking about Peaksville a lot."

Ryan wiped his tears. "Thanks."

Madison covered her eyes to hide tears and walked into the office.

D'Andre whispered. "Is Maddie okay?"

"Ryan mentioned Derrick." Gloria shrugged. "She still misses Derrick."

Ryan changed the subject. "When do you both have to be back onboard?"

D'Andre checked his watch. "We turn into pumpkins at midnight."

Antoine pointed to the Lincoln Liberty Boat station in Star Ferry Terminal ferrying Japan-based sailors back and forth to the anchored, wounded warship. "That's our ride."

"We own you guys until 11:59pm."

Antoine smiled. "Deal."

Seven years had passed since our multiple 2020 treks through The Forbidden Zone to the West Peaksville Neodymium Mine. Charlotte and I packed enough gear, clothes, food and water for three nights.

Charlotte met me west of Peaksville High School with a large, fluffy old dog.

I knelt and greeted my favorite one-hundred-fifty-pound she-wolf. "Kiche!"

Kiche painted my face with giant licks.

"Ruby's mom wanted us to bring her for protection," Charlotte said.

"How was Mrs. Kyle doing?"

"Pretty sad after hearing about the Opera House event. She's worried about Ruby in Sydney."

"I can't blame her."

Charlotte agreed.

I petted Kiche. "Gigi always asks about you, Wolfie. I missed you, too."

Kiche got excited and pushed me over.

Charlotte laughed. "Is your mom all set, Gracie?"

"Josie is going to visit before and after work. How about the Epley farm?"

"Mr. Whipple is going to water our animals, feed them and check on Mom daily."

I smiled. "Let's do this!"

We arrived at Peaksville Creek, excited to use the rope swing linking Peaksville High School and The Meadow.

"It's gone!" I said.

We looked around for ten more seconds.

"Someone cut the rope!"

"Gracie?"

"Yeah, Charlotte?"

"The rope swing's not gone."

I scanned upstream and downstream. "Where is it?"

Charlotte pointed upwards. "Up there."

Mr. Light entered Vice-President Walker's office and closed the door. "Tell me what you found out in the Oval Office, Bud."

"He knows, Ma'am."

"He knows what?"

"Voigt suspects there are rogue actors."

Vice-President Walker sighed. "He said that?"

"Not really."

"What did he say?"

"Voigt *almost* mentioned the Peaksville CABESA Project and our MEDWEAP testing on children."

"Why didn't he?"

Mr. Light shrugged. "Seemed like guilt."

"Guilt. The greatest American flaw. Nations have been toppled by guilt-pushers. I got over that emotion years ago."

"What should we do?" Mr. Light asked.

Vice-President Walker gazed out her window at the Lincoln Memorial. "We push guilt on him."

"Yes, Ma'am."

"Bud?"

"Ma'am?"

"A house divided against itself, cannot stand."

Mr. Light paused. "Did you just make that up?"

Vice-President Walker face-palmed.

"Bud?"

"Ma'am?"

"The Lincoln needs to sink."

I saw the dangling Peaksville Creek rope swing twenty feet above us and gasped. We silently digested the passage of seven years.

"Charlotte?"

"Yeah, Gracie?"

"The trees grew up. Did we grow up, too?"

Charlotte attempted to ignore my question. "Over there, we'll cross."

We forded Peaksville Creek by sitting on a downed 80-foot-long cedar trunk bridge and scooting across.

I laughed as we slow-straddled the suspended cedar. Our Cabela's hiking boots dangled over Peaksville Creek. "Seven years ago, I would have walked on this trunk."

Charlotte started laughing with the cedar between her legs. "You asked if we grew up."

I gradually advanced, foot-by-foot. "Don't even think about answering that right now."

Kiche forded the deep creek down below, swam a bit, breathed heavily and smiled.

I stopped momentarily to point downward. "Charlie, the she-wolf is laughing at us."

Charlie looked around as cedars swayed in the wind. "I think nature is laughing at us."

We eventually removed our twenty-five-year-old bodies from the dead cedar trunk, stood up, struggled to regain lost dignity, and ran across The Meadow like giddy, little school children.

I dropped my pack, jumped in The Boxcar and picked up some school papers. "Charlie!"

Charlotte read a worksheet and handed it to me. "Gigi Becker, sixth grade math."

I picked up more papers. "Jack Kernan! Gigi again! Chloe Epley, English worksheet!"

Charlotte cried. "Sixth-grade. I hope Chloe is okay in Phuket. Do you think they're safe?"

"Jack is as tough as nails. He instructs Muay Thai."

We stuffed the 2020 nostalgia in our pockets, jumped from The Boxcar, slung our backpacks and walked downhill to Liberty Lake with Kiche.

We stood and looked at Deadman's Cliff.

"So many good memories, Gracie."

"So much pain, Charlie."

Charlotte grabbed my hand and smiled. "Let's just remember the laughs."

"And forget the pain?" I asked.

Charlotte shrugged. "Yes."

CHAPTER THIRTEEN

Vice-President Walker greeted her next appointment from INLINE Pharmaceuticals. "Dr. Klein, please have a seat."

"Thank you."

"Can I get you a drink?"

Dr. Klein smiled. "I'm fine, Ma'am."

"Call me Abby, please."

"Very well, Abby."

"You're President Voigt's Opioid Crisis Special Advisor."

"Yes, Ma'am."

"What things do you talk about with President Voigt?"

"Well, since we invaded Afghanistan in 2002, we've lost about 10 million people to opioid abuse or misuse. It's 2027, annual opioid deaths are still strangely climbing. I am trying to reverse this growth by 2030."

Vice-President Walker changed the subject. "Do you speak about the current global health epidemic with President Voigt?"

"In passing, only in an advisory role."

"And?"

No response.

"And what did you advise, Doc?"

Dr. Klein shifted in his seat. "Well, that was a personal conversation, Abby."

"He's going to tell me anyway, I just want to be prepared."

"I told him what I believe."

"And what *do* you believe?"

Dr. Klein looked Vice-President Walker in the eye. "I believe that the global heart attacks are the result of rogue actors utilizing Peaksville Defense and Space MEDWEAP technology developed under our watch in Peaksville under the 2013 CABESA Initiative."

"You really believe that?"

"I really believe that."

Vice-President Walker smiled. "Dr. Klein, CABESA was a very controlled medical study with strict oversight. You're suggesting that 233 million have been slaughtered globally by rogue actors?"

Dr. Klein nodded.

Vice-President Walker laughed. "That's a grand theory."

Dr. Klein shrugged. "The technology exists, Abby. We developed the MEDWEAP's in Peaksville, right?"

"Your theory goes against settled science."

"Abby, it's only an opinion."

"A dangerous opinion."

"Dangerous to whom, Ma'am?"

Vice-President Walker paused then stood up and extended her hand. "Okay then, Dr. Klein. It was a pleasure, as usual."

Dr. Klein exited the office before Vice-President Walker closed the door.

Vice-President Walker dialed her iPhone. "Bud?"

"Yes, Ma'am."

"See me. Today."

"Yes, Ma'am."

Click!

R yan ordered a pitcher of Guinness beer from the waitress in Delayney's Irish Pub. "Do you think she's coming, Antoine?"

Antoine looked at his watch. "She volunteered for duty. Actually, our skipper *volun-told* her. She has Liberty Boat Duty Officer until 8 o'clock. She'll come afterwards."

"Brutal. After a cold swim in the West Lamma Channel wave-pool?"

Antoine joked. "When you're junior in the Navy, you have to basically die to avoid duty on the first night of a port visit."

Madison smiled. "Well then, it's good she didn't avoid duty!"

Gloria smiled. "You told her we're at Delayney's Kowloon, not the Wanchai restaurant, right?"

Antoine nodded. "I told her Kowloon. She's coming."

D'Andre buttered a hot roll. "Apparently LTJG Walker's mom may fly to Hong Kong sometime to thank you guys."

"Her mom might fly to Hong Kong?" Ryan asked.

"I hope she has frequent flyer miles," Gloria said.

Madison nodded. "She must be wealthy."

Antoine tried the spinach and artichoke dip and checked the lobby. "Here comes my DIV-O."

Gloria waved Mercedes towards their long booth.

Mercedes smiled and hugged everyone.

"Mercedes, right?" Madison asked.

"Call me Tater."

Ryan laughed. "You found some dry clothes."

"How are you feeling, Tater?" Gloria asked.

"Petty Officer Jordan got me out just in time," Mercedes said.

Ryan joked. "This is a non-military, first-name-only table we reserved. His name is Antoine."

"Perfect. Let me guess your names." Mercedes pointed around the table.

"Ryan and Gloria. You're married."

The Flynn's smiled.

"Madison?"

"Maddie is fine."

Mercedes smiled. "Maddie."

"Antoine and D'Andre."

The Jordan's smiled.

Mercedes leaned into the Jordan twins and studied the similar faces. "Antoine and D'Andre. Got it."

Ryan ordered Mercedes a drink. "How is the Lincoln?"

"My stateroom is finally air conditioned."

"You guys need dry dock to fix it?"

Mercedes Walker shrugged. "Apparently the Big Navy is talking to the President. That stuff is *way* over my paygrade."

C harlotte and I leapt from boulder to boulder in the Elephant Rocks as the clear, cold spring water perpetually thundered gently beneath us.

I thought the North Idaho boulders would look different since high school. "The rocks. They're still the same."

Charlotte laughed. "What did you expect, Gracie?"

I shrugged. "Maybe seven years isn't a very long time after all."

We walked up the north bank of Coldwater Creek and stopped.

I looked at the cedar trees of Peaksville Forest. "Charlie?"

Charlotte looked.

I pointed. "The parasitic ivy took over. The forest is dying."

"Derrick was right, Gracie."

The wind blew through the cedars. A few remaining live cedars sang beautifully in the breeze.

I grabbed Charlotte's hand and continued upstream. "Let's go."

Charlotte read a posted sign as we circumnavigated Lover's Lagoon. "*By Order of the TSC. Do Not Enter.*"

I laughed. "Scared of the TSC?"

Charlotte shook her head. "No."

I flipped on my flashlight. "Neither am I."

We shined our light into Lover's Cave.

"Kiche, you lead," I said.

We navigated west through the granite cavern for twenty minutes.

"No jelly jars with clues, Charlie."

"I guess we're on our own."

I followed Kiche for another five minutes. "Daylight!"

Charlie stood perched over the steep mountain trail and gazed out at the western TFZ sky. "It's so beautiful."

I nodded. "It's so forbidden."

"Want to take a break?" Charlotte asked.

Kiche galloped down the mountain towards the White River.

"There's your answer."

"Send in the Secretary of The Safety Corps."

Mr. Light entered Vice-President Walker's office. "Ma'am."

"Close the door, Bud."

Click.

"Sit down."

Vice-President Walker joined Mr. Light on the couch and whispered. "How many MEDWEAP Operators do we have working Washington DC?"

Mr. Light counted on his fingers and mumbled for sixty seconds.

"Approximately, Bud."

"Ten percent of Washington DC residents are active, registered MWOP's. That percentage is increasing."

"Training new MWOP's?"

"Terminating non-MWOP's."

Vice-President Walker whispered. "I spoke with Dr. Klein."

Mr. Light patiently listened. "And?"

"Dr. Klein went against settled science. Imagine that, a Special Advisor to the President disagreed with 95% of our nation's top medical professionals and scientists."

"Interesting."

"His divisive rhetoric, hateful vitriol and dangerous discord has no place in a civilized society struggling with such an enigmatic health crisis."

"What do you propose?"

"I propose the problem should go away."

"Go away?"

Vice-President Walker nodded.

"Timeline?"

"Immediately."

Mr. Light cryptically nodded. "Will that be all, Ma'am?"

Vice-President Walker winked and escorted Mr. Light to the door.

"Consider it done, Ma'am."

C harlotte and I continued west along the White River deeper into The Forbidden Zone until we arrived at Rainbow Bridge.

"Charlie?"

"Yeah?"

I stood over a four-foot diameter circle of ten pound rocks.

"Marcus built this fire pit?"

I nodded.

Charlotte attempted to cheer me up. "The campfire rocks are perfectly in position. After all these years, Gracie."

"But the campfire is extinguished."

Charlotte didn't back down. "The foundation remains."

I considered kicking the campfire rocks out of place when suddenly the cedar trees sang beautifully in the northerly breeze.

Kiche smelled high the air with long sweeps of her muzzle and galloped north.

Charlotte yelled. "Kiche, get back here!"

I stared at the fire pit.

"Gracie?"

I was zoned out.

"Gracie?"

I suddenly returned to 2027 after my 2020 space voyage.

"Yeah?"

"Kiche ran ahead. We have to go."

We yelled and ran north towards the Rock Tower. "Kiche!"

My female intuition and a few scars on my body reminded me that we were approaching mountain lion country. "Do you think Kiche's okay?"

We slowed our jog to a walk.

"She's fine, Gracie."

After five more minutes of walking and yelling, we heard footsteps thundering towards us.

Charlotte grabbed my hand, stopped us, and looked around. "Listen."

I grabbed my bear spray and whispered. "Something's coming."

Charlotte lifted her tamarack walking stick. "It's getting closer, Gracie."

"Tex?"

Speaker of the House Bonner picked up his telephone. "Yes, Mr. President."

President Voigt leaned forward on the Resolute Desk. "You asked if I trusted Abby."

"I did."

"Can I qualify my answer?"

"You're the President."

"We're traveling down a very, very dark path."

Congressman Bonner paused. "That's very unfortunate."

President Voigt looked at his American flag in the Oval Office. "Tex, back in Peaksville between 2013 and 2020, we stole some innocence. We killed some mockingbirds."

"I'm sorry to hear that."

"Do you think God will forgive me?"

Congressman Bonner sat down to relieve the pressure on his heart. "I'll pray for you, Mr. President."

President Voigt watched the sunset out his White House window. "I think you better pray for our country."

"Thanks for your honesty, Mr. President."

President Voigt closed out the phone call. "God Bless America, Tex."

Click.

Congressman Bonner keyed his intercom. "Betsy?"

"Yes, Mr. Speaker?"

"Send in my favorite intern. Send in Aaron Webster."

. . .

Charlotte and I stood on the overgrown TFZ path towards the Rock Tower. The galloping noise became louder.

I raised my bear spray.

Charlotte raised her walking stick.

Charlotte laughed.

I looked around. "What is it?"

Kiche cheerfully arrived from behind some boulders with a long animal leg bone. "A doggie with a bone."

"Kiche, don't ever do that again!"

The wolf-dog kept pushing the bone onto my body.

"You want to play catch, girl?"

Charlotte rubbed Kiche's back. "I think she's bringing you a little souvenir, Gracie."

I removed the bone from her long, powerful jaws and examined it. "Smart dog."

Charlotte smiled. "Smart wolf."

Sure enough, two hundred feet north, we arrived at the site of my fateful one-sided clash with the wounded mountain lion. "It's all gone."

Kiche sloppily dug three inches below the sediment and found a rib bone.

Charlotte laughed. "It's not *all* gone."

Charlotte and I began hiking toward the West Peaksville Neodymium Mine again.

"Charlie?"

"Yeah, Gracie?"

"Aaron Webster was right."

"How's that?"

"My physical wounds from the mountain lion are closed up and painless. My moral wounds from CABESA remain wide open. They still hurt, Charlie."

President Voigt waited for General Marsh to pick up his Peaksille Defense and Space CEO office phone. "Swamp?"

"Mr. President! How are you?"

President Voigt sat down and held his aching chest in the Oval Office. "A little tired, Swamp."

"I bet you are. Tough times."

"Swamp?"

"Yes, Sir?"

President Voigt sighed. "You would warn me if there was anything for me to be worried about, right?"

General Marsh did not hesitate. "I got your back, Sir! One-hundred percent!"

President Voigt paused. "I'm considering you for an ambassadorship, Swamp."

"Great, Sir."

President Voigt leaned back in pain and looked around the Oval Office at famous Presidential portraits. "Keep up the great work."

"Yes, Sir."

"Thanks for your loyalty, Swamp."

"Take care of yourself, Mr. President."

Click!

"Hello, Super Jet Pilot."

Mercedes sat in a metal ready room chair holding the VFA-195 squadron duty phone. "Krissy, is that you?"

Krissy Moriarty looked at her FXH News makeup artist. "Can you give me three minutes, Sophia?"

Sophia nonverbally signaled a five-minute warning to Krissy until the next regularly-scheduled FXH Breaking News segment.

Krissy smiled and nodded. "Mercedes, I just wanted to call to make sure you're okay."

Mercedes smiled. "Are we off the record?"

"Oh, please, girl. Tell me about your swim."

"It was no big deal. I got knocked out. I got burned. I got rescued. I got wet. I got rescued again. I got my first helicopter ride."

Krissy laughed. "No big deal?"

"In the whole scheme of things, worldwide, it was no big deal."

"Your mom is awesome, by the way."

Mercedes paused. "You think so?"

Krissy nodded as Sophia gave a two-minute warning. "America is lucky to have Abby as Vice-President. She's such a great leader. I just love her."

Mercedes twirled a ballpoint pen around her fingers. "How's FXH?"

"Awesome! I'm on in one minute. You watching?"

Mercedes clicked FXH News channel on the ready room big screen. "I am, now."

"Got to go, Mercedes!"

Click!

"This is a FXN News Breaking News Alert. Vice-President Walker's expert team of medical physicians and scientists have determined that humans will experience a declining lifespan in the next century, reversing our two-hundred-year trend in America. The lifespan-increase officially reversed in 2016, due to a variety of factors including diet, genetics, and exercise. Some alternative studies attribute irresponsible political loyalties or anti-authority attitudes as possible causes for the shorter life-expectancies. I'm Krissy Moriarty, and you're watching FXH News."

CHAPTER FOURTEEN

Charlotte and I arrived to the West Peaksville Neodymium Mine before sunset.

Kiche frantically smelled the familiar area while wagging her tail.

"She knows," Charlotte said.

"She misses everyone," I said.

"Like we do?"

I nodded. "Like we do."

Charlotte smiled and petted Kiche. "You remember, girl?"

Kiche nervously smelled the mine entrance.

"She'd be better off if she could forget. She looks sad," I said.

Charlotte paused. "She'd be better off without the memories?"

I shrugged. "Probably. Look at her."

Kiche cheerfully joined Charlotte and me and wagged her tail.

Charlotte laughed. "She looks happy to *me*."

I wanted to forget. But I couldn't forget. I wanted to move on. But I couldn't move on. "Why are we here again?"

Charlotte broadcasted our official answer. "Dr. Gunnison suggested a hiking trip."

I sat on a boulder and looked around our campfire site next to the mine. "Charlie, he likely had something to do with Sydney. He told me he was sending fifty PIH Medical Equipment Operators to Australia one day before the Opera House thing happened. He's dirty."

Charlotte nodded. "Maybe so. But —"

"But what, Charlie?"

"But maybe we needed to come to the TFZ one more time. A rite of passage. A way to put the pain behind us. Closure, Gracie."

"Closure?" I asked.

Charlotte nodded.

"No such thing. We're more likely to find a unicorn and pot of gold than closure."

Charlotte looked at me, threw her backpack down and smiled. "Let's gather firewood."

We quietly walked down the mountain to the cold, deep river and wandered along the riverbank. The river speed increased as we continued downstream.

"It smells like smoke, Charlie."

"Probably a controlled burn in Canada."

I licked my finger, held it vertically and looked at the sun for bearing. "The wind is coming from the east."

Charlotte shrugged. "Then it's probably a controlled burn in Peaksville."

We arrived at the river's edge.

"That's the rock, Charlie."

I traversed five large boulders overlooking a one-hundred-foot vertical drop. "Charlie, this is most definitely the rock."

"Be careful, Gracie."

I leaned over and looked down. "Do you think Marcus felt pain?"

"I don't know, Gracie." Charlotte stood on the riverbank and watched me. "I don't think so."

"I need to get closure. Right, Charlie?"

"Let's head back and collect some firewood."

"Without closure, I can't escape the moral wounds of my past."

No response.

I removed my Peaksville High School Class of 2020 24K gold ring and examined it.

"Gracie?"

I held my ring in the air and yelled with all of my might. "I love you, Marcus!"

The sound echoed and reverberated through the North Idaho canyons.

I looked over the edge, kissed the ring, dropped it over the waterfall and whispered. "I'll always love you, Marcus."

I watched it fall one hundred feet.

Splash!

Charlotte waited ten seconds to speak. "Gracie, let's go gather firewood. You're finished here. The thing is done."

I zig-zagged rocks back to Charlotte and wept in her arms.

Charlotte smiled. "You got your closure, Gracie."

We looked at the river's edge one last time.

"I got my closure. Good bye, Marcus."

"Mr. President, your next appointment is here."

"Send him in."

Surgeon General Moriarty knocked and entered the Oval Office. "Sir, you called for me?"

"I'd like to see your latest report on the enigmatic global cardiac arrests."

"Report, Sir?"

"Give me whatever you have."

"Sir, we are still focused on what I said before. You've seen the PSA's on television. The cardiac events are manifested psychosomatically from fear, visual cues and audio cues."

"Not acceptable."

Dr. Moriarty paused. "Okay, Sir. Our experts from PIH, Harvard and Stanford have also developed an alternate scientific theory that the heart attacks are the result of poor diet, lack of exercise, and perhaps hypertension. People that exhibit these traits tend to migrate to the same activities. These subjects, suffering from the same risk factors, are merely suffering their fates together in their own collective demographic group. This creates the illusion of a global health epidemic. In all reality, it's quantitatively a perfectly normal statistical cluster."

President Voigt spun his chair away and faced his window.

"Sir?"

"Surgeon General Moriarty?"

"Yes, Mr. President."

"How many people have died globally from the epidemic?"

"Sir, initially we believed that 233 million people have died this week. But our new alternate theory of statistical clusters negates the theory of a global epidemic. The new number has been adjusted to reflect our new position."

"What is your *new* number of fatalities?"

"Zero, Mr. President."

"Zero fatalities from the global health epidemic?"

Dr. Moriarty paused and smiled. "Correct, Sir. The new alternate theory would eliminate the global health epidemic theory."

"Surgeon General Moriarty?"

"Yes, Mr. President."

"Find the cause of the global heart attacks."

. . .

"The second night in the TFZ was a good idea, Charlotte."

"This hiking and camping gig was Dr. Gunnison's idea, not mine, Gracie."

Charlotte sat with me on a boulder outside the abandoned West Peaksville Neodymium Mine. "I just wish the air wasn't so smoky."

I agreed and lay on her lap. "Otherwise, great trip."

Charlotte yelled into the mine. "What do you think, Kiche? Did you have fun, girl?"

I laughed. "Kiche always has fun."

"Oh, Happy Dog?" Charlotte yelled. "Where are you?"

I looked at Charlotte. "Kiche should have tackled us by now."

Charlotte nodded. "Kiche. Come."

I stood up. "Kiche! Come on, Wolfie!"

"Gracie, you check the mine, I'll look around the campsite."

I yelled inside. "Kiche!"

Charlotte stood on some rocks to look for movement as I entered the cavern.

I gently called my best friend. "Charlie?"

Charlotte guardedly entered the mine and looked down. "Oh, Kiche."

I knelt down, checked for breathing or a pulse, and shook my head negatively.

Charlotte and I wept as we stroked her fur for ten minutes.

"How old was she?"

"Fourteen. That's old for a one-hundred-fifty-pound dog."

I stroked Kiche's ears and whispered. "All dogs go to heaven."

Charlotte cried. "Especially you, Wolfie."

We dug a hole under Ruby Kyle's seat around the campfire. We gave Kiche a proper burial and erected a sign.

Here Lies Kiche Kyle
2013-2027
50% Anatolian Shepherd
50% Canadian Wolf
100% Loyal Friend and Brave Hero

Gloria stood in the Hong Kong Star Ferry Terminal outside the Flynn Brothers Fishing Charter customer service window and dialed Gigi's Tokyo number.

USS Abraham Lincoln sailors in their Liberty Whites shopped and dined in the nearby food court.

"Gigi, this is Gloria, have you seen the news?"

Gigi adjusted her iPhone volume in Japan. "Which news?"

"News about Peaksville?"

"You're crying, Gloria."

"Oh Gigi, it's terrible."

"What happened?"

"Some kind of a fire. A very large fire. Do you have CNH News?"

Gigi ran to her Japanese television remote control in her Ginza apartment. "Okay, I turned it on."

"CNH is confirming that Peaksville has suffered catastrophic damage from a large fire that engulfed the small, North Idaho mountain town. Details of survivors or fatalities are unavailable. Vice-President Walker, a former North Idaho Congressional Representative with very strong ties to Peaksville is reportedly saddened and will be conducting a press conference shortly. We'll provide more details as they become available. This is Skylar Ferguson. You're watching CNH News."

Gigi cried. "What did Grace and Mom say?"

"I can't reach them. I can't reach Charlie. Madison can't reach Mrs. Goodwell. Ryan can't reach Mrs. Flynn."

Gigi paused. "What about the Kernan twins?"

"I called them in Switzerland. They're trying to call home."

"Ruby and Luke?"

Gloria cried. "Trying."

"Did you call Phuket?"

"Jack and Chloe are also trying to call home."

Gigi continued. "Aaron and Tommy Boy in Washington DC?"

"Tommy Boy's trying. Aaron hasn't spoken to his parents since graduation."

Gigi flipped to another news channel. "Gloria, everything looks burned. But I think they're fine."

Gloria cried. "Oh, Gigi. How are they okay?"

Gigi stopped audibly crying. "It's not bad news yet. Keep trying. I bet they survived. Keep trying, Gloria."

"Never again, Charlotte!"

We slow-straddled the Peaksville Creek cedar trunk bridge one last time to conclude our homeward journey.

I stopped to laugh. "Is this the way the settlers arrived into North Idaho two-hundred years ago?"

Charlotte stopped behind me. "Gracie, I'm pretty sure the ladies in the 1830's wore dresses."

"Maybe they side-straddled fallen logs to cross creeks." I smiled and lunged forward. "Unlike us."

We continued towards the finish line. We lifted our bodies with our hands, dangled our feet high over the creek, and scooted forward on the old, fallen tree.

Charlotte laughed. "Oh, the humanity!"

"Are we ladies, Charlie?"

"There was a time, Miss Grace Becker, before today, when we *were* ladies."

We laughed and completed our TFZ journey on a good note.

I walked to the east. "Miss Charlotte Epley, we lost some dignity, but we found some closure."

Charlotte laughed. "It's a tradeoff."

I stopped in my tracks approaching the schoolyard. "Charlie?"

Charlie stopped. "The Peaksville High School. It's gone."

We walked closer to examine the site of our 2020 alma mater.

"It burned, Gracie."

"Not exactly."

We studied the leveled, destroyed structure.

"Gracie, you don't think it burned?"

I shook my head. "It melted."

CHAPTER FIFTEEN

E mma sipped hot chocolate at the Radisson Blu Hotel Reussen Café watching the news about the Peaksville fire and global health epidemic. "You were saying?"

"I was saying what?" Amy asked.

"You were saying that Switzerland is a free country."

Amy paused. "Isn't it?"

Emma wiped her tears. "Freedom is gone. Gone, just like Peaksville."

"What next?" Amy asked.

"We'll teach tourists how to ski and snowboard in Andermatt."

"Shouldn't we help?" Amy asked.

Emma disagreed. "Help who?"

"I don't know."

Emma poured Amy another steaming cup of hot chocolate. "We are helping, Amy."

"We are?"

"Helping tourists learn to ski and snowboard," Emma quipped.

"We should do more."

Emma angrily whispered. "Freedom is gone. Peaksville is gone. Mom is gone. America is gone. We can't save the world, Amy. Give it up. It's all over."

"H ello, Gigi?"

Chloe Epley adjusted her flimsy rental headset inside the Phuket Internet Café. "Gigi, this is Chloe. Can you hear me?"

Gigi Becker answered her iPhone. "Chloe?"

"Do you have a minute?"

"I'm between photo shoots in Ginza. I have ten minutes. Tell me what you've heard."

Chloe held her headset microphone close to her lips. "It's not good. Jack and I are practically living in this 24-hour Thai internet café trying to contact Grace and Charlotte. I hope their phone system is dead and not —" Chloe interrupted herself. "Sorry, that came out wrong. They just don't answer."

Gigi slowly paced in front of ten high-tech Japanese vending machines in the Mitskoshi Department Store lounge. "They survived, Chloe."

"How do you know?"

"I can feel it."

Chloe looked up at the television. "Gigi, do you have CNH? They're talking about Peaksville right now!"

"Go ahead and listen, Chloe. I'll stay on the line."

Chloe held her Phuket Internet Café boom mic up to the television.

"Peaksville's catastrophic fire that engulfed the small, North Idaho mountain town is reportedly the result of International Terrorism. Vice-President Walker, a former North Idaho Congressional Representative has vowed to investigate and bring the terrorists to justice. Secretary Light from The Safety Corps is reporting *zero* residential survivors in Peaksville. TSC Air Patrol Search and Rescue aircrews are searching for survivors."

"Gigi, can you hear it?" Chloe asked.

"Yes, keep it going."

"The Terrorist Electrical Grid Wildfire Attack, or TEGWA, created a high-power surge that ignited virtually every structure in Peaksville. A few surviving structures, including the Peaksville Institutes of Health, PsytoSCOPE Nanotech Corporation, and Peaksville Defense and Space, are fortunate to have been spared. President Voigt's administration continues to be plagued by tragedy and sadness. This is Skylar Ferguson. You're watching CNH News."

Chloe donned her headset again. "Gigi, did you hear it?"

"I heard it."

Chloe cried. "The homes all burned, Gigi. Nobody lived."

Gigi paused. "Chloe?"

"Yeah?"

"I have to run for a photo shoot. Promise me something."

"Okay."

"Promise me you will *believe* our sisters are alive."

Chloe continued to cry. "Gigi, everyone is dying around us in Phuket. It's hard to have hope in this environment."

"Chloe, our sisters *are* alive. Promise me you'll *believe* that with me."

Chloe paused. "I promise."

"Love you, Chloe. Tell Jack that I love him."

"Love you, Gigi."

Click!

"Bud?"

Mr. Light sat alone outside the K Street Starbuck's. "Hello, Ma'am."

Vice-President Walker signaled for her secretary to close her office door. "I'm calling about Peaksville."

"Okay."

"Have you seen CNH News regarding Peaksville?"

"No, Ma'am."

"I just want everyone to be on the same sheet of music, Bud."

Mr. Light whispered. "We're saying it was a wildfire, correct?"

"Yes and no." Vice-President Walker watched CNH Breaking News. "It changed."

"How?"

"Skylar Ferguson told the world that this was a Terrorist Electrical Grid Wildfire Attack, also known as a TEGWA."

"A TEGWA?" Mr. Light whispered as Starbuck's customers passed by. "We're saying it was an electrical grid attack?"

Vice-President Walker laughed. "TEGWA sounds technical, doesn't it? I guess someone didn't get the memo that this was supposed to only be reported as a natural wildfire."

"What now?"

"Skylar said terror attack."

"So?"

"So, it was a terror attack."

"We have to stick with it?" Mr. Light whispered.

"We have to stick with it."

Mr. Light paced back and forth on the K Street sidewalk. "TEGWA. Terrorist Electrical Grid Wildfire Attack. Who makes this crap up, Abby?"

"Someone inside the beltway. It's creative, huh?"

"I'm glad you called, Ma'am."

"One more thing, Bud."

"Okay."

"Skylar said zero Peaksville survivors."

"So?"

"So, ensure there are *zero* Peaksville survivors."

"I'll take care of it, Ma'am."

Click!

"Mom!" Charlotte cried and ran towards her leveled farmhouse. "Charlie, wait for me!" I ran after my sobbing friend.

"Mom! Mom! Where are you, Mom!"

I ran closer to the remains of the Epley family home. "Mrs. Epley! Are you okay? Mrs. Epley!"

The two-story, century-old farmhouse was melted and flattened like cheese in a microwave. The metal, plastic and wooden objects seemed to have melted and mixed together. The substances cooled and hardened into a level, slick, three-foot-tall surface.

I looked at the unburned trees in the yard and mumbled. "This was not a fire."

Charlotte wiped her tears and looked at me with hope. "The barn!"

I tried to smile. "Let's check."

We ran to the perfectly intact, old, red wooden barn. "Mom?"

No sign of damage.

But no sign of life.

Charlotte grabbed my hand. "The shop!"

We ran towards the red, sixty-foot by forty-foot metal workshop.

"Mrs. Epley, are you in here?"

"Mom?"

Charlotte exited the shop and ran to a few more out-buildings. She ran to a small shed. She looked under the farm equipment. She quickly climbed up to the top of her fifty-foot-tall grain silo and yelled inside. "Mom!"

Charlotte worried me atop the tall silo.

"Come on down, Charlie! She's not in the grain. Let's keep looking."

Charlotte thankfully complied.

I cried while Charlotte double-checked and triple-checked every out-building on the Epley Farm.

"Charlie?"

"I have to look around, Gracie. I have to look for Mom. I know she's here. Give me five more minutes."

Suddenly, I remembered. "Mr. Whipple was taking care of your animals for a few days, right?"

Charlotte's face lit up. "Mr. Whipple's farmhouse! That's where Mom is!"

Charlotte sprinted towards the neighbor's farm.
I followed.

V ice-President Walker sat at her desk and answered her phone. "Hello?"
"Abby, check FXH News. It's done."
"Thanks, Bud." Vice-President Walker hung up her phone and clicked on her television.

"We interrupt this program with breaking news. I'm Krissy Moriarty, FXH News Global Public Health Crisis Correspondent.

"It is with great sadness that we report the passing of a great leader in the public and private medical community. Dr. Klein, a Special Advisor to the President, has died of an apparent heart attack in his sleep. The President's administration has struggled to put the brakes on a global crisis that has now claimed the lives of over 233 million people, world-wide. Dr. Klein's heart attack has been preliminarily ruled a result of the great fear and tension surrounding this global health epidemic. Dr. Klein was the CEO of kid-friendly INLINE Pharmaceuticals which helped millions of world-wide children cope with fear and stress."

"Stay tuned for more updates as our enigmatic global health crisis worsens daily under President Voigt. This is Krissy Moriarty. You're watching FXH News."

Vice-President Walker keyed her intercom. "Hold all of my calls, please."

G eneral Marsh leaned back in his Peaksville Defense and Space Chief Executive office and looked at his flag. He thumbed his iPhone and called Mr. Light.

"Swamp, what's up?" Mr. Light asked.
"Just get it over with, Bud."
No response.
"I just spoke with Voigt. I hate this, Bud."
Mr. Light paused. "Are you having second thoughts?"
General Marsh paused and felt the embroidered fabric of the flag. "No, I just hate this."
"Alright, Swamp. I understand."
Click!

C harlotte beat me to the Whipple Farm and froze. "How can it be?"
I caught up with Charlotte and saw the remains.

Charlotte cried. "It's all gone. How do two homes and a high school melt?"

I gently turned Charlotte from the site and led her away. "Let's go, Charlie."

We walked through wooded paths towards my neighborhood as we wept.

Charlotte entered a state of shock. Her pitiful cries had become a series of odd whimpers that combined with mild, rhythmic hyperventilation.

I didn't have any useful consoling words. "It's okay."

It wasn't okay.

We paralleled Peaksville Creek under the cedar canopy to avoid being seen by the dozens of TSC Air Patrol and USAF airplanes.

We arrived. My neighborhood was melted. Only trees remained.

I cried. My poor mother. "Charlie, can you walk with me?"

No response.

"Charlie?"

Charlotte slowly looked at me with her wet face and bloodshot eyes. "Grace, what kind of a forest fire jumps from house to house and leaves the trees?"

"This was sabotage, Charlie."

Charlotte shook her head. "This was murder."

I studied the old neighborhood from our wooded position. "Are there any homes still standing?"

Charlotte leaned on a cedar tree, looked and shrugged her shoulders.

I needed to know if Mom was alive.

"Let's check," Charlotte said.

"Let's not." I was scared.

"Come on." Charlotte squeezed my hand. "We have to check for your mom. We have to know."

We walked and cried. We both knew what we would find.

"He saved us, Gracie."

"Say again?" We walked through my old, unrecognizable neighborhood.

"Dr. Gunnison, the PIH CEO. He advised us to leave."

I remembered. "Oh my God! You're right. But Dr. Gunnison didn't *advise* us to leave Peaksville. He *warned* us to leave Peaksville."

"Dr. Gunnison saved us, Gracie."

"He's not a saint."

President Voigt opened his door and extended his hand. "Come in, Abby."

Vice-President Walker shook his hand and entered the Oval Office.

"Please, have a seat, Abby."

The two sat together on the Presidential furniture.

"Abby, I'm going to be honest with you. I'm not proud of my tenure at

Peaksville Defense and Space. The CABESA Initiative was briefed as a project crucial to national security that was limited in scope and substance."

Vice-President Walker smiled. "I regret a lot of things, Mr. President. But CABESA is not one of my regrets."

"Back in 2013, you recruited me for that PDS CEO position in North Idaho and said, quote-unquote, *we have to crack some eggs to make an omelet.*"

Vice-President Walker didn't respond.

President Voigt prompted her. "Well?"

"Oh, did you ask me a question? If so, I missed it."

"Tell me about the Peaksville fire, Abby."

Vice-President Walker shrugged. "The Peaksville fire was a TEGWA. It is blamed on foreign actors who attacked our electrical grid. Are you suggesting homegrown terrorists from inside your Executive Branch?"

"No."

"I'm on your side, President Voigt. We're all in this together. Together, we will bring the terrorists to justice."

President Voigt clenched his fists and yelled. "I am *not* a part of this!"

"President Voigt, we *are* in this together to bring the perpetrators to justice, aren't we? We don't want your Administration to look weak on terrorism, do we?"

No response.

"Is that all, Sir?"

President Voigt subtly nodded in anger.

"Good day, Sir." Vice-President Walker exited the Oval Office.

"Aaron, you seem to know more about CABESA than anyone around here."

"Yes, Sir."

"Betsy has a line of accounting for you and my son, Bob Bonner. You'll like Bob. He and his Navy SEAL buddies started a very small, very secretive contractor firm that works directly with the House Intelligence Committee. You're the only ones I trust."

"What do you want me to do, Mr. Speaker?"

Congressman Bonner gingerly sat down and looked into the calm, evening sky. "I don't know, Aaron. Funding has been fully-approved by House Intelligence. I'm tired and not feeling well."

Aaron brought the Speaker of the House a cold water.

"Learn more about this so-called, global health crisis, Aaron."

"Then what?"

"You and Bob need to figure that one out."

"Copy, Sir."

The Speaker of the House looked out his Capitol Building window at the beautiful sky towards The West. "The sun is setting on freedom, I'm afraid. I pray that it's not too late."

"Sir, we found two young females wandering around Peaksville."

Mr. Light drove his BMW past the Lincoln Memorial. "How did you not find them yesterday?"

The Peaksville TSC Peacekeeper held Charlotte and me at gunpoint. "Sir, our scanners are not registering any Imaging Probe frequencies in them."

Mr. Light inched forward in beltway traffic.

"Sir, you copy?"

"Anti-Vax?"

"No, Sir. They have childhood vaccine shot records on file in our TSC computers."

"Were they TASED by police?"

"Never, Sir."

Mr. Light adjusted his BMW air conditioning. "Stupid question, but were they struck by lightning or something?"

"Unlikely."

"Completely invisible?"

The TSC Peacekeeper whispered. "Completely. Sir, they wandered around the Peaksville wreckage under TSC Cessnas, Bell helicopters and drones."

"Really?"

"Even USAF Electronic Attack jets couldn't see them."

"How did you find them?"

"They were looking for family."

Mr. Light smiled. "Well, they're going to find their families."

"Sir?"

"The Queen Bee told me *zero* survivors."

The TSC Peacekeeper paused. "Confirm orders, Sir."

"*Zero* survivors are your orders."

"Copy, Sir."

Click!

The TSC Peacekeeper marched Charlotte and me into a cornfield at gunpoint. "Walk!"

I gently held Charlotte's hand, wept and whispered. "This is the end, I guess. No more pain. I love you, Charlie."

The TSC Peacekeeper repeatedly poked us in the back with his rifle muzzle.

Charlotte didn't cry. "I love you, Gracie Becker."

I was ready to join Mom, Dad and Marcus.

I was sad to leave behind Gloria and Gigi to experience this *Brave New World* without me.

We walked towards Schweitzer Mountain under the North Idaho sky.

The sun was quickly setting on our young lives. Too quickly.

The TSC Peacekeeper shouted his last commands. "Stand still! Hands free!"

I wept miserably, closed my eyes tightly and squeezed Charlotte's hand one last time.

He violently separated our hands with his rifle muzzle. "Hands free!"

I cried and prayed. "God, please watch over Gloria and Gigi."

Bang!

Gunfire.

I wasn't shot.

Thud!

I heard a body collapse and whispered. "Oh, Charlie."

My turn.

CHAPTER SIXTEEN

"I need an updated timeline, Abby."

Vice-President Walker looked at her watch and dressed for work in her official residence near the White House. "It's five o'clock in the morning here, Mustafa."

Mustafa Muscat sat near the tee box and accepted a complimentary iced tea from the mobile drink cart employee at Dubai Creek Yacht and Golf Club. "*Timeline*, Abby. Not time."

Vice-President Walker brushed her hair in her bedroom mirror. "Mustafa, the primary element of Operation CHAOS is complete."

"Confirmed?"

She double-checked an early morning text from the Secretary of The Safety Corps. "Confirmed."

"The thing is done?"

"CNH and FXH News reporters have been notified of his death. They're preparing stories. First Lady Voigt hasn't noticed yet. She likes to make breakfast with the White House staff."

"Confirm Operation CHAOS is officially complete, Abby."

"Almost."

Standing behind his golf cart, Mustafa Muscat selected his 3-wood. "Explain."

"The primary element is complete. The rest of CHAOS continues."

"Please excuse me, Abby."

Mustafa walked into the tee box, teed up his Titleist golf ball, performed a practice swing and lined up his shot.

Whack!

He struck his ball 160 yards with an inadvertent left hook then watched his ball's unfortunate trajectory.

"Mustafa?"

Slam!

Mustafa stomped his foot onto the accelerator and raced his customized EZ-GO 2-stroke gasoline golf cart towards the left rough.

"Mustafa?"

"I'm back, Abby. Please, explain."

Vice-President Walker double-checked her makeup in the mirror. "American survivors of the global health epidemic are grieving, suffering, and worried. They deserve a Savior."

Mustafa approached his golf ball and slowed his cart and laughed. "Let me guess, Abby. You will be their savior."

Vice-President Walker fastened her favorite red dress. "I need time. Rome wasn't built in a day."

"Very well, Abby."

She looked outside her Vice-Presidential residence as her security detail waited. "Mustafa?"

"Yes, Abby."

"I completed the primary task —"

"Abby, Syndicate Seat Number Seven will open soon."

Vice-President Walker smiled, clumsily slipped on her shoes, and opened her front door. "Thanks, Mustafa."

R *ing!*
         The electric bell sounded on the Ben Gunn.

"Lines up!"

The twenty deep-sea-fishing customers began reeling up their lines.

Ryan Flynn started the engine, retracted his anchor, and spoke into the intercom. "We're going to give up here and drive to a money-spot near Macau." He smiled at his customers. "No more fishing! Only catching!"

Li Jie helped the slower customers stow their gear. "Ready, Boss!"

Ryan advanced the throttle and steamed northwest from Lamma Island through the highly-congested commercial traffic."

Gloria and Madison climbed the flybridge ladder to join Ryan.

Li Jie supervised and entertained the wealthy customers in the cabin during the transit.

Madison gently smiled at Ryan, sat on the port seat and covered her face.

Gloria leaned her head onto Ryan's shoulder and wiped her tears. "What are their chances?"

Ryan shrugged and negotiated his path through the busy West Lamma Channel traffic.

Madison looked up at Gloria and Ryan in the fifteen-knot breeze, opted not to talk, then covered her face again.

Ryan and Gloria watched the 100-person U.S. Navy repair crew working on the CVN-72 warship's starboard hull.

"Progress?" Gloria asked.

"A little."

Ryan cleared the Navy Liberty Boat route then steered towards Macau. "Shenzhen City got hit last night by a TEGWA only fifty miles north of us. Over 10 million people were instantly melted. I'm fairly certain the 10 *thousand* people in rural Peaksville didn't stand a chance."

Gloria cried and scratched her husband's back. "Maybe?"

Ryan shrugged and plugged some new waypoints into his Garmin GPS. "Unlikely."

Madison looked up and talked over the engine and wind noise. "*Some* people survived in Shenzhen. Maybe some survived in Peaksville, too?"

"CNH News showed pictures of Peaksville. Unlikely, Maddie."

Gloria ran her hand through Madison's hair. "Maybe our moms are okay, Maddie."

Ryan decreased his throttle as he approached a new fishing hole. "Li Jie, you may bait the hooks. Three minutes until lines wet."

Madison wiped her eyes and climbed down the ladder to help.

Gloria kissed Ryan on the cheek. "Maddie probably just lost her mom. Go easy, Ryan."

Ryan closed out the throttle. "In case you're not keeping score, I officially lost *everyone* from my family of five. I'm the *last* Flynn."

"I'm a Flynn, too." Gloria hurried down the ladder.

Ryan slammed his dashboard. "I didn't mean that, Gloria!"

A my sat next to Emma in the Radisson Blu Hotel Reussen's internet café. "Any word?"

"About?"

"Peaksville."

"It was wiped out. I thought we went over this."

Amy logged into the hotel business computer. "Any confirmation on survivors?"

"Besides CNH News?"

"Confirmation from Peaksville friends?"

"Not really. They don't know." Emma opened her Dannon blueberry yogurt and shook her head. "You?"

Amy shook her head. "Nothing. Except for —"

Emma looked up. "Except for what?"

Amy showed Emma her iPhone. "Gracie opened one of my emails."

"Before the TEGWA?"

"After."

"Any response?"

"No. Just a strange code. But it was opened and the code was sent to me."

6-L-O-A-4

E mma grabbed Amy's iPhone to verify. "Probably a fluke. Her phone burned."

"How do you know?"

"Because CNH News reported zero survivors, Amy. I saw the footage. Every home was literally melted."

Amy placed her iPhone back in her ski pants. "Winter Season is over."

"And?"

Amy opened a small, cold orange juice. "Maybe we can go home and check on Mom. We can see for ourselves. Just for a week or two. Maybe Grace and Charlotte are alive somewhere."

Emma disagreed. "They aren't letting anyone close to Peaksville. Nobody survived. And besides, SkiArena Andermatt expects us to be here for Spring Season privates and Summer Season tours."

Amy zoned out and frantically surfed the internet for Peaksville updates for several minutes. "Holy cow! Breaking news!"

"What city got hit?"

Amy gasped. "President Voigt died in his sleep."

"Hmm. Let me guess. Natural causes. Just like Dad."

"Good guess." Amy nodded and read the article. "Heart attack in his sleep."

"This is my shocked face."

"Now what?" Amy asked.

Emma shrugged. "The CABESA Congress chick from Coeur d'Alene probably gets her wish. The kid-friendly humanitarian and champion of industry from North Idaho who experimented on us for years."

"The one who wrote us after Dad was killed and said 'too bad, so sad'?" Amy read more. "You're right, Emma. Walker was just sworn in."

Emma threw her breakfast trash in the recycling wastebasket and tapped her wristwatch. "Amy?"

"Hold on."

"We each have eight o'clock private lessons. They're Swiss skiers. They'll be early. We need to hurry."

Amy sighed and closed her internet browser. "I know, I know. Swiss time."

Emma gave Amy a quick, sisterly hug. "Let it go, Amy."

"Bree are you there?"

"Hi, Ruby."

Ruby Kyle found a private lounge chair in the InterContinental Hotel Sydney lobby during her break. "Have you heard anything about Peaksville?"

Brianna Jordan spoke into her iPhone and inserted a second 500 Yen coin into the Sagami-Otska train station electronic kiosk. "Oh, Ruby. I just can't watch the news anymore."

Ruby rubbed the tears from her eyes. "What happens when you call your mom?"

Brianna inserted her thumb-sized Japanese train ticket into the turnstile, collected the same ticket after it spit out the other end, and walked upstairs to the open-air platform. "I get a Verizon message. Something about system out of service."

"Same."

"What are you hearing when you call your mom's phone, Ruby?"

"Literally nothing."

"Keep trying."

"I will."

Brianna passed on the non-express train and continued waiting on the pollution-stained concrete platform. "I want to believe, Ruby. Oh God, I want to believe! But I'm watching these vans on the Atsugi Naval Air Base park on the street. Sure enough, some military wife on that street dies of a heart attack within twelve hours."

Ruby looked around. "Same here in The Rocks. I try not to let it affect me."

"It's a curse. Knowing what we know is a curse," Brianna said.

"I wish that Aaron never told us about MEDWEAP's."

"Me too, Ruby."

"Why did he tell us?"

Brianna shrugged. "Aaron wanted to help. He's a good guy."

"Unlike his dad."

"True."

"Bree, five thousand people died of heart attacks last night up in Rockhampton, Australia. My co-workers are losing family members."

"Do Aussies suspect anything?"

"Nothing. Sheep mentality. It's like living in a *Twilight Zone* episode. Is Antoine still on the ship?"

"Yes. Stuck in Hong Kong." Brianna boarded an express train towards Tokyo and found a seat. "Right now, I'm traveling to Ginza to see Gigi Becker for lunch."

"How is Gigi?"

"She believes Grace and Charlotte lived."

"Doesn't she have CNH News?"

"Not sure. Regardless, Gigi is going to cheer me up today."

"Lucky you," Ruby said.

Brianna's express train stopped at every fourth station. "How's Luke?"

"He's waiting tables fifty hours-per-week at the American Heritage. He's angry about losing Mrs. Bartholomew. He's scared. He's bitter. He's a lot of things. It's not good."

Brianna "Luke sounds like me."

Ruby laughed. "I'm sugar coating it, Bree. Luke is 'angry-angry.' You sound nothing like him."

"Tell Luke I love him."

Ruby smiled. "Hang in there, Bree. Maybe, later this year, we can see each other."

"Love you, Ruby."

J ack drank a cold can of BOSS milk-coffee in the Phuket Internet café. "Any emails?"

Chloe shook her head negatively. "I'm calling Gigi."

"Hello?"

"Gigi?"

"Hey, Chloe!"

"Any good or bad news?"

"No good news yet, Chloe. Still waiting and hoping."

Jack nudged Chloe and waved.

"Jack says hello!"

Chloe lifted her headset and whispered. "Gigi says hi, Jack."

"What now, Gigi? Does someone in the government notify us if they find our moms' bodies?"

"Just sit tight." Gigi sat at the Ginza train station watching for Brianna Jordan. "Something good has to happen. It's not all bad news."

Chloe smiled. "Thanks Gigi."

"Bree is coming to visit me in Ginza."

"Antoine and D'Andre are still gone?"

"Hong Kong Harbor. They fix the Lincoln aircraft carrier by day. They eat dinner with the Flynn's in Kowloon by night."

"You're right about good things happening. That's a blessing in disguise that they got stranded in Hong Kong near Peaksville friends."

Gigi smiled.

Jack nudged Chloe and pointed at his computer screen.

Chloe read the CNH News article into her headset to Gigi. "Voigt died."

"No way." Gigi continued to wait for Brianna's Japanese train. "Heart attack?"

Chloe nodded. "Bingo."

"Here's Bree! I'll tell her you said hi, Chloe. I have to run."

"Love you."

Click!

Chloe removed her flimsy telephone headset. "Oh, Lordy. Walker's in?"

Jack nodded.

"This means Walker's behind this so-called global epidemic."

"Shhh!"

Chloe shrugged. "It's true. You don't need a PhD to connect the dots. Who benefits? One person. Abby Walker."

"Probably."

She looked at her watch and logged out of her internet café browser. "Walk me to Phuket Equestrian Tours, Jack. Want to take a ride?"

"Beach or mountain?"

"Mountain."

Jack initiated his log-out. "Is Anna available?"

"The Appaloosa?"

Jack shrugged "Sounds right."

"Mr. Bali already texted me to say there are only seven riders." Chloe texted for thirty seconds, waited, then smiled. "Mr. Bali said you get Anna!"

"Let's go, then," Jack said. "Here comes a baht bus."

Chloe smiled and walked to the street with her beau. "Anna is Yul Brynner's favorite!"

Jack nodded. "*Anna and the King*."

Jack and Chloe jumped on the back of the ornately-decorated, Thai pickup truck after it slowed down.

Chloe kissed Jack. "You're my favorite."

. . .

M r. Light successfully connected a satellite call from Washington to his friend in the South China Sea. "Hey, Web."

"Hello, Bud."

"Did you and Nuke see the news?"

Mr. Webster walked aft towards the Sharjah Blue swimming pool deck to avoid satellite phone interference from the island. "The thing is done?"

"The thing is done."

"Now what?"

"Status quo until after the Presidential funeral. Abby wants to let the nation mourn."

"I agree." Web found a comfortable deck chair. "Seems like the most Christian thing to do."

"Are we on a secure line, Web?"

Mr. Webster laughed. "Secure? More or less. The one hundred people in the government listening to us don't want to lose their $150,000 salaries, security clearances or pensions. Yes, it's secure."

"True, whistleblowers have short life spans." Mr. Light stepped outside of the K Street Starbuck's to whisper. "Abby wants the Sharjah Blue to loiter around Hong Kong and execute Operation BLINDSIDE II in deep waters."

"We figured that."

"Abby said port side only."

Mr. Webster laughed. "Is that *Navy port* or *USAF port*, Ensign Major Light?"

"Very funny. Left side. Port side. The side opposite the aircraft carrier tall tower thingy."

Mr. Webster smiled in the warm, South China Sea breeze. "Aye, aye, Cap'n Light! You Salty Dog! Batten down the hatches. Argh!"

Mr. Light chuckled. "Okay, so we're pirates, now. Very funny. Where's Nuke?"

"Swabbing the poop deck."

"I'll let you go, Web."

"Avast, Landlubber!"

Click!

CHAPTER SEVENTEEN

It was my turn to die.

I kept my eyes closed and whispered aloud. "Sorry, Dad. I tried."

Suddenly, I felt a warm, heavenly hand caress my left hand.

Was I dreaming?

Was I dead?

The hand was perfectly comforting.

I slowly opened my eyes and looked to the left. "Charlotte?"

We guardedly turned around. The heavily-armed TSC Peacekeeper lay dead in the cornfield, one mile from Schweitzer Mountain.

"Did you?"

Charlotte shook her head negatively. "You?"

I squeezed Charlotte's hand and wiped the tears from my eyes.

Charlotte pinched herself then pinched me. "So, we lived, Gracie?"

"I think so."

"How?"

"I don't know. What happened, Charlie?"

We looked towards the wooded, North Idaho mountains and scanned the cornfield for movement.

"Gracie?"

"Yeah, Charlie?"

Charlotte looked at the dead TSC Peacekeeper then squeezed my hand. "I'm scared."

"We better run."

. . .

C aptain Scott Smart sat in his Captain's chair on the bridge of the 95,000-ton Nimitz-class warship, USS Abraham Lincoln. He drank coffee and read the Hong Kong Times hand-delivered by the SH-60 helicopter crew from embarked squadron HS-14. "Petty Officer Jordan?"

D'Andre hustled to his side from the Navigation shack adjacent to the Captain's bridge. "Yes, Captain."

He smiled and winked. "How's that second pot of coffee coming?"

D'Andre smiled and quickly retrieved the steaming carafe. "Perfect timing."

Captain Smart, wearing his well-decorated khaki uniform and gold pilot wings, filled his coffee mug displaying his callsign, 'NOTSO.' "Petty Officer Jordan?"

"Yes, Captain?"

"You didn't collapse during the electronic attack."

"Sir?"

"The local Harbor Pilot, the 'Gator, the OOD, and about ten enlisted all dropped with me. You stayed standing. You helped revive me."

D'Andre shrugged.

"Did you not feel dizzy?"

D'Andre smiled. "Maybe I'm invisible to the weapon, Captain. Kind of like a superpower."

Captain Smart laughed and patted D'Andre on the back as banging, grinding and welding sounds could be heard from the repair efforts far below. "You kept your wits about you. You're a fine sailor, Jordan."

D'Andre smiled. "Thanks, Captain."

Captain Smart sipped his coffee and returned to the Hong Kong Times.

"Captain?"

"Yes?"

"The crew is asking about our deployment schedule."

"What's the latest official mess deck scuttlebutt?"

D'Andre shrugged. "Sailors assume we're going home."

Captain Smart laughed. "Well, they're correct. We aren't making it to the Persian Gulf, so we aren't getting tax-free this year."

"Sir, latest mess deck scuttlebutt is RTB Yokosuka for DSRA dry dock repairs in three weeks. Is that accurate?"

Captain Smart conveyed the latest plan. "President Walker wants us patched up and steaming in only *one* week. The straits between Taiwan and the Philippine Islands always throw varsity seas at us. Once we pass Okinawa on our port side we can hug the Kyushu and Honshu coastlines. Then it's smooth sailing up to Yoko."

D'Andre zoned out after Captain Smart's first two words. "*President* Walker?"

Captain Smart held up and rattled the *Hong Kong Times* front page.

"Oh, God."

"President Voigt just died."

"In his sleep, Captain?" D'Andre asked.

"Yes."

"Heart attack?"

"How did you know?"

D'Andre shrugged. "Just guessing. I'll let you get back to reading, Captain. Sorry to hear that. Give me a shout when you need more coffee."

B rianna Jordan exited the train in Ginza, Japan and hugged Gigi Becker. "Cheer me up, supermodel!"

"Sushi-go-round?"

"What else is here?"

Gigi laughed and extended her long, thin arms. "Everything, Bree. Welcome to Tokyo."

Brianna looked around Ginza. "No way."

"What?"

"Wendy's First Kitchen!"

"No."

"Yes."

Gigi held Brianna's shoulders and robotically pivoted her away from the American restaurant. "Beep. Beep. Beep."

Brianna robotically pivoted back towards the Wendy's First Kitchen.

"No, Bree."

Brianna grabbed Gigi's hand and pulled her into the Wendy's. "Yes!"

Gigi and Brianna found a table and waited for their order to be delivered.

"Tell me what it's like to be a supermodel in Tokyo?"

Gigi blushed and held up her small-sized *Frosty*. "Any other profession, and this would be a large."

"Any news from North Idaho, Gigi?"

"Not yet."

Gigi picked up her iPhone and typed.

"Who did you text?"

"Grace."

Brianna smiled. "She's alive?"

"I think so. And if she's alive, she probably would like to read my texts."

"Do you get read receipts?"

"Not yet."

"Let me try." Brianna removed her iPhone from her purse, did a selfie with Gigi and texted.

Gracie, this is Bree. Gigi and I miss you and Charlie. Love you!

Brianna wiped a tear. "Send."

Gigi flagged down the Wendy's employee with their orders.

"Feel better?"

Brianna nodded and ate a French fry. "You got a *Double Baconator*, Gigi?"

Gigi smiled. "We're going to have to walk it off after we eat."

Suddenly, Gigi's phone vibrated.

Gigi looked at Brianna. "Did you hear that?"

Brianna nodded.

"Should I check?"

Brianna nodded. "Check it."

Gigi pushed away her *Frosty* and checked her messages. "It's a code. From Gracie!"

"Can I see?"

Gigi nodded, smiled and showed Brianna her iPhone screen.

4-C-G-R-1

Brianna lost her smile. "It's just some kind of out of service code."

Buzz!

Brianna smiled again. "That's mine!"

The Peaksville natives looked at Brianna's phone screen together.

1-L-N-S-2

Brianna sighed. "Same as you."

Gigi shook her head and pointed at the two phones. "It's not the same. The codes are very different."

Brianna leaned forward and sadly rested her chin in her open palms.

"Those are clues. Believe with me, Bree."

"What?"

"Just believe with me. Believe Gracie and Charlie are alive."

Brianna evaluated and then smiled. "Okay. I'll believe with you, Gigi!"

"How far are you going?" I asked.

The middle-aged man checked his rig in the Missoula, Montana I-90 Flying J Truck Stop. "Rapid City, South Dakota!"

"Got room for two?" Charlotte asked.

"Two people or two cows," the trucker joked.

I looked at his market-bound Hereford and Angus steers in the trailer and laughed. "People."

The trucker politely nodded. "Got room."

Charlotte shook his hand. "Thanks! What's your name?"

"Earl."

"I'm Charlotte."

I shook his hand. "And I'm Grace."

"No luggage?"

"We pack light."

"I'm going to check my tire pressures and brakes. Jump in and make yourselves comfortable."

"Thanks!"

"Hungry, Charlotte and Grace?"

We were penniless and purse-less. "Yes, Sir."

"I buy, you fly?"

I paused. "Okay."

"Here's a twenty. Run into Pilot Flying J truck stop. Grab me two Sausage, Egg and Cheese Maple Griddles and one bottle of Pepsi. You both split and spend the rest."

Charlotte received the twenty dollars and laughed. "We're flying!"

Score!

Earl drove us east from Missoula, Montana via I-90 in the cab of his eighteen-wheeled tractor-trailer towards his Rapid City destination.

Earl looked right from his driver's seat. "You girls don't look like hitchhiker-types."

I smiled. "There's a first time for everything."

Charlotte sat in the middle. "Is this your normal route?"

Earl nodded. "Mondays through Thursdays are cattle drives."

I waited before speaking. "What about Fridays?"

"On Fridays, I'm a bull rider."

Charlotte laughed. "You give them rides four days per week. The bulls let you ride only eight seconds per week on Fridays. That doesn't seem quite fair, Earl."

Earl smiled. "I reckon I never thought of it that way. Besides, they don't really *let* me ride. And half of the time, they only let me ride for about three seconds."

Charlotte spoke livestock lingo, unlike me.

"How far are you ladies heading?"

"Washington DC," I said.

Earl entered some data into his GPS trip computer. "Sixteen hundred miles left after Rapid City."

I looked at Charlotte. "Ouch."

"You really want to go to Washington DC?" Charlotte whispered.

"Aaron and Tommy Boy will know what to do."

"We haven't seen them in seven years. What if they've changed?"

I shrugged and whispered. "They *were* friends. They *are* friends. Right?"

Charlotte shrugged. "I hope."

I read the passing sign. "*Rapid City 650 miles!*"

Earl adjusted the Freightliner's AM radio. "Something happened."

The talk radio host solemnly broadcasted. "That was Vice-President Walker tearfully commenting on the sudden passing of President Voigt. Once again, President Voigt has passed away in his sleep at the age of sixty-one. Please stay tuned for further updates."

Earl sadly switched to country music. "Sixty-one years old. That's so sad. The experts and people in charge of us on television all say people are dying earlier these days. At least Abby Walker is going to be the President. I voted for her when she was our North Idaho Congresswoman. She seems to be very pro-family. She did a lot for children while she was in Congress."

Charlotte and I subtly exchanged looks.

Earl drove his big rig eastbound on I-90 and wiped his tears with his plaid shirt.

Charlotte whispered. "Are you *still* sure about going to Washington DC?"

I was simultaneously sensory-overloaded and void-of-emotion.

Earl's simple, innocent sadness reminded me of my youth. Earl laughed when radio personalities told him to laugh. Earl cried when reporters told him to cry. Earl was inquisitive only when told to be inquisitive. Such a predictably peaceful, perfect existence.

I slid my hand into Charlotte's hand and quietly slept on her shoulder.

. . .

G eneral Marsh flashed his CEO badge to the Peaksville Defense and Space gate guard as he answered his cellphone. "Mr. Bud Light. Somehow, I knew you'd call."

"Swamp."

"It's still early out west. Our engineers and techs are just now hearing the news on talk radio on the way into work."

Secretary of TSC Light paused. "You heard, then?"

"Yeah, brother. Of course."

"It's done."

"America?" General Marsh quipped.

"Yeah, that's done, too."

"Where are you?"

"I walked up the stairs to the Lincoln Memorial."

"Alone?"

"I just needed time to think."

"You good?"

"I'm good."

"You're not going to light yourself on fire and roll yourself down the stairs, are you?"

Mr. Light paused. "No gasoline handy. Maybe next time, though."

General Marsh paused. "Were there any complications, Bud?"

"Zero."

"What's Washington DC like now?"

"I thought it would be chaotic, Swamp."

"And?"

"It's eerily quiet."

"Strange."

"Last night was the worst night of my TSC career or USAF career. Basically, the worst day of my life."

"Did you have someone else do it?"

"You're about the only one that knows about my Queen Bee orders besides a few news reporters who prepared the story."

General Marsh laughed. "Oh, thanks. So, our co-conspirator circle is small and distinguished."

"Like your Johnson."

General Marsh laughed. "Nice one."

"Thanks for being a good friend."

"Bud?"

"Yeah, Swamp."

General Marsh entered his Peaksville Defense and Space CEO office touched at the large American flag. "I cried when I heard."

"Queen Bee sniffles or actual tears?"

"Real tears, Bud."

"Same, Swamp."

"We lost more than a President."

"Understatement." Mr. Light changed the subject. "How's production at PDS?"

"At capacity."

"How did we get here, Swamp? I miss my USAF flight instructor years. I miss taking you to Dogface Field in Oklahoma in the T-37 Tweet and futilely trying to teach you to land somewhere near centerline. I miss the sound my military-issued, old metal kneeboard made on the side of your helmet when you pranged a landing."

"Good times, Bud."

The Secretary of The Safety Corps sighed. "I wish we could go back and do everything differently."

"No 'do-overs,' Bud."

"President Voigt wanted one. I guess that isn't going to happen, now. Is it Swamp?"

General Marsh paused to look at his fast-moving North Idaho MEDWEAP production line. "What word is the opposite of Manifest Destiny?"

"CABESA Initiative."

"See you, Bud."

Click.

I ncluding short car rides, long car rides, short truck rides and long truck rides, Charlotte and I counted thirteen legs on Interstate 90 East towards Washington DC.

Of the thirteen rides, five of the drivers showered us with free food and drinks. Three talked too much. Three never talked.

The driver between Chicago and Cleveland let us borrow his cellphone to research cell numbers. Aaron Webster's number appeared to be unlisted, but we knew he was a Congressional aide in the Capitol Building. Thomas Stallworth's cell number was listed in the law school newsletter at Georgetown.

Our thirteenth and final driver couldn't tell us where he worked, but he was kind enough to drop us off in front of the National Mall. "How's this?"

I smiled. "You're a saint."

He winked. "Trust me, I'm not a saint."

Charlotte and I exited his black Chevy Tahoe and looked around our Capitol in awe.

"Wow," Charlotte said.

I wasn't in Idaho anymore. "It's beautiful."

Charlotte pointed to the Capitol Building. "That's where the 2013 CABESA Initiative was born."

"Don't remind me, Charlie."

Charlotte broke into song. "*I'm just a CABESA bill, and I'm sitting here sitting on Capitol Hill.*"

I tried not to think about it. "Please don't unless you want to die in committee."

Charlotte smiled.

"Where do we start?"

"I think we need to call Tommy Boy."

I was tired. "Can we rest first?"

We found a park bench between the Washington Monument and Lincoln Memorial and sat in the cool breeze. Dozens of pigeons collected around us amid the falling Cherry Blossoms.

"Charlie?"

"Yeah, Gracie."

"We have nothing to feed the birds. And we probably stink worse than them."

Charlotte laughed. "We lost everything, didn't we?"

I nodded. "At least we still have our sisters."

Charlotte pointed down at the ground. "Twelve time zones away, though."

I looked at the freedom-themed monuments. "Maybe we should contact them."

"It's not safe yet, Gracie."

"For us, Charlie?"

"And for them. We're supposed to be dead."

I sighed and leaned on Charlotte. "I'm scared."

"I hope our sisters are okay."

"Gigi and Gloria probably think we're dead."

Charlotte shrugged. "I don't blame them. We officially died in Peaksville."

Mr. Webster stood on the Sharjah Blue deck and dialed his satellite phone. "Mustafa, the Queen Bee wants us to loiter in the north end of the South China Sea for Operation Blindside II."

Mustafa sat in the executive lounge of the Dubai Creek Yacht and Golf Club. "Abby didn't tell me that, Web."

"I'm sorry."

"Do you have a timeline, Web?"

"The aircraft carrier is undergoing repairs in the Hong Kong Harbor. Our TSC sources in the Pentagon confirmed that the repairs will continue for only one more week. Abby ordered the Commander of Seventh Fleet to hurry the Lincoln back to Yokosuka."

"Good." Mustafa paused. "I need the Sharjah Blue moored in Dubai for my daughter's Sweet Sixteen surprise birthday party."

"When?"

"Three weeks."

Mr. Webster looked at his watch. "No worries. Expect the Sharjah Blue to return home in two weeks. I'll pass the word to Captain Farsi."

"Web?"

"Yes, Mustafa."

"The Sharjah Blue is executing a very predicable operation. The only difference between BLINDSIDE and BLINDSIDE II is going to be the surrogate ship, correct?"

"Affirmative, Mustafa."

"Don't you think this is risky?"

"No, Mustafa."

"The element of surprise is gone, Web."

Mr. Webster explained. "The Sharjah Blue's offensive and defensive weapon systems are both silent and invisible. Even the ship's NEXTGEN Nuclear Propulsion and Power is stealth."

Mustafa emptied a pack of sugar into his iced tea. "Please make sure Captain Farsi returns my Sharjah Blue in two weeks in one piece."

"As you wish, Mustafa."

CHAPTER EIGHTEEN

"Thomas?"

"Speaking."

I smiled at Charlotte as I spoke into the kind National Park Ranger's phone. "Tommy Boy! It's me, Gracie."

Thomas paused. "Gracie Becker?"

"Yes."

"Are you in Peaksville?"

"I *was* in Peaksville. Charlotte is here with me. We're on the Lincoln Memorial stairs, borrowing a nice NPS ranger's phone."

I smiled at the park ranger and tried to hurry.

"Okay, your caller ID said *federal government*. You had me worried for a second."

"Are you in DC, Tommy Boy?"

"Yes."

"Meet us here."

Thomas paused and covered his mouth. "Meet me in the Air and Space museum. First floor. In the dimly-lit flight simulator area. There's renovation going on. I'll be there in ten minutes."

Click!

I handed the phone to the National Park Service Ranger. "Thank you, Officer."

The ranger pleasantly smiled and said goodbye.

Charlotte waited for privacy. "What did Tommy Boy say?"

I paused. "That was kind of weird. He wants to meet inside the Air and Space museum. Then he hung up."

"He must be in a hurry," Charlotte said.

I nodded. "Or maybe Washington DC makes him nervous in general."

R uby smiled at the Ottoman Grill Kebab restaurant in Sydney, Australia. "I miss our mothers."

"Same here. I miss our mothers. And our fathers, too." Luke took a bite of his Beef and Chicken Doner Kebab. "But they're all dead."

Ruby gently placed her hand on Luke's arm. "Do you want to get some ice cream after this?"

Luke shrugged and chewed his kebab.

"Maybe we could go see a movie. We haven't been to a real movie theater in years."

"No way. Our bartender at the Australian Heritage just died in a movie theater at age twenty-four." Luke took another bite, set his kebab onto his plate and flashed finger quotes. "Heart attack."

"Want to go to Bondi Beach tomorrow?"

Luke shrugged.

"We both have a day off."

Luke took another bite of his kebab.

"It's topless."

Luke stopped chewing and almost went out of character. He quickly regained his grumpy demeanor and continued chewing.

Ruby whispered. "I'm sorry about your mother, Luke. The good news is that she's in a better place with your father, now."

Luke ignored Ruby's sentiment.

Ruby Kyle continued. "I wish we could have stopped the Peaksville TEGWA. Or even predicted it. But we couldn't. Our moms are in heaven with our dads."

Luke stopped chewing again. "It's not fair. It's not fair that Grace and Charlotte stayed back to help their moms and died. It's not fair that I feel guilty leaving my mom. It's not fair that we survived because we abandoned our moms. It's not fair that I don't have any parents. Nothing is fair. Everything sucks."

Ruby whispered. "I want to make it better."

"You can't. Things suck all over. Darwin just had a Terrorist Electrical Grid Wildfire Attack up north. Darwin's gone. A quarter of the Gold Coast has died from heart attacks. Why can't we tell people the heart attacks are from MEDWEAP's? Why can't we help? Why can't we warn people that two plus two does not equal five? It's not healthy to sit and watch. It's not ethical. It's not human. Derrick died years ago trying to make a difference. We're sitting here eating kebabs in The Rocks while people are dying."

Ruby looked around and tapped Luke's knee. "Patience."

Luke shrugged.

"There will come a time when we can help. But we aren't there yet."

Luke annoyingly tapped the table. "When? How?"

Ruby held Luke's hand. "I don't know when. I don't know how. But things are going to change. Somehow."

"Let me know when that day arrives."

"F NG!"

Mercedes looked at her favorite VFA-195 Lieutenant Commander as she finished her Steak and Surf dinner in the O-3 Level Officer's Mess while anchored in the Hong Kong Harbor. "Yes, Sir?"

"Call me Burner, F'ing New Guy."

Mercedes smiled and issued an open-handed salute. "Sir, Yes, Sir, Burner, Lieutenant Commander, Sir."

Burner looked around the table at the other pilots. "Tater thinks she's Sierra Hotel now that mommy is Commander in Chief."

Mercedes mocked her OPS-O under her breath.

"Where are the Airman Evals for the Powerplant Division?"

Mercedes wiped her mouth with the white cloth napkins. "Petty Officer Jordan and I will get them to you in about three days. Dotting I's. Crossing T's."

Burner leaned back and waited ten seconds. "Finished your meal?"

She nodded at the Officer's Wardroom table.

"Why are you sitting here, FNG?"

She shrugged. "Because someday I want to be: Just. Like. You."

Burner tried not to smile. "What are we forgetting?"

She shrugged again.

"Dog report!"

"Forgot!" Mercedes quickly slid her seat back and walked to the large, metal ice cream soft serve machine. She pulled the lever and studied the consistency of the chocolatey 'Auto-Dog' swirling into her dish. She returned to the wardroom table.

Mercedes tasted the soft serve and swirled it around in her mouth.

Burner tapped his fingers. "Well?"

Mercedes took her time for comedic effect.

An SH-60 pilot, named HIRF, laughed. "Burner, VFA-195 obviously doesn't have control of its F'ing New Guys."

"Chocolate in color."

HIRF laughed. "Great observation, Tater. You've got the Right Stuff! I'm going have to send you to Top Gun. Outstanding dog report! Future astronaut, Burner!"

Tater winked. "Not exceptionally rich."

"Are you talking about Burner or the ice cream?" HIRF asked.

Burner flicked HIRF's earlobe.

"Ouch."

Mercedes took another bite. "No ice particles. No dime store, stealthy lemon additive today like yesterday."

"Okay, keep going."

A second HS-14 helicopter pilot, named Spooner, yelled from the Wardroom phone. "LTJG Walker! Telephone!"

"Stand fast!" Burner held up a closed fist. "Tater will be right there. She's performing a Naval ritual."

Mercedes swirled her third bite around. "Creamy, but not watery. I'll rate it an eight. Good dog. I recommend it."

Burner stood up to visit the Auto-Dog. "Go answer the phone, FNG."

Spooner bowed and handed the CVN-72 wardroom phone. "The royal telephone, m'lady."

Mercedes smiled. "LTJG Walker." She waited for the one-second transmission lag.

"Mercedes! It's Skylar!"

"Hey! How's New York!"

Skylar Ferguson shrugged. "It's okay. Starbuck's Coffee stores are everywhere."

Mercedes looked at the one million Yen, Japanese-built, CVN-72 Officer's Wardroom Cappuccino machine. "We have only *one* coffee store on the boat."

"You all good? I heard you did a Triple Lindy from the Lincoln after you swapped paint with the supertanker. Show-Off!"

"I do things for attention."

"I miss you, Mercedes."

"I miss you, Skylar. How's CNH News?"

"I'm like Ron Burgundy. You put it in front of me, I'll mindlessly read it. The news is all bad anyway. Kind of bittersweet about your Mom stepping up to the Oval Office, huh?"

Mercedes nodded. "No comment."

Skylar paused. "Krissy Moriarty drank the Kool-Aid."

"I know. I spoke with her. Krissy acted like my Mom was the second coming of Christ."

"I'll let you go, babe. Fly safely. No more swimming unless you're on liberty."

"Our ship is dead in the water (*DIW*) anyway. I'm like Buzz Lightyear. *This is not a flying toy.*"

Skylar Ferguson laughed. "Love you, Mercedes."

"Love you, Sky!"

Click!

I pointed to the sign. "This is it, Charlie. Smithsonian National Air and Space Museum."

"Fancy."

I smiled. "And thankfully for us, free."

Charlotte held my hand as we walked through security. "Nothing is *really* free."

"Phones, metal, belts, keys in the baskets please." The Smithsonian guard stopped us. "No purses or phones?"

We smiled and shrugged. The last person who asked for our things was the TSC Peacekeeper who now lay peacefully in an Idaho cornfield as mulch.

"Step through the machine."

We entered and turned to our left.

I read the exhibit signs. "*Space Race, Lockheed Martin IMAX Theater, How Things Fly, Explore the Universe —*"

Charlotte found it. "*Simulators!*"

We walked into a dark, cold room with random exhibits allowing tourists to simulate landing on aircraft carriers, dogfighting, or lazily flying small airplanes around Washington DC.

Charlotte stood near the night carrier landing exhibit. "Tommy Boy said flight simulators?"

I nodded. "The dark simulator area."

We waited another five minutes.

"Gracie?"

"Yeah, Charlie?"

Charlotte looked around at the hundreds of people. "Do you think —"

"Do I think what?"

"No."

"Say it, Charlie."

"Do you think Tommy Boy is setting us up?"

"No chance, Charlie."

"I shouldn't have said it."

We waited another ten minutes.

"Charlie?"

"Yeah, Gracie."

"I'm starting to get scared. I don't like being in Washington DC."

A tall, well-dressed young man arrived in a business suit and stood directly in front of us.

I examined his handsome face in the dim lighting. "No way! Thomas?"

Charlotte laughed. "Tommy Boy, is that you?"

Thomas smiled, hugged us and cried. "God, I missed you guys."

I squeezed him so tightly. "Oh, Tommy Boy."

Thomas wiped his eyes. "Have you heard the news?"

Charlotte wiped Thomas' tears. "About Peaksville?"

Thomas nodded and cried.

"We were there, Tommy Boy."

"I figured you were there." Thomas looked around and whispered. "You're supposed to be dead. The TSC said no survivors."

I whispered in his ear. "Someone tried to kill us."

Thomas looked around nervously. "Really?"

Charlotte got closer. "Someone saved us and killed the bad guy."

"Who?"

We shrugged. "We had our eyes closed."

Thomas whispered. "Charlie? Gracie?"

"Yeah?"

"Did you see my home? Did you look for my mom?"

I hugged Thomas. "We looked. Our moms are all together in a better place, buddy. No more pain."

Thomas cried. "I needed to know."

Charlotte wiped his tears. "I'm sorry, Tom."

Thomas looked around the museum, reached into his wallet and whispered. "Here's some lunch money to get you both started. I just met with Aaron. That's why I was late. Web has something big going on. He wants you to be a part of it."

"Thanks. What about you?" Charlotte asked.

"I'm out. I just passed the bar exam this week. Let me know if you need a lawyer. That's the only way I can help. I don't recommend calling anyone. The TSC in this town is bad news, and you're supposed to be dead."

"How do we contact Aaron?" I asked.

"Go to the Capitol Building. Find the Speaker of the House's office. The secretary's name is Betsy Ross."

I smiled. "You're kidding."

Charlotte laughed. "Betsy Ross?"

Thomas nodded. "Aaron was Speaker Bonner's intern for two years. Betsy and Aaron are workmates."

"We go to Betsy."

"Betsy is waiting for you."

I hugged Thomas. "We love you, Tommy Boy."

"**M**r. Bali said he will take the tour riders back to the stables for me, Jack. When does Dragon Muay Thai Camp expect you back to work?"

Jack sat atop Anna the Appaloosa on the north end of Kata Beach in Phuket, Thailand. "I have a private lesson at three o'clock."

Chloe looked at her watch and smiled atop her trusty, Thai steed named Yul Brynner. "Want to take a longer ride?"

"Just you and me?"

Chloe Epley pointed uphill towards the lush, tropical Phuket landscape. "A secret trail."

Jack smiled and held Anna's reins. "Lead the way!"

After ten minutes of riding up a gradual incline, Jack and Chloe summited a small peak featuring a tropical waterfall and lagoon overlooking Karon beach, Kata beach, and Nai Horn beach.

Chloe dismounted, secured Yul Brynner, helped Jack secure Anna and extended her open hand. "Let's rest."

Jack and Chloe shared their last water bottle in the picturesque Thai setting.

Chloe leaned her head on Jack's shoulder as colorful birds flew from tree to tropical tree. "This place reminds me of Idaho."

"Tall trees, waterfall, swimming holes. *This* is the only difference." Jack pointed to the expansive, panoramic views of the Gulf of Thailand and the Indian Ocean.

Jack and Chloe enjoyed the hidden, private lagoon tucked away on the busy, touristy island in southern Thailand.

Chloe looked and pointed. "I can't believe that beach was underwater in 2004."

Jack nodded. "Only two-hundred and fifty died here in Phuket from the tsunami. But thousands have died of heart attacks in the last few weeks."

"Are we safe here, Jack?"

"For now. But the Phuket ER doctor didn't paint an optimistic picture." Jack suddenly wept. "My Mom was going to visit this summer. She always dreamed of traveling to Thailand. I miss her."

Chloe wept. "I miss her, too. And I miss Charlie. The best sister ever."

Jack wiped his eyes. "Charlie taught me how to ride horses."

"I think Charlie's alive with Gracie."

Jack didn't respond.

"I love you, Jack." Chloe kissed Jack on the cheek. "I'm hungry. Pad Thai Shop?"

Jack nodded. "Again?"

Chloe nodded.

"Okay, Pad Thai Shop."

"Saddle up, partner!" Chloe helped Jack stand up, mount Anna his Appaloosa and ride her down the mountain towards Phuket Equestrian Tour stables.

CHAPTER NINETEEN

Amy Kernan sipped a complimentary Swiss Alps spring water at Andermatt Restaurant Natschen. "How was your private?"

Emma leaned back into her seat and whispered. "He was scared."

"Scared of skiing?"

Emma looked at the nearby Swiss locals and foreign tourists and shook her head negatively. "Scared of dying."

Amy took her sandwich half from the plate. "I still wish we could help."

"We can't."

"We know things other people don't know."

"Ha! Like that's a *good* thing."

Amy typed into her iPhone on the open-air deck overlooking the Swiss Alpine Mountains.

"What are you doing?"

"Texting."

"Texting whom?" Emma asked.

"Grace and Charlotte."

Emma shook her head. "Text Mom and Dad. Text Elvis Presley and Jim Morrison, while you're at it."

Amy looked up from her phone and sternly pointed at Emma. "That's not funny."

Emma finished her sandwich half. "Why?"

"Why isn't that funny?" Amy asked.

"No. Why did you text Gracie and Charlie?"

"Because maybe they survived."

"Nothing wrong with wishful thinking. But there's a point when you will need to —" Emma noticed the restaurant big screen television, tapped her identical twin on the knee and interrupted herself. "Amy."

Amy shook her head. "An electrical grid terror attack on Independence, Missouri. Let me guess. Totally not related to the heart attack epidemic."

Emma continued to watch silently.

"They killed the whole town, Emma."

Emma shrugged and stopped watching CNH News.

"Look at the pictures, the homes melted but trees are still standing. Just like Peaksville. How did they do that?"

Emma shrugged again and refilled her Alpine spring water.

Amy watched the television screen. "Oh, God. Independence was the hometown of Harry Truman."

Emma shrugged. "The New American Homeland. Courtesy of President Walker, humanitarian and child advocate."

Amy collected her trash and stacked the silverware. "We should tell someone."

Emma stood up. "Go tell your noon private from France all about CABESA. Tell me what she writes on your instructor critique."

Amy looked away and stood up.

"Come here, sister."

Amy followed Emma to the Andermatt Alpine overlook. "You're not going to push me over the edge, are you?"

Emma looked around. "Too bright out. Too many people."

"Good."

Emma whispered. "Amy, here's the deal. The victims *don't* know. The perpetrators *do* know. We're anomalies. We're invisible. Let's *stay* invisible. Let's just keep our mouths shut and stay alive."

"And we let innocent people continue to die around us?"

Emma nodded. "We have *zero* control over that."

Amy watched the Schneehuenerstock-Express gondola lift cars summit over the scenic Oberalp Pass.

Emma grabbed Amy's hand. "Amy, grab your skis and go do what you do best."

"You want me to get high score on Candy Crush?"

"No." Emma laughed. "Go make your private lesson customer laugh."

Charlotte and I waited as the Capitol Hill Policeman called up to the Speaker of the House Office.

"Yes, Ma'am. Yes Ma'am. Right away, Ma'am." The policeman returned to us and smiled. "Do you know your way?"

I squeezed Charlotte's hand and shook my head no.

"Follow me, ladies. Betsy Ross is waiting for you."

Charlotte laughed. "Does everyone in Washington DC name their children patriotic names?"

The Capitol Hill Policeman held the door open for us. "Yes, my name is Francis Scott Key."

"Really?" I laughed.

The policeman pointed at his badge.

Arnold.

Charlotte smiled at we reached the fifth floor. "Your first name isn't Benedict, is it?"

"No." He laughed. "It's Tom."

"Like the actor," I said.

He nodded. "I'm older than Tom Arnold. So, I'm the *real* Tom Arnold."

We approached a series of regal, important-looking Congressional offices.

Capitol Police Officer Arnold pointed. "Here you are ladies. Speaker of the House."

I smiled. "You're a kind man."

Charlotte shook his hand before he returned to the elevator. "Thanks!"

I looked around. "Look at this place."

"The floors and the walls are made of marble and granite, Gracie."

The expansive hallway was covered with famous works of American art. "I feel like Katniss who just traveled from Sector 12."

Charlotte laughed. "That makes me Peeta. No fair."

I smiled. "Peeta's a cool name."

"It is?"

I approached a door labelled *Speaker of the House.* "Aaron actually works here?"

Charlotte nodded.

"Are you ready to do this thing?"

"What thing, Gracie?"

I laughed. "I've been following *you* from Idaho. I thought you were running this show."

Charlotte smiled, knocked on the door, and whispered. "The blind leading the blind."

A sweet, motherly woman answered the door. "Grace Becker and Charlotte Epley?"

I nodded. "Betsy Ross?"

She smiled. "Come sit down. The new President is finishing her Emergency State of the Union."

Betsy's secretarial office was fit for a king or queen. Charlotte and I sat and watched the CNH News live coverage.

"Each congressional district nationwide has been affected. This emergent crisis is not accidental or happenstance. Congress clearly has *not* kept you safe. The New American Homeland will retain Congressional Representatives and Senators on the Homeland payroll in an *advisory* nature, only. Our legislature is no longer entrusted with lawmaking duties, nor is our judicial branch entrusted with making meaningful decisions. State governors and legislatures will also be retained in an *advisory* nature, only.

"The new Ministry of Health will solve the negligence-induced fatal cardiac crisis. The Ministry of Safety, formerly known as The Safety Corps, is forced to shut down our Homeland electrical power grids in residential and non-governmental areas for installation of necessary TEGWA-preventing reinforcements."

I whispered to Betsy Ross. "Did President Walker just say New American Homeland?"

Betsy solemnly shook her head.

President Walker continued. "We will persevere through this unfortunate, man-made State of Emergency. We will prosper. We will rebuild. We are Strong. We are United. We are the New American Homeland!"

Charlotte and I sighed.

"God bless you, Homelanders! And God bless the New American Homeland!"

"Hit me."

The Bellagio dealer dealt Dr. Moriarty a Queen of Diamonds.

He sighed. "Dang it."

Charity Ferguson whispered. "Hitting on seventeen?"

Dr. Moriarty smiled. "I told myself I could lose three thousand dollars then stop."

"What else did you tell yourself you could lose in Las Vegas?"

The dealer collected the losing wagers.

Dr. Moriarty placed ten $100 bills on the table. "Change please."

Charity sipped her drink and looked around the casino. "You're the new Minister of Health. Are you sure this Las Vegas vacation was a good idea?"

An older woman sitting on the Blackjack table's 'First Base' leaned closer. "Didn't mean to intrude. Did you say you're the new Minister of Health?"

Dr. Moriarty nodded. "I'm a better doctor than gambler."

The woman smiled. "You must be working so hard to solve this global health epidemic, Doctor."

"If you only knew."

Charity laughed, accidentally dribbled her martini and wiped her chin. "Whoops."

Crash!

A middle-aged man collapsed from a neighboring Blackjack table.

Someone shouted. "He's having a heart attack! Is there a doctor in the house?"

The woman sitting on 'First Base' pointed at Dr. Moriarty. "Here's a Doctor!"

Dr. Moriarty looked at his watch and collected his chips. "It's been grand, dealer."

Dr. Moriarty and Charity Ferguson stood and speed-walked fifty feet in five seconds towards their escape.

Charity held his hand through the marble Bellagio lobby exit and found an open railing to marvel in the Fountains of Bellagio Water Show. "*I'm a better doctor than gambler* said the PhD!"

Dr. Moriarty nervously caught his breath and laughed. "I can't believe the lady at our table exposed me."

"Doctor, you exposed yourself, Minister of Health, PhD."

"That lady at our table almost gave *me* a heart attack."

Charity laughed and watched the orchestrated fountains dance to the music. "Maybe you need mouth to mouth? You're *are* a PhD, right?"

"Yes, a Doctor of Philosophy."

Charity smiled. "You're sure that PhD doesn't stand for *Pizza Hut Dude*?"

Dr. Moriarty watched the Bellagio Water Show. "Now you're messing with me."

"What discipline did you study for your PhD, Mr. PhD?"

"Urban Studies."

"That's rich."

"Why?"

Charity laughed in front of the Bellagio. "You got your doctorate in Urban Studies. From the University of Idaho. And now you're the Homeland's Ministry of Health? Do you have a Bachelor's Degree in Agriculture from the University of Brooklyn?"

Dr. Moriarty smiled. "And what exactly qualified you for the Ministry of Youth position?"

"I was the President's childhood friend. In my youth. And I feel very youthful."

The Bellagio Water Show ended. "Ready to walk back to the Mandalay Bay?"

Charity shook her head negatively. "The night is young."

. . .

"Gracie and Charlie! You're from Peaksville, Idaho."

We smiled in the Speaker of the House's Congressional Secretary's office. "Yes, Ma'am."

Aaron told me lots of fun stories about you guys. Monkeys. Wolves. Horses. Cattle. Grace, you fought off a mountain lion once?"

I blushed. "I didn't exactly fight it off."

"Oh, you're being modest." Betsy leaned forward and whispered. "Aaron thought you both died in the Peaksville TEGWA."

"We're glad Aaron is wrong."

Betsy smiled. "Funny. Aaron was so happy to hear you survived, he cried."

I smiled and looked at Charlotte. "We know the feeling."

"How did you survive?"

"We're still trying to figure that out."

Charlotte pointed to the television. "The Presidential Address. What was that about?"

Betsy Ross whispered. "We knew it was coming. It's a sore subject in this building. Have you heard about Speaker Bonner?"

"I've seen him on television a few times."

Betsy shook her head. "Tex died in his sleep last night."

Charlotte and I gasped and subtly looked at each other. "We're sorry."

Betsy stood up to close the doors. "I know that look you gave each other, Charlotte and Grace. Aaron told us what's happening around the world. There are no secrets in this office. Aaron showed us some things."

I sighed. "I'm sorry about Congressman Bonner. I'm sorry you learned about it. Knowing changes your life."

"Gracie, that's the wisest thing I've ever heard during my thirty years in the Capitol Building. Before last week, I thought that I've heard everything and seen everything. Then Aaron brought us these CABESA books." Betsy patted the large 2020 NASDA and MEDWEAP Operator Master List.

"Scary stuff."

Betsy nodded. "Understatement of 2027. This 2020 book predicted my husband's heart attack in 2023. Mr. Ross died on Christmas Eve, 2023."

"I'm sorry."

Betsy gently smiled. "Thanks."

"What now?" Charlotte asked.

"A poignant question, young lady. Aaron is running some errands. Tying up some loose ends that Tex Bonner was working on. He'll be back soon."

"So, we wait for Aaron?"

"Please." She nodded. "Water and snacks are in the fridge. Make yourselves at home."

Betsy seemed like family.

G igi Becker smiled and stood in the Navy Base Atsugi Food Court atrium overlooking the ball fields and movie theater. "Bree?"

Brianna Jordan couldn't decide which military food court restaurant to patronize. "Yeah, Gigi?"

"Visiting you on Atsugi absolutely rocks."

"It's okay."

Gigi laughed and ogled the passing sailors. "Okay? Your home is a three-minute walk to Taco Bell, Subway, Popeye's, and Pizza Hut!"

"Yeah, it's okay."

"When you visit me in Tokyo, plan on Sushi or Yakisoba. When I visit you out here in the Kanto Plain, we're eating in the Food Court. Deal?"

Brianna shrugged and studied the multiple restaurant menus near the Navy NEX Exchange shopping mall. "Wendy's First Kitchen was good, though."

"I've decided!" Gigi declared with a smile. "Popeye's!"

Brianna laughed. "Okay, Miss Tokyo Supermodel. Wasn't there a funny rap song from the 1990's with lyrics about red beans and rice?"

"We'll walk it off."

Brianna smiled and got in line with Gigi. "It's okay. Popeye's is secretly my favorite. Probably because it's Antoine's favorite."

Gigi and Brianna ordered their spicy chicken and found a seat.

"Antoine's coming home soon on the Lincoln, Gigi. Persian Gulf is cancelled."

"That's good, Bree."

"CNH said repairs would be finished within one week. It just got faster. They were saying one month before."

"Bree, look." Gigi pointed at the Atsugi Food Court television.

"FXH News is reporting that a Lincoln, Nebraska high school experienced 500 student fatalities during a Tuesday morning Multiple Cardiac Arrest Fatality Incident, also known as a MCAFI. Initial reports indicate that one student in the cafeteria experienced a fatal cardiac arrest. Then, over 500 fellow students died from fear-induced psychosomatic heart attacks. Minister of Safety Light has charged the school administrators with felonies for failure to properly implement Homeland-mandated *Crouch, Close and Cover Technique* training to avoid MCAFI's. This is Krissy Moriarty, Global Public Health Crisis Correspondent. You're watching FXH News."

"*Crouch, close and Cover*, Bree?"

"The Heart Attack Avoidance Procedure (HAAP). They're teaching it to the Officer and Enlisted personnel on base. Someone falls down with a heart problem.

Other sailors in the room shall get under the tables, close their eyes and cover their ears *or* suffer UCMJ charges."

"They outlawed bravery?" Gigi handed Brianna some Popeye's napkins. "For real?"

"Gigi?"

"Yeah, Bree?"

"Don't choke on your chicken bones." Brianna smiled, closed her eyes and covered her ears. "My Homeland military base MCAFI training will kick in."

CHAPTER TWENTY

"Betsy, what kind of monkey business is going on in here?"

"Aaron Webster!" I smiled and jumped up from the Congressional Office's plush leather couch.

Charlotte and I hugged Aaron and cried.

I whispered. "Oh, Aaron. Peaksville was destroyed."

Charlotte cried on Aaron's tailored suit. "Our moms."

Aaron hugged and comforted us. "I'm so glad you both survived."

I didn't want to let go of Aaron.

"Were you both out of town when the TEGWA happened?"

Charlotte nodded and wiped her tears.

"Were you in Spokane?"

I shook my head negatively.

"Coeur d'Alene?"

I let go of Aaron. "Closer."

Aaron smiled. "The neodymium mine?"

I wiped my tears and smiled. "The PIH Chief Executive Officer advised us to leave town. We camped in the TFZ for two nights. We thought Dr. Gunnison was being altruistic."

Charlotte sighed. "Then he killed our moms."

Aaron hugged us. "I'm sorry you had to go through that. I've heard the name Gunnison before. He goes by Raygun. He seems to be in Walker's inner circle."

Betsy smiled and exaggerated her keyboard actions. "And, print!"

Charlotte whispered. "What is Betsy doing?"

"The question is more like 'What are *we* doing'?"

I paused. "Okay. What are *we* doing, Aaron?"

Aaron sat with us on the couch, drew us in closely for comedic effect and quietly whispered into our ears. "It's classified."

We laughed.

"Tommy Boy said you were up to something," I said.

Betsy walked to the printer, winked at Aaron and picked up ten pieces of paper from the outlet tray. "Viola!"

Charlotte nudged me. "Aaron is definitely up to more monkey business."

Representative Gus Bryant, an Alabama Congressman, poked his head in the Speaker of the House secretarial office. "Aaron, are we good?"

"We're good, Sir."

"You know how to find Bob?"

Charlotte and I listened to the cryptic conversation.

Congressman Bryant looked at Betsy. "The House Intelligence Committee accounting data should be in your inbox."

Betsy smiled and held up the newly printed documents.

"Perfect."

"Signature Flight Support at Reagan National, right?" Aaron asked.

Congressman Bryant nodded. "My driver is standing by downstairs to take you to your jet. Charlotte and Grace, where's Tommy Boy?"

The Congressman knew our names. Charlotte and I sprung to our feet.

I laughed and looked at Aaron. "Not sure, Sir."

"Here's my card." Congressman Bryant handed us three official business cards. "Call if you need more funding."

Charlotte and I shook his hand. "Thank you, Sir."

"Aaron?"

"Yes, Sir?"

"Good luck."

"Thanks, Gus."

Congressman Bryant exited the office.

Aaron looked at Charlotte and me. "You have no idea. Do you?"

We shook our heads.

Aaron smiled. "It's better that way."

We stood patiently with blank faces.

Aaron finally fed us some information. "Gus is a good old boy from Mussel Shoals, Alabama. Every day in the House of Representatives for the last decade, Tex and Gus discussed college football, Washington Nationals baseball, you name it. Gus is Chairman of the House Intelligence Committee. Speaker Bonner and President Voigt briefed Gus on CABESA, TEGWA's, MEDWEAP's, MCAFI's, the MWOP, everything. We're going to pick up Tex's son, Bob Bonner. He owns a jump school and security firm in Texas."

"Then what?"

Aaron looked at Betsy. "I told you everything I know."

Charlotte raised her hand.

Aaron smiled. "Charlie, speak your peace."

"We didn't pack."

"That's because you don't have anything to pack."

"True."

"Where *is* Tommy Boy? It's time to go."

"He said he's out," I replied.

"Really?" Aaron immediately called Thomas. "Tommy Boy, meet us at Washington National Airport. Follow signs to Signature Flight Support Fixed Base Operator. Pack light."

Thomas declined. "I'm out, Aaron. I just passed the bar. Tell everyone I love them."

"You sure?"

"I'm sure."

"Alright, Tommy Boy. I understand."

"He's not going?"

Aaron shook his head. "Seems scared."

T he Minister of Youth and Minister of Safety arrived early to the White House Situation Room for the noon briefing.

"Abby's angry with you, Bud."

Mr. Light sighed. "What did I do now, Charity?"

Charity whispered. "Abby's secretary's daughter attended college in Charlottesville."

Mr. Light shrugged. "Her cousin's neighbor's teacher's uncle is probably a professor in Charlottesville. Big deal."

"I guess her secretary's daughter was one of the three thousand student heart attack fatalities on campus last weekend."

"You heard Abby last week. She wanted me to cut ten percent from every college." Mr. Light leaned back and feigned blowing smoke from his right index finger. "Mission accomplished."

Charity whispered. "Abby also said to exclude colleges in the Washington DC area."

"Charlottesville is in the Washington DC area?"

"It's in Virginia."

Mr. Light looked Charity in the eyes. "Have you made that drive, Charity?"

The Minister of Youth shook her head.

"Get in your car. Leave the beltway. Keep driving. For several hours. When you arrive in Charlottesville after dark, call me and tell me it's in the local area."

She shrugged. "Abby thinks it's local. She thinks you messed up."

The Minister of Safety whispered. "Abby always thinks I messed up."

The Minister of Health entered the Oval Office.

"Speaking of mess-ups." Charity Ferguson whispered then broadcasted her greeting. "Introducing the new Minister of Health, Kenny Rogers. Hitting on seventeen lately, Doctor?"

Dr. Moriarty chuckled. "Hey, I won five hundred dollars last night in Vegas."

"Yeah, but you lost two thousand."

Minister of Truth Michaels entered the Situation Room. "Abby is running thirty minutes late."

Mr. Light laughed. "Is that *The Truth,* or is it fiction?"

The Minister of Youth nudged the Minister of Safety. "The Minister of Truth is infallible. He's physically incapable of telling a falsehood."

Mr. Light chuckled. "Abby injects scopolamine truth serum into his arms daily."

Secretary of Truth Michaels inarticulately mumbled in pain. "The Minister of Youth wishes she had the divine wisdom of the Minister of Truth! Anyhow, give me a break. I just got back from the dentist. Root canal."

Charity laughed. "They pulled his wisdom truth."

Mr. Light smiled. "The tooth shall set you free."

Congressman Bryant's personal driver, Paul, stopped the black Chevy Suburban with dark, limousine-tinted windows in the Washington DC airport parking lot. "Aaron, ladies, Signature Flight Support FBO."

"Thanks Paul!" Aaron said.

We disembarked from the official vehicle.

"Aaron?"

"Yeah, Paul."

"Be careful, buddy."

Aaron shook Paul's hand and led us into the Ronald Reagan Washington National Airport's luxury FBO.

I looked around at the Reagan National facility. "Is this a small terminal?"

"It's a gas station for small jets." Aaron opened the door for us. "This is how the other side lives."

A young woman approached us with a stack of paperwork. "Mr. Webster?"

"Aaron is fine."

"I'm Kelly Cross. I'm your pilot, today."

Aaron shook the young lady's hand.

Kelly looked at Charlotte and me then shook our hands. "Kelly Cross."

"Charlotte Epley."

"Grace Becker."

"Just you three?"

Aaron nodded.

"One bag?"

We smiled.

"You ladies have bags?"

We shook our heads.

"Well then, you have no luggage for me to lose. Piece of cake. We're in the red, white and blue G-5 on Alpha Ten. I'm topping her off with Jet A, getting weather, getting NOTAMS and filing my FAA flight plan. You've got the whole jet to yourselves. Light chop on the climb. After that, smooth sailing. Flight time to Fort Worth is nineteen hours."

We all looked at each other.

"Nineteen hours?" Charlotte asked.

Kelly laughed. "Two hours. Just kidding. Gus Bryant ordered meals and drinks for us. The KDCA Flight kitchen just delivered six box lunches to our Gulfstream. Save one for me. And don't steal my dessert." Kelly looked at her watch. "Wheels in the wheel well in twenty minutes. Okay?"

Charlotte and I smiled. "Thanks, Kelly."

I looked at Aaron. "Kelly's nice."

R esting back on her elbows, Ruby whale-watched on Bondi Beach (*pronounced bond-eye*) in her two-piece bikini.

"Thanks for taking me to Bondi, Luke."

Luke silently responded with a quick half-smile.

"The train ride from Sydney wasn't too bad. Was it?"

Luke shrugged.

"It took about thirty minutes from The Rocks. Don't you think?"

Luke shrugged.

Ruby rubbed suntan lotion on her belly and legs. "I can't believe how big the Pacific Ocean is. This water goes all the way to Seattle."

"Don't try to swim it," Luke said. "Sharks will eat you before you get past the coral reef."

"Take your shirt off, Great Pasty White Shark. Stay a while."

Luke didn't smile. "I'm good."

Ruby relaxed in the sand. "It's nice to be out here away from Sydney. Just you and me. And the whales."

Luke shrugged. "And sharks."

"I bet I can make you smile, Luke."

Luke shook his head and stared into the South Pacific.

"Smile if you noticed any topless girls here on Bondi Beach."

Luke turned his smiling face away.

Ruby sat up to look. "Exposed!"

Beep-beep!

Ruby laughed. "You keep smiling, Mr. Creep-a-Sneak-Peek. I'm going to check my iPhone."

Luke closed his eyes and soaked up the Gold Coast sunlight.

"That's weird."

"Who is it?"

"It's from Charlie's phone. I texted her and Charlie ten times in the last few days. I finally got this reply." Ruby held up her phone.

2-I-I-H-2

R uby sat up and dialed an international phone number. "Hello, Amy? It's Ruby. How are my favorite Swiss Misses?"

"I'm awesome. Top of my game, as expected. I look good, Ruby. Emma is jealous in a distant second place."

Ruby laughed. "I got a reply from Charlie's cellphone."

"For real?"

"Just five digits. It's a code. 2-I-I-H-2."

Amy paused. "Nothing else?"

"Nothing."

"I got a code, also. Maybe it's a good sign."

"This is costing us. Say hi to Emma. By the way, Luke took me to a topless beach today. We're on Bondi Beach."

Amy paused to think. "Make that creep take off his sunglasses."

"Good idea. See you, Amy."

Click!

"What did Amy say?"

Ruby lay back on the beach. "She called you a creep and wants you to remove your sunglasses."

Luke smiled and turned away.

I sat on the plush, leather couch in Ronald Reagan Washington National Airport's Signature Flight Support executive lounge. "Kelly's cool."

Aaron nodded. "Kelly always flew Speaker Bonner and Gus Bryant around."

FXH News broadcasted a Breaking News report on the FBO's courtesy television. "Once again, Cardiac-Related Discussion, also known as CRD, is considered a felony offense by the Minister of Safety for non-medical and non-governmental Homelanders. Violators will be charged with second degree murder if a nearby Homelander becomes nervous and experiences a fatal heart attack after nearby CRD."

FXH News continued. "In other news, a Registered Service Squirrel named Larry and its owner were told to leave the Golden Corral in Pensacola, Florida by a group of unkind, unwelcoming Homelanders. Sixty-eight percent of polled viewers believe the Registered Service Squirrel's removal was unjustified. The Ministry of Safety is investigating and considering hate crime and animal cruelty charges against the restaurant employees and inhospitable patrons. What do you think should happen to the disruptive and unwelcoming Homelanders? Visit our website to participate in the polling. I'm Krissy Moriarty, Global Public Health Crisis Correspondent. You're watching FXH News."

Charlotte smiled. "I wonder if the Larry the Squirrel left without a struggle."

Aaron smiled. "Larry will bury those nuts in a lawsuit."

I laughed. "Maybe President Walker should invite Larry to the White House. Her new Vice-President could be a squirrel to prevent future uprisings."

Charlotte looked at her watch. "Aaron? Should we walk to the jet?"

Aaron nodded.

"Wait!"

We turned around and smiled. "Tommy Boy!"

"Got room for one more?"

"Absolutely!" Aaron said.

I hugged Thomas and whispered. "Thanks for coming."

Charlotte smiled. "What made you change your mind?"

"This is for my parents." Thomas looked at Aaron. "Reciprocity."

We happily led Thomas to the Gulfstream.

Kelly was completing her pre-flight. "Sorry, no room for the straggler. Too late, buddy."

We sighed in disappointment.

Aaron smiled.

"For real?" Charlotte asked.

"Just kidding." Kelly looked at Thomas. "Saddle up, partner!"

CHAPTER TWENTY-ONE

"Dr. Braun?"

Dr. Braun adjusted his satellite phone volume and walked from the Sharjah Blue executive cabin onto the swimming pool deck. "President Walker. That has such a nice ring to it."

President Walker smiled.

"How is life in the New American Homeland?"

She laughed. "Probably not as good as life on the Sharjah Blue."

"How can I help you, Abby?"

"I'm prepared to push some monthly money at you."

Dr. Braun laughed and replied in his elderly, East-German accent. "Monthly money? That's my *favorite* kind of money."

President Walker spun her chair around and looked outside her Oval Office onto Pennsylvania Avenue. "Can PsytoSCOPE Nanotech Corporation increase production capacity by 250 million monthly shots within a week?"

"Of course."

"How much are we talking, Abby?"

"Let's call it an even ten dollars per shot. My napkin math brings that up to $2.5 billion monthly, $30 billion annually."

Dr. Braun paused. "Cost per shot increasing by five percent annually?"

"That's fair," President Walker said.

"Deal."

Dr. Braun lounged on the Sharjah Blue deck and watched dozens of supertankers on the South China Sea horizon. "I'll notify my CFO in Peaksville immediately. Do you have my bank routing data?"

"Yes. Expect the first payment tonight. One more thing."

"Anything for you, Abby."

President Walker clicked her 24K gold, ballpoint pen on the Resolute Desk. "Mustafa promised me a Syndicate Seat after my inauguration. He's dragging his feet on confirmation, though."

"I'll catch a helicopter-ride to Hong Kong International and fly to Dubai tonight. It is best if I ask him on the golf course tomorrow."

"That's so kind. Thanks."

"Abby, a $30 billion annual contract is very kind."

"That's what friends are for, Dr. Braun."

"Goodbye, Abby."

A aron reached out and momentarily held our hands at thirty-six thousand feet in the Gulfstream Five. "What an amazing thing. You survived because of your trip to The Forbidden Zone. And then you were both saved by a Good Samaritan gunshot."

Charlotte nodded.

"And you don't know who saved you?"

I shook my head. "We had our eyes closed in Farmer Youngblood's thousand-acre corn field under Schweitzer mountain. The TSC Peacekeeper kept jabbing the rifle into our backs. Then, someone killed him."

Charlotte agreed. "We were goners."

Thomas looked out the G-5 passenger window at North Texas from his leather seat and mumbled. "That's twice, Grace."

I wasn't sure what he said. "Say again, Tommy Boy?"

Thomas looked at the three of us. "Grace was saved twice by a magic bullet."

Aaron and Charlotte nodded.

Thomas put his hand on my knee. "You were supposed to die twice. God's not ready for you, Gracie Becker. You still have work to do on this earth."

"You're going to make me cry, Thomas."

Charlotte gently smiled. "We actually talked about reversing fate during our 2300-mile hitchhiking adventure. We were *so* ready to die in the Youngblood's cornfield that day. We had witnessed too much pain in Peaksville."

I agreed. "We feel like the person who shot the TSC Peacekeeper cheated us out of something. We were so sad. We were ready to join our parents in heaven. It was as if the Good Samaritan interfered with our fate."

Charlotte nodded. "I still have survivor's guilt. For being alive. Isn't that strange?"

Aaron squeezed our hands and kissed Charlotte and me on the cheek. "Thomas said it best. God wasn't ready for either of you."

Kelly spoke to us through the jet's PA system. "We'll be on deck at Fort Worth Meacham International Airport in about seven minutes. Weather's good. Clear skies and eighty degrees. The radio operator at American Aero Fixed Base Operator said Bob Bonner is waiting for us. Make sure you fasten your seatbelts on final approach. Technically, I'm legally blind, and my landings are usually a bit rough."

Click!

Kelly unclicked the PA button.

Thomas ran from an executive lounge chair to a regular airplane seat to strap in. "Legally blind?"

I cinched down my seatbelt strap. "Kelly didn't just say that."

Everyone except Aaron followed my lead and tightened their straps.

Charlotte laughed. "Our pilot's blind as a bat? God can't save us now."

Click!

Kelly laughed on the intercom. "Just kidding! Everybody relax and enjoy. Technically, I'm not *legally* blind. Talk to you on the ground."

"Operation CHAOS has worn out its welcome according to my wives here in Dubai. They have lost parents and young siblings in their home countries."

President Walker paused and clicked her ballpoint pen on the Resolute Desk. "I need a more time, Mustafa."

"How much time?"

"One week."

Mustafa Muscat leaned back in his golf cart and stirred sugar into his iced tea in the hot United Arab Emirates sun. "The world has apparently lost one billion people to heart attacks in the last two weeks."

"I will slow the operation, Mustafa. Trust me."

Mustafa sipped his iced tea. "Dr. Braun arrived in Dubai."

President Walker looked at her American flag in the Oval Office. "His PsytoSCOPE nanotech firm is part of the Operation CHAOS drawdown."

Mustafa paused. "I understand. You are developing a cure. I trust you, Abby."

"Thanks, Mustafa."

Click!

President Walker dialed her telephone and waited. "Hello, may I speak with the Minister of Truth, please."

"One moment, Ma'am."

Mr. Michaels picked up his phone. "President Walker?"

"When was the last time you spoke with Krissy or Skylar?"

The Minister of Truth laughed. "They were just on conference call with me."

"Call them back. I need a televised press conference for the Homelanders."

C hirp!

Kelly greased our landing at Fort Worth Meacham International Airport.

I laughed as the reverse thrust roared through the fuselage skin. "Kelly's not blind. She nailed it."

Aaron unbuckled and looked out the windows. "There it is. American Aero FBO. The one with the big *TEXACO* sign."

Thomas looked around. "What are we doing here?"

Charlotte and I immediately looked at Aaron.

Aaron grabbed his backpack. "We're here to see Bob Bonner, the son of the late Speaker of the House Tex Bonner."

"Why?" Thomas asked.

Aaron watched Kelly intercept the parallel taxiway towards American Aero. "Because Bob is waiting for us."

"Why is Bob waiting for us?"

"Because Bob's going with us."

"Where?"

Aaron smiled as Kelly taxied into the line and shutdown the Gulfstream engines. "Actually, we're going with Bob!"

I looked at Charlotte and Thomas. "Huh?"

Kelly broadcasted into the PA system before losing generator power from the winding down engines. "Welcome to Fort Worth."

Aaron opened the port cabin door hatch and was greeted by an American Aero lineman. "Hi, there!"

The FBO employee smiled. "Top it off?"

Aaron leaned into the cockpit. "Kelly? Top it off?"

Kelly checked her kneeboard cards. "Tell him five hundred gallons of Jet A."

Aaron leaned out the cabin door and repeated the order.

The American Aero gave a 'thumbs up,' grounded the airplane with a thin metal cable, and began pumping gas from his truck.

"Aaron Webster!"

Aaron saw a young man in black, tactical gear driving towards the G-5 in an electric utility cart. "Bob?"

Bob Bonner smiled. "How was the flight?"

"Great."

We followed Aaron down the stairs.

Bob looked at the four of us. "I'm Bob Bonner. What are your names?"

We all shook his hand.

"Grace."

"Charlotte."

"Thomas."

Bob pointed at us one by one. "Peaksville survivor, Peaksville survivor, new lawyer."

I laughed. "You did your homework."

Bob yelled into the Gulfstream. "Kelly! Get this cargo door open! You lazy, sandbagging, hack!"

Kelly leaned out the cabin door hatch. "Open it yourself, Bub! You good for nothing jerk!"

Bob winked. "Kelly flew my father around."

Aaron shook Bob's hand. "Sorry about Speaker Bonner."

"Thanks. I guess that's part of the reason why we're all here." Bob walked towards the back of his electric cart. "Can you all help me out?"

"Sure!" Charlotte and I grabbed one of his large, black canvas duffle bags and lugged it towards our Gulfstream 5.

I struggled and laughed. "This is *heavier* than a hay bale."

Thomas and Aaron grabbed an even heavier bag.

"Bob, did you bring your whole childhood rock collection?" Charlotte asked as we loaded the multiple items.

Bob winked.

Thomas heaved a bag into the Gulfstream cargo bay. "What's in here?"

"Little bit of this. Little bit of that."

Kelly poked her head out of the airplane. "Bob thinks he's *Mary Poppins*. Just go along with it or he gets mad."

Aaron looked at me after lifting a canvas bag onto the G-5. "Bob was on a Navy SEAL Team, then Delta Force."

Bob changed the subject, tapped his watch, and clapped his hands. "Student Pilot Kelly, how soon until you can get this bag of bolts off the ground?"

Kelly checked the fuel truck transfer meter. "We can be wheels in the well in *fifteen* minutes. Bob, *you* board in *twenty* minutes."

Bob looked at us. "It's obviously impossible to find a competent pilot these days. We found Kelly wandering around a dumpster licking the inside of yogurt canisters. We raised money for her flight training and bought her those thrift store shoes. People can be so charitable for the underprivileged."

Kelly looked at Charlotte and me. "There are bathrooms in the FBO if you need to vomit after looking at Bob's face."

It was fun to laugh again.

"Why did we summit Mount Fuji, again?"

Brianna laughed. "I thought it would be fun."

One by one, Gigi picked the cinders out of her old, Cabela's hiking boots. "I'll never climb Fuji again."

Brianna sat with Gigi on her front porch of the Liberty Lane base housing on Atsugi. "We did it! It was pretty cool at twelve thousand feet overlooking Tokyo and the Pacific Ocean, right?"

Gigi shrugged and took her socks off. "We were lucky the volcano didn't blow. Every step on the way down the mountain spilled one hundred more cinders into my boots. The Atsugi MWR tour company should have paid *us*, Bree!"

Beep!

Brianna stood up. "Come inside, Sir Edmund Hillary. Our pizza's ready."

Gigi left her shoes and socks on the porch and walked inside. "Have Antoine or D'Andre summited Fuji?"

Brianna shook her head and removed the pizza from the oven. "I wouldn't recommend it to them."

"What?"

"I said that I wouldn't recommend it."

"Why?"

"Because they'll get cinders in their boots. Duh!"

Gigi smiled. "Oh, so it's okay for Gigi to have cinders in her boots. But not AJ or DJ?"

Brianna shrugged. "Check out the television. President Walker is speaking on FXH News."

"I have initiated development of Fear Suppression Shots (FPS) through the creation of my Multiple Cardiac Arrest Fatality Incident (MCAFI) Task Force.

"Medical and Scientific Leaders from INLINE Pharmaceuticals, PsytoSCOPE Nanotech Corporation, Harvard, Stanford, Peaksville Defense and Space, and the Peaksville Institute of Health have responded to my demand for a cure to the psychosomatic secondary heart attacks. Together, these kid-friendly institutions have developed specialized Fear Suppression Shots (FPS), causing an end to the pain, death, and misery that previous Presidential Administrations and Legislatures negligently brought to the Homeland. Testing on Homelanders has already commenced."

"That was our leader, President Walker in the Oval Office. This is Krissy

Moriarty, Global Public Health Crisis Correspondent. You're watching FXH News."

Gigi looked at Brianna. "Shots for everyone, Bree?"

Brianna nodded. "Peaksville Defense and Space was mentioned."

Gigi shrugged. "Everything old is new again."

CHAPTER TWENTY-TWO

The Gulfstream PA system energized as we waited for takeoff clearance."

"Thank you for flying Kelly World Airlines. There is a one-hundred-knot tailwind to New Orleans generated by Bob Bonner's Tex-Mex lunch-exhaust. Flight time is only one hour, but you will be required to don oxygen masks and toggle one hundred percent."

Bob shielded his smile as we laughed in the executive jet.

Click!

Kelly wasn't finished. "Your pilot today is *very* hot. Be sure to stay hydrated with *very* wet, cold water to avoid overheating."

Charlotte nudged me. "Amy Kernan Part II?"

I laughed and nodded.

Ding!

The fasten seatbelts light energized.

Kelly advanced the power levers from idle, checked her engine instruments on the roll after takeoff clearance from Fort Worth Meacham Tower, and achieved maximum power within five seconds.

Once airborne and after completing a steep turn to the east, the fasten seatbelts light extinguished.

Ding!

I looked at Bob. "Where exactly are we going?"

"Wichita, Kansas. To swap this airplane out."

I paused. "Kelly said New Orleans."

"True. First, we have to pick up my Delta Force friend."

"He's in New Orleans?"

"He's in jail."

I maintained eye contact with Bob Bonner, waiting for him to flinch.

The smile never came.

"You're serious?"

Bob nodded. "You'll like him."

"What's his name?"

"Lurch."

"Lurch?"

"Lurch."

"And Lurch is in jail?"

Bod cracked a slight smile. "Lurch is in jail."

Charlotte nudged me. "Where are we going, Gracie?"

I leaned towards her. "We're going to New Orleans. To pick up Lurch. Lurch is in jail."

We sat quietly for ten seconds to digest the plan.

Then we laughed.

R uby smiled in the New South Wales sunlight in wine country. "This is lovely."

Luke shrugged. "It's okay."

"It's good for us to get away on a holiday."

Luke looked away and mumbled. "Wine country doesn't bring my mom back."

An elderly, Australian gentleman pulled out the seat for his lovely wife and joined Luke and Ruby for breakfast. "Mind if we join you?"

Ruby and Luke stood momentarily to greet the couple in the elegant deck overlooking Shiraz vines of Hunter Valley Cooperage Bread & Breakfast. "Please."

"Good brekky?"

"Great." Luke said.

Ruby smiled. "The Eggs Benedict and Ricotta pancakes are phenomenal."

"American?" asked the elderly woman.

"Technically, I think these foods are European," Luke said.

Ruby tapped Luke's knee and smiled. "Yes, *we're* from America."

The man prepared his breakfast napkin. "Just visiting Hunter Valley?"

Ruby looked at Luke.

"We've lived in Sydney for a few years," Luke said.

"Ah!" The man smiled. "We live in Newcastle."

Ruby poured the woman some caffeinated coffee and smiled. "We saw you both on the grass tennis courts at sunrise."

The woman smiled and held her husband's hand. "That's our routine. We play tennis on Tuesdays and Thursdays. My name is Edna. This is Steve."

"Hi, I'm Ruby. This is Luke."

"Pleasure."

Edna generously salted her buttery hash browns and looked at Ruby. "Which wineries have you visited, dear?"

"We did Mount Pleasant's full tour yesterday. Today is Tyrrell's and Glen Oak."

"Our favorites."

"How long have you been married?" Ruby asked.

"We've been married since before Steve went away to fight in the war."

Luke wiped his mouth with a napkin. "World War II?"

Steve laughed. "We're old. But not *that* old. Vietnam. My battalion served alongside American soldiers."

"Thanks for your service," Ruby said.

"Sixty-five years of marital bliss this year," Edna said.

Steve salted his eggs for twenty seconds. "What do you think of that Abby Walker?"

Edna tapped Steve's leg. "Steve."

Luke and Ruby made eye contact.

"I think Walker —"

Edna interrupted Steve and looked around. "Manners, Steve."

Steve continued. "All of my old Vietnam buddies at a Newcastle ANZAC picnic on Saturday decided that Walker is behind the billion heart attacks."

Edna nodded quietly in agreement.

Ruby placed her hand on Luke's leg. "Why do you think they are induced?"

Steve pointed at a leg wound then raised his shirt to show a stomach wound. "My generation didn't need to see the gun to realize you've been shot."

Ruby carefully studied Steve's wisdom. "And why President Walker?"

"Seven hundred days in Vietnam honed my ability to determine good guys from bad guys."

Aaron, Charlotte and Thomas slept at flight level two-three-zero in the New Orleans-bound Gulfstream while Bob Bonner reviewed computer documents on his laptop.

I woke up, leaned over and smiled at Bob. "You're a Navy SEAL?"

Bob closed his computer and nodded. "I *was* a SEAL."

"My dad was a Marine. My mom was an Army medic."

"West coast?"

I nodded. "Mostly Pendleton and Okinawa for my dad. Mom always tried to get nearby Army orders. Were you west coast, Bob?"

Bob nodded. "Coronado."

I paused. "That's down in San Diego?"

"The island over the tall bridge. Seventy degrees year-round. It didn't suck."

"Sorry about your dad."

"Thanks. Before Dad died, he showed me some things that may be familiar to you." Bob opened a duffle bag and showed me the 2020 North American Scheduled Depopulation Agenda and MEDWEAP Operator Master List. He also flashed a very familiar MEDWEAP.

I suddenly and strangely missed my parents. "Looks familiar."

"Aaron told me about your parents, your friends, and his father the PDS engineer."

I looked out the window. "Where are we going, Bob?"

"Someplace warm and far."

I smiled. "Tell me about Lurch."

"He and I went through BUDS together. Later, we each got shot up pretty bad waiting for air support in the sandbox. Both of us got medically retired and tried to start new lives."

"You own a jump school in Texas?"

Bob nodded. "And a security firm. Congressman Gus Bryant's House Intelligence Committee secretly hired my firm about three years ago."

"Lurch works for you?"

"Sometimes."

Kelly lowered the nose and started her descent into New Orleans.

Bob looked out the right window at the Gulf of Mexico and continued. "I did some homework on Charlotte, Thomas and you. You'll have a lot in common with Lurch. He was an experiment."

Someone just called me an experiment.

Bob looked at me. "Are you alright with danger, Grace?"

"I never really thought about it."

Bob smiled. "Aaron said you wrestled a lion."

I laughed. "Actually, the lion wrestled me."

Click!

Kelly utilized the PA as the private jet experienced mild buffet during descent. "We'll be on deck in Lakefront in fifteen minutes. The jet stream is kicking us in the pants. I'm looking at a ground speed of six hundred knots. That's ten miles per minute." Kelly momentarily unclicked the intercom then continued. "That's roughly one mile of travel for every breath you take."

Charlotte, Aaron and Thomas began to wake up.

Click!

Kelly wasn't finished on PA. "That's one mile traveled per breath. Bob, do *not* try to hyperventilate yourself. It won't get us into New Orleans any faster. It just doesn't work that way."

Charlotte laughed. "Poor Bob!"

Bob reached up and rapidly cycled his Gulfstream *PASSENGER ASSISTANCE* button ten times to annoy Kelly.

Ding! Ding! Ding!

Kelly descended into New Orleans Lakefront at six-hundred knots ground speed and joked. "Bob, please fill out your *Hurt Feelings Report* prior to landing and hand it to ground personnel to declare your airborne case of *Butt-Hurt*."

I leaned towards Bob in the Gulfstream Five cabin. "Kelly's brutal."

D r. Moriarty sighed and yelled over the loud, Key West live band inside Sloppy Joe's. "It's a *real* shame that your husband died last week, Madam Secretary Minister of Homeland Youth."

Charity Ferguson squeezed a lemon onto her raw oyster plate and smirked in the warm Caribbean night breeze. "Yeah, I'm really going to miss him."

Dr. Moriarty stirred his Captain Morgan Rum and Coke.

"Have you come to terms yet, Dr. Moriarty, Homeland Provincial Minister of Health, PhD, with the death of *your* lovely spouse during the Peaksville TEGWA?"

He shrugged. "She should have come to Washington DC to live with me."

"Oh, please. You didn't invite her, Moriarty, Doctor of Urban Studies."

"She knew she was welcome to live in DC."

"Maybe she didn't want to."

"Her loss." Dr. Moriarty sipped his drink. "Anyway, this is my first time in Key West. Don't ruin it."

"You like it?"

He held his drink and looked around. "What time is the thing supposed to happen?"

She checked her watch. "The Safety Corps is running late."

Dr. Moriarty looked around Duval Street in the warm evening breeze. "I'm thinking about staying down here and growing a grey beard like Ernest Hemingway."

"For whom does your bell toll, old man of the sea?" Charity rubbed Dr.

Moriarty's clean-shaven chin, looked at a Hemingway portrait on the Key West tavern wall then kissed him. "It tolls for me."

K elly entered New Orleans Lakefront's Signature Flight Support FBO lounge and threw me a set of keys.

I smiled. "Chevrolet?"

"It's our loaner car. Choices were a Prius or Suburban. Lurch won't fit in a Prius."

Kelly plopped down between Charlotte and me on the courtesy couch then turned to the boys. "You boys stay here. It's Ladies' Night in New Orleans."

Bob stood up and looked at his watch. "Is the jet secure?"

Kelly nodded.

"Load up the 'Burban. We're going to get Lurch."

I threw Bob the Suburban keys.

Bob quickly threw them back to me. "You drive, Gracie."

Kelly laughed. "Bob's in serious mode."

Bob sat in the passenger's seat and typed into the Chevy GPS. "*J-A-I-L.*"

I laughed and waited to leave the FBO parking lot. "Jail. Too funny."

Bob pointed at a large green sign. "New Orleans. Follow the signs to downtown for now."

I adjusted my seat, began driving and immediately ran over a curb. "Sorry!"

Aaron yelled out from the third row. "Curb check!"

Laughter.

"You're doing fine." Bob figured out the GPS. "Seventeen minutes."

Bob sat in the passenger seat and scribbled on his notepad. "Kelly?"

"Yes, Ma'am?"

Bob turned around.

Kelly hid behind Thomas in the second row of seats. "I made the SEAL angry. I hope he doesn't disappear me."

Bob looked at Kelly. "Fun fact. New Orleans Lakefront was one of Amelia Earhart's last stops ninety years ago in 1937. Almost to the day."

Kelly slouched down, tried to hide and whispered to Thomas. "Protect me from the passive aggressive man in the front seat who just threatened me with a historical fact."

"Kelly."

Kelly sat up straight and saluted. "Sir, Yes, Sir!"

"Tell me about your pilot crew day."

Kelly looked at her watch. "I turn into a pumpkin in three hours. My pilot crew day unfortunately started at sunrise."

Bob opened his laptop and checked some data. "How early can we be airborne tomorrow if we stay in downtown New Orleans?"

Kelly shrugged. "Six o'clock is sunrise."

"Aaron?" Bob asked.

"Yeah?"

"Can you hand me the accounting data from Betsy?"

Aaron passed it forward.

"Kelly, call Signature at Lakefront. Make sure we're topped off tonight. Tell them our new plan."

Kelly saluted with a ridiculous open hand and called on her iPhone.

I whispered as Kelly called. "Bob?"

"Yes, Gracie."

"How are we bailing out Lurch?"

"The New Orleans District Attorney played football and did ROTC with my dad at Texas A&M in the eighties."

"He'll let Lurch out of jail?"

Bob looked at me. "He'd let Al Capone out of jail for my dad. Besides, Betsy told him our mission."

This was my chance. "What *is* our mission?"

Bob began to explain then stopped himself. "Nice try."

"Dad!"

Across the street from Sloppy Joes in Key West, Dr. Moriarty looked down from the second floor of Rick's Bar into the Duval Street crowd. "Did you hear that?"

"Dad!"

"It's Krissy, your daughter. You don't recognize her voice by now?" Charity Ferguson looked below as they sipped mugs of beer on bar stools and smiled. "Hey, Krissy!"

Krissy Moriarty looked up at the Minister of Health and Minister of Youth and subtly pointed down Duval Street towards Irish Kenny's and the Hard Rock Key West.

Dr. Moriarty sipped his beer. "It happened."

Charity leaned forward and looked down Duval Street. "Ambulances are arriving."

"Should we go watch? Maybe give interviews?"

"Optics. Abby would strangle us." Charity held up her beer. "We should never be at the scene of an active MCAFI."

Dr. Moriarty nodded. "True."

Charity watched the news truck arrive. "Besides, Krissy is handling it. She's going live, now."

"This is Krissy Moriarty, FXH News Global Public Health Crisis Correspondent coming to you live from Duval Street in Key West, Florida on the scene of a Multiple Cardiac Arrest Fatality Incident. An elderly Homelander reportedly collapsed and died in Irish Kenny's. Dozens of nearby young tourists became severely frightened and collapsed of secondary, psychosomatic heart attacks. The rapid onset of fear rapidly spread onto the street and next door to the Hard Rock Café.

"In related news, President Walker is reporting incremental success with PsytoSCOPE's new Fear Suppression Shots (FPS). They were tested on 100,000 primary, middle and high school Homelanders in fifty states. These particular schools have since been free of MCAFI's.

"Minister of Youth Charity Ferguson has implemented Monday through Friday twenty-four hour lockdowns at selected New American Homeland public and private schools to avoid inter-generationally triggered MCAFI's at home with their parents. This measure has reduced Homelander heart attacks by ten percent.

"Four Homelanders in Lincoln City, Kansas were arrested for irresponsibly jeopardizing Public Safety by voicing uncertainty about President Walker's expert and effective handling of the global MCAFI crisis at a town hall event. They have been charged with felonies for inciting a riot.

"In unrelated news, a Terrorist Electrical Grid Wildfire Attack (TEGWA) leveled Springfield, Illinois, the boyhood home of Abraham Lincoln. The historic Lincoln House did not remain standing. President Walker pledged to bring the foreign perpetrators to justice. I'm Krissy Moriarty. You're watching FXH News."

CHAPTER TWENTY-THREE

"Eight!"

The six-foot-eight, two-hundred-fifty-pound city jail prisoner yelled and strained on the metal bench press in the hot sun. "Ah!"

"Nine!"

The four rough characters in the southern Louisiana sunlight encouraged him. "Push it, Lurch! Push it!"

Lurch struggled to lift the bar off his chest. "Ah!"

"One more! You can do it, Squid!" A man with a large USMC tattoo on his left forearm encouraged his cellmate. "One more for the Corps!"

Lurch pushed. "Ah!" He extended his arms and exhaled.

The Marine and two local New Orleans gang members helped Lurch stow the bar.

Lurch sat up and laughed. "For the Corps?"

The Marine shrugged. "It helped."

A city Correction Officer entered the prison yard. "Lurch!"

Lurch replied as he stood up from the bench press in the moist, southern breeze. "Yes, Sir?"

"You're out of here."

One of the gang members complained in his Mexican accent. "Officer, Lurch has two more sets."

"Next time." The Correction Officer smiled and looked at Lurch. "There *will* be a next time, right?"

Lurch shook his head negatively. "I've learned my lesson. I can honestly say that I'm rehabilitated. I'm a better man."

"Cut the crap." The Officer laughed and led Lurch inside the stone structure from the fenced prison yard."

Lurch cleaned out his jail room and joked at the Correction Officer. "I was going to start digging my way out this evening. I'm a procrastinator. But tonight, though! Tonight, I was going to start excavating for sure."

"You've only been here for three days." The Officer winked. "Besides, Andy Dufresne. You're too big to crawl through our prison sewer to freedom."

"True." Lurch smiled and zipped his duffle bag. "That's everything, Boss."

The Correction Officer walked Lurch to the front security gate of the city jail. "This call came directly from the District Attorney. A gentleman is here to pick you up in Duty Office."

Lurch smiled and hugged Bob. "Hey, brother."

Bob walked Lurch outside to our Suburban.

I looked at Kelly. "Do you know Lurch?"

Kelly smiled. "I've flown with him a few times."

Aaron watched the extremely large, bearded man approaching the Lakefront Signature loaner SUV. "You've flown him?"

"Flown with."

"He's a pilot?" Thomas asked.

"Mainly a SEAL. The Navy taught Lurch to fly pretty much everything, just in case. Float planes. Single engine props. Helicopters. Commercial jets like our Gulfstream."

Bob opened his door.

Kelly sighed. "I thought the deal was a one-for-one trade. We spring Lurch. Bob goes to jail for fashion crimes."

Bob smirked and whispered. "I saw some of your ex-boyfriends in there, Kelly."

I started the Suburban, looked in the rearview mirror and smiled. "Hi, Lurch."

Bob sat in the front passenger seat and looked back. "Lurch, this is Grace, Charlotte, Aaron, and Thomas. And you know Amelia Earhart."

"Hey everyone."

Charlotte found herself sitting next to Lurch in the second row. "Unpaid parking tickets?"

We laughed.

Lurch shook his head. "I was cited for being excessively handsome."

Kelly whispered. "An honest jury would never convict him."

I looked in the mirror and defended Lurch. "Guilty as charged!"

· · ·

E mma took off her snow boots in the Kernan twin's Radisson Blu Hotel Reussen two-bedroom suite in Andermatt, Switzerland. "I can't even watch anymore. Turn the channel."

Amy sat in the small living area as FXH News broadcasted from Key West, Florida. "Okay. Hold on."

"We're here on Key West's famous Duval Street in front of Sloppy Joe's, known to be a regular hangout of Ernest Hemingway. A second Multiple Cardiac Arrest Fatality Incident has just occurred at the Hog's Breath Saloon. Twelve young people reportedly became fearful and suffered heart attacks while illegally engaging in felony Cardiac Related Discussion about an earlier MCAFI at Hard Rock Café.

"In related news, President Walker has successfully tested Fear Suppression Shots (FPS) on two million federal Homelander prison inmates. These shots are in high demand. President Walker is committed to ensuring global safety. Long lines, riots and civil unrest is expected when her FPS shots become available. President Walker insists that these shots will soon be available for all. Homelanders should remain calm and patient.

"The New American Homeland is *finally* in good hands. I'm Krissy Moriarty, Global Public Health Crisis Correspondent. And you're watching FXH News."

Emma sighed. "Please change it."

Amy clicked the remote to the local ski report. "Do you think Americans suspect anything?"

"They're Homelanders, now."

"Do you?"

Emma shrugged. "Nope."

Amy checked her cell phone for more world news. "We should help."

Emma shook her head. "How?"

Amy shrugged.

I looked to my right as Bob Bonner continued a laptop computer chat session. "Are you online?"

"Satellite connection." Bob pointed at our GPS navigation. "Loyola Avenue. Turn right here, Gracie."

"Whoops." I turned onto the busy, downtown New Orleans street.

"Need help navigating?" Aaron asked from the third row of our Suburban.

Bob nodded. "Everyone look for the Hyatt Regency."

"Hyatt?" I smiled. "Sounds nice. Peaksville doesn't have one of those."

Charlotte nodded. "Peaksville doesn't have anything, now."

"Betsy secured two suites for us."

"Sounds *very* nice."

"Hyatt Regency." Thomas pointed. "On the right."

I followed the signs and stopped the car.

A well-dressed employee greeted me. "Valet parking?"

I looked at Bob.

Bob nodded.

"Yes, please."

"When you leave, bring this tag and we'll pull your vehicle."

We followed Bob into the lobby.

Bob threw Lurch one key. "Dude's room. Presidential Suite."

Twenty seconds later Bob threw Kelly a key. "Chick's room. Superior Suite."

Kelly looked at the key. "Wait a minute, wait one minute, Mister! Which is better?"

Bob smiled at Aaron, Lurch and Thomas. "Superior. The ladies have the better room."

Kelly looked at Charlotte and me as the seven of us entered the elevator. "Let's trade, then."

I stood with Kelly. "You guys should have the *superior* room."

Charlotte nodded. "There are four of you. You deserve the best."

Bob shrugged and held the elevator door open for us. "Too late. Thanks, though."

Lurch quickly opened their door and ushered in Thomas and Aaron.

Kelly crossed her arms and tried to force her way inside the Presidential Suite. "Let me see your room!"

"They're all suites, Earhart. They just have different names. They're all the same. Step off or I'll call the authorities, Ma'am," Bob said entering his room.

Kelly laughed. "Okay, fine. Then tell me about dinner."

"Betsy reserved a table at Restaurant Revolution for us. We'll come get you in thirty minutes."

Kelly entered the Superior Suite and smiled. "Woah."

Charlotte looked around. "We're definitely not in Peaksville anymore."

Mustafa waved down the Dubai Creek Yacht and Golf Club drink cart girl. "Iced tea, Dr. Braun?"

"Please."

The two golfers ogled the small teenager as she poured their drinks.

The elderly East German doctor sipped his iced tea. "The Seventh Seat has opened, Mustafa."

Mustafa nodded and threw a few bags of pretzels in his golf cart and winked. "Of course."

"Abby has patiently waited for a seat since the 2013 CABESA Initiative. She has successfully developed the weapon capabilities of The Syndicate for fourteen years."

Mustafa smiled. "I agree, my friend."

Dr. Braun walked behind the cart and selected a seven-iron. "What do you think, Mustafa? About one hundred yards?"

Mustafa touched the high-tech screen of his golf cart GPS. "Five-knot headwind component, three-knot left crosswind component, ninety-two yards, and of course we are twelve yards above the pin."

Dr. Braun smiled. "Of course."

Mustafa laughed. "You do not like my golf computer."

Crack!

Dr. Braun struck his ball onto the putting green.

"You're on the dance floor, my friend."

"Technology is fine, Mustafa. I have made tens of billions from my five-micron PsytoSCOPE Nanotech RFID's floating around in everyone's bloodstream."

Mustafa selected his six-iron and lined up his shot. "Then what is wrong with knowing the winds and distances exactly?"

Crack!

Mustafa struck his golf ball into the left bunker.

"I began my career in the East German secret police."

Mustafa plopped into the cart and stepped on his gas pedal. "Explain."

"Public technology eventually leads to disorder and revolution. The internet is the worst development in the history of mankind."

"What about your nanotechnology?"

"That's private technology." Dr. Braun waved his finger. "PsytoSCOPE nanotech is secretive. Secret technology maintains order."

Mustafa nodded and stopped the cart near the putting green.

Dr. Braun selected his putter. "What is the timeline for Abby assuming the Seventh Seat of The Syndicate?"

Mustafa grabbed his sand wedge.

Dr. Braun tried to hand him a putter. "You'll need this putter soon, my friend."

"Not yet." Mustafa declined. "Patience, Dr. Braun."

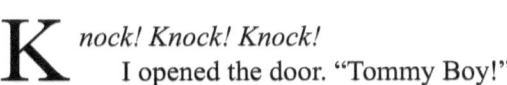

K nock! Knock! Knock!
    I opened the door. "Tommy Boy!"

Thomas politely spoke for Aaron, Bob, and Lurch. "May we squire you ladies to fine Cajun dining at Restaurant Revolution?"

"How romantic." I laughed and shouted into our large Superior Suite. "Kelly! Charlie! You ready?"

Charlotte sat in front of the television with Kelly. "Something happened."

The boys entered our Superior Suite to watch the news.

Bob looked around. "Nice and cozy."

Kelly sneered. "Cozy? Your suite *is* bigger. I knew it."

"This is Skylar Ferguson reporting from Kansas. CNH News Military Correspondent. The small town of Lincoln Center, Kansas has been destroyed by a horrifying TEGWA. The entire town has been completely destroyed by terrorists. There are zero survivors of the thirteen hundred residents.

"Today, in the New American Homeland, over eight hundred small towns have been completely leveled. The terrorists struck each and every House of Representatives district in the Homeland, exploiting gaps in protection and security caused by a century of negligence from incompetent legislatures.

"President Walker, on the other hand, is actively responding to the TEGWA's by tracking down the terrorists around the globe. Over five hundred dangerous individuals have already been found and killed today by elite teams of The Safety Corps called Tactical Victim Units.

"In unrelated news, President Walker's Fear Suppression Shots (FPS) have now been successfully tested on over ten million low-income Homelanders. PsytoSCOPE and PIH are preparing to make President Walker's effective, life-saving solution available for the benefit all Homelanders.

"I'm Skylar Ferguson. This is CNH News."

Aaron turned off the Superior Suite television with the remote control. "Pure, unadulterated horse crap."

"True." Bob nodded. "Time for some Cajun."

CHAPTER TWENTY-FOUR

I woke up in the Superior Suite of the Hyatt Regency New Orleans and reached over to turn on the light.

Click!

Charlotte lounged in the living area while checking her iPhone for morning news. "Don't bother. President Walker secured the Southern power grid."

Kelly laughed. "Oh please, President Walker. Please protect us helpless, scared Homelanders from bad, evil terrorists. I'm so scared. I think I'm having a heart attack from fear!"

We laughed.

Kelly continued. "Help me, Abby One, you're my only hope!"

"You're too much." I smiled and lay back in my bed. "What time is it?"

Charlotte checked her watch. "Five o'clock in the morning."

Kelly took a bite of Cajun food and intentionally spoke with her mouth full of leftovers. "Bob wants us airborne by six."

"Ouch."

Charlotte threw a new duffle bag onto my bed. "Aaron had the Hyatt Regency deliver us two new outfits. Tops. Bottoms. Socks. Shoes. Undies. The works."

I sat up, smiled, and flipped through the clothes. "That was nice."

Kelly laughed. "You cross-country fools were starting to get a little ripe. Who knows what's on your smelly clothes, you dirty pirate hitchhikers."

Charlotte nudged Kelly and smiled.

I grabbed the new clothes, walked into the bathroom to start my shower, and yelled. "What time did we get home?"

Charlotte yelled into the steamy, marble bathroom. "Nine o'clock."

Kelly continued to eat her leftover Grilled Swordfish and Flash-fried Oysters from Restaurant Revolution. "Our four gentlemanly squires squired themselves to Bourbon Street after dinner."

Charlotte opened her box of Creole Cioppino and began to eat. "Dinner was amazing."

Knock! Knock! Knock!

Bob stood at the door. "Let's go, we have to stop somewhere on the way to the airport."

I yelled from the shower. "Five minutes, Bob!"

Click!

The door closed.

We hurried downstairs and looked inside the Suburban and counted heads. "Where's Lurch?"

"We have to pick him up."

"Where?"

Bob looked at me. "Just drive."

I looked in the rearview mirror as I followed Bob's directions. "Aaron, thanks for the new clothes."

"Yeah, thanks!" Charlotte said.

Aaron smiled. "Courtesy of Betsy and Gus."

After several left and right turns, the environment looked eerily similar.

"Stop here." Bob ran into the New Orleans City Jail.

"No way."

Kelly nodded. "Yes way."

Bob returned with Lurch and quickly punched the Lakefront Airport waypoint into the GPS.

"Thanks." Lurch slapped the back of my seat. "Good to go."

I complied and followed the GPS instructions.

Charlotte and Kelly stared at Lurch with smiles.

Lurch slapped his large biceps. "I had to finish my last two sets."

The boys laughed.

Kelly whispered in my ear. "Gracie, drive these sinners to the nearest New Orleans parish to bathe in holy water."

Gloria Flynn sat in the Hong Kong MTR Train Station food court booth eating Mrs. Field's Cookies. "Maddie?"

"Yeah?" Maddie delicately broke her White Chocolate Chip Cookie.

Gloria took a bite and sighed. "We told Ryan we were getting lunch."

Maddie smiled. "This *is* lunch."

Gloria played with the melting chocolate. "Grace loved chocolate."

Maddie nodded.

Gloria stared off into space. "I miss her."

"Don't give up."

"It's been almost a week, Maddie. She would call."

Madison shrugged. "Maybe —"

Beep!

Gloria looked at her iPhone. "Maddie. You're not going to believe who just texted me." She held up her screen.

"No way!"

Gloria smiled and cried tears of joy. "It's a code!"

5-O-B-J-1

" A T&T codes don't look like that. Let me see." Madison confirmed the Idaho phone number. "That's definitely from Gracie's phone."

Gloria shrugged and wiped her tears. "Why wouldn't Grace just text me proof of life? Why send a code?"

Maddie smiled. "It's better than *no* text."

"It's probably just a code."

"Maybe, Gloria. Maybe it's a coded clue with deeper meaning."

Gloria looked at the remaining portion of her Mrs. Field's cookie, packaged it, and saved it in the paper bag. "I'll save this. For Gracie. Just in case."

C *lick*!

Kelly keyed the Gulfstream PA fifteen minutes after takeoff from New Orleans Lakefront. "We're level at thirty thousand feet eleva-*shun*. Rest your eyes for some relaxa-*shun*! Eat your leftovers from Restaurant Revolu-*shun*!"

Click!

Kelly secured the PA.

I waited. "Is she finished?"

Aaron smiled. "Doubt it."

Charlotte laughed. "Poor Emma has a second twin."

Kelly rekeyed the intercom.

Click!

"Please ridicule Bob. Utiliza-*shun* of persecu-*shun* and humilia-*shun* towards Bob will bring you satisfac- *shun*."

"Cajun Pilot?" Bob chuckled and almost smiled while he communicated with Betsy Ross on his satellite-connected laptop. "That's great."

Lurch woke up and looked at Aaron and Thomas. "What was that about?"

They boys shrugged.

I smiled. "Kelly's bored."

Lurch stood up and sat next to me in the luxurious Gulfstream cabin. "Awesome food last night, huh?"

I nodded. "My family passed through New Orleans when I was a child. We all loved the Cajun food. I felt guilty enjoying it again. Without them, that is."

"Parents?"

I shook my head. "My parents retired from the military. Peaksville didn't work out. They're both passed on to a better place, I guess."

"Brothers and sisters?"

I nodded. "Gloria is married in Hong Kong. Gigi is a model in Tokyo."

Lurch looked out the window. "You miss them?"

"Bob says I can't contact them yet. Since I'm officially dead."

Lurch zoned out and stared below at Oklahoma through the cabin window.

"How about you, Lurch? Parents or siblings?"

"My parents died in a house fire when I was seven. It was arson. They were great parents. Damn. That was almost twenty years ago. Then I got passed around annually in the foster care program."

"I'm sorry."

Lurch nodded. "When I was about fifteen, I started realizing that all of my previous parents were either TSC, adolescent medical researchers, or in the pharmaceutical industry."

His epiphany sounded familiar.

"They shopped for me at Goodwill. They shopped for themselves in fancy malls."

"What did you do?"

The Gulfstream buffeted through a rough pocket of air. I tightened my seatbelt. Lurch didn't flinch.

"Once I started figuring out what they were doing to me, I was passed around six more times in my final two years. I became taller, stronger and more aware, while they became more afraid of me."

I placed my hand on his knee. "Then what?"

"On my eighteenth birthday, I said goodbye to our dog and walked outside. I walked to the Navy recruiter. I never looked back."

"You ran away?"

Lurch shrugged. "Eighteen years old. Technically, I just left. They had very sinister plans. Many foster children don't fare well in society after aging-out."

"Amazing."

Lurch looked around and whispered. "Bob took me under his wing at BUDS in Coronado. I wanted to ring the bell. Bob wouldn't let me quit. Bob's a good guy."

I whispered. "Do you know our mission?"

Lurch smiled. "You really want to know, don't you?"

I nodded.

"Me, too."

"You don't know?"

Lurch shook his head. "That's the way Bob operates. It keeps everyone safer."

"I figured Bob didn't trust Charlotte, Thomas and me."

Lurch laughed. "Can I call you Gracie?"

I smiled. "Of course."

"Gracie, go to the cockpit. Kelly will teach you how to fly."

I coughed and laughed. "Excuse me?"

"Do you know how to fly already?"

I shook my head. "Of course not."

Lurch nudged me. "Then you better get up there and learn."

Gigi Becker loaded her third load of laundry into Brianna's American-sized Kenmore washer on Atsugi base. "Last load."

"Won't Gaijin2Ginza Modeling Agency do this for you?"

Gigi nodded affirmatively.

Brianna waited for an explanation.

Gigi laughed. "What are you looking at?"

"Then why are you taking a two-hour train ride to Atsugi base each week to wash your clothes?"

"I don't trust them with my clothes."

Brianna sighed.

"Besides, it gives me a chance to visit you on the base."

"Now you're talking. Do you want to go to the Zama sushi-go-round for lunch?"

Gigi laughed. "We already talked about this, Bree. Here in Atsugi, we eat Popeye's Chicken. Up in Tokyo, we eat Japanese food."

Brianna sighed and turned on FXH News. "Popeye's Chicken again?"

Gigi nodded. "And red beans and rice. New Orleans-style."

"Check it out. President Walker is talking."

"My Fear Suppression Shot (FPS) program has lowered cardiac arrests below the pre-epidemic 2026 baseline. The mandatory FPS shot program has commenced and will hereby be administered monthly to the surviving 250 million New American Homelanders. First come, first serve. Please be patient. Twelve shots per year will prevent felony indictment for jeopardizing Public Safety of fellow Homelanders.

"Also, the Electrical Grid is back online across the Homeland and stronger than ever. Homelanders are resilient, despite prior legislative failures and judicial incompetence. God bless the New American Homeland."

Gigi folded clothes as she watched. "The Peaksville CABESA shots."

Brianna agreed. "It's happening. Everywhere."

Gigi stopped watching and matched her socks.

Brianna leaned back on the couch and changed the television channel. "The military is always first."

"I'm sorry, Bree."

Brianna nodded. "Gigi?"

"Yeah?"

Brianna stood up. "I'm ready for Popeye's Chicken."

"Shadow two-two, Wichita Approach. Descend and maintain three thousand. Proceed direct NAMZU. You are cleared for the ILS Runway One Right approach to Wichita Mid-Continent Airport."

Kelly keyed the microphone as I flew the twin-engine Gulfstream jet. "Out of four thousand for three thousand. Cleared for the approach. Shadow two-two."

I squeezed the yoke. "What now?"

Kelly smiled. "Roll into a right turn. Perfect."

I flailed.

"Pull these two power levers back halfway. Set sixty percent for now. Trim upwards to make it easier." Kelly pointed to the engine gauges and helped me adjust the power. "I have the controls."

I released my hands from the yoke and power levers. "You have the controls."

"Shake it out." Kelly laughed. "Your knuckles are white from squeezing too hard."

I flapped my hands to regain circulation.

"Wiggle your toes."

"Huh?"

"Wiggle the toes. Relax!"

"Shadow two-two, contact tower."

Kelly keyed the VHF microphone and popped the wheels down. "Switching tower, good day."

Kelly looked at me. "You got this call. Say 'Tower, Shadow two-two, wheels down and locked, full stop."

"Tower, Shadow two-two, wheels full, down stop."

Kelly laughed.

Bob yelled from the Gulfstream cabin. "Cleared to land, Grace! This is Bob Tower!"

Kelly laughed and helped me toggle to VHF from Cabin PA. "Now tell *tower*."

"Tower, full stop, Shadow two-two."

The local FAA controller spoke in a Kansan accent. "Shadow two-two, cleared to land on the right."

Kelly smiled and pointed. "Read me the airspeed."

"One hundred thirty."

I saw the runway approaching

"You take the controls back."

"Huh?"

"I trimmed it up. Just fly for a bit. Loose grip, Gracie. Like you're holding eggs in your hands and you don't want to break them. Airspeed. Centerline. Airspeed. Centerline. Eyes focus inside close. Eyes focus outside far. Focus close inside to airspeed. Focus far down the centerline. Airspeed. Centerline. Airspeed. Centerine." Kelly verbalized the landing checks.

I waited for Kelly to take the controls back as my eyes got tired from the rapid scanning. "I don't know how to land a plane."

"You're looking good. Two miles. Touchdown Zone Elevation is 1331 feet. You're below two thousand. Six hundred to go. These needles are your crosshairs. Inside, outside. Focus near at airspeed and crosshairs, focus far at centerline."

"Shake it out." Kelly took the controls and retrimmed for me. "Okay, Gracie, you got it back. One mile."

I smiled. "This is fun."

"See those skid marks?"

I nodded.

"That's your aim point. When we get close, we trim up, pull back lightly, and reduce some power, and drive it down the road. Keep going inside and outside."

I flailed. "Kelly?"

Kelly helped transition into the flair. "You got this, Gracie. Now look one mile ahead. Pull the dashboard to the tree at the end of the runway, like driving a car. Only outside, don't look inside. Straddle the centerline with your legs. Look way ahead, down the road. Use your feet to drive it like a tank. Let it settle nicely onto the runway."

Chirp! Chirp!

Kelly close out the power levers. "Rest your feet on the *lower* portion of the rudder pedals." Kelly kicked the rudders for me. "See how we turn on the ground like a boat? Okay, Gracie. I got it from here. Good job."

I nodded and exhaled as we slowed. "I think I held my breath for the last minute."

"Shadow two-two, when able, turn left, contact ground."

Kelly pointed at me. "Say 'switching'."

I keyed my mic. "Shadow two-two, switching, good day."

Kelly laughed. "Nice, Gracie! You even threw a *good day* in there."

We eventually shut down engines parked at Signature Flight Support FBO. "Wow, that was fun! Scary, too! Thanks Kelly!"

Lurch poked his head in the cockpit. "How did she do?"

Kelly shrugged. "We lived."

Bob hustled towards his mysterious contact outside Signature.

Aaron, Thomas and Charlotte approached the cockpit. "Did you land it?"

"Yeah." I looked at Kelly. "Did I actually land it?"

"Grace needed a little divine intervention. But it was mostly her."

Charlotte gave me a 'high five.' "Girl power."

Bob climbed back into the airplane and looked at his Casio G-Shock. "New bird on Spot Bravo Three. Everyone grab your gear. Carry it into that white Gulfstream 650 Extended Range jet."

CHAPTER TWENTY-FIVE

M r. Light, the Homeland Minister of Safety, sat in The Safety Corps luxury box at the Washington Nationals baseball game. "Worldwide, Ma'am?"

President Walker rode in the back of her limousine. "Yes, worldwide."

"Timeline?"

"Indefinitely."

"What type of rate are we talking?"

President Walker waved back at smiling, thankful pedestrians. "How many Homelanders are left?"

"250 million."

President Walker covered her mouth and whispered. "Let's start with two million per day domestically. Ten million globally."

Mr. Light looked at the seventh inning, three to three score on the big screen. "It's going to take about three hours to get that rate initiated."

The crowd cheered.

"Bud, where are you?"

"I'm at the Nationals game."

President Walker paused. "How many Homelanders are FPS Shot Compliant so far?"

"Ninety-seven percent have received their first PsytoSCOPE FPS shot."

"245 million shots were administered today?"

"Yes, Ma'am."

Mr. Light covered his iPhone to applaud the Nationals' stolen base.

"Have you identified the non-compliants?"

"Say again, Ma'am?"

"Did Dr. Moriarty provide a non-compliant roster?"

Mr. Light snagged one last bratwurst from the luxury box silver tray before the ballpark employee removed the food cart. "Yes, Ma'am."

"Target those five million holdouts."

Bud took a very small bite to avoid being rude to the President. "Understood, Ma'am."

"Bud?"

"Yes, Ma'am."

"Commence Operation STORMWATER."

C hloe Epley jumped off the baht bus, dropped ten baht in the driver's hand, and ran into Dragon Muay Thai Camp. "Jack! Jack Kernan!"

Jack looked at Chloe. "Yes?"

Jack's opportunistic Muay Thai student promptly kicked Jack in the side of the head.

Thud!

Chloe cringed. "Sorry, Jack."

Jack unsnapped his head gear and patted the young Aussie student on the back while Chloe waited for her beau. "Nice kick, Dan. Take five."

"Sure thing, Jack."

Jack jumped out of the sparring ring. "You frightened me. What's up?"

Chloe frantically pointed at her phone. "I got a text from Charlie. I texted her yesterday. She responded. I got a text! I got a text!"

"For real?"

Chloe nodded with a wide smile. "Look!"

3-N-N-A-1

J ack leaned back. "She texted you a code?"

Chloe beamed with happiness and shrugged. "She's trying to tell us something. She's alive!"

"Okay. Maybe, just maybe she's alive. God, I hope so, Chloe."

"Gigi said she's alive, this is proof. This means Gracie is alive, too!"

Jack wiped the sweat from his face with a white towel. "Hopefully."

"I just know it!"

Jack looked at the phone again. "Is that Charlie's number?"

Chloe smiled and jumped for joy. "Yes! Do you believe?"

"I believe she's alive, Chloe."

"Thanks!" Chloe jumped for joy and hugged Jack. "I have a beach tour in twenty minutes. I've got to run. Your words mean a lot to me. I love you, Jack!"

Chloe ran outside and jumped in the back of the next baht bus heading towards Phuket Equestrian Tours.

Dan returned from his water break. "Wife?"

Jack shook his head.

"Girlfriend?"

Jack shook his head again and smiled. "Never seen that Sheila before in my life."

"Yeah, right." Dan laughed and donned his kickboxing head gear. "I know love when I see it."

Jack smiled. "Maybe so, Dan."

"Bud?"

Mr. Light sat in Washington DC Beltway traffic. "Hey, Swamp."

General Marsh closed the door of his Peaksville Defense and Space CEO office. "Queen Bee secured Operation CHAOS."

"Yeah."

"I now have ten thousand nervous employees."

"Contracts are *not* cancelled, Swamp."

"I know, but they're just nervous about possible layoffs. They have families to feed in Peaksville, children to raise."

"My International MWOP Union President just expressed the same concern."

General Marsh watched his production crew in action. "What do I tell my technicians and engineers?"

"Tell them we recently commenced Operation STORMWATER."

"I've heard it's limited in duration and scope."

Mr. Light bullied his way into the Beltway HOV lane towards Bethesda, Maryland. "Have any PDS MEDWEAP technicians ever lost their jobs since the 2013 CABESA Initiative?"

"No."

"That's what you tell them."

"Okay."

"We've experienced fourteen years of MEDWEAP growth, Swamp."

"Fair enough, Bud."

Bud changed lanes again. "How's Peaksville?"

General Marsh paused. "Are you serious?"

"Yes."

"It's all gone. All we have left is PDS, PIH, and PsytoSCOPE."

"I forgot. Sorry."

"Some of the employees are upset, by the way."

"Why?"

General Marsh looked at the scribble on his CEO office whiteboard. "I have a list of post–Peaksville TEGWA complaints. Youth Sports leagues cancelled. Our PDS parents all need to homeschool. The churches, grocery stores, gas stations, friends' homes, babysitters' homes, et cetera, et cetera were all melted."

Mr. Light arrived home to his wealthy Bethesda neighborhood. "First world problems."

"How does this all end, Bud?"

"Extinction."

General Marsh looked around his executive Peaksville office. "The previous PDS CEO went the way of the Dodo Bird."

Bud cleared his throat. "What are you saying?"

"Do you see that in my career progression?"

Bud paused. "Not on my watch, Swamp."

"What if Queen Bee orders my extinction?"

"Like I said, Swamp. Not on my watch."

"Thanks, Bud." General Marsh sighed. "Do you think monkeys will rule the world someday? Just like Planet of the Apes. But instead, Planet of the Spider Monkeys."

No response.

"Sore subject? I'm just trying to inject a little levity."

"Enjoy it. Injecting levity will soon be a crime, Swamp. You committed an LIDC. Levity Injected During Crisis. Same penalty as Cardiac Related Discussion."

General Marsh nodded. "We're almost there, unfortunately."

"I think we *are* there." Mr. Light clicked his Bethesda mansion's garage door opener. "Take care, Swamp."

B ob poked his head into the cockpit on the Wichita flightline. "How much more time do you need?"

I helped Kelly page through the Gulfstream 650 ER Operator's Manual while she entered waypoints into the touch-screen, high-tech, Multi-Function Displays on the instrument panel.

Kelly turned around from the left seat and smiled at Bob. "This 650 is amazing."

Bob tapped his watch. "Thirty minutes? Three hours? What's your timeline?"

"Thirty minutes." Kelly paused then looked at me in the right seat. "Bob?"

"Yes?"

"There's a problem."

"Let it rip."

"The first MFD is engine instruments, warning and caution lights. MFD-1 is easy. Keep temps and pressures in the green."

Bob nodded. "Okay."

"The second MFD is Communications and Navigation. Grace, a total noob, quickly figured out how to dial in ATIS, Flight Service, Ground, and Tower VHF frequencies. Here's our next route. MFD-2 is almost as easy as MFD-1."

I smiled at Bob. "And here's the Standard Instrument Departure and routing on MFD-2."

"Nice work, Gracie. For a noob." Bob smiled. "What's our hangup?"

Kelly pointed to the right-side cockpit dashboard. "MFD-3 is kicking our butts."

"Why?"

I held up the Operator's Manual as I attempted to gain access to MFD-3. "It requires an access password."

Kelly nodded. "Did that fellow give you a code?"

Bob tapped on the MFD-3 glass, shrugged then yelled to the back of the new Gulfstream. "Lurch?"

Lurch quickly walked forward. "Hey, Bob."

"Ever seen an MFD that needs a password?"

Lurch shook his head negatively. "I was wondering how to get in the rear cabin. Charlotte, Aaron and Thomas and I realized there is a window-less, ten-foot-long cabin in the back."

Bob looked aft from the cockpit area. "Cargo bay?"

"Negative."

"Kelly, can you get airborne without MFD-3?"

Kelly checked her fuel gauges, ground electrical power, and looked at her patient lineman from Signature. "Ten minutes until engine start."

Bob tapped on the MFD-3 glass one last time. "I'll message Betsy and Gus about a password on my laptop."

Kelly waited for Bob and Lurch to leave the cockpit then tapped the MFD glass with her finger. "Caveman Bob tap large pterodactyl with finger to fix looking glass."

I laughed. "Poor Bob."

Kelly handed me a laminated eight-by-ten Gulfstream checklist-card. "Checks, please, Noob."

The Minister of Safety entered the Oval Office for the Operation STORMWATER update and FXH News press conference. "Good morning Charity, Mr. Michaels, Dr. Hands, and Dr. Moriarty!"

Charity smiled. "Hey, Bud."

Mr. Light smiled when he saw the FXH News crew near the George Washington portrait. "Krissy Moriarty, newscaster extraordinaire."

Krissy waved. "Good morning, Mr. Light."

"What is it like being the daughter of the Minister of Health? Is he always telling you to wash your hands, brush your teeth, eat lots of vegetables?"

Krissy laughed. "Dad parties with me in Key West sometimes, right dad?"

Dr. Moriarty smiled.

The Minister of Truth checked his cell phone. "Abby is running a few minutes late. She's on her way."

Charity poured a glass of water for herself. "How do we know if that's true?"

Mr. Light pointed his index finger high in the air. "Because the Minister of Truth *says* it's true."

Charity looked around. "Dr. Hands, our resident Minister of Comfort, did the Minister of Truth's words comfort you?"

Dr. Hands smiled and quietly shuffled his papers.

Dr. Moriarty nodded. "We were all comforted, but only psychosomatically."

Charity held her throw pillow in the air. "Perhaps the Minister of Comfort would like to fluff my pillow?"

Dr. Hands looked around. "I got here early enough to fluff your pillows before you sat down. It's part of my job. I also ensured the restrooms have extra-soft, two-ply toilet paper. Bud, I got the Aloe kind. Just as you requested. For your tender bottom."

Oval Office laughter.

Click!

President Walker opened her door, walked in the Oval Office and looked around. "Sorry I'm late, brief me quickly and then we'll run cameras. Hi, Krissy."

"Good morning, Ma'am," Krissy said next to her FXH News cameraman.

President Walker pointed. "Minister of Comfort. Go!"

"Weekly *Crouch, Close and Cover Training* will continue in perpetuity in each Homeland school for MCAFI's, our new crisis, or any future crisis."

"Good. Minister of Youth, go!"

"I'm working with the Minister of Safety to ensure uniformity and equity between youth and adult fatalities and strokes. I'm ensuring compliance with the 1964 Civil Rights Act."

"Thanks. Minister of Safety, what do you have?"

Mr. Light smiled. "Good morning, Ma'am. Operation STORMWATER has claimed two million domestic lives from strokes in the last fifteen hours. We had a slow start last night, but our MWOP's are at full force today."

President Walker paused. "Minister of Health, how many Homelanders die annually from strokes?"

Dr. Moriarty looked at his papers. "About one hundred and forty thousand, Ma'am."

"What do you have for the group, Minister of Health?"

Dr. Moriarty stood up to present a list of cooperative partners. "These medical institutions are standing by with approved messaging regarding the global stroke crisis."

President Walker reviewed the list of universities, hospitals, non-profits and corporations. "Krissy, did you get a copy of approved opinion-holders at FXH News?"

Krissy nodded and held up her copy.

"Okay. Who else?"

Charity smiled. "The truth!"

President Walker laughed. "Minister of Truth, what do you have for me?"

Mr. Michaels stood up. "Good morning, Ma'am. Your 2028 reelection campaign is underway. We have worked with CNH and FXH News to ensure that you are always filmed with a cross or halo in the background."

Mr. Light smirked. "Like in the movie *The Omen*?"

Charity slapped his leg. "That was a stake."

President Walker turned to Mr. Michaels from her Resolute Desk. "A cross. Like a crucifix?"

"No, Ma'am. More like two subtle intersecting beams of light. In this case, the Oval Office window panes have crosses pre-installed in them. News cameramen and photographers have been trained to insert halo effects around your head. And the reporters will begin using historically biblical words to describe you and your actions."

President Walker looked at the cameraman. "Am I going to have a halo, today?"

The FXH News cameraman extended a 'thumbs up.'

Charity laughed. "I can't wait to see this."

President Walker smiled. "Let's do this, Krissy."

Krissy stood in front of the camera. "This is Krissy Moriarty, Global Public

Health Crisis Correspondent on FXH News. President Walker is poised to deliver her Homeland Salvation address from the Oval Office."

President Walker faced the camera from behind the Resolute Desk. "Good morning Homelanders. This week, my administration has saved the Homeland and the world of the MCAFI epidemics with successful FPS shot distribution. Unfortunately, a new crisis has developed in its wake. In the last day, two million Homelanders have mysteriously died of strokes.

"I quickly built a team of experts from the Ministry of Health, the Ministry of Safety, the Peaksville Institutes of Health, PsytoSCOPE Nanotech Corporation, and dozens of top hospitals and universities to investigate.

"My Task Force quickly revealed that the New American Homeland was struck by thousands of simultaneous Water Contamination Incidents, or WCI's, orchestrated by terrorists. We have brought those terrorists to justice. PsytoSCOPE Nanotech Corporation quickly developed a reservoir additive for all Homeland water facilities.

"Our nanotech water additive has worked. Homelanders who have consumed this water have evaded strokes. The stroke epidemic has quickly been brought to an end. Homelanders who drink of these reservoirs shall not perish. God bless you. And God bless the New American Homeland."

"And cut." Krissy smiled. "That's a wrap, Mrs. President."

Mr. Light covered his mouth and whispered. "Pah-raise the Lord."

Charity smiled and sipped her water. "I'm healed!"

President Walker laughed. "Can it, Bud and Charity."

CHAPTER TWENTY-SIX

B etsy Ross logged into her computer. "Gus, I'm on the House Intelligence network."

Congressman Gus Bryant stood up and closed the door to the Congressional Office. "What's Bob saying?"

"They're airborne from Wichita."

Gus smiled and watched. "The new jet?"

Betsy typed and waited. "He said it looks like it's only worth $70 million. Kelly the pilot hasn't figured out Multi-Function Panel Three yet."

Gus nodded and smiled.

Betsy looked at Gus. "How much *is* that Gulfstream worth?"

Gus shrugged. "After-market weapon upgrades cost about $600 million."

Betsy whistled her surprise and watched Bob Bonner text a question. "A code for MFD-3?"

Gus laughed. "TEX. Three letters. All caps."

Betsy typed and waited. "Bob typed 'LOL'."

Gus looked at Betsy. "Ask Bob if the goods were delivered from GM?"

"Who is GM?"

Gus smiled. "Our Peaksville contact."

"Oh, forgot."

Betsy typed into her computer and waited for a response. "Bob said he loaded three boxes of MW and assorted gear. Bob also said GB is learning to fly."

Gus nodded. "Tell Bob thanks."

Betsy typed and waited. "Bob said 'No, thank you'."

. . .

C harlotte poked her head into the cockpit at altitude and smiled. "Hi, Gracie! Hi, Kelly!"

I slid my left headphone above my ear and turned with a smile. "How do you like the new airplane, Charlie!"

"It's like a dream."

Charlotte looked around. "Where are we?"

Kelly pointed at MFD-2, dedicated to communication and navigation, then pointed outside. "We're overflying Moab, Utah soon."

Charlotte nodded and studied the cockpit.

Kelly turned to us from the left seat. "Want to get lower?"

We smiled.

Kelly keyed her VHF microphone. "Salt Lake City Center, this is Shadow two-two with request."

Then FAA controller promptly responded. "Go ahead with request, Shadow two-two."

"Shadow two-two, request descent to one-six thousand."

"Shadow two-two, Salt Lake Center, cleared to descend from flight level three-two-zero to one-six thousand."

Kelly dumped the nose, reduced power and read back the FAA clearance. "Leaving flight level three-two-zero for one-six thousand."

Charlotte waited for the radio calls to end. "Bob's finally asleep. Aaron and Thomas are playing Doom on the big screen. Lurch is reading."

Kelly laughed. "What's Lurch reading? *Shawshank Redemption*?"

Charlotte winked at me. "Or *Count of Monte Cristo*, another great prison escape book."

Kelly transmitted on VHF. "Salt Lake Center, Shadow two-two, cancel IFR, proceed VFR to Page, no flight following required."

"Shadow two-two, I show you passing one-seven-thousand over Moab VORTAC. Radar service terminated. Proceed VFR."

Kelly keyed the VHF. "Good day."

Kelly smiled, dumped the nose even lower, and reduced power to avoid over-speeding the new jet. "Woohoo!"

I smiled at Charlotte. "That's Bryce Canyon."

Charlotte looked outside. "It's like a post card!"

Kelly leveled the new Gulfstream just five hundred feet above the famous sloped red rocks of Moab and pointed. "The Colorado river will take us to Page, Arizona after it opens up into Lake Powell."

Charlotte leaned forward to marvel at the cut canyon walls. "What's in Page?"

"Vic."

"Short for Victor?"

"Short for Victoria. The most decorated female Navy SEAL in history."

Kelly gave me the controls for the seventy-mile canyon river run into Lake Powell.

I smiled. "This is amazing." The Colorado River gradually widened into Lake Powell near Bullfrog Basin. Green, picturesque water and two-thousand feet red, rock walls.

Kelly pointed at Page and a nearby dam. "The Glen Canyon Dam feeds the Grand Canyon and provides hydro-electric power for the four-corner region."

Charlotte looked at Kelly over Antelope Island. "Want me to go strap in for the landing?"

"Stay and watch." Kelly keyed her mic. "Page Muni, Shadow two-two is a Gulfstream jet setting up for a six-mile final, anyone in the area please advise."

Crickets.

Kelly took the G650 controls and smiled. "It's just us. I'll take the first landing in this beast. Not that I don't trust your airmanship, Gracie. Ride the controls very gently. You'll take the next landing."

"Are we high?"

Kelly nodded and reduced power. "Good eye, Gracie. Fixing it. Confirm three down and locked."

I checked. "Three down and locked." I lightly rested my right hand on the right yoke as Kelly talked through the frequent, tiny corrections to maintain glide path and lineup.

"Remember, Gracie. Inside for airspeed, outside for lineup. Near vision, far vision."

My feet lightly monitored her rudder inputs. My left hand monitored her power lever manipulations through the flare.

"Eyes outside to the end of the runway, now. Keep the runway centerline between your legs."

Chirp!

Charlotte tapped me on the shoulder and smiled. "Nailed it!"

Kelly slowed the Gulfstream and taxied to a lineman waiting near his fuel truck for shutdown in Page, Arizona. "Looks like we're the only show in town."

I looked outside the cockpit at the rocky, arid terrain as Bob opened the left Cabin door. "Does Vic know we're coming?"

Kelly yelled into the cabin. "Bob, does Vic know we're coming?"

Bob smiled. "Of course not."

Kelly looked at me and smiled. "Of course not, Gracie."

. . .

D'Andre welded alongside his VFA-195 brother, Antoine, during the all hands effort to repair the CVN-72 hull.

Antoine checked his gas tank gauge then lowered his large, metal welding face shield when he heard his name.

"Petty Officer Jordan!"

Both D'Andre and Antoine raised their face shields.

Mercedes laughed. "Ha! Let me be more specific. Petty Officer *Antoine* Jordan?"

Antoine smiled and stood up. "Good afternoon, Ma'am."

"Chief Petty Officer Smith told me where to find you." Mercedes held up the Airman Evaluations. "I've been working on these for the last three days."

"How are they looking?"

Mercedes shrugged. "Chief helped me. I hope they're okay."

"Thanks, Ma'am."

"Hello, Antoine's brother."

D'Andre stood up. "Good afternoon, Ma'am."

Mercedes looked at the USS Abraham Lincoln repair efforts. "Welding? Is it difficult?"

Antoine shook his head negatively. "My brother, DJ, is ship's company, so I got permission to help us get home sooner than later. Welding is kind of fun."

Mercedes examined the instruments and safety gear. "Can I try?"

D'Andre looked at Antoine. "She's not qualified."

Antoine laughed. "Neither am I."

D'Andre looked around for supervisors. "Do you really want to try, or are you just asking to be a polite, young Naval Division Officer?"

"I want to weld." Mercedes laughed. "For one week, during this repair in Hong Kong Harbor, the wire brushers, welders, hammerers, drillers, scrapers, zombies, vampires and motorcycle chain gangs have all kept me awake all night. Now it's *my* turn to make some noise."

D'Andre smiled. "Okay."

The Super Hornet pilot from Coeur D'Alene, Idaho donned a face shield, protective jacket, gloves, and a fresh cloth respirator.

"How do I look?"

Antoine sighed. "Like a first-tour Hornet pilot dressed in oversized welding gear."

Mercedes laughed. "Let's do this."

D'Andre lowered her metal welding face shield and did a final safety check. "This mask protects those perfect pilot eyes."

She smiled.

D'Andre handed her the welding tool. "Hold it two inches from this seam, pull this trigger, and run the flame at two inches per second. Calmly release the trigger if something is unsafe."

She nodded.

The brothers supervised the young Navy Lieutenant Junior Grade until she finished welding the line.

Mercedes raised her mask and laughed. "Awesome!"

Antoine smiled. "You liked it?"

"Can I keep working?"

D'Andre walked to his newly-arrived supervisor to speak in private.

Antoine whispered. "That's his CVN-72 ship's company boss."

D'Andre returned. "My chief said he knows who you are. He said you can do anything you want."

Antoine smiled. "Are you a celebrity, Ma'am?"

D'Andre studied the pilot. "Who are you?"

"I'm just a sailor from Idaho, like you guys." Mercedes Walker lowered her metal face shield. "But today, I'm a *welder*!"

The Page, Arizona fourth graders in Navajo Mission Elementary classroom sang in unison. "Eleven twelves are one-thirty-two! Twelve twelves are one-forty-four! Thirteen twelves are one-fifty-six!"

Bob peeked in the classroom.

Aaron and I waited in the hallway.

The young teacher smirked and blushed. "Keep going, class! All the way to twenty!" She stood from her desk, and walked outside on titanium legs.

Bob hugged her tightly and almost smiled. "You look good, Vic."

Vic whispered and joked. "How can I look good? I have no legs, Bobby."

Bob hugged her again. "I missed you, Vic."

Vic nodded and instructed us to peek inside her classroom. "I have a new life, now. These kids are my life."

"Nineteen twelves are two-twenty-eight! Twenty twelves are two-forty."

"Okay, kiddos. Finish the worksheets, then you'll get an early recess."

The children cheered. "Yeah!"

Bob looked at Aaron and me. "Aaron, Gracie, this is Vic."

I shook her hand and whispered. "Adorable children."

Aaron agreed.

Vic smiled. "Thanks. They're all children from the local Navajo reservation. Very, very poor. I'm trying to end that poverty cycle during this generation."

Aaron and I looked at Bob.

Bob looked at Vic.

"No, Bob. I have a life, now."

Bob maintained his silent, cryptic posture.

"No, Bob. Absolutely not. I'm medically retired."

Bob smiled.

Vic paused. "Where?"

Bob shrugged.

"Bob, I can't go with you. Look at me. I have no legs."

Aaron and I took a step back from the persuasive negotiation.

Vic pointed. "Bob. These kids. I can't leave my students."

Bob showed Vic a text from his iPhone. "Betsy found a substitute. College grad, veteran, speaks Navajo dialect."

Vic smiled. "Betsy found a Wind Talker?"

Bob nodded.

"What's the mission?"

Bob shrugged.

Vic turned away from the students and cried. "I saw that they killed your father. They killed my dad this week, also."

"I heard."

Vic cried. "We just buried him down in Flagstaff, Bobby."

"What's it going to be, Vic? The substitute is standing by in the office."

"Not sure."

"For our dads."

"I'll miss my schoolchildren."

Bob nodded.

"Where are we going?"

"Someplace warm."

"For how long?"

"As long as it takes."

"Are we going after the people who killed my dad?"

Bob nodded.

"I have a service dog."

Bob paused. "What kind?"

"Thor's a one-hundred-pound German Shepherd."

"Thor sounds mean."

"Thor was a military working dog. He knows good guys from bad guys."

Bob nodded. "We have a new white Gulfstream 650 at Page Muni. How soon can you be there?"

Vic looked at me and laughed. "Did I agree to go?"

I smiled. "Please go with us, Vic."

Bob waited silently for an affirmation.

Vic looked at her watch. "Thor and I will be at KPGA in twenty-five minutes."

T he Minister of Truth sat in the Oval Office briefing President Abby Walker. "Ninety-two percent is the highest approval rating in recorded history."

President Walker tapped the Resolute Desk. "Are those fake numbers?"

Minister Michaels shook his head negatively. "The sixty-five percent number last week *before* your MCAFI and Water Contamination Incident resolutions was falsified. But then you 'saved' the Homelanders. The ninety-two percent survey is very, very real."

President Walker spun her chair around to look at the balloons, cardboard signs, and dancing on Pennsylvania Avenue.

"You cured the heart attacks with the FPS shots. You cured the strokes with the reservoir water additive. Look at them. People are grateful."

The thousands of Homelanders on Pennsylvania Avenue celebrated like New Year's Eve partiers on Time Square.

President Walker watched her fans. "They believe it?"

"Our research indicates that eighty percent believe that the shots and water additive work. Twelve percent, we estimate, don't believe it but still told the phone screener they approve of you."

"They lied?"

The Minister of Truth nodded. "Of course, Ma'am."

"Why?"

He laughed. "You don't know?"

"Tell me."

"Fear." Minister Michaels leaned forward and whispered. "Guilt placed the Homelanders in the palm of your hand when you were Vice-President. A constant drumbeat of fist-clenching fear will hold them there during your Presidency."

"Guilt and fear." President Walker smiled and looked outside at dancing Homelanders. "Emotions of peasants."

CHAPTER TWENTY-SEVEN

Aaron whispered to Charlotte as the German Shepherd leaned on her knees at thirty-six thousand feet. "Thor. He looks like a Thor."

Vic gradually opened her eyes and looked out the window. "Where are we?"

"Mid-Pacific." Charlotte whispered. "I just visited Grace and Kelly up front. We're northwest of Hawaii."

Lurch snored and Bob communicated on his satellite laptop.

Vic looked at Lurch. "Lurch is still asleep?"

Aaron smiled. "Lurch slept through Gracie's hard landing in San Francisco, refueling, *and* takeoff."

Vic laughed. "Some things never change."

Charlotte looked at Thor. "Your service dog has been sitting on my feet. I didn't pet him."

"You can pet him. He's seven years-old and set in his ways pretty well. Fairly stubborn and predictable." Vic looked at Bob. "Just like Bob."

Charlotte promptly rubbed Thor's ears and laughed.

Bob looked up from his laptop momentarily, delivered a blank, thousand-yard stare through Vic, then continued typing.

"Your students are math wizards," Aaron said.

Vic smiled. "Thanks. I try."

Charlotte studied Vic's small frame and titanium legs. "I'm trying to figure you out. You seem like a humble, gentle schoolteacher —"

Bob interrupted without taking his eyes off his laptop. "Don't let her fool you.

That Navy SEAL sitting next to you is ninety-percent warfighter, ten-percent schoolteacher."

Charlotte winked at Vic and continued to pet Thor.

Ding!

Kelly keyed the intercom. "Ladies. Gentlemen. Dogs. Bob. Gracie is beginning our descent into Midway Island. Grace has assured me that this landing will be a big improvement over her previous landing. Please complete your tasks before Grace's landing. Bathroom breaks. Securing luggage in the overheads. Last will and testaments."

I heard laughter from the cabin as I concentrated on a smooth descent over the deep, blue Pacific Ocean as the evening sun finally stopped blinding us. "Is that a white cloud around the island?"

"Thousands of giant birds live on Midway." Kelly explained. "The Gooney Birds fly and fish for their babies until sunset."

"Gooney Birds?"

"Albatrosses."

I looked at my instruments. "We're five miles from Midway. Are they huge?"

"These albatrosses can have eight-foot wing spans when soaring. And right now, there may be over ten thousand flying. I think they got the nickname Gooney Birds during World War Two."

The mid-Pacific, white atoll was fascinating. "Midway Island isn't very big. It's just a runway on a circular white beach with a green lagoon in the middle."

"Level off." Kelly nodded. "Let's hang out up here."

We loitered for another twenty minutes until the cloud of birds subsided. Then we set up for final approach. Kelly talked me through my much-improved landing.

Chirp!

Kelly helped me slow the large Gulfstream 650. "Nailed it, Gracie."

We parked and shut down.

Charlotte and I followed Bob onto the Midway Island tarmac.

"Is this our destination?"

"Just a gas and go."

"What next?"

"We need to pick someone up in a southeast Asian town."

I smiled and looked at Aaron. "Gigi is in Tokyo! So is Bree! Can we —" I didn't finish my question.

Aaron shrugged. "This trip is a secret."

I sighed. "I understand."

Actually, I didn't understand anything.

Charlotte, Thomas and I took a stroll on the Pacific atoll.

The four hundred thousand pairs of albatrosses lay on the ground in makeshift nests everywhere on the island raising a young, fluffy chick.

I smiled. "They're everywhere. And they don't get scared."

Thomas laughed as he zig-zagged around the Gooney Bird nests. "Not a care in the world."

Charlotte placed her hand in front of a sitting albatross.

I tried not to watch. "Careful, Charlie."

Honk! Honk! Honk! Honk!

The tall albatross placed Charlotte's hand inside its long beak and gently chomped.

Honk! Honk! Honk!

Thomas picked up a fully-grown, thirty-pound, docile Gooney Bird and cradled it in his arms. "It's okay, Gooney."

Honk! Honk!

I laughed and petted the large majestic birds in the civil twilight after the sun had set. "They're too trusting. They can't distinguish predators from non-predators."

Honk!

Vic arrived with well-behaved Thor on a leash. "Neither can New American Homelanders."

I sighed.

Bob concluded a satellite phone call. "Kelly!"

The two conversed near Aaron and Lurch next to the newly topped-off Gulfstream.

"Homelanders!" Bob yelled. "Gather 'round!"

Vic laughed as we wandered through the albatross nests. "What did he just call us?"

We walked to the airplane.

Bob explained the plan. "We traveled from New Orleans to Midway, sunup to sundown. But we chased the sun."

Kelly nodded. "Long day."

"Two more flights. Betsy's Department of Interior contact arranged billeting for us on Midway. Kelly's looking a little haggard. Therefore, we'll sleep here. But we have to be airborne *before* sunrise to avoid the Gooney Bird gaggle launch. Any bitches, moans or gripes?"

Vic lifted her hand.

Bob pointed. "Go."

Vic smiled. "Kelly looks awesome."

. . .

T he Minister of Safety waited for President Walker to finish her Oval Office phone call with the Peaksville Institutes of Health CEO.

President Walker swiveled her leather chair and continued her call. "Okay. Yes. Okay."

Mr. Light admired the Presidential artwork then read an email from his son, Ben, as he waited on the couch.

"Okay. Thanks for the heads up, Raygun. Goodbye."

Click!

"Bud!"

Mr. Light looked up from his device and smiled. "Mrs. President!"

"What can I do for you, Bud?"

"I'm making sure we're on the same sheet of music. The PsytoSCOPE Nanotech Fear Protection Shot program is perpetual, correct?"

President Walker rapidly clicked her ballpoint pen and nodded. "Monthly. Forever."

Mr. Light visually verified the secured door then whispered. "MEDWEAP heart attacks?"

"Back to baseline, only as required. Whistleblowers, political opponents, their families, etc."

"Strokes?"

"Same."

"Is Cardiac Related Discussion still a speech violation in the post-Operation CHAOS Homeland?"

President Walker swiveled her chair to look outside at thousands of thankful fans. "Bud?"

"Yes, Ma'am?"

"Get our CRD speech violators the help they need."

"Ma'am?"

"Handle unregulated CRD as a mental disorder. Convert the violation from criminal to medical. Do not *jail* malcontents. *Commit* malcontents."

Mr. Light scribbled onto his notepad. "Get dissidents and malcontents the help they need. Soviet-style. Got it! What about TEGWA's?"

President Walker paused. "One more for now."

"Strategic target?"

"Symbolic."

"Another Lincoln TEGWA?"

President Walker clicked her ballpoint pen on the Resolute Desk. "That's all I have, Bud."

"Copy all." Mr. Light clapped his notebook closed, stood up and smiled at the Homelander's celebrating on the streets. "I'll let you get back to work, Abby."

President Walker gently raised her hand. "Hold on. Tell me about Swamp."

Mr. Light shrugged. "Swamp's good."

"That was Raygun in Peaksville. He told me General Marsh may be developing a conscience. Similar to his predecessor, Voigt."

"Negative. Swamp's good to go."

"I have a replacement CEO standing by to run Peaksville Defense and Space. Are you sure about Swamp?"

Mr. Light nodded. "Swamp is solid. Loyal to the cause."

"Thanks, Bud."

C harlotte and I walked towards the new, high-tech Gulfstream 650 ER one hour before sunrise on Midway Island with a Department of Interior's continental breakfast box.

The mid-Pacific moonlight illuminated the only airplane on the island. "It looks like Kelly beat us there."

Charlotte fed two lucky albatrosses a warm, blueberry muffin and laughed. "I dreamed about these Gooney Birds last night."

I stepped around the nests on the way to the runway. "I didn't sleep long enough to dream because of their all-night honking."

"It's nice to dream about something other than Peaksville."

I sighed. "Are you going to make me cry at five in the morning?"

"Sorry, Gracie."

We stepped onto the concrete tarmac.

I stopped. "My dreams are still only about Peakville. The good dreams *and* the bad dreams."

Charlotte held my hand and pulled me towards our jet. "Do you think Bob and Aaron will eventually let us call our sisters?"

I nodded. "Eventually. I hope."

"Where do you think we're going, Gracie?"

We approached the Gulfstream lit up on ground electrical power by a Midway Island portable yellow start cart.

"Probably Asia or Australia."

Charlotte laughed. "That narrows it down. Do you want to throw Europe and Africa into that mix?"

I looked upstairs into the jet and yelled. "Paging pilot-extraordinaire Kelly Cross!"

No response.

"Huh." I walked upstairs into the cabin and looked around. "Oh, sorry. Wrong jet."

I walked outside to Charlotte. "Wrong jet."

Charlotte looked around the Gulfstream 650 Extended Range jet. "This is ours. Look around. There's one airplane here."

"True."

Bob, Thomas and Aaron arrived. "Good morning."

"Bob, someone's inside."

"A man?"

I nodded.

"Average height, average weight, average looks?"

I nodded again.

"Did he talk?"

"No."

"That's Casper."

"Casper's good?"

Bob nodded. "Casper's going with us. He's pretty quiet."

Kelly arrived with Lurch, Vic and Thor. "Pretty quiet? Understatement of the year."

Charlotte and I walked upstairs to introduce ourselves. "Hi, Casper. I'm Grace."

"And I'm Charlotte."

Casper typed into his iPhone and showed us the screen. "*Good morning.*"

Lurch plopped down in a leather cabin seat. "That's all you're going to get."

Vic let Thor approach Casper to lick his face. "Hey Casper. This is my new Service Dog."

Casper smiled and quietly whispered. "Good doggie."

Casper typed into his iPhone and showed it to Vic. "*You look good, Vic.*"

Vic smiled. "You see, Gracie and Charlie. Casper speaks."

Casper typed into his iPhone. "*Only to dogs.*"

"Gracie! Get your checklist-reading, co-pilot butt up here."

I sighed and whispered to Charlotte in the early morning darkness. "You want to fly?"

Charlotte theatrically yawned, closed her eyes and leaned back. "Too early."

"Some friend you are, Charlie." I flicked Charlotte in the earlobe after she closed her eyes.

She didn't flinch.

"Nice to meet you." I whispered to Casper. "I'm coming, Kelly!"

Kelly walked me through a quick pre-flight.

I helped her with record-time pre-start through takeoff checks in the moonlight to beat the giant Gooney Birds into the air.

Kelly chose a westbound takeoff since there was no wind and no runway slope.

Passing three-thousand feet, we climbed into the sunlight. After reaching cruising altitude, Kelly kicked on the auto-pilot. "Time to put some Department of Interior glazed donuts into Kelly's Interior."

I smiled and looked at Kelly. "Tell me about Casper."

"He's a good guy. Just not a great communicator."

"His name is Casper?"

Kelly nodded. "He technically doesn't exist. He was a teenage computer hacker. He did hard time after breaking into multiple Government D-Bases. Some very bad people sprung him and used him for his computer expertise."

"He still works for bad people?"

"He escaped. Actually, we emancipated him. Now, Casper freelances for the House Intelligence Committee and Bob's security firm."

I smiled. "Casper the friendly ghost."

"Pretty much. He has a 150 IQ. He's a millionaire. Probably a billionaire. Nobody really knows. I don't think Casper knows or cares. Most computer geeks play PlayStation, Xbox, and iPhone games during their free time. Casper trades Bitcoins."

Lurch tapped me on the left shoulder at altitude as the sunrise chased us from behind. "Miss Becker, I'll take over co-pilot duties. Go sleep. Kelly, say goodnight to Gracie."

"Goodnight, Gracie."

I looked at the MFD-2 as I unbuckled my co-pilot harness. "Where are we going, anyhow?"

Kelly smiled as Lurch winked at me. "You'll see."

I looked at the ginormous former Navy SEAL. "You're not going to fit." I set my green *Dave Clark* headset on the dashboard, lowered my seat all the way down, slid my seat all the way back and slid the rudder pedals all the way forward.

Lurch smiled. "Great cockpit etiquette."

I winked, walked back to the cabin and grabbed the first open seat.

Bob closed his laptop and leaned towards me. "Get some rest, Gracie. You're going to need it."

"Petty Officer Jordan!"

D'Andre hustled to the Captain's Chair on the bridge of the anchored aircraft carrier. "Yes, Captain!"

"I understand you've been plotting our course down the West Lamma Channel with the Navigator."

"Yes, Captain. The Gator, current Officer of the Deck, and myself have a workable plan that is almost ready for your review."

Captain Smart looked around at the dozens of Supertankers. "Something new coming down from The White House. They want us to get underway *after* civil twilight ends within the next week."

D'Andre tilted his head. "Night departure, Captain?"

The salty, ex-Hornet pilot nodded.

"Copy, Captain."

Captain Smart sighed and whispered. "The order apparently originated from non-Navy bureaucrats with forty-pound brains who have never navigated the West Lamma Channel. The White House has been sold on this plan. They even ordered a departure under twenty-percent lunar illumination. I'm still trying to confirm if this is a *requirement*."

D'Andre paused. "Copy all, Captain. Night, no-moon passage into the South China Sea later this week. I'll pass to Gator and prepare."

CHAPTER TWENTY-EIGHT

I woke up fully-reclined in the Gulfstream cabin as Kelly and Lurch taxied into a sunny, Asian FBO for gas. I looked at Charlotte. "Morning?"

"Yes."

"China?"

Charlotte smiled and shook her head negatively.

I looked at Thomas. "Taiwan?"

Thomas shrugged and winked.

Aaron looked out the windows. "Seoul maybe?"

Charlotte nodded. "Could be Manila."

Bob leaned towards his window. "Looks like San Francisco again. Maybe Chinatown?"

I looked at Vic and petted Thor. "Vic, everyone's messing with me."

Vic smiled and ran her fingers through my hair. "Gracie Becker, you're in for such a treat."

Kelly bagged the engines after the lineman chocked the main mounts then keyed the PA system. "We have two new passengers near the port wingtip. One of them looks like a supermodel. Out the starboard window, you can see Tokyo Tower."

I looked at Charlotte. "Tokyo Tower? A supermodel? Gigi and Bree?"

Charlotte wiped her tears and smiled. "Go tell your sister you're alive, Gracie."

"Oh, God!" I stood up, screamed, cried like a baby, jumped, screamed again, then ran onto the tarmac to greet Gigi and Brianna. "Gigi! Bree! Oh, God!"

Gigi jumped up and down while she hugged me. "I knew it! I knew it! I knew it!"

Charlie came down the stairs and cried in the morning Tokyo sun.

Brianna hugged us so hard. "Gigi told me you two were alive. I believed. I believed thanks to Gigi!"

Gigi ran around in circles repeatedly hugging us and screaming. "Gracie and Charlie! I knew it!"

Aaron and Thomas walked down the stairs and smiled.

Our new friends, Bob, Lurch, Casper, Vic and Kelly enjoyed watching the Peaksville reunion at Haneda Airport perched atop the cabin stairway.

Brianna hugged Aaron and Thomas. "Aaron! Tommy Boy! God bless you guys for setting this up."

Aaron pointed at Bob Bonner. "Bob's the one to thank!"

Gigi and Brianna ran up to hug and kiss Bob.

Bob stoically tried to maintain his predictable Navy SEAL military bearing while blushing.

Gigi looked at Bob and whispered. "Can I call our sister in Hong Kong yet?"

"Not yet."

Aaron helped the Japan residents with their small bags. "Bree, what did you tell Antoine?"

Brianna smiled. "I emailed AJ and said Gigi and I are taking an Atsugi MWR 5-day tour. I said Gigi was surprising me with the location."

Bob looked at Aaron and nodded. "Good cover."

Gigi smiled at me. "Bree and I are coming with you."

I sighed. "You don't even know where we're going."

Bree laughed. "And?"

Charlotte laughed. "Neither do we, Gracie!"

"True."

Vic set Thor loose on the tarmac.

I couldn't stop crying.

"Thanks everyone!" Gigi instinctively knelt to pet Thor. "You remind me of Wolfie!"

Charlotte looked at me, parsed her lips and whispered to me. "Poor Kiche."

I hugged Gigi again and cried. "I'm sorry that we didn't tell you we were alive."

"Aaron explained about the need for secrecy." Gigi whispered a sad, one-word question into my ear. "Mom?"

I shook my head negatively.

Charlotte immediately cried with Brianna.

Brianna wiped her eyes. "Did you see my home?"

"She's gone, Bree. Mrs. Lopez is gone. The Jordan's are gone. Everyone in Peaksville is gone to a better place. They're all together in heaven, now. I'm sorry, Bree."

Brianna hugged Charlotte. "I needed to know for sure. Thanks, Charlie."

"AJ is on the ship?"

Brianna nodded. "The Lincoln is in the Hong Kong Harbor being repaired before steaming home to Yokosuka dry dock."

Bob looked at Kelly as the lineman mounted the large, brass, Jet-A fueling nozzle onto the fuselage port. "Airborne in twenty minutes, Kelly?"

Kelly nodded.

Gigi and I managed to stop crying and hugging. "When did Aaron and Bob call you?"

"Last night."

Aaron laughed. "While you guys were playing with the Midway Gooney Birds, I called Ginza and Atsugi."

I hugged Aaron and whispered into his ear. "I love you for that."

"Gloria Becker!"

Gloria waited for the telephone lag time between Southeast Asia and Europe. "Amy Kernan is that you?"

Amy smiled from her Radisson Blu Hotel Reussen room in the Alps. "It's great to hear your voice, Gloria. How's Hong Kong?"

"Great. Except when we turn on CNH or FXH News. How's Switzerland?"

"Andermatt is okay." Amy paused. "Any word on Gracie or Charlie?"

Gloria sat in the Flynn Brothers Fishing Charter kiosk at Star Ferry Terminal. "No word."

"I'm praying so hard," Amy said.

"Me too."

"Emma needs a vacation." Amy whispered. "The Peaksville news about our moms really messed her up."

Gloria sighed. "Poor thing."

"We wanted to thank you for the airline tickets."

"What tickets?"

"You bought us KLM airline tickets from Switzerland to Hong Kong. And the JW Marriott Hotel Hong Kong reservations are awesome, too."

No response.

"I'm sorry. Was it supposed to be a surprise?"

Gloria whispered to Ryan and Maddie. "Anyone buy the Kernan twins airline tickets to Hong Kong?"

Ryan and Madison shrugged.

"Sorry, Amy. It wasn't us. We'd love to see you, though."

"We should come anyway." Amy whispered. "Emma needs closure."

Gloria sighed. "Just love her, Amy."

"I'm trying."

"Then bring Emma to us."

Amy paused and checked her itinerary. "I guess we'll see you tomorrow night, Gloria."

"Yeah!" Gloria smiled at Ryan and Madison. "The Kernan twins are coming!"

Madison smiled.

"Text me your flight information, Amy!"

"Okay. See you soon, Gloria."

"Love you."

B ob visited Kelly and me in the Gulfstream cockpit during our Tokyo Haneda Airport engine start sequence. "Kelly?"

Kelly turned around and provided detailed instructions to our visitor. "I'll take decaf and two cubes of sugar, Coffee Boy. Make sure it's hot this time. Chop! Chop!"

I laughed.

Bob didn't.

Kelly looked at me as she energized the right starter motor. "Bob's in serious mode, again."

Bob almost smiled. "No radar services. No flight following. No transponder."

Kelly smiled and monitored rising turbine speed. "No problem."

Bob returned to the cabin.

"Check right side clear."

I looked out my window at the engine intake. "Clear."

Kelly introduced fuel to the starboard engine and watched the turbine temperature spike with N1 passing 50%.

I whispered. "Where are we going?"

Kelly flipped the #2 Generator on after engine start, checked for proper power distribution and signaled the Haneda lineman to disconnect the large, yellow electrical start cart.

"Kelly?"

No response.

"Okay, fine, 007. Then I'm going to type in direct to Tokyo Disneyland on MFD-2."

Kelly ignored me and keyed the PA system mic. "Welcome to Kelly Cross

Executive Airlines a division of Hot Chick Corporation and subsidiary of Perfect Body Travel Company. Flight time to our destination is five hours. Gigi and Brianna, we do have a Service Animal on board this flight. His name is Bob."

Bob looked up from his House Intelligence computer chat session for three seconds then returned to his work.

Kelly continued on the cabin intercom. "Please do not attempt to pet Bob, aggravate him or feed him. Bob requires a special diet. As you can see, he is off the diet."

Laughter from the cabin.

Kelly checked the left side clear. "Do you like monkeys, Gracie?"

I smiled. "Monkeys are cool."

Kelly signaled the Haneda International Airport FBO lineman and started our port engine. "How cool are they?"

"Very cool."

"That's where we're going. Type in direct Okinawa in MFD-2 for now. That's eight hundred and forty miles southwest. Okinawa is almost halfway to our monkey-friendly destination."

"Monkey-friendly?"

Kelly nodded. "Monkeys. Lots of them."

"What kind?"

Kelly signaled the lineman to pull our wheel chocks. "That's classified."

Everything old was new again.

J ack Kernan stirred his noodle dish at Pad Thai Shop restaurant. "You look confused."

Chloe Epley closed her iPhone mail application and reopened it. "This must be a mistake."

Jack set down his silverware and looked. "What?"

"Tickets." Chloe held up her screen. "I got an email from Cathay Pacific with tickets. Phuket to Hong Kong. Leaving tomorrow."

"Junk mail?"

"No."

"Did they charge you?"

Chloe shrugged. "It looks like you're going, also. Jack Kernan. Chloe Epley. First Class."

"First Class?" Jack smiled and took her phone. "That costs a fortune. Let me see."

Ding!

"You just got another email, Chloe."

216

Chloe `opened the second email. "JW Marriott Hotel Hong Kong? We have reservations."

"Open your bank app. Make sure you weren't charged."

Chloe spend a few minutes checking for online VISA and checking account charges.."I didn't pay for it. I should call Maddie or Gloria. Maybe Ryan bought us tickets for a reunion or surprise party."

Jack took a bite of his Pad Thai noodles. "We shouldn't call."

"Why?"

"Simple." He shrugged. "We would ruin the surprise."

Chloe disagreed. "Let's just call Gloria."

"Maybe it's Gloria's party. A phone call would ruin it."

"True." Chloe looked at her phone one last time then mixed her Prawn Pad Thai Fried Noodle dish. "We should go to Hong Kong."

Jack stirred his tapped-open coconut with a bamboo straw and smiled. "Let's go to Hong Kong."

"M rs. President, the Minister of Safety is on Line One."

"Thanks." She finished her email then leaned forward over the Resolute Desk to answer her phone. "Bud, you called?"

Mr. Light stood outside the K Street Starbuck's. "Quick question."

"What is it?"

He whispered. "Are you aware of any House Intelligence Committee operations requiring the movement of over $700 million?"

President Walker paused. "No."

"No knowledge?"

"Negative. What's up, Bud?"

"I was hoping you had the answer, Abby."

President Walker peered outside at the celebratory activity on Pennsylvania Avenue and sighed. "Call Congressman Gus Bryant."

Mr. Light looked around, covered his mouth and whispered. "Negative, Ma'am. Gus was best friends with Tex. Gus knows what happened."

President Walker paused. "Should I be worried?"

No response.

"Bud?"

"I'll handle this."

"Should I be worried, Bud?"

"Abby, I'll handle this. Don't worry."

She clicked her ballpoint pen. "Keep me informed."

Click!

. . .

Gigi and Brianna scrunched on the cockpit floor between Kelly and I during our thirty-eight-thousand-foot-high straits-transit between the Philippines and Taipei.

I rubbed Gigi's knee. "Having fun?"

Gigi smiled.

Brianna kept looking at me and crying. "Tell us about the miracle that saved you and Charlie."

I slid my green *Dave Clark* headphones above my left ear and smiled. "Bree, I didn't witness the miracle. My eyes were closed."

"You don't know why you lived?"

I shook my head. "Charlie and I were in the TFZ during the Peaksville attack. We returned. We found our homes and neighborhood destroyed. All melted."

I started crying in the right seat. "Sorry, Kelly."

Kelly rubbed my shoulder.

Brianna cried with me. "Then what?"

I wiped my eyes. "Then we were captured and targeted for execution. Then someone intervened."

"Who?"

I shrugged. "An angel."

Gigi gently leaned her head on my shoulder and closed her eyes.

Brianna cried. "I'm so glad you and Charlie were spared. Gigi never lost hope."

I smiled. "Thanks."

Brianna looked at Kelly. "Sorry we made your co-pilot cry. We'll leave you both alone. See you on the ground."

Kelly smiled as the Gulfstream 650 ER transitioned from the West Pacific into the South China Sea above Manila and below Taiwan.

Bob's *'no flight following or radar services'* instruction made for a very, very boring flight. No radio-chatter. No Position-Time-Altitude calls on HF radio.

I heard a polite knock on the open cockpit door. "Casper!"

Casper smiled, scribbled and showed us his phone screen. *"Hi Gracie! Hi, Kelly!"*

Kelly looked at Casper. "What do you have going on?"

Casper typed into his phone. *"TEX."*

Kelly looked at me. "Tex?"

I shrugged. "What's that?"

Casper studied our instrument panel. MFD-1 and MFD-2 were energized and operable. He pointed at MFD-3 and made typing signals with his fingers.

Kelly laughed. "TEX. Our missing password?"

Casper nodded and typed quickly. *"Bob got TEX from Gus in DC."*

Kelly quickly typed it into MFD-3. "It worked."

The third Multi-Function Display went through a series of initialization steps.

"Oh Gosh." Kelly keyed her intercom. "Bob?"

Bob looked in the cockpit. "Did it work?"

Kelly nodded. "It wants some extra data. *Auto* or *Manual*?"

Bob leaned over my left leg and pressed *Manual*.

Kelly read the next screen. "It wants a MEDWEAP Imaging Probe FREQ. What's that?"

Bob winked at me, backed out, and selected *Auto*.

Kelly watched. "Scan radius. One, two or five nautical miles, Bob?"

Bob held up one finger.

I selected '*1 NM*' on the screen.

MFD-3 suddenly provided a God's Eye map view of seven manned ships six nautical miles below our jet.

Kelly gasped. "It wants to display MEDWEAP Imaging Probe FREQ report. What?"

Bob and I calmly nodded.

Kelly squirmed in the left seat.

I selected *View*.

Bob pointed at the screen. Of the forty-two sailors and fisherman within six thousand feet of our jet horizontally and thirty-eight thousand feet vertically, forty people have nanotechnology frequencies in their blood. "These are the blood nanotechnology frequencies of the fishermen and sailors directly below us."

"Nano-what?" Kelly nervously laughed during her epiphany. "Start talking Bob."

Bob looked at Kelly. "This harmless-looking business jet you are flying, Miss Cross, has more advanced weaponry than an F-35."

Kelly's jaw dropped.

Bob patted us both on the shoulder. "One last thing. Grace, select the *OPEN MWOP BAY* button on MFD-3."

I complied.

Bob looked aft.

Lurch yelled from the cabin. "Open!"

Bob and Casper smiled and left the cockpit.

CHAPTER TWENTY-NINE

During her thirty-minute lunch break, Ruby Kyle walked to the Australian Heritage Hotel restaurant from the InterContinental Hotel Sydney's Café Opera restaurant.

Luke finished taking orders from a young Chinese couple then met Ruby in the lobby. "Hey, babe. Lunch break?"

Ruby nodded and smiled.

"Why are you smiling?"

"The tickets."

Luke checked his tables and shrugged. "Tickets?"

Ruby smiled, flashed her iPhone screen and hugged Luke. "You bought us airfare and hotel to Hong Kong."

A businessman and his girlfriend at Table Five signaled for Luke. "Hold on, Ruby."

Ruby sat in the foyer and double-checked her emails.

Luke hustled back. "Show me."

Ruby pointed. "Qantas roundtrip. First Class. Marriott hotel. You and I leave tomorrow. You bought this for us. Right?"

"First class?"

Ruby nodded.

"Marriott?"

Ruby nodded again and smiled.

Luke patted his front and back pockets. "I don't have ten thousand dollars for a trip like that. Sounds like a scam. Delete it."

Ruby shook her head. "I called Qantas. I emailed the JW Marriott near Wanchai. It's real."

Luke threw his hands in the air. "What are we supposed to do about it?"

"Someone wants us to go to Hong Kong."

"Okay, maybe it's not a *scam*. Then it sounds like a *trap*."

Ruby sighed. "Sounds like a *scam*. Sounds like a *trap*. Come on, Luke. Someone bought us first class tickets and a fancy suite."

Luke watched his tables. "I have to go wait tables."

"Are we going to Hong Kong?" Ruby asked.

"Yeah, sure. I don't really care." Luke shrugged and backed into the restaurant from the foyer. "Fine. I'll tell my boss."

L urch flew right seat for me during the last hour because I was *so* exhausted from the reunion.

Our main mounts touched down on a slender runway.

I watched coconut trees and tropical vegetation speed past my cabin window as the G650 reverse thrust shook the airframe.

Gigi studied the environment and put on her sunglasses to look outside. "Wow, you can feel the hot, equatorial sun heating up the fuselage skin."

Aaron nodded. "It's bright."

Thomas looked out the cabin windows. "Where are we?"

Charlotte smiled. "It looks like paradise."

We exited the jet onto the lonely landing strip after Kelly bagged our engines.

Brianna looked around. "Singapore?"

Charlotte guessed. "Indonesia?"

Gigi smiled. "Down under?"

Thomas took a guess. "Alaska?"

We all laughed. "Alaska?"

Bob Bonner smiled and yelled in a romantic, Mexican accent. "Welcome to Proboscis Island!"

I envisioned the funny looking monkeys with large noses. "Did you say Proboscis?"

Kelly and Lurch smiled.

Bob nodded.

Vic looked at Kelly. "Kelly, you flew us. Where are we?"

Kelly donned her 'serious face.' "Yes, Lurch and I were flying. And then a dark cloud swallowed up our jet. Unicorns were flying in the cloud. Dorothy's house flew by. We passed out. Then we woke up on the ground."

Vic whispered to her service dog. "Bite her in the leg and you'll get a cookie,

Thor."

Thor barked and wagged his tail after hearing his favorite word.

Vic smiled and threw Gigi a treat.

Gigi whispered and delivered. "I'm going to call you Wolfie."

Bob walked to the cargo bay under the Gulfstream. "We're just north of Brunei."

"Oh, Brunei." Brianna looked at Charlotte. "Where is Brunei?"

Charlotte shrugged. "Borneo?"

Bob brought up a map on his satellite laptop. "Brunei is at the lower end of the South China Sea. It shares the same land mass with Malaysia."

Charlotte smiled. "Malaysia touches Thailand. Chloe lives in Phuket. We're close to my sister!"

Bob nodded. "Yes and no. Western Malaysia has Kuala Lumpur, near Phuket. Eastern Malaysia touches Brunei."

Aaron looked around. "We're near Hong Kong?"

"That's one thousand miles directly north of us."

I smiled. "My middle sister lives in Hong Kong!"

"I know."

"You know?"

Kelly talked with a deep voice. "Bob *knows*."

Bob nodded. "Gloria is fairly far from Proboscis. Two hours by Gulfstream. Two days by boat."

I whispered. "Bob knows *ev-er-y-thing*."

Kelly laughed. "Not everything."

Bob gave her 'the look.'

Vic let Thor run free around the runway.

Gigi chased him and played catch with a fallen coconut. "Go fetch, Wolfie."

"What next, Bob?" Lurch asked.

"Overwatch."

Thomas held up his iPhone. "The game?"

Bob looked at Thomas. "You passed the bar exam in DC?"

Thomas lowered his iPhone.

"Where's Overwatch?" Aaron asked.

Bob looked up at the island's highest mountaintop, lush with green vegetation. "Up there."

Casper typed onto his iPhone and showed us. "*6,300 feet above sea level*."

Bob nodded. "We have to get Casper full access to the House Intelligence Committee network."

Brianna threw her backpack over her shoulder and looked at the jungle. "Let's hike."

"Before we beat feet," Bob opened the Gulfstream cargo hatch, "I need Sherpas."

"I agree." Kelly looked at the heavy gear. "Let's go hire Sherpas."

Bob shook his head. "Only monkeys live on Proboscis Island."

Kelly shrugged. "Let's go hire monkeys."

Bob lifted a bag. "*These* bags go up *that* mountain."

Brianna, Gigi, Charlotte and I immediately pointed fingers at Lurch.

Lurch flexed his biceps then smiled at Aaron and Thomas. "The ladies bought tickets to the gun show."

Thomas subtly looked at his own arms and sighed.

Aaron grabbed a heavy bag of tactical gear and slung it over his shoulder. "Let's get this done."

M ercedes Walker caused a storm of sparks on the USS Abraham Lincoln's starboard inner hull then secured the gas. "Light show. Dig it."

Antoine laughed. "Pretty awesome welding, Ma'am."

D'Andre supervised the VFA-195 Division Officer's daily contribution to the CVN-72 repair efforts. "How exactly do you know Max Burns, again?"

"Max saved me in Atsugi from taking a dirt nap." Mercedes raised her face shield. "Technically, he saved me from a *water* nap."

Antoine helped her prepare for welding the next seam. "He lives in Tokyo?"

Mercedes nodded. "He's a Yokota F-35 guy. Max just emailed me yesterday. He may be down here in the area this week."

"Where?" D'Andre asked.

"Max said 'nearby.' I think it was classified."

Antoine checked the area clear and looked at his Division Officer. "Ready for another light show?"

Mercedes almost lowered her face shield. "I forgot to mention. My mom is coming to Hong Kong tomorrow to thank you, Antoine. She wants to thank you, D'Andre since you helped Captain Smart regain control of the Lincoln. She also wants to thank the Flynn Brothers Fishing Charter crew who pulled me out of the water."

Antoine sighed. "I have to work."

Mercedes smiled. "Captain Smart and our VFA-195 skipper cancelled your watch for the Hong Kong meeting."

"Will there be pizza?" D'Andre asked.

"Mom reserved a fancy restaurant in Hong Kong." Mercedes held up the welding wand. "Better than pizza."

D'Andre smiled. "Great."

Mercedes Walker lowered her welding face shield. "Ready for the light show?"

Antoine laughed. "Born ready."

Thomas set his large, black tactical bag down on the tropical jungle floor of Proboscis Island. "We found the tar pits. Which way now, Bob?"

Bob silently studied his map.

I rested my head on Aaron's shoulder during our short break.

Aaron put a friendly arm around me in the ninety-five-degree heat and opened a plastic bottle for me. "Water?"

I nodded and drank. "It's good. Still cold. Thanks."

Bob stood on a rocky peak and pointed his high-tech, portable GPS handheld into the sky. "We need to track two-three-zero towards a crashed World War II airplane for twenty-two hundred feet."

Lurch pivoted around with his compass and pointed up a steeper slope. "Two-three-zero. This way, gang."

We continued through the equatorial jungle with our heavy gear.

Brianna and Gigi walked with Vic and Thor.

"Gigi, I can tell you're a huge dog lover."

Gigi nodded and smiled with her personal bag and a larger, heavier bag.

Brianna laughed. "Gigi loves dogs. Dogs love Gigi."

Gigi looked at Vic's titanium legs. "What happened?"

Vic shrugged. "This happened in a gun fight when I was a SEAL."

"You lost?" Brianna asked.

Vic smiled. "I was with Bob and Lurch. Lurch carried me to the H-60. What was left of me, that is. We won the fight. But I lost my legs."

Gigi scratched Thor's back as she trekked southwest. "Wow."

I saw a dark blue, metal object about one hundred feet ahead. "Is the airplane blue?"

"Probably." Bob checked the hand-written map provided by Congressman Gus Bryant. "Gus didn't say."

I pointed at our potential checkpoint. "Is that it?"

Casper utilized his binoculars, typed and showed Bob Bonner his phone. "*Bearcat.*"

Bob nodded and kept walking.

We arrived at the crashed U.S. Navy propeller airplane overgrown with tropical vegetation.

I looked at Aaron. "Survivable crash?"

Aaron looked up at the hundred-foot-tall dense, treetop canopy. "Unlikely because of the secondary fall."

Bob checked his map and GPS. "Track three-zero-five to a tropical lagoon at the base of a five-hundred-foot waterfall."

Charlotte smiled as Lurch led our adventuresome group to the northwest. "Sounds romantic."

Kelly agreed. "Do we have time to skinny-dip, Bob? Only the attractive people, of course. Everyone except —"

Bob interrupted with a blank expression.

"Bob secretly loves me." Kelly whispered to Gigi and Brianna. "Not *fairytale-love*. It's a different kind of love. More like a *tough-love*."

Bob and Lurch found the lagoon then led us on a two-seven-zero heading up a mountain to a broken-down, concrete-walled power station.

Aaron tried the door. "It's jammed, and the door knob is rusted."

Bob pulled Aaron and Thomas away from the door. "Lurch has this."

Thomas backed up. "Lurch picks locks?"

Bob smiled.

Lurch broke the door with one powerful kick.

Thomas smiled. "Oh."

Casper quickly traced the propane lines and electrical leads.

Bob watched Casper study the 1940's technology. "What do you think?"

Casper typed into his phone. "*Open propane valve outside.*"

Aaron ran outside and yelled from the rusty piping overgrown by tropical plants. "Found it! This propane gas seems to tap an underground tank, Casper. Open the valve?"

Casper nodded.

Bob helped and yelled outside to Aaron. "Yes!"

Aaron complied. "It's open!"

Casper found a five-gallon jug of oil and lubricated an old engine.

Lurch found the lawn mower-style starting cord. "Ready?"

Casper quickly removed a sparkplug, scraped off corrosion with his pocket knife and replaced it with a 'thumbs up.'

Lurch pulled the cord.

Bob watched. "Careful. It's old."

Casper manipulated the generator's choke.

Lurch tried again.

Vroom!

Kelly joked. "We have ignition."

Gigi sang. "*It's Electric!*"

I looked at Bob. "Is this our destination?"

Bob shook his head negatively, threw large bags over his shoulder and pointed to a mountain peak. "This building powers Overwatch."

CHAPTER THIRTY

Ruby held Luke's hand after clearing customs and immigration at Hong Kong International Airport. "Qantas is now officially my favorite airline. The upgraded seats were phenomenal."

Luke shrugged and followed signs to Baggage Claim. "It was okay."

"I can't wait to see Ryan, Gloria, and Madison."

"Yeah, it's been a while."

Luke and Ruby found Baggage Claim and found an open bench.

"The JW Marriott is a five-star hotel, Luke."

No response.

"Aren't you excited, Luke?"

"Ruby, look." Luke pointed towards the Cathay Pacific Baggage Claim.

"No way."

Luke stood up and focused his eyes. "Yes way."

"Here come our bags."

"They're leaving, Ruby. Let's run and catch them."

Ruby led the way. "Jack! Chloe!"

Jack stopped wheeling the cart towards the taxi stand. "I heard our names."

Ruby tried again. "Jack! Chloe!"

Chloe turned around and screamed. "Ruby and Luke are here!"

The twenty-five-year-olds from Down Under hugged the nineteen-year-olds from Phuket.

"How did you get here?" Ruby asked.

Chloe smiled and wiped her tears of joy. "We don't know. Did you do this?"

Luke laughed. "So, the four of us all got surprise tickets."

Jack nodded and pointed at Ruby and Luke. "JW Marriott Hotel?"

Ruby smiled. "It must be a surprise party. Possibly organized by Ryan."

"Come with us, kiddos." Luke looked back at the Qantas Baggage Claim. "We can ride together to Wanchai."

B ob held his handheld GPS high in the air under the jungle canopy on his tippy-toes.

Kelly laughed as she toted two large canvas bags of gear. "Hey Bonner! The GPS satellites are two-hundred miles above us in the Exosphere. Make sure you stretch for optimum reception. Maybe jumping would help."

Bob almost smiled.

"Kelly's right." Lurch teased his SEAL buddy. "Maybe I should hold it. I'm a lot taller than you."

Bob looked at Lurch. "The overabundance of electrons in your head will scramble the signal."

"Really?"

I laughed as we eventually continued uphill.

We heard a strange noise from the jungle.

"*Ooh, ooh, ooh. Ah, ah, ah!*"

Gigi pointed into the trees. "Look!"

Charlotte smiled. "Proboscis monkeys!"

Kelly stopped walking and looked at her watch. "Bob, we're going to give you ten minutes. Climb up there. Say hello to your family. Catch up on old times. Eat a banana. Have them check your scalp for bugs. Slide down on a vine. Then, we'll continue."

No response from Bob.

Laughter from the peanut gallery.

Bob kept trekking up the hill along a series of warning posts signifying underground powerlines.

The monkeys in the trees became more and more excited as we passed under their jungle home. "*Ooh, ooh, ooh! Ah, ah, ah!*"

"Bob." Kelly pointed up. "They're talking."

Gigi and Brianna soaked in the wild adventure alongside Thor the leggy German Shepherd.

Aaron pointed at the mountainside. "It's becoming steeper."

Lurch nodded. "That means we're getting closer."

Bob looked back at the group. "Found it."

I looked around. "Found what?"

"Overwatch?" Thomas asked.

"The railway," Bob pointed. "This two-thousand-foot, World War II mountain trolley will take us up to the peak."

We approached the antiquated cable and track system as the monkeys yelled.

"*Ooh, ooh, ooh! Ah, ah, ah!*"

Aaron looked at the rusty track and smiled. "They're laughing at us."

I looked at Bob. "Are you sure this is safe?"

"Climbing the final steep incline with gear would take twelve hours." Bob studied the WWII equipment. "The answer to your question is 'no,' though."

T he polite, cheery taxi driver parked his yellow Toyota Crown, the Asian version of the Avalon, in the grand entranceway to the JW Marriott Hotel Hong Kong. "Here we are. JW Marriott."

"It's beautiful," Amy said.

Emma agreed. "This is too fancy. Ryan, are you sure you didn't pay for this?"

Ryan looked at Gloria and Madison as he paid the taxi driver. "We swear, it wasn't us."

Gloria smiled at the Kernan twins. "Let's get you both checked in."

Emma and Ryan walked to the customer service area as Madison and Gloria entertained Amy in the magnificently decorated lobby.

"Tell us about Switzerland," Madison said.

Amy laughed. "What do you want to know about?"

Gloria looked to make sure Ryan was not nearby and whispered. "European guys."

Amy shrugged. "European guys? They love me just as much as American guys love me."

"Good." Gloria laughed. "You haven't changed."

Amy winked. "I'm working on Emma. The so-called TEGWA or Terrorist Electrical Grid Wildfire Attack on Peaksville really freaked her out. I think she's clinically depressed after Mom died."

Madison sighed. "She lost her mom. It's called grieving."

Amy nodded. "We all did. Why is Emma so distant?"

Gloria whispered. "It's traumatic, Amy. Everyone takes it differently. Some people *totally* shut down."

The three North Idaho natives talked as CNX News flashed *Breaking News* on a nearby television.

Gloria pointed. "Look."

"Former President Voigt's hometown of Tulsa, Oklahoma has been completely destroyed and burned to the ground by a TEGWA. The Ministry of Safety found the perpetrators overseas in a small cave near a remote, southern Omani village. The TSC Tactical Victim Unit sent by President Walker raided the electrical grid terrorists and killed their leader in his family cave."

Amy joked. "Yeah, cave dwellers burned Tulsa to the ground from Oman."

"Amy!"

Madison tapped Amy. "Someone called you."

Gloria shook her head and pointed to the JW Marriott customer service counter. "Ryan and Emma are getting keys. Someone else, maybe?"

"Amy! Gloria! Maddie!" Ruby came running from the elevators.

Ryan and Emma returned with the key and saw Ruby. "Ruby Kyle!"

The girls made a scene with very high-pitched screams in the luxury, five-star hotel.

Ryan put his hands in the air. "Easy, girls."

"What are you doing here?" Amy asked.

Ruby shrugged. "Luke and I are in Room 2502. Guess who's next door?"

Amy shrugged. "Jackie Chan?"

Ruby paused. "Wow. Good guess. Close. But the answer is your brother. Jack and Chloe are in 2503."

Emma and Amy screamed.

Ryan tossed Room Key 2501 to the Kernan twins. "Who did this?"

Ruby looked around. "Nobody knows."

Ryan flashed his phone. "Something's going on. Antoine just emailed me while Emma and I were getting the key. Tonight, at seven o'clock, we're all invited to a fancy dinner at Gaddi's restaurant."

Gloria gasped.

"What's Gaddi's?" Emma asked.

Madison smiled. "Gaddi's is a five-star French restaurant the Peninsula Hotel in Tsim Tsa Tsui. It's across the street from Flynn Brothers Fishing Charter at the Star Ferry Terminal."

"Something is happening," Ryan said.

"Good or bad?" Emma asked.

"Good so far." Amy looked around the elegant JW Marriott lobby and flashed the room key. "Let's go upstairs and mess with Jack, Chloe and Luke."

C asper inspected the small, two-seat metal carriage and associated trolley control panel.

"Who is first?" Bob asked.

Aaron raised his hand.

I quickly raised my hand and got a wink from Charlotte.

Lurch and Casper double-checked the cables.

"Saddle up," Bob said.

Aaron and I climbed inside the rusty cage and sat on the rusty bench on the small, mountain trolley car. "What's the cage for?"

Vic looked around with Thor at her side. "Wild animals."

Kelly winked at me. "T-Rex's and Velociraptors."

Brianna couldn't resist. "Pigmy head hunters."

I squeezed Aaron's hand and waved from inside the cage. "Thanks everyone."

Bob slammed our cage closed. "You guys know the procedure if the cable snaps?"

I looked up the forty-five-degree incline. "Pull the hand brake?"

Bob shook his head. "Scream loudly so we know to get out of the way."

"How far up?"

Casper typed into his iPhone and showed Aaron.

Aaron gasped. "Two-thousand feet?"

Casper typed a message again. "*Expect a ten-minute ride.*"

"Thanks Casper."

I looked at Bob. "We're screaming *your* name the whole way down if the cable snaps."

Lurch reached in, checked our seat belts, acted like he took tickets, banged on our cage like a Carny and gave a 'thumbs up' for laughs.

Casper energized the electric motor with a rusty lever.

I squeezed Aaron's hand tighter. "Oh, God. Here we go."

Aaron joked as we left the lower Proboscis Island station. "I'm getting too old for this!"

I bumped Aaron with my shoulder. "Too old? We're only twenty-five."

The 1943 metal trolley stressed and strained.

I leaned towards Aaron. "You're right, we *are* getting too old for this."

M r. Light sat outside the K Street Starbuck's in Washington DC on a small table. "Is Ben getting you up to speed, Mr. Sharjah Blue Weapon's Officer?"

Mr. Murdstone climbed two ladder wells and stepped onto the starboard deck for better satellite phone reception. "This yacht's weapon system is enigmatically complex *and* simple at the same time."

"Have you met Omar?"

"I have."

Mr. Light laughed. "Thoughts?"

Mr. Murdstone paused. "No comment."

"Hey listen, Nuke. Your son, Tony, has been doing great as a TSC Peacekeeper. I'm going to send him out to the Sharjah Blue. If that's okay with you."

"Timeline?"

"As soon as you approve."

"I approve," Mr. Murdstone said. "Let's give him a shot out here."

"Tony's been leading the cleanup and cover in Peaksville. I'll send him your way immediately. What's the nearest Port of Call for arrival?"

"We're still near Hong Kong. Half an hour via the TSC H-53."

"Perfect. I'll have my secretary cut Tony some orders right now."

"Thanks, Bud."

"See you, Nuke."

T he metal mountain trolley became more predictable and less scary as Aaron and I approached the highest peak of Proboscis Island.

"It's beautiful Aaron."

Aaron nodded and gazed at the South China Sea to the north.

I was no longer scared, but consciously decided to maintain my strong grip on Aaron's hand.

"Are you still scared, Gracie?"

I shrugged and smiled.

"You can let go, now."

"Maybe I don't want to."

"That's okay, too."

I smiled and whispered. "Are you sure?"

Aaron nodded. "This little carnival cage from World War II is quite romantic."

I laughed as our trolley creaked and moaned through a large group of Proboscis monkeys.

"*Ooh, ooh, ooh! Ah, ah, ah!*"

Aaron watched the odd primates overhead. "They're warning each other. Listen."

The monkey calls extended up the mountain as we traversed upwards.

I smiled and scooted closer to Aaron on the creaking trolley car. "I like them."

Everything was now perfect. Lush, tropical vegetation, colorful flowers, thousands of birds. Fascinating wildlife. Aaron and I were together again.

I pointed. "Toucan?"

"Hornbill."

"How do you know?"

Aaron shrugged. "I did my homework on Brunei before arriving."

I nodded and rested my head on his shoulder. "Are there tigers on this island?"

"Not anymore."

"Good."

"Only jaguars."

"Only what?"

"We're reaching the top." Aaron pointed. "When it stops, exit quickly before Casper reverses the trolley."

We opened the cage, exited, unloaded bags and gear, and secured the cage. Aaron studied two buttons on a rusty stanchion in the ground. Aaron depressed the lower button. The trolley traveled down the tropical island's primitive railway towards the others.

"Aaron!" I pointed at an old, three-thousand-square-foot concrete building with multiple satellite dishes on the roof. "What's that?"

Aaron smiled. "Overwatch."

"Raygun! Over here." General Marsh lowered his right hand as the Peaksville Institutes of Health CEO joined him for lunch at the Cosmic Cowboy Grill.

"Hi, Swamp." Dr. Raymond Gunnison shook his hand.

"How are things?"

"SSDD." Dr. Gunnison ordered an iced tea. "It's pretty sad that we have to drive to Coeur d'Alene to find a good restaurant for lunch."

The Peaksville Defense and Space CEO nodded. "I didn't realize that the TSC was going to destroy every restaurant within ten miles."

Dr. Gunnison agreed. "Wasteful."

General Marsh studied the menu. "I wonder what happened to those two young girls in Peaksville Bread Company?"

Dr. Gunnison spilled sugar into his glass. "You're talking about Grace and Charlotte?"

"Yeah."

"Maybe they went camping."

"Hope so." General Marsh sighed. "We should have submitted a personal request to save the Peaksville Bread Company. They were good people."

Dr. Gunnison nodded. "I don't think the TSC cares."

"Bud cares."

The Peaksville Institutes of Health CEO whispered to the USAF General. "Two months ago, I submitted DNK Request Forms to the TSC for my family and my wife's family. My mother, her father, our sisters. Their new families. And my two brothers."

"DNK forms are supposed to be honored." General Marsh solemnly set his drink down. "What happened, Raygun?"

"Guess where my family lived, Swamp."

"You're from Oklahoma City, right?"

"Tulsa." Dr. Gunnison pointed at the television in the Cosmic Cowboy Grill.

FXH News repeatedly scrolled the news. *"Former President Voigt's hometown of Tulsa, Oklahoma has been completely destroyed by a TEGWA."*

General Marsh gasped. "No."

Dr. Gunnison nodded. "Yes."

"How many?"

Dr. Gunnison cried. "They're all gone, Swamp."

"Did you tell Bud?"

"Yes."

The young waitress smiled. "Are you gentlemen ready to order?"

General Marsh pointed at his watch and signaled for five more minutes. "What did Bud say, Raygun?"

"He said it was Abby's call, Swamp. One final, symbolic, signature strike to erase the Homeland's memory of Voigt."

"But it's customary to allow TSC, PIH, and PDS families advance notice before terminal operations."

"Not this time." Dr. Gunnison dried his tears. "Abby said no warnings. No honoring DNK requests. No survivors."

"Damn."

Dr. Gunnison regained his composure. "It was nothing personal, though. Right, Swamp?"

General Marsh sighed. "Sorry, Raygun."

CHAPTER THIRTY-ONE

Ruby lounged in the luxurious Hong Kong suite and paged through her messages. "Gloria and Chloe. Check this out. I got this text from Peaksville after the TEGWA."

Gloria leaned over Ruby and grabbed her phone. "I got one."

Chloe smiled. "Same! Just different numbers."

Amy turned off the complimentary blow dryer and joined her friends. "Here's what I got. Do you think Grace and Charlie are alive?"

Ryan checked the four phones and handed the girls a JW Marriott pen and notebook. "Write them all down."

Luke clicked the television channel. "Ryan, don't get their hopes up."

Emma nodded. "I agree."

Madison winked at Ryan and sat with Luke.

Amy held up the paper. "Here are the codes."

5-O-B-J-1
3-N-N-A-1
2-I-I-H-2
6-L-O-A-4

Jack studied the codes. "The only word that I see is LION. Sentosa Island of Singapore was just leveled by a TEGWA. The tall *Merlion* statue completely melted."

Ruby smiled. "I tutored this boy. Smart as a whip."

Jack smiled.

Ryan shrugged. "It doesn't explain the other characters. It seems incomplete."

Amy read the codes. "Or it's a very high-concept code."

Jack shook his head. "My vote is simple and low-concept."

Gloria leaned back. "Or maybe it's nothing."

Luke coughed. "Bingo!"

Emma agreed. "My vote is Verizon codes indicating no service."

Chloe disagreed. "There has to be a reason for these texts. Grace and Charlie are alive. I'm sure of it!"

Emma shook her head. "The Peaksville TEGWA wasn't survivable."

Chloe stood her ground. "They both lived."

"Sometimes, Chloe." Luke shrugged and set his drink down. "Sometimes, people just die, Chloe."

Chloe cried. "Take that back, Luke."

Luke quietly watched television.

Chloe clicked the television off. "Take it back, Luke!"

"Okay, I'm sorry. I take it back."

Aaron jimmied the door to Overwatch. "I'm in!"

I looked around and smiled. "We have a barbeque grill!" I kicked two propane tanks. "This is odd. We have full tanks."

"Good!" Aaron yelled from inside. "Two refrigerators are stocked!"

"Wow!"

"It looks like someone recently delivered food." Aaron flipped the power on. "Must have been today. The food is still cold."

I peeked inside. "Are you kidding?"

Aaron swung a door open. "Look! Beef and chicken. Fruits and vegetables. Bob told me that Betsy always plans ahead."

I smiled and rubbed my belly. "I'm starving."

"Same."

"I'll wait outside." I sat atop the mountain trolley's upper station for another twenty minutes.

"Ooh, ooh, ooh! Ah, ah, ah!"

I yelled inside to Aaron. "Next group is approaching!"

I saw Bob and Charlotte. "Charlie!"

Charlotte waved and sat awfully close to her mountain guide. "Hi, Gracie!"

Bob reversed the trolley after they stepped outside the cage.

Vic and Gigi rode with Thor. Kelly and Thomas. Brianna and Casper.

Over one hour later, last and certainly not least, Lurch arrived.

I smiled, opened the door for him and greeted him with a cold drink. "Thanks for waiting so long, Lurch."

Charlotte agreed. "Lurch, you're a gentleman and a scholar."

"This ride needs a Fast Pass." Lurch popped open the cold can of Pepsi. "Thanks!"

Gigi wore Thor down playing fetch with a banyan tree branch. "Now what?"

Aaron presented his deep metal tray filled with piping-hot burgers, dogs, potatoes, and corn on the cob. "Now, we eat."

Lurch smiled. "You read my mind, brother."

Casper whistled from atop Overwatch near the multiple satellite dishes.

Bob looked up.

Casper delivered a 'thumbs up.'

I looked at Bob. "What's that?"

"We're online, Gracie."

"Online with what?"

"HICSON."

"What's HICSON?"

"House Intelligence Committee Satellite Operator Network."

I looked at Aaron. "Sounds like a movie."

Aaron winked at me. "We're glad you're here, Gracie."

I grabbed a hotdog, added mustard then sat next to Charlotte.

Charlotte whispered. "Why *are* we here?"

I shrugged and took a bite.

Vic sat down with her hamburger. "You're here because Bob trusts you."

Thor chose to sit near Gigi over Vic.

Vic smiled. "Would you look at that. I have beef and cheese. Gigi has no food. Thor *still* chooses her. I like your little sister."

"Thor does, too." I smiled and winked. "And I like her, too."

Bob stacked our gear inside with the help of Thomas, Aaron and Lurch. "We have ten bunk bed structures. One of us has to take a top bunk."

Silence.

"Nobody wants the top bunk?" Bob asked.

I stayed perfectly still.

"Get some nourishment. You're all going to need it." Bob positioned two large, wooden boxes forty feet apart and placed ten burlap bags filled with corn kernels nearby. "2027 Corn Hole Tournament starts after dinner. Loser gets the top bunk.

You're all about to find out what it's like to go head-to-head with a highly-trained Navy SEAL."

"Ha!" Kelly laughed. "Bob cheats. *And* Bob loses. Why don't we just forgo the Corn Hole ritual and you humbly climb up into your top bunk, Bob."

We laughed.

Bob looked at Kelly with a serious face. "First round in fifteen minutes. Eat up, Amelia Earhart."

Kelly shrugged.

"Things are about to get *real*," Bob said. "*Real* soon."

D'Andre leapt onto the violently-rocking, sixty-foot Hong Kong liberty boat from the eleven-hundred-foot aircraft carrier's makeshift dock aft of the stern.

Antoine and the duty officer caught him. "Gotcha!"

Mercedes sat with the twins and pointed to Captain Smart's personal liberty boat. "There goes your Lincoln boss, DJ."

D'Andre smiled. "Where are we going again?"

"The Peninsula Hotel. My mom rented us a large room for dinner at Gaddi's."

Antoine looked at his VFA-195 Dambuster Division Officer. "I have one hundred dollars left from my last trip to Wanchai. Is that enough?"

Mercedes laughed. "You don't need a dime, AJ. You're the guest of honor."

Antoine looked at D'Andre and Mercedes. "Lieutenant, Ryan Flynn said he is bringing six extra people in addition to Gloria and Madison. Is that okay?"

"Of course."

The liberty boat filled, the CVN-72 Deck Department duty personnel untied the mooring lines, and the Chinese liberty boat pilot accelerated towards Star Ferry Terminal.

D'Andre nervously held onto a rail as the boat slammed against the choppy wake of the dirty Hong Kong Harbor.

Antoine made small talk. "I can't wait to meet your mom, LTJG Walker. Does she look like you?"

Mercedes shrugged. "A little bit."

D'Andre nodded. "Is she nice?"

Mercedes paused. "Depends on who you ask."

Antoine stared at the USS Abraham Lincoln's starboard side from their speeding liberty boat. "We're almost seaworthy for the trip home."

Mercedes nodded. "Mom wants us to leave soon."

D'Andre rapidly turned his head. "Excuse me? Did you say your *mom* wants us to leave soon?"

Mercedes flashed her Coeur d'Alene prep school smile and placed her hands on the shoulders of the Jordan twins. "You'll understand in an hour."

"Mr. Light, the CEO Of Peaksville Defense and Space is on Line One."

"Thanks, Jill."

Click!

"Swamp! How are you?"

General Marsh walked from his executive desk to close his door. "Can't complain."

"Nobody will listen anyway."

"Exactly, Bud. How are things in the belly of the beast?"

"Finally stepping down from the high operation tempo."

"What now?"

The Minister of Safety looked out his window at the Washington Monument. "I guess we prepare for the next crisis."

"Prepare for it or create it?"

"Both." Mr. Light laughed. "All the world's indeed a stage, and we are merely players."

"One of my favorite songs from the eighties. God, I miss those days. No internet. No cell phones." General Marsh watched his PDS production line technicians create MEDWEAP's. "Hey, Bud?"

"Yeah, Swamp?"

"Are there background checks for the MEDWEAP Operators? We have several million of these things issued. I've seen the MWOP. Pretty decent controls. It's mostly filled with law enforcement, medical, and scientific personnel, while informants, parolees and foreigners account for only thirty percent of MWOP Operators."

"Correct."

"But do the Operators get checked out, first?"

Mr. Light leaned back. "Good question."

"Do you know the answer?"

"I know that the MWOP's are checked out for loyalty before training and before taking possession of a MEDWEAP."

"Loyalty to the United States of America?"

Mr. Light paused. "We're the Homeland, now."

General Marsh continued. "Loyalty to the Constitution?"

"Another good question, Swamp. Abby recently nullified the Constitution for public safety, didn't she?"

"Yep."

"Maybe we need to take a look at the MEDWEAP oath." Mr. Light stood up and closed his door.

"Maybe, Bud."

"There is one technique that preserves loyalty after MEDWEAP issuance."

"What?"

Mr. Light whispered. "The new MWOP Operators are required to terminate several Homelanders within one week. And the Operator doesn't get to pick the victim. It usually ensures a long and honorable MEDWEAP career."

General Marsh paused. "I was just thinking about President Voigt. He was a pain in the ass, but —"

Mr. Light recited the punchline together with his old Air Force buddy. "*But he was OUR pain in the ass.*"

"I'll let you go, Bud."

"Swamp?"

"Yeah."

"Quit worrying so much."

"See you, Bud."

K elly proudly stood among the nine lower bunk survivors as the contest neared the end. "The 2027 Top Bunk Corn Hole Tournament isn't looking so good for Bob 'Top Bunk' Bonner."

Bob ignored Kelly while competing with Gigi in the loser bracket.

Gigi smiled and petted Thor between tosses in the hot, equatorial island humidity. "This is fun!"

Vic looked at Bob. "Your opponent doesn't agree."

Bob led the third tie-breaking round by sinking the small, burlap bag of corn kernels in the wooden hole. "Yes!"

"I've never played this game before." Gigi matched Bob's toss. "And we're on a tropical island. Good food, also! Thanks Bob!"

Bob prepared for his second throw and ignored the Tokyo supermodel's flippant, cheerful banter.

Kelly interrupted. "Bob, want me to wipe the sweat from your brow?"

Bob ignored Kelly and missed.

Brianna laughed. "That one's going to leave a mark."

Lurch looked around. "Kelly, does this island have an Aloe plant for Bob after he loses?"

Kelly shrugged. "It's going to be a really deep burn. I'm not sure if Aloe will heal his wounds."

Everyone cheered for Gigi except Bob.

Gigi was winning two Corn Holes to one.

I leaned on Aaron and laughed. "Uh oh."

Lurch patted Bob on the shoulder. "You can do it."

Bob sneered. "You were just cheering for Gigi."

"I was?"

"I saw you." Bob nodded before tossing his third bag. "Duly noted, SEAL Team shipmate."

Bob missed.

Kelly laughed and slapped her knee. "The agony of defeat."

Gigi knelt down to pet Thor and looked at Bob. "It's okay. I want the top bunk anyway. I'll take it."

Kelly stepped forward. "That's a protocol violation, Gigi. Bob lost fair and square. We have to abide by Corn Hole by-laws."

Gigi winked at Bob, walked inside and threw her Tokyo Mitsukoshi bag on a top bunk. "It's okay. I call top bunk."

Aaron held my hand in the setting equatorial sun. "Let's take a walk, Gracie."

Charlotte winked at me.

I smiled. "Sure thing."

CHAPTER THIRTY-TWO

Antoine and D'Andre Jordan approached the Peninsula Hotel with Mercedes Walker from the Star Ferry Terminal and noticed twenty large, black limousines.

"American flags on limos," Antoine said.

D'Andre corrected him. "Homeland flags."

"I forgot."

A Secret Service Agent shouted as Mercedes, Antoine and D'Andre crossed Salisbury Road towards the famous Hong Kong Peninsula Hotel. "Mockingjay!"

Mercedes waved and yelled back to the agent. "Hey, Brian!"

Antoine observed the traffic pattern on Salisbury. "They stopped traffic for us."

D'Andre walked with LTJG Walker. "Mockingjay?"

"That's me."

"Brian?" Antoine asked. "That guy is Secret Service."

"I knew him in Annapolis."

Antoine looked at the massive security detail. "I thought your Navy callsign was Tater."

Mercedes smiled and shrugged. "It still is. Come on inside, I'm starving."

The Jordan twins walked Mercedes into the lobby as reporters snapped pictures.

Antoine saw friends at a large table waving and smiled. "DJ! They're here!"

D'Andre ran to hug his Peaksville friends. "Luke and Ruby! Chloe and Jack! Kernan twins, also?"

Antoine began to cry. "I'm so happy."

Emma comforted Antoine and wiped his tears. "Sit with us, hero."

Antoine quickly regained his composure. "Lieutenant Junior Grade Walker, meet our Peaksville friends."

Ruby flashed her beautiful smile. "Behold the President's daughter."

D'Andre lost his smile. "LTJG Walker? As in President Walker?"

Mercedes nodded. "I try to keep it a secret."

Emma looked at Luke as they subtly shook their heads negatively.

Ryan was not amused. "Mercedes, you should have told us."

Gloria squeezed Ryan's hand in the elegant, Hong Kong restaurant. "You just want privacy, right?"

Madison winked. "We understand."

Mercedes smiled as numerous aides helped the young adults find their seats near Captain Smart. "I'm not your average President's daughter."

President Walker entered the Gaddi's banquet room with her security detail as the CVN-72 Navy Band played traditional Presidential music. She shook everyone's hand and joined them for dinner.

Amy chuckled after the music stopped. "We're eating with the President."

President Walker nodded. "The pleasure is all mine."

Emma looked at President Walker. "Our parents all used to vote for you."

President Walker smiled uncomfortably.

Amy pinched Emma's leg.

"Well, then. Which one of you is Antoine?"

Antoine smiled and stood up at the table in his Navy whites. "That's me. Madam Mrs. President Walker, Ma'am."

"Relax, Antoine."

Antoine stood at military attention as Captain Smart laughed. "Yes, Ma'am."

President Walker smiled. "I'll tell you what, Antoine. And this goes for all of you. No more standing. Call me Mrs. Walker or Abby. Whichever you are more comfortable with."

Antoine sat. "Yes, Ma'am. I mean Mrs. Walker. I mean Abby."

Captain Smart, the Commanding Officer of the USS Abraham Lincoln and former Topgun instructor pilot, cleared his throat.

Antoine quickly corrected himself. "Yes, President Walker."

Jack and Chloe giggled at the military exchange.

Mercedes looked around the large table and pointed at her friends. "Mom, Antoine ran into my burning stateroom to save me. D'Andre, his twin, helped Captain Smart maintain control of the Lincoln. Ryan pulled me out of the harbor onto the Ben Gunn. Gloria and Madison gave me medical attention until the HS-14 crew gave me a ride back to my boat."

President Walker smiled as the first course of five-star, French cuisine was brought to the table. "You are truly all heroes. And tonight, you will all eat a hero's dinner."

Ryan, Luke and Emma sat expressionless as Gloria, Ruby and Amy covertly reprimanded them under the table.

Introductions continued.

President Walker looked around the table. "Please, tell me your names and hometowns. Ryan, you begin."

"Ryan from Peaksville, Idaho." Ryan looked at Gloria.

President Walker squirmed in her seat. "Peaksville."

"Gloria from Peaksville." Gloria looked at Jack.

"I'm Jack." Jack looked around the table. "President Walker, I'll cut to the chase. Everyone at the table is from Peaksville."

Captain Smart raised his hand. "Except for me, President Walker."

"All from Peaksville, Idaho. And you, Captain Smart hail from which town?"

The Navy O-6 paused and stoically nodded. "Tulsa."

Five seconds of uncomfortable silence.

President Walker held up her wine glass after learning the rest of the names. "I would like to propose a toast. To our heroes, to fellowship, to family, and to the Homeland."

Ryan reluctantly followed along with the toast as Charity Ferguson joined the Presidential table for a moment.

"Friends, this is Charity Ferguson. Charity is from North Idaho also. She worked in the weapons industry up there."

Charity pinched President Walker's arm lightly.

"Charity worked in other industries and jobs also. She is now the Homeland's Minister of Youth."

Charity peered around the table curiously. "Some of you look very familiar."

President Walker smiled. "They're all from Peaksville."

Charity nodded. "I just wanted to say hello." Charity quickly left.

Amy looked around the table and patted her left inner elbow. "I could use a shot. I mean my dinner is nice and hot. I like it a lot. Do you not?"

Captain Smart laughed. "You're funny, Amy."

Emma face-palmed and rubbed her eyes.

President Walker made eye contact with Mercedes. "Interesting that you deploy to southeast Asia and wind up running into so many people from Peaksville."

Mercedes nodded and looked at the CVN-72 Commanding Officer. "And Tulsa, Mom."

"Correct, Mercedes." President Walker lost her smile. "And Tulsa."

. . .

Ryan, Jack and Luke helped the girls exit the two minivan taxis in front of the JW Marriott Hotel Hong Kong.

Ruby smiled. "Thank you, gentlemen."

Madison walked with the Kernan twins. "That was really, really strange. Dinner with the President."

Ruby nodded. "Charity Ferguson remembered us."

"Fergie looked like she was going to faint when she saw the Kernan twins," Chloe said.

Amy held her nose high in the air. "My beauty is unforgettable."

Emma continued towards the elevator. "It's dangerous seeing the CABESA Lady. Fifty million Americans died this month."

Luke nodded. "And they hate *us* the most."

"The guy who hated spider monkeys is always on the news," Ryan said. "He was the worst."

Emma agreed. "Ben Light's dad."

Luke looked at his Peaksville friends. "Do you guys trust Mercedes?"

Madison nodded. "Yes."

Gloria agreed. "Luke, she's like one of us."

Luke shrugged. "I hope so."

Emma shook her head negatively. "She denied getting us airline tickets and hotel reservations. Maybe she's lying. If she didn't arrange it, then who did?"

The Peaksville friends looked at each other with puzzled looks.

"Ooh, ooh, ooh. Aah, aah, aah."

Ryan looked around. "What was that?"

Amy laughed. "It was a monkey sound."

"Ooh, ooh, ooh. Aah, aah, aah."

Madison saw the distant perpetrators hiding behind marble pillars and collapsed into tears. "Oh, God."

"Ooh, ooh, ooh. Aah, aah, aah."

Gloria hugged Madison. "What is it? What did you see?"

Madison cried. "Gloria and Chloe. You're not —"

Chloe looked around. "Gloria and Chloe what?"

Madison pointed. "Your sisters are —"

Gloria cried. "Our sisters?"

Chloe smiled as Charlotte, Kelly and I appeared from behind the lush vegetation of the JW Marriott lobby. "I knew it!"

The girls screamed and cried and hugged for five minutes. "Gracie! Charlie!"

Gloria wiped her eyes. "How?"

I cried. "We were in The Forbidden Zone during the Peaksville attack. Everyone, this is our pilot, Kelly."

Amy laughed. "Your pilot, Grace? Do you have a driver and hairdresser, also?"

Kelly shook her head. "I do it all."

Charlotte sat on a lobby couch with her nineteen-year-old sister. "Someone saved our lives in Peaksville."

Chloe nodded. "I just knew it. And the texts?"

"What texts?"

"You sent us texts."

I looked at Charlotte. "Chloe, our phones were taken in Peaksville by TSC Peacekeepers after the TEGWA. It wasn't us."

Chloe looked at Jack. "Then who?"

Jack looked at me. "Did you arrange our airfares and hotel rooms?"

I smiled at Charlotte. "Tomorrow, you'll meet the organizer who set that up. His name is Bob Bonner."

Ryan looked at me. "They're in Hong Kong?"

"No."

"They're coming here?"

Charlotte smiled. "Kelly is going to fly you to meet them."

"When?"

"At four o'clock in the morning." I looked at my watch and smiled. "In four hours."

Chloe smiled. "Where?"

I looked at Charlotte and Kelly. "It's a secret."

President Walker removed her headphones and light-blocking eyewear to stroll around the Air Force One cabin.

Charity Ferguson looked up and whispered in the peaceful cabin. "Hey, Abby. Couldn't sleep?"

"My internal clock is scrambled."

"Same." Charity closed her laptop. "Mercedes looked good in her Navy whites and Wings of Gold."

President Walker smiled. "Thanks."

"She seems to be doing well."

"I agree."

Charity put her hand over her mouth. "Her new friends."

President Walker whispered. "What did you find out?"

"Bud almost had a heart attack when I read him the roster of attendees."

"And?"

Charity waited for the wandering Press Corps members to vacate the area. "Do you remember the five 2020 CABESA Initiative fathers who tried unsuccessfully to obtain whistleblower status?"

President Walker remained still and silent.

"Bud checked. Kernans, Beckers, Flynns, Epleys, and others. You literally ate dinner with our CABESA Projects."

No response.

"Abby?"

"CABESA Projects saved my daughter?"

"Apparently."

"The irony is rich."

Charity covered her mouth and whispered. "Do you need Bud to eliminate this problem?"

No response.

Air Force One chased the darkness across the Atlantic towards Washington DC.

"Abby? We can make this go away. The twins remembered me."

"I noticed."

"Say the word."

"Mercedes seems to have befriended them."

Charity nodded. "Exactly. That's my point."

"I'm not worried about them."

"Bud and I are worried. They could harm your administration."

"How?"

Charity reminded her boss. "These so-called 'children' got the CABESA Initiative defunded in 2020."

"Don't hurt the Peaksville Projects," President Walker said. "Not yet, at least."

K elly leveled off at flight level three-six-zero while heading one-eight-zero, engaged the autopilot, and grabbed a JW Marriott French croissant from her flight bag. "Nine hundred miles to Proboscis Island. Time to eat."

I studied the instruments and sighed. "Two hours. Ugh!"

Kelly placed her right hand on my left shoulder. "Gracie, you can sleep. Nice job helping me get airborne at Hong Kong International."

I looked at MFD-2. "When is sunrise?"

Kelly punched a few buttons. "In sixty minutes."

I sighed.

Kelly reached down and pulled a handle on my seat. "Have you seen this lever?"

I looked down. "What is it?"

"Lean back."

My co-pilot seat slowly reclined as I smiled. "Ooh, nice. Haven't found that lever."

"I'll wake you if we're on fire or starting our descent."

I smiled and closed my eyes. "Thanks, Kelly."

After a few minutes, I vaguely heard Gloria's voice in the cockpit. "Is Gracie asleep?"

"Gracie." Kelly whispered into our ICS. "Smile if Kelly is awesome."

I smiled.

Gloria sat on the cockpit floor and touched my left shoulder.

"Hello, Gloria."

"I just wanted to come up to see you. I was worried this all was just a dream."

I slid my left headphone a few inches above my ear. "It's real, sister."

"Amazing. It's a miracle."

Kelly checked the autopilot and mowed down her Marriott blueberry bagel.

Gloria studied the glass cockpit display. "Is that our destination? That little island?"

Kelly nodded and purposefully spoke with her mouth full with spittle. "Phro-bhosph-schicph I-lanph."

Gloria looked at me. "Amy's other identical twin?"

I nodded. "What my esteemed colleague tried to say was 'Proboscis Island.' It's near Brunei, which is near Malaysia and Indonesia."

Gloria studied the Gulfstream flight information. "Wow."

I pointed to the different instruments to teach Gloria. "Altitude 36,000. Heading 180. Groundspeed 420. That's 7 miles per minute. Distance 700. ETA in 100 minutes. These are just oil pressures, temperatures, turbine speeds, etc. Simple, huh?"

Gloria shrugged. "Gracie?"

"Yeah?"

"I have a problem."

"What's that?"

"Ryan doesn't know, yet."

"Is it bad?"

Gloria nodded her head.

"Do you want to tell me?"

Gloria nodded and cried. "My breast cancer from high school re-manifested in my liver and bones."

Kelly heard the bad news and stopped eating. "I'm sorry."

"Oh, God." I cried. "Are you sure?"

"My doctor told me yesterday. One hour before the fancy dinner with the President. Maddie is the only one who knows."

Kelly looked at me as I wept. "We'll need to get her back to Hong Kong soon."

I held my sister's hand. "Why did you come on this trip?"

"To be with you."

"We'll beat it." I wiped my eyes and hugged my sister. "We beat it before. We'll beat it again, Gloria. I promise."

"I'm sorry," Gloria cried.

I smiled and caressed her beautiful face. "It's not your fault, sister. It's not your fault."

CHAPTER THIRTY-THREE

K elly and Amy were appropriately designated Corn Hole captains for multiple afternoon rounds of fun and games.

Aaron, Thomas and Lurch prepared the best BBQ burgers, dogs, and steaks on Proboscis Island since WWII.

Bob, Casper and Vic communicated with Gus Bryant and Betsy Ross on HICSON base via the Overwatch rooftop satellite dish.

Kelly yelled inside. "Bob, come out here and play! It's no fun without you!"

No response from inside Overwatch.

Amy tried. "Bob, Kelly said that when you play sports, you always end up on top. On the *Top Bunk*, that is!"

No response.

Charlotte looked inside and laughed. "Bob's not playing Corn Hole anytime soon."

Jack, Chloe and Gigi played catch with Thor with coconuts and branches.

Ruby stood and watched. "Just like old times."

Gigi yelled and giggled. "Go get it, Wolfie!"

Emma smiled. "God, I missed that giggle."

Brianna watched Jack. "Your brother is a Thai kickboxer. Has he kicked any mountain lions, lately?"

Emma smiled.

Thor didn't appear to show fatigue.

Madison looked at Charlotte. "Why are we here?"

"I think it's classified."

Ryan evaluated the situation. "It sounds dangerous."

Luke nodded. "I don't really want to mess with the people who messed with our childhoods."

Emma agreed. "Way too dangerous."

Gloria gently walked Ryan away from the Overwatch building, Corn Hole games and barbeque for privacy.

Charlotte whispered. "She's going to tell him."

Amy, Emma, Ruby and Brianna huddled with Charlotte and me.

"Do you think Ryan will take the news okay?" Ruby asked.

Ryan screamed into the Proboscis Island jungle

"Noooo!"

The Proboscis monkeys quickly reacted.

"Ooh, ooh, ooh! Aah, aah, aah!"

I sighed. "There's your answer."

M ercedes sat with fellow pilots in the CVN-72 Officer's Wardoom after midnight during Midnight Rations. She took a large bite of her One-Eyed Jack cheeseburger. "I love MIDRATS. This makes four square meals in one day."

Burner shrugged. "FNG, why didn't you order a Barney Clark? How do you expect to upgrade if you display dietary weakness?"

Mercedes studied her beef, cheese, and fried-egg One-Eyed Jack burger. "What's on yours?"

Burner opened his bun. "Same as yours, but with bacon. If you can't eat bacon, you can't upgrade in the Super Hornet."

Mercedes looked at Spooner. "What did you get?"

"Barney Clark."

"HIRF?"

Burner laughed. "My whirly-bird man here from HS-14 ordered *two* Barney Clarks. With *extra* bacon!"

Mercedes looked at HIRF. "Why do they call you HIRF?"

HIRF shrugged and chewed his Barney Clark. "It stands for His Royal Fatness."

"You're not fat."

Spooner feigned a cough while eating. "He's not thin."

Mercedes slid her chair closer to HIRF and whispered. "I like men who can eat as much as you at twelve thirty in the morning and still be in great shape. Burner went to Top Gun and can only eat *one* Barney Clark."

Burner pointed at the Wardroom phone. "That discussion is what I'd like to call

OVER! Tater, you apparently have a phone call from some other ocean where someone may actually care about your thoughts or opinions."

Mercedes kissed HIRF on the top of the head. "Mmm-mah!"

HIRF smiled and chewed his Barney Clark burger.

Spooner looked at his helicopter buddy. "That was really weird."

"LTJG Walker." Mercedes answered the phone and waited for the overseas lag.

"Hey girl, it's me."

"Skylar?"

"Yeah."

"How are you?"

"I'm good." Skylar Ferguson looked around her CNH newsroom and paused. "Mercedes, are you on speaker phone?"

"No?"

"It's your ship. Something's planned. Something bad."

Mercedes looked at her Operations Officer while speaking. "How bad?"

"It's going to be a rerun of before when your ship got —"

Click!

The shipboard phone call was cutoff.

"Skylar?" Mercedes hung up and returned to her table.

Burner looked at Mercedes. "Everything okay?"

Mercedes sighed. "No."

B ob Bonner looked around our Proboscis Island group after three-hour mountaintop training. "Does anyone have any questions about their gear?"

Thor slept at Gigi's feet as Bob, Lurch and Vic finished their demonstrations.

I raised my hand.

"Gracie."

"Everyone gets one of each?"

"Yes. Every operator will carry a battery backpack, MEDWEAP, SATCOM radio, Emergency Beacon, and multiple EMP grenades."

Ryan raised his hand. "What about Gloria?"

Kelly gently placed her hand on my sister's shoulder. "Gloria Flynn flies Kelly Cross Airlines to the finest Hong Kong hospital in two hours."

Ryan nodded. "What about me?"

Bob looked at Ryan. "You've lost the most, Ryan. If you want out, if you want to attend Gloria's appointments with her, you have that right."

Lurch agreed. "You *had* a family in Idaho. You *lost* your family in Idaho. I know how that feels, brother."

Luke looked at Emma and raised his hand. "Emma and I volunteer to attend

Gloria's appointments with her. We'll get her to the hospital and won't take her out of our sight."

Ryan held Gloria's hand and looked at Luke and Emma. "Are you sure?"

They nodded.

Ryan stood up. "Then count me in. I'm not seeking revenge or justice." Ryan looked at Aaron. "Just reciprocity."

C aptain Smart reviewed stacks of Post-Maintenance Inspection (PMI) paperwork regarding the successful temporary repair of the USS Abraham Lincoln's starboard hull. "Petty Officer Jordan!"

D'Andre paused cleaning the six-inch-thick, blast-proof windows of the bridge. "Yes, Captain."

"That was quite a dinner in Hong Kong."

D'Andre smiled. "Yes, Sir."

"LTJG Walker welded with you and your brother for the last seven days, didn't she?"

"She's from Idaho, Sir. We're all potato farmers. Potato farmers stick together."

Captain Smart laughed. "It's probably the only way to survive the winters up there."

D'Andre continued window maintenance and then paused again. "Captain?"

"Yes, Petty Officer Jordan?"

"We're getting underway soon?"

Captain Smart nodded. "CHENG is working with the Navy Norfolk Shipyard (NNSY) Inspectors to safely bring the nuclear reactor online again. Expect to be underway tomorrow night. After dinner, LTJG Walker's mother personally reminded me of her desire to get underway in total darkness."

"Is it safer with zero illumination?"

Captain Smart shrugged. "Orders are orders."

D'Andre scrubbed the windows again.

Captain Smart shuffled more NNSY Inspection paperwork in his elevated, steel Captain's chair. "Tomorrow night, there's no moon. That's when we'll steam for Yokosuka."

I rode the Liberty Boat from Star Ferry to the aircraft carrier in Hong Kong Harbor. "Is it always this rough?"

Bob smiled. "This harbor is worse than most due to shipping traffic."

I held onto the rails and leaned on Bob for support. "Is the carrier like this?"

"The carrier is rock solid. Except when underway in rough seas like near Guam, in the north Atlantic, or between Melbourne and Tasmania."

"I'm worried about Gloria."

Bob winked. "Kelly is taking Gloria to the finest cancer center in Hong Kong. Luke and Emma backing out of the mission actually works. They can stay with Gloria. No worries."

I smiled as rogue waves bumped me into the former Navy SEAL.

Our Liberty Boat approached the back of the Navy ship. Multiple sailors helped me leap from the rocking boat onto the small, temporary platform.

I jumped with extreme assistance. "Thanks!"

Bob adjusted my fictive NNSY Inspector nametag. "You good?"

"Good." I nodded. "Wow. That was literally a leap of faith."

Bob nodded. "Lots of ways to accidentally die on a carrier. Stay close to me. This way to Hangar Bay Two, Inspector Becker."

I looked around the seven-hundred-foot-long airplane garage filled with Baby Hornets, Super Hornets, Hawkeyes, Growlers and Seahawks. "It's huge! You could play football in here!"

Antoine and D'Andre arrived in their work uniform. "Gracie!"

Bob whispered to me. "No screaming and carrying on. Remember, we're NNSY Inspectors."

"AJ! DJ!" I tapped my fake nametag and hugged them.

D'Andre smiled and whispered. "We couldn't believe it when we heard."

"Charlotte is alive, also! This is Bob Bonner."

The Jordan twins shook his hand.

Antoine whispered to me. "Did you see my Peaksville home?"

I quietly nodded. "Mrs. Jordan is in very good hands, now. I'm sorry."

Officers, sailors and inspectors frantically prepared for deployment in the busy hangar bay as the Jordan boys subtly shed tears. "Thanks, Gracie."

"Antoine, this note is from Bree. She didn't go on an MWR trip with Gigi. They're both with us. Bree's safe."

Antoine smiled and pocketed the note. "Thanks."

Bob looked at his watch. "AJ, please take us to your infamous Division Officer."

"This way."

General Marsh greeted his old friend for lunch at the Cosmic Cowboy Grill in Coeur d'Alene, Idaho. "Raygun, over here."

Dr. Gunnison smiled and walked to the table. "Swamp!"

"How is my favorite Peaksville Institutes of Health CEO?"

Raygun shrugged. "My wife is grieving and nearly catatonic. She isn't taking the death of her family in Tulsa very well."

"I don't blame her."

Dr. Gunnison looked around. "I've always been loyal to Abby since CABESA. I helped her secure the Vice-Presidential spot under President Voigt."

General Marsh nodded. "I remember."

Dr. Gunnison whispered. "I even helped her get Voigt out of the way."

General Marsh stayed silent.

"Sorry, I'm venting. How is life at Peaksville Defense and Space?"

General Marsh shrugged. "My loyalty meter also dropped, but MEDWEAP production is at full capacity, as usual."

The two North Idaho industry leaders ordered from the menu.

General Marsh leaned over the table. "Something's going down in the South China Sea."

Dr. Gunnison paused. "You mean something *did* go down. Operation BLINDSIDE put a hole in the Lincoln two weeks ago."

"It's happening again, Raygun."

"No."

General Marsh nodded.

"Mercedes is on that carrier." The PIH CEO whispered. "Is Abby trying to kill her own daughter?"

"A group is trying to stop it."

"Who?"

"Think, Raygun."

"House Intel?"

General Marsh looked around and shrugged. "I didn't say it."

Dr. Gunnison stirred sugar into his iced tea. "How?"

"MEDWEAP's. Other hardware."

The PIH CEO paused. "PDS MEDWEAP's?"

General Marsh shrugged. "Can I trust you?"

"The Tulsa TEGWA changed everything." Dr. Gunnison pointed at his drink. "I'm not a Kool-Aid drinker anymore, Swamp."

B ob Bonner briefed Captain Smart in his private cabin as Mercedes and I listened. "Do you have any questions, Captain?"

Captain Smart shook his head.

"Bob's intel is solid, Sir." Mercedes politely addressed the CVN-72 Commanding Officer. "Skylar Ferguson, my friend from CNH News, tried to warn me about this on the phone before someone disconnected our call."

"Bob, you're telling me that tomorrow night, my aircraft carrier will be under attack. And I can't warn my crew."

"The attack is political. Of three hundred Officers on this ship, how many are politically loyal to President Walker?"

"Most."

Bob nodded. "Definitely over half."

Captain Smart sighed.

"Your own Officers would sabotage your defense. If you mentioned the Commander in Chief's intentions, you would be relieved of command within one hour."

Mercedes nodded. "It's true, Sir."

"We live in interesting times." Captain Smart looked at Mercedes. "I'll need two Super Hornets airborne. And one SH-60. Who do you trust?"

Mercedes quickly replied. "Burner and I can fly in a Super Hornet section. We'll call it night landing proficiency. HIRF and Spooner are already scheduled for SH-60 Channel Guard."

Bob handed Captain Smart a SATCOM walkie-talkie and charger. "Grace and I need to take a Liberty Boat to Hong Kong to prepare the defense. The Jordan brothers are aware of the plan. Contact us with questions. House Intelligence is on this SATCOM network. Mercedes, you'll brief Burner, HIRF and Spooner?"

Mercedes and Captain Smart nodded.

I tapped Mercedes on the knee and pointed to the Captain's television. "Is this the Skylar you're speaking about?"

Mercedes gasped at the CNH Breaking News. "No."

The reporter delivered the somber message. "We regret to inform you that Skylar Ferguson, a young CNH journalist, has died in her sleep of cardiac arrest. Her mother, the Minister of Youth, is deeply saddened and has asked all Homelanders to join her in prayer and remembrance."

I hugged Mercedes as she wept.

"Skylar was my friend. Not fair."

Captain Smart watched the sobering news. "I'm sorry, Tater."

Mercedes pointed at the television. "They killed her. Because of the warning."

Bob stood up, tapped his SATCOM unit and pointed to his watch. "Gracie, Liberty Boats are running for thirty more minutes."

Captain Smart stopped us before we left his cabin. "Bob?"

"Yes, Sir."

"Good luck. And thank you."

CHAPTER THIRTY-FOUR

M r. Light entered the Oval Office and closed the door.

President Walker noticed his demeanor. "Something's wrong."

Mr. Light nodded. "My old friend from the USAF."

"Swamp?"

"Yes."

"What happened."

Mr. Light whispered. "I have received intelligence from confidential TSC sources that General Marsh has illegally distributed NEXTGEN MEDWEAP's from PDS outside of normally approved Syndicate channels."

"Are you sure, Bud?"

"Fairly certain."

"Who received the MEDWEAP's?"

"We're not sure. House Intel is definitely involved, though."

President Walker sighed. "Hundreds? Thousands? How many weapons are we talking about?"

"Dozens."

President Walker laughed. "We've engineered and built five million MEDWEAP's since the 2013 CABESA Initiative. And you're worried about a few dozen?"

Mr. Light shrugged.

"What do you want me to do? Are you saying you don't trust Swamp?"

"That's exactly what I'm saying."

"Is that all you have for me?"

Mr. Light stood up. "Yes, Ma'am."

"Thanks for the update, Bud."

G igi played with Thor on the Proboscis Island peak. "Charlie!"

Charlotte joined Gigi as the boys played another round of Corn Hole. "Yeah?"

"We never solved the text message puzzle."

Amy, Ruby and Brianna sat with Gigi as Casper listened to the conversation.

Charlotte got a pen and paper. "There has to be a meaning to these numbers."

Ruby smiled. "And you're absolutely sure that you and Gracie didn't send the messages?"

"Promise. The TSC took our phones."

Casper overheard the riddle and showed us his iPhone. *"Can I see the codes?"*

Charlotte handed Casper her paper.

2-I-I-H-2

1-L-N-S-2

6-L-O-A-4

3-N-N-A-1

5-O-B-J-1

4-C-G-R-1

C asper scribbled for thirty seconds and showed Charlotte the rearranged codes.

1-L-N-S-2

2-I-I-H-2

3-N-N-A-1

4-C-G-R-1

5-O-B-J-1

6-L-O-A-4

"*S imple.*" Casper typed into his phone and showed Charlotte. "*Who got text message #7?*"

Amy looked around. "Atticus Finch! Get your skinny lawyer butt over here."

Thomas walked from the Corn Hole match. "Yeah?"

"Did you get a text from Gracie or me after the Peaksville TEGWA?" Charlotte asked.

Thomas scrolled and showed Casper a text. "This one?"

7-N-9-H-3

R uby sighed. "Tommy Boy!"

"I didn't know."

Charlotte read the coded messages aloud from Casper's notepad. "Lincoln. Ningbo9. Sharjah. 2211143."

Gigi watched with one hand on Thor's back. "Casper, you're a genius."

Casper winked.

Amy threw her hands in the air. "Casper makes me feel twenty IQ points dumber."

Casper flashed his phone again. "*Lincoln is the target. Ningbo 9 is a Supertanker. Sharjah Blue is a weaponized, nuclear yacht. N22.1 E114.3 is a LAT LONG just south of Hong Kong Harbor.*"

Brianna laughed. "Wow. Make that forty IQ points dumber."

P resident Walker called the Peaksville Institutes of Health CEO. "Raygun?"

Dr. Gunnison tucked his grieving wife into bed and whispered into his cell phone. "Hello, Abby."

"How's Peaksville?"

"Great." The PIH CEO looked at his wife then left the room. "Just great. Living the dream."

President Walker smiled. "That's the spirit."

"How can I help you?"

"Mr. Light recently told me that Swamp may have performed an unsanctioned weapons transfer to Gus Bryant over at HICSON."

Dr. Gunnison stepped outside and sat on a lawn chair. "Bud is lying, Ma'am."

"Raygun, you told me last week that Swamp was off the reservation."

"I was wrong."

"Wrong?"

"I got bad intelligence."

"Bad intel?"

"More like misdirected. I have many sources inside and outside of The Safety Corps that have confirmed Bud is participating in seditious and treasonous behavior."

"Really?"

Dr. Gunnison paused. "It should come as no surprise to you, Ma'am. You and Bud have a long history that dates back to CABESA. How many times has Bud failed to deliver after receiving direct orders?"

"Go on, Raygun."

"Bud's routine failures always *conveniently* go down in the record books as incompetence, not sedition."

President Walker looked out the Oval Office window. "I'm sorry to hear this. What about Swamp?"

"I observe Swamp daily in Idaho. He's loyal and dedicated. Bud is a threat to the Syndicate. Swamp is an asset."

"Thanks, Raygun. I appreciate your candor."

"You're welcome, Abby."

Click!

Captain Smart sat on the bridge, continuously receiving, reviewing and signing Inspection forms from the NNSY, CVN-72 Chief Engineer, and other Department Heads.

Beep!

He picked up his small, high-tech SATCOM phone to read a message.

> *CAPT: Sharjah Blue = weaponized nuke yacht.*
> *Ningbo 9 to impact CVN @ N22.1 E114.3.*

Captain Smart yelled into the Navigation shack. "Petty Officer Jordan!"

D'Andre ran to his side on the bridge.

"Read this."

D'Andre shook his head. "Give me five minutes, Sir."

Captain Smart began to dial his Executive Officer's 4-digit shipboard phone number. "Damn." He hung up his phone and waited for D'Andre.

D'Andre returned with a marked-up NAV Chart and whispered to his Commanding Officer. "Here is our planned route. Here is that LAT LONG on our route south of the harbor. Here is the Sharjah Blue current POSIT. Here is the Ningbo 9 current POSIT."

Captain Smart nodded and whispered. "Thanks, Petty Officer Jordan. Go throw that paper in the shredder and keep an eye on those ships."

"WILCO, Sir."

P resident Walker welcomed Mr. Light into the Oval Office. "Bud, thanks for visiting on short notice."

Mr. Light sat on the couch. "Anytime, Abby."

"Tell me about the CABESA Projects."

"You apparently had dinner with them, right?"

"But you said you would investigate them."

"I did?"

No response.

"What would you like to know about them?"

"For one, I want to know how these North Idaho CABESA Project dropouts ended up at my dinner table."

Mr. Light took out a notebook and penciled some notes. "I'm going to find out."

"Thanks."

Mr. Light stood up. "Anything else?"

President Walker motioned for Mr. Light to sit back down. "Tell me about Skylar Ferguson's death."

Mr. Light shrugged. "She died?"

"Do you realize that Skylar was my God Daughter?"

Mr. Light shook his head negatively. "Skylar was *reliability-challenged.* That's what I heard."

"But you don't know how she died?"

"No, Ma'am."

"Reliability-challenged. That's an interesting way to describe someone." President Walker stared at Mr. Light for ten seconds. "That's all, Bud."

B ob Bonner bought me a Diet Coke in the Hong Kong International luxury FBO and tossed it to me. "Gracie, catch."

I cracked it open and drank. "Thanks! Who are we waiting for?"

Bob looked out the window as a Navy SH-60 Seahawk landed onto the

Signature Flight Support flightline. "HIRF and Spooner. Let's go greet them so they don't need to shut down."

Bob arranged clearance from their HS-14 lineman to enter the port side door with the rotor blades turning.

I followed Bob and ducked. "Is this safe!"

Bob couldn't hear me.

We jumped in and exchanged pleasantries.

"I'm Bob! This is Grace!"

The Navy pilots leaned towards the cockpit door. "I'm HIRF! This is Spooner!"

The noisy, vibrating Seahawk helicopter smelled like jet fuel, motor oil, hydraulic fluid, saltwater, and body odor.

Bob handed them two SATCOM radios, two MEDWEAP's, and two beacons. "Did Mercedes and Burner brief you guys about the Sharjah Blue and Ningbo 9?"

"Yes!" The two Navy helicopter drivers nodded. "It's a House Intel mission, right?"

Bob pointed to the controls on the SATCOM radios. "HICSON Base is in the Capitol Building. Overwatch is in the South China Sea on an island. You know how to work these?"

HIRF nodded and shook our hands.

Spooner handed us two large HS-14 squadron coins and looked at me. "Drinking coins! If I see you in a restaurant or bar and you don't have your coin, you're buying the round!"

I laughed and pocketed the souvenir. "Deal!"

Bob slapped the pilots on their shoulders. "Thanks, guys!"

We ran out the port side holding hands after obtaining clearance from their rescue swimmer.

M r. Light finally fell asleep on his favorite lounge chair in his grand, Bethesda home at midnight. He woke up with severe heartburn and indigestion then flipped on FXH News.

"This is Krissy Moriarty, the Global Public Health Crisis Correspondent on FXH News."

Mr. Light walked into the kitchen, took two aspirin with water, then returned to watch television.

"FXH News Medical Team, in conjunction with the PIH and Peaksville State University Medical School, have recently released a study revealing a high correlation between excessive oxygen intake and early mortality. Doctors and scientists determined that Homelanders that reside in lower elevations are now experiencing shorter lifespans due to higher oxygen levels, increased gravity, and dangerous compression of vital organs."

"Ministry of Truth, no doubt." Mr. Light sighed, turned off the television and grumbled. "Why do people believe his hogwash?"

Click!

He rolled to his left side, the pain continued. He rolled to his right side. His chest was visibly thumping with rapid palpitations. He suddenly sat up and looked around. "Damn."

Mr. Light stood up, grabbed a weapon, and ran to the front door.

Screech!

A yellow Dodge Challenger sped away from his home.

Mr. Light holstered his weapon and talked to himself on his front porch. "Nice try, Charity."

C ongressman Gus Bryant and Betsy Ross keyed their SATCOM radio microphone. "Overwatch, this is HICSON Base, checking in for a SITREP."

Casper nodded to Gigi and smiled.

Gigi keyed the microphone and smiled. "HICSON Base, this is Overwatch. We have you loud and clear. Personnel are moving into place. Gettysburg has been briefed."

Thomas gave a 'thumbs up' to Gigi. "Sounded good."

Gus keyed his mic. "Overwatch, I have you loud and clear. We are standing by to render assistance as required."

Thor rested his long, heavy German Shepherd snout on Gigi's leg. "Thanks, HICSON Base. Over and out."

Casper smiled, typed into his iPhone and showed Gigi. "*Over and out?*"

Gigi laughed. "Pretty good for a ditsy supermodel, huh?"

Thomas rolled his eyes.

C harity joined her lifelong friend in the Oval Office. "Bud saw my car."

"Are you sure?"

"Yes."

President Walker paused. "It was after midnight. Did Bud see your face?"

"Doesn't matter."

"Why?"

"I was in my Yellow Challenger."

"You're probably right." President Walker laughed. "Can you try again?"

Charity shook her head. "No. Bud has too many connections. And he's ready for me now. I'm in a lot of trouble."

President Walker clicked her pen on the Resolute Desk. "You're afraid?"

"Bud killed President Voigt for you. Aren't *you* afraid, Abby? Because you *should* be."

"Damn. What should I do?"

Charity shrugged. "If you try to kill him, don't miss. Because he'll kill you. I missed. And he's probably going to kill me."

"I'll send Bud away."

"Where?"

"Twelve time zones away." President Walker paused. "Hong Kong."

"Probably a good plan."

CHAPTER THIRTY-FIVE

L urch completed his fifth touch and go in the right seat of a new Airbus H225 Super Puma. "This helicopter is amazing!"

Brianna studied the Multi-Function Display from the left seat while on the ground at Hong Kong International's Signature Flight Support FBO. "Can you teach me this again?"

The former Navy SEAL and Special Operations Command helicopter pilot smiled. "Okay, Bree. This button scans for nearby nanotech RFID in people's blood."

"Okay."

Lurch pointed at the Chinese FBO fuel truck employee fueling a nearby Cessna Citation. "That guy over there. 215.445 MHz is his personal Imaging Probe frequency."

Brianna gasped. "Wow."

Lurch pressed more buttons. "Here, you get a picture of his head and heart. This is how to zoom in. You can see his heart beating right here. This is how to select *PAIN*, *AFIB*, or *FLATLINE*. This is how to select *manual* or *continuous fire control*. And if you press this, he dies."

Brianna gasped and looked at Lurch. "Don't even have your finger near it."

"Of course not."

"Scared me."

Lurch looked at his inexperienced co-pilot. "You will be in charge of fire control, tonight."

"I can do it." Brianna looked at the weapon controls on the MFD. "They want to sink my husband's boat. I'll sink them first."

"That a girl, Bree."

P resident Walker closed her door. "Have a seat, Bud."

Mr. Light guardedly walked to a couch. "What's this about?"

"You've been working hard lately."

Mr. Light shrugged.

"I need you to oversee something for me."

"Say the word."

"Operation BLINDSIDE II."

"In Hong Kong?"

President Walker leaned on the edge of the Resolute Desk. "I don't have a 'warm and fuzzy' about the operation. Weapons have been moving around. House Intelligence seems to be involved. And a few nights ago, I ran into multiple CABESA Projects in Hong Kong."

"You want me to be more hands-on with BLINDSIDE II?"

"I want you to be *there*."

Mr. Light sighed. "When?"

"I have a 767 standing by at Andrews AFB for you and Dr. Hands. It started engines five minutes ago. My Marine Corps Two helicopter will take you to the jet from the lawn."

"Doctor Hands? I work better alone."

No response.

"So right now?"

"Dr. Hands is at Base Operations at Andrews waiting for you." President Walker pushed away from the Resolute Desk and extended her hand. "Thanks, Bud."

Mr. Light shook her hand, returned a polite smile, then ran towards the White House landing pad.

President Walker called his cell phone before he boarded. "Bud?"

"Yes, Abby?"

"Mustafa needs the Sharjah Blue in Dubai next week for his daughter's birthday party."

"Copy."

"Mustafa *needs* it back, safe and sound."

Mr. Light boarded Marine Corps Two. "Copy that. Safe and sound."

.   .   .

"Understood. Okay, thanks Emma." Ryan hung up his iPhone.

Madison discontinued hosing down the Ben Gunn deck. "How is she?"

"Emma and Luke are staying with her at the hospital. The cancer doctor recommended immediate chemo and radiation treatments."

"That's good. She's in good hands, Ryan."

Ryan entered multiple waypoints and frequencies into the Ben Gunn's shipboard GPS and radio electronics. "This timing sucks."

"Gloria will be fine." Madison smiled. "I promise."

Ryan looked at the SATCOM radios inside the Ben Gunn cabin. "Have you tested those things out yet?"

"Let me try." Madison dialed in pre-briefed frequencies. "HICSON Base, this is Amber Jack One. Radio check."

Gus Bryant answered the call from the Capitol Building. "Amber Jack One, this is HICSON Base. Loud and clear. How me?"

"Loud and clear, thanks. Break, break. Overwatch, this is Amber Jack One. Radio check."

Casper and Thomas looked at Gigi and pointed to her SATCOM radio.

Gigi keyed her mic from Proboscis Island. "Thor and I have you loud and clear."

Madison laughed. "Same here, Overwatch. Thanks!"

Brianna keyed her mic from the new Airbus H225. "Amber Jack One, Harbor Watch."

Madison looked at Ryan and keyed her mic. "Go ahead."

Brianna transmitted. "Maddie, look up."

Ryan, Madison and Li Jie curiously exited the Ben Gunn cabin.

Lurch buzzed the Star Ferry Terminal at four hundred feet with Brianna in the co-pilot seat.

Madison keyed her mic. "Looking good in your shiny new toy, Harbor Watch!"

Ryan continued his launch preparations on his fishing boat and watched the Liberty Boats speed towards the USS Abraham Lincoln in the Hong Kong Harbor. "The aircraft carrier is raising the anchor soon."

Li Jie watched the naval activity and pointed to various Chinese husbanding agent boats. "Agree, Boss. The local water and trash barges just disconnected from Lincoln one hour ago."

"This is dangerous, Maddie. This isn't a game. We're in a fishing boat among warships. You can back out now, if you want."

"I'm in, Ryan."

. . .

B urner sat with Mercedes in the VFA-195 Ready Room briefing space. "Tater, you and I are getting a touch and go trap in one hour. Then officially a night proficiency flight. Are you sure you want to take this flight? We can get a senior Lieutenant or an O-4 instead. Captain Smart might feel more comfortable. It's going to be dangerous."

Mercedes whispered. "I can do this."

"I *know* you can do this. But you aren't even fully-qualified. Eighty-percent of your three hundred hours of flight time is TRACOM or FRS time. You literally have only fifty *fleet* hours. This is real world stuff. NOTSO is scared to death about getting sunk tonight. Why don't we replace you with a TOPGUN instructor? You're the FNG. I was once an FNG. It's not your fault."

Mercedes looked at Burner. "I got good grades in flight school. Besides, *I* was the one who asked *you* to go on this mission."

Burner leaned close to Mercedes and rubbed his eyes for ten seconds. "Okay, Tater. Stay tight on my wing. If I call knock it off, you knock it off then RTB to mom immediately."

"Okay. I mean Roger. I mean WILCO." Mercedes smiled.

Burner sighed and looked at his SATCOM radio. "Have you tried this?"

"Not yet."

Burner looked at his watch. "Alright. Let's go sign our A-Sheets in Dambuster Maintenance Control. The Yellow Shirts in V-3 are bringing our jets up to the flight deck from the Hangar Bay on Elevator-2. We'll test our SATCOM radios from the flight deck."

Mercedes smiled, grabbed some kneeboard cards and hugged Burner. "Thanks!"

I van Smirnov, in full tactical gear, quickly ran into the noisy TSC helicopter.
    Captain Farsi broadcasted on his 5MC loudspeaker warning from the Sharjah Blue bridge. "Heads up on the stern. Lifting H-53 from Spot One. Stand well clear."

The TSC pilot lifted off with the Tactical Victim Unit and executed a left turn out.

Mr. Murdstone sat with Ben Light in the Sharjah Blue Weapon Control Center. "I heard your father is airborne on a 767 flying to Hong Kong."

Ben nodded. "That's the word on the street."

Omar Muscat stormed into the high-tech WCC and hollered. "Why haven't we already taken control of the Ningbo 9?"

Ben slouched down in his seat to hide.

Mr. Murdstone stayed erect in his seat.

"Nuke! Why are we not in control of the Ningbo 9 already?"

Mr. Murdstone looked at the Dubai oil tycoon's son. "The H-53 has lifted, Omar."

"Why not earlier?"

Mr. Murdstone looked at Ben.

Ben turned away and covered his face.

"Omar, I believe the H-53 was waiting for the Ningbo 9 to steam closer. Also, I believe the Lincoln is raising the anchor as we speak."

"You *believe*, Nuke. What else do you *believe*?"

Mr. Murdstone shrugged.

"I *believe* I am the only smart person on the Sharjah Blue." Omar Muscat exited the Weapon Control Center and slammed the door.

Ben sat up straight and monitored his radar scope. "You handled that well, Nuke."

"Thanks for the backup."

"Omar has a few issues."

"A few?"

Ben linked to the TSC body cameras to the WCC big screen. "The H-53 is approaching the Ningbo 9. Let's watch."

B ob instructed Jack and Ruby on the E-SOC-1 Riverine boat as Vic, Aaron and Charlotte listened from their docked E-SOC-2. "Vic and I operated these boats when we were SEAL's. They are very *forgiving*, but the South China Sea is extremely choppy in the shipping lanes and very *unforgiving*. Wear your harness. Or you *will* be ejected at high speeds."

Jack raised his hand. "In the movies, these Riverine boats have 50 cals and machine guns. What do we have?"

"Those are SOC-R boats. Gus arranged for these two E-SOC's here in Macau. This is not a shooting war. The attack on the Lincoln will be covert. We will defend covertly." Bob walked to the weapon station. "On our boat, E-SOC-1, Jack drives while Ruby operates the E-SOC mounted MEDWEAP's. Vic, how are you dividing duties on E-SOC-2?

Vic stood up on E-SOC-2. "Charlie said it reminds her of her John Deere tractors. She drives. Aaron operates the MEDWEAP."

"Perfect." Bob summarized his brief. "At high speeds, expect two hours of gas. At low speeds, expect six hours of endurance. Tight MEDWEAP beams will save power. EMP will quickly get you out of a pickle. But beware, using the EMP function will require over ten minutes of normal ESOC operation for the engine generators to recharge your weapon batteries. Questions?"

The E-SOC operators shook their heads negatively as nearby hydroplaning evening tour boats ferried gamblers between Hong Kong and Macau casinos.

Bob keyed his SATCOM mic. "Overwatch, Stingray One and Stingray Two, checking in from Macau. Up and ready. Standing by for tasking."

Gigi watched her scope and keyed her mic. "Stingray One and Stingray Two, this is Overwatch. I see you on HICSON satellite link. Gettysburg raised the anchor and is entering the West Lamma Channel. Harbor Watch and Amber Jack One have mobilized. Proceed to rendezvous location when ready."

Aaron signaled the E-SOC drivers to start engines and signaled Vic to check her SATCOM radio. "Stingray One and Stingray Two are underway."

"Copy!" Gigi said.

Mercedes stood with Burner on the elevator as 304 and 307 rode from the hangar bay to the flight deck. "There's HIRF doing a walk-around with Spooner."

Burner waved to his HS-14 buddies. "Tater, did you brief them on the Overwatch frequencies."

"They're good to go."

Burner removed his SATCOM radio from the lower, outboard leg pocket of his green Navy flight suit. "Lightning, this is Dambuster, you good?"

HIRF keyed his mic. "Locked, cocked, ready to rock."

Burner smiled and looked up.

Captain Smart gave a 'thumbs up' from seventy feet above the flight deck through the bridge window and keyed his mic. "Gettysburg is up and ready. You guys need a touch and go trap before proceeding on your night mission, right?"

Burner keyed his mic from the flight deck. "Affirmative."

Captain Smart checked his weather reports. "We'll have recovery winds for you once we're pointing south and out of the harbor."

"Copy, Sir." Burner stowed his SATCOM and looked at Mercedes in her G-suit, torso harness and SV-2 survival vest. Burner checked her emergency beacon for operability. "You good?"

"I'm good."

Burner looked her in the eyes. "It's okay to be scared."

"I know."

"You will essentially be going against your Mom. Are you sure you don't want me to find someone else, Tater?"

"I'm only ten percent scared."

"Say again?"

Mercedes smiled as an aircraft tow tractor drove past on the flight deck. "The first day we met, before our first Area Familiarization flight in Atsugi around Mount Fuji. You told me to be 90% arrogant and cocky and 10% scared shitless."

Burner laughed. "You remember that?"

Mercedes nodded.

"Then let's do this."

"Thanks, Burner."

The Lieutenant Commander pointed to Dambuster 304 and 307 as Antoine Jordan executed a daily inspection on LTJG Walker's airplane. "NOTSO spotted us behind catapult four. Let's go finish our brief, top off our water bottles, and get in the zone. Remember Tater, no working on Airman EVAL's or awards once you're in the zone. Take *off* your Division Officer hat and put *on* your Aviator hat in the zone."

Mercedes smiled. "Let's go get in the *zoooone*. I'm getting in the *zooone*."

Burner laughed. "Petty Officer Jordan will have our jets ready for preflight in ten minutes. Let's hurry."

CHAPTER THIRTY-SIX

Gigi looked at an Overwatch monitor on Proboscis Island. "What are you guys watching, Tommy Boy? Looks like a *John Wick* movie. Do we have satellite television here?"

Thomas whispered. "Casper hacked the TSC Supertanker raid. This is a live feed from the Ningbo 9."

Gigi gasped. "Body cameras?"

Casper nodded.

"Oh, God. They're killing that crew."

Thomas nodded. "This is tough to watch."

Amy keyed the mic from the weapon station of the Gulfstream 650 ER. "Overwatch, this is Shadow two-two. Radio Check."

Gigi somberly keyed the mic. "I have you loud and clear."

"We are airborne, climbing through twenty thousand."

Casper nodded.

Gig keyed her mic. "We see you, Shadow. Be safe up there."

Kelly winked at me in the cockpit then keyed her SATCOM mic. "Question. All the attractive people ended up in the Gulfstream. Was this on purpose?"

Gigi laughed on the radio. "Copy that, Kelly and other attractive Gulfstream people! Say hi to my attractive sister!"

I keyed my mic. "Hey, Supermodel."

Chloe keyed her Gulfstream SATCOM mic. "Overwatch, are you getting this video feed?"

"Affirmative, we linked it up to you."

"What is that?"

Gigi transmitted. "The TSC is taking control of the Ningbo 9. HICSON Base, are you copying this?"

A female voice replied from Washington DC. "HICSON Base copies. We have a visual."

Casper and Thomas looked at Gigi.

Gigi called HICSON Base. "Betsy, is that you?"

No response.

"Gus? Betsy? This is Overwatch. Are you there?"

Betsy replied. "Gus Bryant's family was just killed in a house fire. Wife and three children. Gus is driving to Alexandria to the scene. Destiny Jamison made that radio call. You'll like her. She's a junior Congresswoman from Georgia. Gus selected her for her House Intelligence Committee position."

"Sorry about Congressman Bryant's family." Gigi keyed her mic. "Welcome to the team, Destiny."

Destiny keyed her mic. "Gus and Betsy briefed me. We got your back."

"Thanks!" Gigi leaned back and looked at Casper and Thomas. "Poor Gus."

C harity leaned into Dr. Moriarty as he finished his fifth Captain Morgan's rum and Coke. "I don't think Abby will be requiring the governmental services of Bud much more."

"Au contraire." Dr. Moriarty wiped his mouth with his sleeve in their Washington DC Ritz Carlton restaurant booth. "Abby just sent him to Hong Kong."

"Abby sent him *away*. Not to *help*."

"This happens every year. Abby and Bud have been like fire and ice since CABESA started in Peaksville. Don't exaggerate."

Charity Ferguson poured herself another beer from her pitcher and wiped a tear. "Things changed."

"How?"

"Bud killed my daughter."

The Minister of Health sipped his mixed drink. "You're sure? I thought she died of natural causes."

Charity sneered at the Ministry of Health.

"Maybe you're mistaken."

"I was told by a much more reliable source than you, *Doc*. Bud killed Skylar."

Dr. Moriarty ordered another rum and Coke. "He did?"

Charity audibly cried and nodded.

"I'm not sure if this helps you grieve, Charity. But Skylar *did* reveal Operation BLINDSIDE II to Mercedes."

Charity wiped her tears and sat up rigidly straight in the Ritz Carlton booth. "That knowledge will help me grieve?"

Dr. Moriarty shrugged.

"Did you just imply that my deceased daughter, Skylar, was a traitor."

He sipped his drink and slouched.

"My only daughter?" Charity slapped Dr. Moriarty in the face.

"What was that for?"

"Because you're an insensitive a-hole." Charity threw her draught beer in his face and left the Ritz Carlton restaurant.

Dr. Moriarty wiped his face and drunkenly mumbled to himself. "Well, she *was* a traitor."

L uke keyed a SATCOM mic from a small waiting room in the Hong Kong Cancer Center. "Amber Jack One, this is Home Guard."

Ryan carefully navigated south from Kowloon towards the West Lamma Channel as Madison and Li Jie served as evening traffic spotters. "Go ahead, Home Guard. How are things?"

Luke checked the hallways then transmitted. "Gloria is asleep. She's fine. There is some other information I want to pass. Is this network secure?"

Casper signaled Gigi to respond from Proboscis Island. "A-firm, Luke. This is Gigi. HICSON is secure."

"Okay. Our nurse got Gloria in her chemo booth. Emma and I never left Gloria's side. Gloria sat in the recliner. Nurse plugged her port. Chemo began. All good. Then —"

Ryan made minor steering adjustments from the flybridge tracking one-eight-zero from Hong Kong. "Then what?"

"We had a visitor. Gloria was half asleep. Remember that doctor from Peaksville that Dean Michaels always tried to push on the students?"

"Moriarty?"

"The other guy."

"Hands?"

Luke snapped his fingers. "Yes! He asked the three of us about ten questions. Told us he grew up in Spokane and Seattle. Emma and I tried to deflect. Gloria acted like she was asleep from chemo. Dr. Hands studied Gloria's chart. He kept asking us about Idaho."

Ryan looked at Madison. "Damn."

Luke continued. "There's more. Emma and I saw Ben's dad in the hallway."

"Ben who?"

"Ben Light."

Bob keyed his SATCOM radio. "Home Guard, that man was the Homeland Minister of Safety. He runs the TSC."

Ryan turned around and observed his Star Ferry Terminal open parking spot. "Luke, do you want me to turn around?"

Luke paused. "Not sure."

Emma grabbed his SATCOM radio. "Ryan, we got this. Gloria is safe. Luke and I will guard her. Two words. Do. Not. Worry."

"That's three."

"You get the picture."

Madison nodded her head and whispered to Ryan. "Emma has this."

Ryan looked straight ahead as he followed the USS Abraham Lincoln from the Hong Kong Harbor. "You won't let Gloria out of your sight?"

Emma spoke softly. "All is well, Ryan."

"Thanks, Home Guard."

President Walker invited Charity Ferguson into the Oval Office. "Charity, I'm sure you heard about Dr. Moriarty."

"Heart attack, right? I saw the news."

"Walking out of the Ritz Carlton."

Charity shrugged. "Was he drunk?"

"You tell me. You were seen with Dr. Moriarty in the Ritz two hours ago. He was my Minister of Health."

"And?"

"How do you think this looks?"

"What do you mean?"

"The optics. My overweight Minister of Health died of cardiac arrest. How secure do you think this makes my Homelanders feel? I'm trying to pacify my Homelanders and your cavalier and reckless stunt flew in the face of my policies and messaging."

"He looked unhealthy. Nobody will question it."

"That's my point. *My* Minister of Health looked *unhealthy*. Your actions are painting that picture." President Walker looked out her window at her thousands of supporters waving flags on Pennsylvania Avenue. "I'm supposed to be their Savior."

Charity remained silent.

President Walker spun her chair towards Charity. "This news has already dropped my approval rating. I'm now sub-ninety percent. The west coast hasn't even been polled yet."

"I'm sorry, Abby."

"How about a little respect. Call me Mrs. President."

Charity looked at her lifelong friend. "I'm sorry, Mrs. President."

"That will be all, Minister of Youth Ferguson."

T he VFA-195 duty officer intercepted Mercedes as she walked to preflight. "Miss Walker, you have a call from CONUS."

Mercedes removed her Navy flight helmet and skull cap to take the call. "Hello?"

"Don't interfere with progress, Mercedes. My dad interfered. And he is dead."

"Krissy?"

"Yes."

"Are you threatening me?"

Krissy Moriarty paused. "No, I'm not threatening you. I'm just saying that Skylar talked to you then had an unfortunate health problem. My father got in the administration's path. He died. I'm your friend, Mercedes. I don't want you to go down the wrong road."

Mercedes saw Antoine standing by for the planeside brief on the port side of 307. "I have to run, Krissy. Thanks for calling."

"Remember Mercedes. I'm your friend. Just be careful."

"Bye, Krissy."

Mercedes re-donned her gear and walked to 304 to intercept Burner, who was mid-preflight. "You beat me up here."

"Tater, no phone calls after the brief. You're in the zone, remember?"

"Sorry."

"Who was that?"

"Just another Kool-Aid drinker. Let's roll."

B ud looked at his watch in the JW Marriott Hotel Hong Kong lobby and spoke into his satellite phone. "Abby wants me dead."

General Marsh laughed from his Peaksville Defense and Space office. "Join the club."

"I miss experimenting on those loveable PIH spider monkeys. We should have never retired them in 2013. Those were the days. What was the name of that friendly monkey who loved me? Jerome. That's it. He was my favorite."

"Are you drinking, Bud?"

"I'm one hundred feet from my Hong Kong hotel bar. I have a TSC platinum VISA card. Don't provoke me."

General Marsh smiled. "Why Hong Kong?"

"Abby sent me here. I found some CABESA Projects."

"Where?"

"Here in Hong Kong. Something's going on. They seem to be organized."

"Who funded it?"

"Congressman Gus Bryant and House Intelligence."

"Tell me more."

"His family just died in a tragic house fire."

General Marsh broke his pencil and threw it against his wall.

"Swamp?"

The PDS CEO regained his composure in his Idaho office. "I wouldn't worry about the CABESA Projects. They have no formal training."

"I'm not. I'm worried about the Queen Bee."

"And spider monkeys?"

Mr. Light paused. "To be painfully honest, I still have bad dreams about Jerome the PIH spider monkey. Jerome haunts me at night. He comes at me like a spider monkey when the lights go out."

"The Boogey Monkey."

"Jerome is my kryptonite."

"Bud, I knew you weren't serious when you reminisced about the PIH CABESA monkeys."

"You know me to well, Swamp."

I transmitted on HICSON Base from our Gulfstream 650 ER. "Overwatch, this wasn't fair. I've got Kelly *and* Amy in the same airplane. There's a lot of tomfoolery on the ICS."

Chloe keyed her mic. "But Gracie and I secretly like it."

Gus checked in. "Overwatch, this is HICSON Base. I'm back online. Destiny will stay online, also. Let me know if you need anything."

Bob transmitted. "Gus, we're all sorry about your loss."

"Thanks, Bob."

Gigi waited ten seconds after the warm sentiment then looked at her scope with Casper and Thomas nearby. "Can we get an 'up and ready' report from everyone?"

Thor barked into the radio. "Arf!"

Gigi laughed. "That's our Overwatch 'up and ready' call."

Bob watched Jack drive and Ruby navigate ESOC-1 south from Macau. "Stingray One. Up and ready."

Vic coached Charlotte and Aaron in ESOC-2 as they trailed in loose formation. "Stingray Two. Up and ready."

Ryan got a 'thumbs up' from Madison and Li Jie on the Ben Gunn. "Amber Jack One. Up and ready."

HIRF and Spooner flew the HS-14 Lightning 615 at three hundred feet in right hand turns in the Lincoln's Starboard Delta pattern. "Channel Guard. Up and ready in Starboard-D."

Brianna keyed her mic as Lurch piloted the new Airbus H225 Super Puma. "Harbor Watch is up and ready."

Captain Smart subtly leaned away from the Gator and OOD to covertly make his transmission from his chair in the bridge. "Gettysburg up and ready. 614 is northbound, returning our local Harbor Pilot to Star Ferry. HIRF and Spooner in 615 are going to stay by my side in Starboard D."

Gigi looked at Casper and keyed the mic. "Dambuster up?"

Burner keyed the mic and climbed into the darkness with Mercedes on his starboard Super Hornet wing. "Dambuster 304 and 307. Up and ready, passing angels ten for angels twenty."

Amy keyed her mic again. "And Shadow two-two, of course, is up and beautiful."

"That's everyone!" Gigi put her pencil down and looked at the scope. "Okay, Ningbo 9 has been commandeered by the TSC. Consider the supertanker hostile to Gettysburg."

Bob sped southbound in ESOC-1 "Stingray One copies. Overwatch, cleared to execute Operation ELECTRONIC SHELL GAME."

"Copy." Gigi looked at Casper who nodded in return. "Commencing Operation ELECTRONIC SHELL GAME."

M r. Murdstone looked at Ben Light. "Your dad is in Hong Kong."

"One second, Nuke." Ben studied the Weapon Control Center monitors of the Sharjah Blue and made a call. "Bounty Hunter One, this is Solar Flare."

Ivan Smirnov keyed his mic from the bridge of the Ningbo 9. "Solar Flare, this is Bounty Hunter One."

"Say status."

"Up and ready. Ningbo 9 crew neutralized. TSC Tactical Victim Unit in control of vessel."

Ben smiled at Mr. Murdstone. "Nuke, check this out. The Sharjah Blue GPS system is giving me some erratic signals. It's probably the Chinese military or local hackers."

Mr. Murdstone nodded. "We're okay for the impact?"

"Oh, yeah. I was just showing you. For training. We're good."

Ben Light keyed his mic to call the Russian oligarch and former KGB agent. "Verify ready for impact."

We are accelerating through thirteen knots. She's very heavy. This is probably maximum velocity. Setting up for Operation BLINDSIDE II."

Ben flipped multiple switches on his panel and called the bridge. "Captain Farsi, can you confirm that we are midnight."

Captain Farsi stepped outside to view the luxury, weaponized yacht. "Midnight."

"Thanks." Ben toggled back to satellite communications with Ivan. "Bounty Hunter One, be advised that the Solar Flare is midnight. Please confirm when you have extinguished all exterior lighting on the Ningbo 9."

"There's one light outside of our bridge. I can't find its controls."

Ben looked at Mr. Murdstone.

"Standby, Solar Flare." Ivan walked outside the bridge and un-holstered his Makarov pistol.

Bang!

Ivan missed.

Bang!

Ivan returned and transmitted. "Ningbo 9 midnight. Lights are secured. Ready to proceed inbound."

Ben studied his instruments in the Sharjah Blue WCC. "We have the Gray Lady on our scope. Be advised Gray Lady is also midnight. You are cleared to commence Operation BLINDSIDE II. Initial course two-seven-zero to Gray Lady."

"Commencing Operation BLINDSIDE II."

CHAPTER THIRTY-SEVEN

K elly pointed to MFD-3 as we circled overhead at thirty thousand feet. "Are you watching this?"

I leaned forward and adjusted the Gulfstream cockpit and instrument panel lighting. "Okay. This is Ningbo. This is the Lincoln. And this is the Sharjah Blue?"

Kelly smiled.

Amy kicked her feet up next to Chloe in the Gulfstream weapon bay and watched her scope. "I need popcorn to watch this."

Kelly laughed. "Wish I had a lawn chair."

Chloe keyed her ICS. "Kelly, is it really going to happen the way that it looks like it's going to happen?"

Kelly zoomed into the Ningbo 9. "It's doing fifteen knots. I don't think anything can stop it."

Amy called Gigi. "Overwatch, this is Shadow two-two."

Gigi replied from Proboscis. "Go ahead Shadow."

"Impact expected in one minute. Make sure you guys record this for the blooper reel."

Gigi smiled at Thomas and Casper. "Copy."

Bob transmitted from Stingray One. "Maintain radio silence until impact."

I van Smirnov called from the Ningbo 9. "Solar Flare, this is Bounty Hunter One. Impact with Gray Lady imminent. Accelerating through sixteen knots."

Ben smiled at Mr. Murdstone in the WCC. "Copy that Bounty Hunter. You're looking good."

Mr. Murdstone studied his scope. "Ben, their icon keeps jumping around. The Ningbo 9 appears on my screen here, then it moves to here. And then it moves back."

Ben looked at Mr. Murdstone's screen. "It's definitely having trouble tonight. Isn't it, Nuke? I'll have a PDS Tech Rep fly from Idaho to Singapore Changi International Airport tonight. Probably a linkage problem with PDS or NASA satellites. I'll tell Web. He's in Dubai."

Mr. Murdstone nodded. "Okay. The GPS is not *wrong*, it's simply *erratic*. Right?"

"We're good." Ben keyed his mic. "Ningbo, status?"

"Ten seconds from impact."

Ben Light looked at Mr. Murdstone. "Queen Bee ordered Operation BLINDSIDE II to happen on the darkest night of the year. The Lincoln bridge won't even see the Ningbo 9 coming. Is Abby a genius or what?"

The Sharjah Blue shipboard 1MC radio speaker energized with a frantic voice. "Turn them away! Turn them away!"

Ben called the bridge. "Who said that?"

"Abort! Abort!" Captain Farsi called the Weapon Control Center. "Turn the Supertanker away! They think we're Gray Lady!"

Mr. Murdstone looked at Ben Light. "What's Captain Farsi yelling about from the bridge!"

Ben shrugged. "Farsi's probably drunk."

Crunch!

Ben and Mr. Murdstone were knocked out of their seats onto the floor by the collision.

Squeel! Screech! Crunch! Squeel!

Captain Farsi sounded the Sharjah Blue GQ alarm. "General Quarters! General Quarters! Secure all watertight hatches and scuttles!"

A my watched with Chloe in the back of our Gulfstream. "Overwatch, this is Shadow. We have a visual on the impact."

Bob keyed his mic. "Casper, you're a genius. This concludes Operation ELECTRONIC SHELL GAME."

Chloe cheered into her ICS mic from our Gulfstream weapon bay. "We did it!"

Captain Smart watched from his captain's chair on the bridge with D'Andre and keyed his SATCOM button. "I'm glad we're back to normal on that GPS spoof. My sailors down in Combat Systems and were just beginning to take apart our CVN-72 computers to find the root cause of the GPS errors."

Gigi gasped. "Shadow, this is Overwatch. We have a problem."

Amy replied. "Shadow."

Thomas transmitted from Probosics. "It's not over yet."

Gigi keyed her mic and relayed Casper's analysis. "Apparently the Ningbo 9 bounced off. Standby. Yes. The Ningbo 9 bounced off and is now pointing at Gettysburg. They kept their speed. Impact in four minutes."

Captain Smart conferred with his OOD after the nearby collision and fireball. "OOD. Those two ships had a collision and one of them has trained its nose on us. Engines all ahead full."

The OOD replied. "Understood. All ahead full. Aye, aye, Captain."

D'Andre exited the Navigation shack to watch the Sharjah Blue evening fire.

The OOD pointed to the impact sight. "Captain, ship in distress. Shall we render assistance?"

Captain Smart pointed to the Ningbo 9 and quietly whispered to the OOD. "This supertanker was involved in the impact. It is now accelerating towards us. Do you concur, OOD?"

"Visual on inbound supertanker." The OOD studied the mysterious situation. "Concur, Captain."

"Do you concur with my decision to accelerate from this situation?"

"OOD concurs, Captain."

Ruby looked at her Mission Commander on their ESOC-1. "Now what, Bob?"

Bob jumped on the SATCOM radio. "This is Stingray One. The TSC crew on the tanker probably switched to inertial navigation to overcome Casper's GPS spoof."

Burner checked his young Hornet wingman in position. "307, this is 304."

Tater studiously maintained rock-solid bearing and distance on her night Super Hornet lead with rapid power, aileron, and elevator adjustments. "307."

"307, disable exterior lights. Go Master Arm HOT on your MEDWEAP."

Tater complied. "307."

Burner called Bob. "Stingray One, this is Dambuster flight of two. Request clearance to commence Operation BROKEN BRIDGE."

Bob accelerated ESOC-1.

Charlotte, driving ESOC-2, matched Bob's power addition to stay in night formation.

Bob keyed his mic. "All HICSON assets, this is Stingray One. Commence Operation BROKEN BRIDGE."

. . .

D'Andre woke up on the floor of the bridge and looked around. "Captain? Gator?" He stood up and saw ten bodies on the floor. "OOD!"

He quickly ran to the telephone to call DC Central.

"Good evening, this is DC Central, how may I help you Sir or Ma'am?"

"This is Petty Officer Jordan on the bridge. I work in Navigation. The Captain, Gator and the OOD were all knocked out. Everyone on the bridge is on the deck except me. Recommend General Quarters and request medical and backup OOD's to the bridge to drive the ship!"

"DCA copies all."

The USS Abraham Lincoln 1MC sounded the alarm from DC Central. "General Quarters. General Quarters. All hands man your battle stations."

D'Andre dialed the assistant Navigator stateroom as GQ sounded. "Lieutenant Commander Halsey?"

"Speaking."

"This is Jordan, Sir. Gator, Captain and the OOD are down. Request your immediate presence on the bridge."

"On my way, Jordan."

Click!

I van Smirnov ran to the Ningbo 9 bridge, saw the TSC Tactical Victim Unit laying on the deck, and took over the helm.

"Solar Flare, this is Bounty Hunter One."

Ben keyed his radio. "Go, Bounty Hunter One."

"The TSC bridge team is down. I am taking over visually and continuing BLINDSIDE II on my own. Repeat, all TSC crew members are down."

Ivan utilized his night vision goggles and drove towards the Lincoln.

"Bounty Hunter One, our ship is compromised and badly damaged. Nuke and I took out the Lincoln bridge. You will have one chance as they pass you. Lincoln speed twenty-nine and accelerating."

Ivan checked the Ningbo 9 heading. "Say Lincoln course."

Ben studied his degraded equipment. "Zero-nine-zero."

The Russian oligarch studied his gauges, pointed the commandeered supertanker directly south and gambled on a successful T-bone impact heading. "Solar flare, Lincoln in sight, I have one chance at this."

Ben and Mr. Murdstone ran from watertight hatch to hatch, scuttle to scuttle to salvage the Sharjah Blue and secure flooding. "Copy all!"

Ivan continued forward and suddenly collapsed.

"The Ningbo 9 bridge straggler is down!" The Super Hornets, Airbus H225, Navy SH-60 and ESOC Riverines discontinued their MEDWEAP attacks.

Amy watched from our Gulfstream and disengaged her MEDWEAP attack. "Concur. Bridge Straggler is down. Ningbo 9 heading one-six-zero. Speed, thirteen knots. Distance from Lincoln, three thousand feet."

Casper, Thomas and Gigi studied the potential impact. Casper typed into his phone recommended instructions for Gigi.

"Gettysburg, this is Overwatch. Check your nine o'clock. Recommend turn south to avoid Ningbo 9."

D'Andre heard the SATCOM call and checked his port side. "LCDR Halsey, tanker at ten o'clock! That tanker already had a collision with that middle eastern yacht."

The Assistant Navigator took evasive action and quickly spun the ship's rudders for a right turn. "Damn. This turn will be slow. And our port tail is going to kick out."

Bob studied the collision profile. "Overwatch, this is Stingray One. Boarding the Ningbo 9 to steer away from Gettysburg."

"Copy!"

Bob and Jack launched a cable up to the Ningbo 9 and boarded with an electric winch. "Ruby, stay alongside! Don't crash! We'll come down this same cable in a few minutes!"

Solo on ESOC-1, Ruby nodded nervously in the choppy, no-moon South China Sea. "Copy. Don't crash, he says."

Amy watched her scope from our Gulfstream. "Careful Bob and Jack. That straggler stood up and exited the bridge. Whereabouts unknown."

Bob looked around the dark, abandoned deck of the Chinese supertanker with Jack and transmitted. "Proceeding to the bridge."

Omar kicked the Sharjah Blue bridge door open.
Wham!

"The Americans damaged my yacht, my precious yacht. Follow the Lincoln. Sink the Lincoln."

Captain Farsi continued the crippled, luxury yacht homebound to the southwest. "Ivan is on the Ningbo 9 steering towards the Lincoln. Ivan will sink the Lincoln."

Omar ran to the controls. "Heading two-three zero? Negative! Turn zero-eight-zero! Chase the Lincoln! Sink the Lincoln!"

The Iranian ship captain challenged the Dubai oil tycoon's son. "Our ship is damaged and taking on water, Mr. Muscat. We need to keep her afloat and proceed home to your father."

Omar screamed and spun the steering wheel to the left. "Negative! We have a four-billion-dollar, nuclear-powered weapon onboard the Sharjah Blue! We will use it the weapon! We will burn a hole in the American carrier!"

Captain Farsi complied with the order and called Ben. "Weapon Control Center, this is the bridge."

"Go ahead."

"Ben, do we have operable weapons?"

Ben and Mr. Murdstone examined the system. "Degraded but operable, Captain."

The yacht violently listed to the starboard.

"You will notice that we are turning east to follow the Lincoln. We will follow the Lincoln, and sink the Lincoln with our nuclear-powered MEDWEAP."

Ben looked at Mr. Murdstone and called the captain. "We're slowly sinking."

Captain Farsi looked at Omar Muscat attempt to steer the yacht. "Those are the orders."

"Whose orders?"

"Mr. Omar Muscat's orders."

"Copy." Ben energized the nuclear-powered QUAD-Capacitors to prepare for attack. "I'll need a few minutes to bring the weapon system online."

B ob kicked the Ningbo 9 bridge door open and cleared the area. "Jack! Steer to the right!"

Jack ran to the controls and spun the large ship's steering wheel. "How to I chop power?"

Bob ran to the throttle control system and pulled the levers.

"Are we going to hit?"

"Not sure. We're merely passengers, now. We've done all we can."

The Ningbo 9 gradually steered right as the Lincoln accelerated in a starboard turn.

Jack began to smile. "We're going to miss it. We're going to miss it to the right!"

Bob watched the supertanker nose miss the aircraft carrier's stern by three hundred feet. "We did it." Bob confirmed zero thrust on the Ningbo 9. "Ruby, returning to ESOC-1 in two minutes."

No response.

"Ruby?"

"Damn." Bob Bonner looked at Jack Kernan. "Let's run!"

CHAPTER THIRTY-EIGHT

D'Andre picked up Captain Smart's SATCOM radio as LCDR Halsey redistributed the bridge duties among the replacement personnel. "Shadow two-two, this is Gettysburg."

I looked at Kelly. "That's DJ's voice."

"Go ahead Gettysburg," Kelly replied.

D'Andre looked out the bridge windows into the zero illumination, moonless night. "We're taking on water on our aft, starboard side. Is anything happening that we need to know about?"

Amy called us on ICS. "I see it." She keyed her SATCOM radio. "Gettysburg, there is a linear heat signature coming from the Sharjah Blue. Standby."

Amy and Chloe studied the scopes.

Kelly keyed her ICS. "What else, Amy?"

"Gettysburg, the Sharjah Blue is now following your ship. It's doing forty-five knots. This might be an error. Overwatch? Are you watching this?"

Gigi replied from Proboscis Island. "A-firm. Casper said the yacht is it's nuclear-powered. The speed is accurate. They're intentionally burning a hole in your starboard side at the waterline."

Burner called from his Super Hornet. "Let's light up the Sharjah Blue. 304 and 307 engaging."

Amy agreed. "Shadow two-two engaging."

Lurch nodded at Brianna and fired at the Sharjah Blue bridge from the Airbus H225 Super Puma.

Brianna made the call. "Harbor Watch, engaging."

HIRF called from his Navy Seahawk as Spooner fired his MEDWEAP. "Channel Guard, engaging."

Captain Farsi was immediately knocked down.

Amy confirmed partial success. "There was one person in the bridge. He's now horizontal. But the heat signature remains fixed on the Lincoln."

B ob and Jack ran aft on the supertanker deck and reached the tactical cable and winch. They yelled down to their ESOC-1 teammate. "Ruby!"

No response.

"I don't see the boat." Jack yelled. "Ruby Kyle!"

Bob keyed his SATCOM radio. "Ruby come in!"

Amy called from our Gulfstream high up above the South China Sea darkness. "Oh, God. Bob, we saw ESOC-1 drive away. We figured you were in it. ESOC-1 is approaching the Sharjah Blue and appears to have one passenger. It's not Ruby. The occupant strangely has zero Imaging Probes. Similar to a Project. But the person's *not* one of us."

Bob looked around. "Damn. Then we lost Ruby."

"Ruby!" Jack yelled into the dark sea. "Ruby!"

Brianna called Bob from the Airbus H225. "Stingray One, Harbor Watch. We found Ruby. Picking her up now."

"Hang on, Bob." Lurch initiated a hover over Ruby. "We'll swing by to pick you both up in three minutes."

"Copy. Lurch, there is a helicopter landing pad aft on the Ningbo 9. We'll meet you there."

Bob looked at Jack. "Ideas?"

Jack nodded. "We join Vic, Aaron and Charlie on ESOC-2. We board the Sharjah Blue. We disable the weapon. We save the Lincoln."

Bob smiled. "Sounds easy. Doesn't it?"

Jack shrugged. "We have to try."

"Concur." Bob nodded as the Airbus H225 Super Puma approached the landing pad. "Overwatch, is the Lincoln still under attack?"

Gigi replied. "A-firm."

D'Andre keyed his mic from the bridge. "We're taking on more water. The repair locker teams are starting to fall behind."

Bob watched the Super Puma land on the Ningbo 9. "You're right, Jack. We have to try."

Jack and Bob jumped inside the cabin.

Bob looked at Ruby, who was thoroughly drenched. "How's the water?"

"Dark and scary." Ruby smiled and towel-dried her face. "I lost the ESOC. A

Russian gentleman came down the line and made me jump. He kindly let me inflate first at gunpoint."

"A Russian?"

Ruby nodded.

Lurch pointed the Airbus nose towards ESOC-2 and accelerated.

Jack looked at Ruby. "You good?"

"Lots of stars. Zero moon. I like swimming. But that was just too lonely. Too scary."

Jack crawled over to hug Ruby. "Glad you're okay."

Bob looked at Ruby. "Ready for more?"

"More what?"

"More action. The Lincoln is still under attack."

Ruby Kyle took a drink from her water bottle and towel-dried her hair. "Sure. Why not? I'm ready."

"Harbor Watch, this is Overwatch."

Lurch hovered over ESOC-2 as Ruby, Jack, and Bob were lowered onto the boat by Brianna out the starboard-side helicopter cabin door.

"Go ahead."

"The solo rider is back onboard the Sharjah Blue. ESOC-1 was abandoned. The attack on the Lincoln continues."

Lurch looked below after the quick offload. "ESOC-2 now has six operators and is speeding up the wake of the Sharjah Blue."

I keyed my Gulfstream ICS. "Amy and Chloe, you're both still lighting up the Sharjah Blue, right? ESOC-2 is about to board."

"We're trying. It just keeps firing, though," Amy said.

I looked at our altitude as ESOC-2 closed in on the weaponized yacht. "Kelly, should we get lower to increase our effectiveness?"

Kelly didn't answer.

"Kelly, check your toggle, I didn't hear you." I looked at Kelly's face in the dark cockpit. "Kelly?"

"Amy and Chloe! Kelly's knocked out."

Chloe tried to call her on ICS. "Kelly? Can you hear me?"

I studied the autopilot and took control of the orbiting airplane and mumbled to myself. "Okay. Twenty thousand feet. Two hundred knots indicated airspeed. Shallow left turn. Hold what you got. Nice and easy."

Chloe poked her head in the cockpit and tended to Kelly. "Kelly Girl. Wake up."

No response.

"She's out, Gracie." Chloe checked her pulse. "Only knocked out. She's breathing and has a pulse."

I called Overwatch. "Gigi, Kelly's knocked out. We're going to continue this flight. At least for a while."

"Gracie." Lurch called me on SATCOM. "You can fly. Right?"

"I got this. I can do it."

"Call me if you need me. Just orbit while your backend keeps firing. Nothing fancy."

I wasn't ready for a solo flight. Not at night. Not out to sea. Not even close. "Thanks, Lurch."

Chloe tapped my shoulder. "Are you okay?"

I looked at Kelly, reclined her Gulfstream pilot seat and nodded. "I can do this. Get back there with Amy. Save the Lincoln."

"Overwatch, this is 307."

"Go ahead, 307," Gigi replied.

Mercedes took a loose cruise position behind Burner's F/A-18E. "Burner's knocked out. He's in a descending, shallow left turn."

Gigi looked at Casper and Thomas. "We're not sure what to do, Tater."

Mercedes tried to call her lead. "Burner, this is Tater. Radio check."

No response.

"304, this is 307."

HIRF attempted comms. "Dambuster 304, this is Lightning 615, over."

No response.

Mercedes mumbled to herself. "Thump him."

"Overwatch, 307, I'm going to try to thump Burner."

Amy keyed her ICS. "She's going to what?"

Chloe slapped her knee. "Amy!"

HIRF called Mercedes. "Tater, it's dark. Do not pull up until your exhaust stacks are *well clear* of his nose cone. Copy?"

"Copy."

Mercedes crossed under his jet, added power, and stayed ten feet below his fuselage. She jammed both PCL's into afterburner, cleared his nose cone, and hand-fistedly pulled up and through his flight path.

Burner woke up and keyed his mic. "What —"

"Burner, this is Tater. Say status."

"What are the —"

Mercedes regained starboard parade position. "304. Say status."

"Vision. Can't see —"

"Burner. Listen. Look at your HUD. Pull nose up. Level your wings. Put your velocity vector on the horizon. Nice and easy."

"Can't see."

"Ok, buddy. Five pounds backstick on now. Stop backstick."

Burner transmitted. "It hurts. Head hurts."

"Little more backstick, Burner."

Burner complied.

"Hold it there."

Burner achieved stabilized, straight and level flight. "Still hurts."

Mercedes spoke calmly. "Now reduce power."

Burner complied and Mercedes reduced accordingly to stay in loose cruise.

"Good. I'm showing us ten miles south of mom. Angels six. Two hundred and twenty knots. Reset your power one inch forward."

Burner complied.

"How are you feeling, now, Burner?"

Burner paused then keyed his mic. "Can't see —"

Mercedes gave Burner ten more seconds to regain consciousness. "Burner, what's six times eight?"

No response.

"Burner?"

"Twenty-seven."

HIRF called Mercedes. "Tater, say POSIT."

Mercedes looked at her Lincoln TACAN. "We're on mom's two-four-zero at nine. Angels six. Are you nearby?"

HIRF keyed his mic. "Spooner and I are in Starboard Delta."

No response.

Mercedes analyzed the situation. "Dambuster rep, this is Tater in 307."

"Tater, this is Gordo in CATCC. I've been listening. Either Burner bingos to Hong Kong International or he ejects. Skipper said no shipboard landing."

Mercedes maintained parade position on her lead. "Burner, you copy?"

Burner double-clicked.

"Burner, Hong Kong is north up the harbor. Do you think you can take a field landing with no cables?"

"Not really." Burner paused. "I think I'm toast. Getting darker. Can't see or think, Tater."

"Do you want to punch?"

Burner double-clicked.

Mercedes spoke softly and took a cut away from him. "Burner, reduce power. Sit up nice and straight, buddy. Put your head way back. Okay good. I'm showing one-seventy. Keep those arms in. No flailing. I'm backing off. I'm with you, buddy. You do what you have to do."

Bang!

The ejection lit up Tater's plane like the fourth of July. Burner's rocket seat went up the rails. Two seconds later, Burner was hanging from the straps.

"HIRF! Burner punched out! 304 has ejected!"

Spooner took the Seahawk radios. "We've got his seat pan beacon on our scope. Proceeding inbound for water rescue."

C harlotte sped westbound from the Sharjah Blue. "Overwatch, Stingray Two." Gigi checked her scope. "Go ahead."

"Five operators have boarded Sharjah Blue. Alpha, Bravo, Juliet, Romeo, and Victor are onboard the Sharjah Blue."

"Copy. Say intentions."

Charlotte looked around the pitch-black South China Sea. "I'm turned back towards Hong Kong on the ship's wake and —"

Gigi looked at Thomas. "Did she stop transmitting?"

Thomas nodded. "Try her again."

"Charlie? You good?"

"It's really dark. Can you guys keep an eye on me?"

Thomas keyed the mic from Proboscis Island. "Charlie, we got eyes on you from satellite. You're clear to cut engines right there and wait."

Chloe keyed her mic from Shadow. "Hey big sister, Amy and I are watching you. We'll let you know if you have any company."

"Okay." Charlotte slowed the ESOC. "I'll be on the radios. I'll wait for them. Cutting engines to idle."

"Charlotte, this is Grace. Sit tight. We're watching you like a hawk."

"Thanks, Gracie."

T he Navy Rescue Swimmer pulled Burner into the SH-60 Seahawk. "Flight, Aft. We are good. Package is aboard."

HIRF didn't respond.

Petty Officer Washington keyed his ICS. "Flight, Aft. You copy?"

"HIRF, you good?" Spooner looked at his pilot. "Aft, Flight. HIRF is hard down. This is Spooner. I have the controls. Departing rescue scene with Burner onboard."

Spooner drove towards the aircraft carrier. "Lincoln Marshall, this is Lightning

615. We have one package on board. One Lightning pilot unconscious. Declaring emergency. We're on mom's two-one-zero at twelve miles."

"615, Marshall. Say needles."

"Fly up, fly right."

"Concur. Radar contact. Fly Bullseye. Expect a ready deck. Switch tower."

Spooner replied. "Switching."

Brianna looked at Lurch. "Sounds like HIRF is down but Spooner's heading to the Lincoln with Burner."

"615, Lincoln Tower, winds are twenty-one knots, right down the angle. Deck has a two-degree starboard list. Deck is steady. You are cleared to land Spot Four."

No response.

Lurch listened carefully. "Bree, I'm going to fly towards the carrier. Just in case."

"615, Tower."

No response.

Captain Smart wearily got on the radios while being medically treated. "615, this is Charlie Oscar. Are you experiencing difficulties?"

The CVN-72 Commanding Officer called the HS-14 Lightning Skipper. "Goober, are you listening to tower?"

"Affirmative, Sir. 614 is hard down for Reduction Gear Box. My only up bird is 612 down in the barn."

"Damn. Copy that, Goober."

Crash!

Spooner lost control of the SH-60 and splashed into the South China Sea. The Navy Rescue Swimmer's training kicked in. Washington waited until the motion stopped, grabbed a reference point in the cold, dark water, and unbuckled his harness. After clearing his cabin door in the dark, lifeless water, he pulled Burner from the wreckage.

Burner coughed up saltwater and yelled. "I'm good! Get HIRF! Get Spooner!"

The rescue swimmer stuck the HEEDS bottle in his mouth, kicked his feet up in the air, pulled HIRF through his ditching hatch and surfaced. "Burner, take HIRF."

Washington discarded his spent HEEDS bottle, took a breath, and dove again. He found Spooner wrapped in cords. The swimmer unsheathed a large knife from his outer calf and cut cords until Spooner cleared the sinking Seahawk.

I watched our Gulfstream scope from twenty-thousand feet. "Four heads floating in the water."

Amy watched. "Should we call them?"

Chloe shook her head. "Not during the rescue."

Washington reached down and pulled HIRF and Spooner's lanyards to inflate their vests. "Burner, you good?"

"Two crashes." Burner nodded, coughed and bobbed in the swells. "That sucked."

Lurch switched frequencies. "Lincoln Airboss, this is Harbor Watch."

"Harbor Watch, Airboss. Go ahead."

"Sir, we are an Airbus H225 Super Puma rigged for rescues. Request permission to rescue the four swimmers in your airspace."

"Air Boss." Captain Smart quickly called down to the tower from the bridge. "They're friendlies. Pilot was a SEAL in his previous life."

"Harbor Watch, Air Boss. We are currently Sea SAR-limited and we thank you. You are cleared to enter our airspace and rescue our four swimmers."

Lurch sped inbound. "Harbor Watch is inbound. Swimmers in sight."

CHAPTER THIRTY-NINE

Bob Bonner led the team of five operators around a corner, heard footsteps and whispered. "Weapons set to EMP."

A TSC Peacekeeper patrolling the Sharjah Blue mindlessly approached and raised his hands. "Don't shoot."

Aaron recognized the uniformed Officer and lowered his MEDWEAP towards the deck. "Tony Murdstone?"

Bob looked at Aaron. "You know this guy?"

Ruby looked at Tony. "We all do."

Jack lowered his MEDWEAP. "His dad is upper level TSC."

Vic kept her MEDWEAP trained on Tony's chest. "Bob, we need to keep moving. What should we do?"

Bob pointed at his watch and nudged Aaron's shoulder. "We don't have time for prisoners."

"Follow me." Tony pointed to a vacant guest lounge. "Hurry."

Bob and Vic kept their weapons pointed at the 2020 Peaksville High School graduate and followed him into the luxurious lounge.

Bob looked at Tony. "Why shouldn't we waste you right now."

"The text messages. I sent them from Charlie and Gracie's phones."

"Prove it." Vic lowered her MEDWEAP. "What did the messages say?"

Tony shrugged. "I sent a simple code. Lincoln. Sharjah. Ningbo 9. And the planned impact LAT LONG. Don't kill me. Aaron, you know I'm good."

Ruby got closer to Tony. "How did you get their phones?"

"I shot the TSC Peacekeeper before he could execute them. Don't you believe me?"

Jack nodded. "He's telling the truth, Bob."

Aaron nodded. "Concur."

Ruby hugged Tony. "You saved my friends. That makes *you* my friend."

Bob checked the passageway outside. "The Sharjah Blue is burning a hole in the Lincoln's hull. How do we get to the Bridge? And how do we stop the Weapon?"

"Bridge is up four levels to O-7 then forward. The Weapon Control Center is down two levels on the O-1 level. It's roughly mid-ship. About frame one-hundred. Look for WCC signs in the Blue Tile area. My dad is in the WCC. Don't kill him. Also, you'll see Ben Light there."

Vic looked at her watch. "Other threats?"

"The Russian. Old KGB Oligarch. Ivan Smirnov. He's older than dirt. And like dirt, he doesn't ever really die, so be careful."

Ruby nodded. "The Russian made me go night swimming after he stole my boat."

"Sounds like Ivan. He was on the Ningbo mission."

Bob looked down the passageway. "Let's do this."

Ruby hugged the Peaksville alum again. "Thanks, Tony."

Captain Smart called DC Central from the Lincoln bridge. "DCA, Captain. Damage report."

"Sir, we have dozens of burned sailors. Every time we come close to shoring the holes, another hole appears. We are taking on water between frames one-eight-zero and two-two-zero. It's contained for now. What's going on outside?"

Captain Smart looked at the Chief Engineer who just entered the bridge. "DCA, Captain. CHENG just got on the bridge. Keep shoring up the flooding. You'll get a full debrief from CHENG. Keep up the great work, Shipmate!"

The Chief Engineer approached Captain Smart. "Captain, we can't continue to stay afloat if this continues. What *exactly* is happening?"

Captain Smart pointed outside into the darkness. "What do you see?"

Chief Engineer looked around the crippled aircraft carrier. "Nothing."

"Welcome to 2027, CHENG. What you are *not* seeing with your human eyes is the future of warfare. Just go take care of your sailors. Make sure they are getting medical attention."

The Chief Engineer exited the bridge. "Aye, aye, Captain."

. . .

B ob quickly led the five operators to the bridge and looked inside. "It's clear."
Vic observed the path ahead of the Sharjah Blue and studied the radar scope. "There's the Lincoln at six miles. You can just make out the red hot, melting metal on the hull. We're matching its speed."

Aaron nodded. "Gettysburg is getting hit bad. How do we steer this thing?"

Jack ran to the helm. "I already did this tonight on the Ningbo 9." He quickly spun the wheel clockwise.

The yacht began to list as it achieved a high-speed right turn.

Ruby watched the heading. "Zero-nine-zero. Okay there is zero-nine-five. It's working."

Ben called Ivan from the Weapon Control Center on a walkie-talkie. "Ivan, something's happening."

"I've got it!" Ivan mobilized up and forward.

Bob looked around. "We need this ship to turn to the southwest. A final course of two-three-zero will build separation and put the Sharjah Blue over the horizon and out of firing range. We *also* need to disable the weapon."

Vic nodded. "Ruby, Aaron and I will monitor the turn on the bridge towards the southwest. You and Jack find and destroy the WCC."

Jack looked at Bob. "Blue tile area on the O-1 level, mid-ship."

Bob agreed. "Let's go."

B rianna operated the winch, pulled up Petty Officer Washington first and yelled over the rotor noise. "Can you pull yourself in?"

The Navy Rescue Swimmer nodded and swung inside the new Airbus H225. "Do you know what you're doing?"

Brianna shook her head. "No clue!"

Petty Officer Washington secured Brianna via a gunner's belt and studied the Airbus hoisting system. "Okay, Ma'am. I got it from here!"

Washington expertly rescued Burner, Spooner, and HIRF as Brianna watched. He carefully strapped them into the helicopter.

HIRF and Spooner were out cold.

Burner was barely coherent after two dips in the South China Sea.

Washington yelled to Lurch. "Are you taking us to the carrier?"

Lurch was slouched forward in his seat as the Airbus automatically hovered in place. "Flight, Aft! Are you okay?"

Washington yelled to Brianna. "He's knocked out. That's what happened to my pilots."

Brianna pulled Washington closer to yell into his white Navy Helmet. "Can you fly?"

Washington shrugged. "No, can you?"

"No!" Brianna jumped into the co-pilot seat. "Overwatch, this is Harbor Watch. Lurch is out cold. We rescued four Navy swimmers but Lurch is down. We're in an automatic hover. We're so low. There is sea spray. What do I do?"

I monitored my scope as we orbited in the Gulfstream and spoke with Chloe and Amy on ICS. "Bree's at fifty feet. If she messes up, she's going in the water with six people."

Amy watched. "Lurch, this is Shadow two-two. Radio check."

Lurch was unconscious.

Washington poked his head in the cockpit and yelled to Brianna. "You're really not a pilot?"

Brianna tried to smile. "No! My husband is a mechanic in VFA-195. Antoine Jordan, do you know him?"

"I know AJ!" Washington yelled over the night rotor noise as he dripped gallons of water onto the new Airbus floor. "I've seen you at Popeye's with him. What are you doing in this fancy helicopter?"

"Long story. Don't you have three Navy pilots back there in the cabin with you? Are they *all* knocked out?"

"Let me check!" Washington walked to the back of the Super Puma.

Burner walked to the cockpit. "What's going on?"

Brianna yelled and pointed at Lurch. "He's passed out. We're in an automatic hover. Are you a pilot?"

"I'm a *Hornet* pilot!"

Bree yelled from the cockpit into the doorway. "I'm a *nothing* pilot!"

"Damn." Burner looked at the helicopter cockpit on the no-moon, 0% illumination-night. "Keep it steady!"

Brianna yelled. "It's hovering automatically. I'm not touching it."

"That's right. You said that. Where's the automatic pilot?"

Brianna shrugged and pointed to the lower console. "That's the *area* for the autopilot."

Burner sighed. "Unstrap your harness! Ready to trade spots?"

Brianna nodded.

"Now!"

Burner helped Brianna out and slid his feet onto the rudder pedals and looked at the altimeter. "Fifty feet, Lurch! I need you! Wake up!"

No response.

"Damn. Looks like I'm logging some helicopter night time." Burner, soaking wet and wearing his automatically inflated SV-2 float coat, placed his hands on the controls and immediately realized that his F/A-18E training, habits, and techniques were counterintuitive to flying helicopters.

Brianna sat between Lurch and Burner. "Can you figure it out!"

Burner shrugged and continued to study the cockpit. "I hope so!"

President Walker waited for Mr. Light to answer his cell phone. "Bud?"

"Yes, Ma'am."

"Where are you?"

"Hong Kong Marriott."

"You need to get out to the Sharjah Blue right now, it sustained serious damage. Your TSC Tactical Victim Unit apparently rammed the Sharjah Blue instead of the Lincoln."

Mr. Light dropped his jaw. "No."

"Yes. The TSC H-53 has departed the area towards a different strategic target. I've arranged different transportation for you. Your hotel has a landing pad on the roof. Be up there five minutes ago. A Bell Jet Ranger is waiting for you."

"On my way, Mrs. President."

Captain Smart drearily sat in his chair with his Motorola walkie-talkie as the Ship's Senior Medical Officer finished tending to him. "CHENG! Damage report update!"

The Chief Engineer replied. "Multiple additional breaches. Largest waterline breach is four feet in diameter."

"How are we doing?"

"My repair locker teams are kicking butt, Sir. Lots of practice shoring up the hull in the last few weeks. But we're still getting hit! This is unprecedented."

Captain Smart leaned back in his chair. "Thanks CHENG!"

The Senior Medical Officer continued to monitor Captain Smart's heart using a mobile EKG monitor. "Improving, Captain. Still dizzy?"

"SMO, you're a lifesaver. Literally."

"Call me if you feel nauseous or faint, Captain."

The Captain patted the SMO on the back. "Tell me about the injuries you are seeing down on the water line."

"Lots of burns, Captain. Bad burns. They don't teach this stuff in Med School."

"They don't teach stuff this at Boat School in Annapolis, either." Captain Smart looked into the dark nothingness of the South China Sea. "Thanks, SMO. Go make sure the sailors are well taken care of."

. . .

"Lincoln Airboss, this is Burner from 307. I'm learning how to fly this Airbus. HIRF, Spooner and the original Airbus pilot are knocked out. Washington is also in the back with a civilian."

The Lincoln Airboss keyed his mic. "Burner, understand *you* are piloting the helicopter?"

"A-firm, Sir. I exited the hover and climbed to one thousand feet."

"Good. Stay up there for now." The Airboss looked at his HS-14 lineman standing by to assist with the night recovery onto Spot Four. "Say intentions."

Brianna pointed at Hong Kong on the MFD.

Burner struggled to learn the controls. "I've got Hong Kong International NAVAID's dialed in. A night carrier landing is unwise, since this is my first ever helicopter flight. Do you concur?"

Airboss keyed the mic. "Concur. You need a nice long runway. Call us when you're safe on deck. Be careful, Burner. You can do this."

Captain Smart called from the bridge. "Burner, this is Gettysburg."

Burner cruised northbound at one thousand feet. "Go ahead, Sir."

"Practice landings at altitude before you descend for your actual landing. Practice slow flight. Practice waveoffs. Practice hovering. All *above* three thousand feet. Just like Pensacola Flight Training. Burn some gas. Learn how to fly that Airbus *before* you set up on final approach."

Burner studied his controls and gauges and continued his climb towards three thousand. "WILCO, Sir. Good call."

Bob looked at Jack. "Blue tiles. WCC. O-1 level. This must be the place."

Jack nodded. "Concur."

Bob held two EMP grenades in his hand. "Ready, Jack?"

"I'll kick it open. You toss the EMP's."

Bob nodded. "One. Two. Three!"

Jack kicked and yelled. "Muay Thai!"

Wham!

Bob set the EMP grenades and rolled them into the Weapon Control Center.

Mr. Murdstone dove away from the grenades, Ben Light opened fire with a handgun towards the doorway.

Bob shut the door to keep the EMP's from being volleyed back into the hallway.

Bang! Bang!

"That should work, Jack. Let's go to the bridge. We stopped our right turn. That's not necessarily a good thing."

Jack followed Bob to the bridge.

Suddenly, their MEDWEAP's were nearly simultaneously kicked from their hands by the old Russian.

Wham!

Ivan knocked Bob down with an elbow and fought with Jack Kernan.

Jack entered his Muay Thai stance and proceeded to unleash multiple high, spinning kicks at Ivan.

Wham! Wham! Wham!

"Thailand. Probably Phuket or Phattaya." Ivan struck Jack in the face. "But definitely not Bangkok. Correct, thin one?"

Bob stood up and joined the fight.

"Military trained." Ivan laughed and fought Bob. "Tattoo from the Philippine Islands. Are you a Navy SEAL, large one?"

The two-on-one fight continued.

Bob smiled as he wrestled with the old Russian. "Krav Maga."

The two untangled quickly as Ivan pulled a handgun. "You recognize this weapon, Navy SEAL?"

Bob nodded and raised his hands. "Makarov." Bob rapidly slammed the Makarov from Ivan's hand, ejected the magazine, cleared the bullet in the chamber, and threw the old Russian weapon. "Let's go."

"Not yet." Jack retrieved their MEDWEAP's. "Okay, let's go."

Bob and Jack ran forward towards the bridge and abandoned the fight.

"Large one! Thin one!" Ivan Smirnov yelled. "You won't find them, my Fight Club friends!"

"Lincoln Marshall, Dambuster 307."

"Go ahead 307."

"Marshall, 307. Checkin' in on your two-two-zero at thirty. Level at Angels seven."

"307, Marshall. Descend to Angels six. Marshall radial two-five-zero. Expected BRC zero-seven-zero. Say fuel state."

No response.

"307, say fuel state."

Tater mumbled into her mic. "I'm —"

"307, Marshall, say again your last. Broken and unreadable."

No response.

"307, Lincoln Marshall. Radio check."

"Declaring emergency —"

The young petty officer on the aircraft carrier inquired for more details. "Say nature of emergency, 307."

"My vision. My consciousness. I'm fading —"

The Air Ops petty officer clicked the microphone then unclicked.

The CVN-72 Air Operations Officer keyed the microphone. "Tater, confirm fading level of consciousness."

Mercedes pulled her power levers and decelerated her jet. "Sir, I'm —"

The Air Ops Officer spoke in a calm voice. "307, I'm showing you level at Angels six and four hundred knots, Tater. Give me a power reduction. Level your wings."

"Yes, Sir."

The jet slowed below two-hundred knots.

"Okay, now reset your power levers up to sixty-five percent. Can you see your HUD velocity vector?"

Mercedes advanced her power levers a bit. "Dizzy —"

The Air Operations Officer yelled into group of junior pilots. "Dambuster Rep!"

"Here, Sir."

The ship's company Air Ops Officer whispered. "I can't order Tater to eject. Can you speak with her?"

The VFA-195 Skipper quickly entered CATCC. "Air Ops, what's up with Tater?"

"She's losing consciousness. I recommend ejection before she's totally gone. I just can't order it."

The Skipper grabbed a transmitter. "Tater, this is Skipper."

No response.

"307, how copy!"

Mercedes clicked her mic for four seconds and breathed into the mic.

"Tater!"

"It hurts, Skipper. Need to punch —" Mercedes unclicked the microphone for three seconds. "Can't see —"

"Tater, Sit up straight!"

"Okay."

"Are you in position?"

Tater double-clicked.

"You're below two hundred knots. I want you to eject. You're 'feet wet.' We'll coordinate a water rescue. Sit up straight."

No response.

"Tater! Eject, eject, eject!"

CHAPTER FORTY

"*Zoom!*"

Madison listened from the bow of the Ben Gunn. "Ryan, look up!"

Li Jie observed the light show in the night sky. "What is that?"

"Is that a shooting star?" Madison asked.

Ryan watched. "A shooting star named Mercedes." Ryan keyed his SATCOM handheld. "Dambuster, this is Amber Jack One. How copy?"

No reply.

"Tater, double-click if you can hear me."

"You're right, Ryan." Madison watched. "That was an ejection. That was Tater."

Ryan added power and drove in her direction. "Overwatch, Amber Jack One. Did our second Super Hornet eject?"

Gigi looked at her scope. "We can't see her anymore on our satellite."

Captain Smart keyed his SATCOM handheld. "Amber Jack, this is Gettysburg. Air Ops is reporting a controlled ejection from CATCC."

I watched MFD-3. "This is Shadow. We see her floating down. Ryan, you're roughly heading her way."

Amy called Ryan. "Say heading, Ryan."

"One-three-five."

Amy studied the intercept. "Ryan, turn right thirty degrees to one-six-five. You're about two miles away. She's descending through one thousand feet."

Ryan added more power. "Right thirty degrees. Looking."

Madison and Li Jie energized strong flashlights. "We'll take the bow! Looking, Ryan!"

"Yell if you see her, Maddie!"

"Okay!"

G igi called us in the Gulfstream from Proboscis Island. "Shadow two-two, Overwatch."

Amy keyed the mic. "Go!"

"Do you see the low, slow rider at five-hundred feet approaching the Sharjah Blue?"

"A-firm."

"It's a helicopter squawking the MEDEVAC code on the transponder. It originated from Hong Kong downtown."

Amy prepared her MEDWEAP from our Gulfstream. "Do you want me to light up the pilot?"

Gigi paused. "Casper said negative. Possible MEDEVAC."

Chloe keyed her microphone. "We all know it's a trick. Let's splash that sucker."

Gigi carefully watched the scope with Thomas and Casper. "It just landed. Someone got out. It's lifting off."

Gus Bryant keyed his SATCOM microphone from the Capitol. "Shadow two-two, you have a green light to splash the helicopter. Consider *all* Sharjah Blue traffic hostile."

"Shadow two-two, engaging."

Amy and Chloe directed our powerful MEDWEAP from our Gulfstream 650 ER at the pilot during liftoff from the Sharjah Blue. "Helicopter is down. Repeat. Syndicate helicopter is down."

Gigi keyed her mic. "Overwatch copies."

T he USS Abraham Lincoln Chief Engineer ran to the bridge. "Captain! The attack has stopped. Our sailors are containing the flooding. Recommend Hong Kong Harbor to receive maintenance support."

Captain Smart evaluated the situation. "CHENG?"

"Yes, Captain."

"Ever watch *Groundhog Day*?"

The Chief Engineer smiled. "Yes, Captain."

"Hong Kong Harbor appears to be hostile and dangerously repetitive. Do you concur?"

CHENG nodded.

"Are your Engineering Department and DC Repair Locker sailors able to get us home to Yokosuka? Or at least around the bend from Taiwan to Okinawa?"

The Chief Engineer called DC Central on his Motorola walkie-talkie. "DCA, CHENG."

"Go ahead, Sir."

"Can our sailors shore this damage on the go?"

No response.

"DCA, how copy?"

"A-firm, Sir. We can do this!"

Captain Smart smiled. "Get back down there, CHENG. Let's get the Lincoln home."

President Walker keyed her intercom. "Please send in my next appointment."

The Minister of Truth walked into the Oval Office. "Hello, Abby. How is your day going so far?"

"Ha!"

Mr. Michaels paused. "Do you want me to come back later?"

President Walker clicked her ballpoint pen incessantly. "It depends. Why did you schedule the appointment?"

Mr. Michaels pointed to his folder. "Krissy Moriarty and I prepared a preliminary Breaking News report regarding the sinking of the USS Abraham Lincoln."

President Walker stopped clicking her pen. "You didn't get the memo, did you?"

"No, Ma'am."

"There *was* no second accident. There *is* no second accident. And there *will be* no second accident."

Mr. Michaels nodded. "I'm sorry."

"Is that all you have for me?"

"Yes, Ma'am."

"Then I guess that's all. Thanks for stopping by."

The Minister of Truth quickly departed the White House.

Jack led with his MEDWEAP around the corner to the bridge. "They're gone."

Bob transmitted on HICSON base. "Overwatch, this is Stingray One. Sharjah Blue has three teammates in captivity. Juliet and Bravo are searching for Romeo, Victor and Alpha."

Gigi paused. "Understood."

Bob transmitted. "Stingray Two, you there?"

Charlie keyed her mic. "I'm near the Sharjah Blue. About five minutes away."

"Do not hang around. The Russian is too dangerous."

"Copy."

"You and Jack find those three, Bob." Charlotte stared into the dark, lonely South China Sea. "Then call me. I'll come back. Please find them!"

Bob whispered into his SATCOM. "Thanks, Charlie."

"Amber Jack, this is Burner in the Airbus Super Puma." Ryan carefully advanced towards Tater in the South China Sea as Madison and Li Jie searched off the nose. "Go ahead Burner."

Burner sloppily maintained control of the Airbus H225 helicopter ten miles south of Hong Kong International at three thousand feet. "I'm just getting the hang of flying this beast. Do you need me to turn around and help you with search and rescue? I have Washington onboard. He's a SAR swimmer."

Ryan looked into the zero-illumination night. "I can't make that call, Burner. Do you have enough gas?"

Burner studied his Airbus glass cockpit gauges and high-tech MFD's. "I'm pretty fat. Got over two hours of gas remaining."

Captain Smart keyed the mic. "Burner, this is Getttysburg. The HS-14 skipper is standing right next to me. Goober wants you to get HIRF, Spooner and Washington to Hong Kong International. HIRF may be injured."

"Gettysburg, Tater's in the water. I want to help. Maybe if I just spot her and then let Amber Jack pick her up."

No response.

"Gettysburg, you copy request?"

Captain Smart paused. "Burner, I am talking with Goober. His four-thousand hours of helicopter experience says continue north to Hong Kong International after getting comfortable. SMO has an ambulance waiting for you guys at Signature FBO. Just land the Airbus safely. We'll find Tater."

Burner nodded and studied the Hong Kong International rabbit lights pointing at the runway. "WILCO, Sir. Continuing north."

Mr. Light ran up to the Sharjah Blue bridge after watching the Hong Kong Medical Center helicopter crash into the South China Sea. "Tony, you're here."

"Ivan just told me to head the ship back to Dubai." Tony showed Mr. Light his southwesterly course towards Singapore and the Straits of Malacca.

"Where's your father? Where is Ben?"

"Mr. Light, Ben and my dad were recently hit by EMP's in the Weapon Control Center."

"By whom?"

Tony stood at the helm of the large yacht. "I don't exactly know. There are intruders onboard. Ivan has some of them in captivity. Be careful."

Mr. Light looked at the floor. "Captain Farsi got hit?"

Tony Murdstone nodded. "He's dead."

"Use the shipboard 1MC to warn me if you see the intruders again."

"Yes, Sir."

A my called from the Gulfstream 650 ER weapons bay. "Ryan, you're three hundred feet from her beacon. She's in the water. Turn right twenty."

Ryan keyed his mic and slowed the vessel. "Right twenty. Looking."

Li Jie and Madison used powerful searchlights. "Are we near?"

Ryan yelled down from the flybridge. "Very near!"

"Boss!" Li Jie yelled. "I see helmet!"

Madison and Li Jie utilized the reflective properties of Tater's Navy helmet to guide Ryan closer.

Ryan decelerated. "Maddie, get up here! Switch!"

Madison climbed up the ladder like a spider monkey as Li Jie trained his light on the President's daughter. "Got the controls!"

Ryan briefed Madison. "Be ready to cut the engine to idle. Steer slightly right of Mercedes. Miss her by twenty feet. Keep her helmet in sight or you're too close."

Madison nodded. "Drive to the right. Be ready for idle. Keep her in sight. Got it."

Ryan donned a float coat and tethered a large life ring bearing the name 'Ben Gunn' to a rope. "Maddie, go to idle!"

Madison immediately closed the throttle.

The engine noise quickly subsided.

Madison yelled. "We're at idle!"

Ryan threw the rope ladder over the port side. "Li Jie, be ready to help."

"Yes, Boss!"

"Tater!"

No response.

"Tater!"

Mercedes was unconscious and bobbing in the dark sea.

"Maddie, call Overwatch! Tell them I'm going in after Tater!"

Splash!

Madison keyed her handheld SATCOM mic. "Overwatch, this is Amber Jack One. Tater in sight. We put our swimmer in the water."

The CVN-72 bridge and CATCC personnel cheered. "Gettysburg copies."

Gigi keyed her mic. "Overwatch copies."

"Amber Jack, this is Gettysburg."

Madison keyed her mic on the flybridge. "Go ahead."

"Be advised Lightning 612 is inbound towards your position. Please have your swimmer wait for our trained Navy rescue swimmer. Tater may have back injuries. Repeat, do *not* attempt to rescue Tater due to potential spinal injuries from ejection. How copy."

"Copy! Standby!"

Madison yelled down to Ryan in the water. "Ryan! That noise is another Navy helicopter! They say wait! Ejection can hurt her spine!"

"Okay!" Ryan gently kept Tater's face above water as the SH-60 searchlight beam painted Tater's reflective helmet for the inbound Seahawk. "I'll wait!"

"Hello?"

Mr. Light spoke into his satellite phone. "President Walker?"

"Bud?"

Mr. Light stood on the starboard deck of the Sharjah Blue. "There is a lag. I'm on the Sharjah Blue. It's damaged. Took on water. They isolated the flooding and it will remain afloat. The Murdstone boy is driving. The Weapon Control Center is destroyed. Nuke and my son are injured. Mission is aborted. Repeat, mission aborted."

President Walker spun her chair around to look outside the Oval Office.

"Abby, are you there?"

"Has Tony ever driven an eight-hundred-foot yacht?"

"No, Ma'am. Captain Farsi and his bridge team were killed."

"Who killed them?"

"Some Hornets were involved. Other aircraft, too. House Intelligence has their fingerprints on this. There are apparently CABESA Projects involved."

No response.

"President Walker?"

No response.

Mr. Light waited ten seconds before speaking again. "Abby?"

I got a call from SECNAV. "Mercedes ejected. She's apparently in the water near Hong Kong."

"Copy."

"Bud." President Walker looked at an Oval Office portrait of President Lincoln. "I specifically remember asking you to terminate the CABESA Projects in 2020."

"Don't worry, I'm —"

Click!

President Walker discontinued the satellite phone call and rested her head on the Resolute Desk as she continued to click her ballpoint pen.

"Listen." Gigi removed her headset at the top of Proboscis Island in the Overwatch building. "What's that noise?"

Thomas stopped moving. "Monkeys?"

Gigi shook her head negatively.

Casper calibrated his radar screen for the immediate Brunei area and rapidly snapped his fingers.

Thomas looked at the screen as a low, slow flyer approached their mountaintop Overwatch location. "I'll go see." Thomas ran outside.

Casper typed on his phone screen and flashed it to Gigi. "Danger."

Gigi keyed her mic. "Shadow two-two, this is Overwatch. We have company here."

I monitored the autopilot and called my little sister. "Oh, God, Gigi! The H-53 that raided the Ningbo 9. Kelly's still knocked out and we stopped tracking it. Amy pulled up the historical flight track. It's coming for you guys. Get out!"

Thor barked at the noisy red and green NAV lights.

Thomas ran inside. "It's a very large helicopter. It landed at the south end of the mountain."

Casper typed into his phone. "*EVAC & DESTROY.*"

Gigi got on the radio. "We'll be at Point Delta. Repeat. Evacuating Overwatch to Point Delta."

Thomas ran outside as the Proboscis monkeys screamed and hollered. "They're approaching!"

Gigi petted Thor as the Overwatch operators hurled backpacks over their backs. "This way."

Thomas looked at Gigi. "Where's Casper?"

The two waited twenty seconds with Vic's service dog before Casper ran outside.

Gigi looked at Casper. "You're smiling. Why are you smiling?"

Casper winked and led Gigi, Thomas and Thor down the north side of the mountain.

The Navy Rescue Swimmer from Lightning 612 dropped from the SH-60 into the dark, violent sea and swam towards Ryan and Mercedes.

Ryan yelled over the rotor noise as sea spray sand-blasted his face. "Tater's out cold."

The petite, female SAR swimmer smiled. "We have it from here! Thanks!"

Ryan back-paddled towards the Ben Gunn.

The small rescue swimmer let the metal stokes litter touch the water before grabbing it. She pulled Mercedes into place and expertly strapped her limp body onto the stretcher.

Ryan continued towards the Ben Gunn's rope ladder as Mercedes lay unconscious in the sea spray.

The hovering SH-60 Seahawk was rock-solid as eight-foot seas tossed Ryan, the rescue swimmer and Mercedes upwards and downwards.

The rescue swimmer thumped her own sternum and delivered a long-armed 'thumbs up.'

The metal cable became taught and lifted Mercedes with the small, female rescue swimmer kneeling on her chicken-wire, stokes litter cage.

Ryan returned to the Ben Gunn, climbed the ladder and collapsed on the deck.

Li Jie ran to his side. "Boss, are you okay?"

"I'm fine." Ryan sat up, coughed out a mouthful of seawater and watched the SH-60 continue the rescue. "I'm fine."

Madison watched Mercedes and her stokes litter rider get pulled inside then keyed her SATCOM mic. "HICSON Operators, Tater's safely inside the Navy helicopter!"

CHAPTER FORTY-ONE

"*Ooh, ooh, ooh! Aah, aah, aah!*"
Monkeys screamed from the top of Proboscis Island as Gigi, Thomas and Casper descended into the dark jungle with Thor.

"They're yelling." Gigi whispered to Thomas and Casper during their emergent EVAC. "The TSC helicopter crew found our base."

Kaboom!

Overwatch burst into flames after a grand, mountaintop explosion on the small, South China Sea island.

Thomas looked up the hill. "What happened?"

Gigi held Thor tightly. "They blew it up?"

Casper smiled, shook his head negatively and typed into his cellphone. "*Curiosity killed the cat.*"

Amy keyed the internal Gulfstream ICS. "Gracie, Bad news. Overwatch just —"

"Just what?"

"Just exploded."

Kelly began to wake up and keyed her mic. "Huh?"

I rubbed Kelly's knee. "Kelly's awake. Amy, call Gigi for me."

"Overwatch, Shadow."

Gigi scrambled to reduce her SATCOM radio volume as she navigated through the jungle then whispered. "Go ahead, Shadow."

"Are you okay?"

"Affirmative. We are descending to the north. We don't think we're being followed anymore."

Amy studied the satellite imagery in the back of the Gulfstream. "Confirm you're all okay."

"Affirmative. Casper left a surprise for the intruders. Proceeding to Point Delta."

Kelly woke up and rubbed her forehead in the Gulfstream pilot seat. "What happened?"

I looked left and smiled. "You got knocked out. Are you okay?"

"Ouch."

Kelly sat up straight. "The Lincoln! Is it okay?"

"It's forty miles east of us. She's going to make it home to Japan just fine."

"Can I fly?"

"Please!"

Kelly kicked off the auto-pilot, shook out her hands, and wiggled her toes in her steel-toed flight boots. "Ah. This is better." Kelly looked at me. "Who's in back?"

Amy keyed her mic. "The awesome one. And Chloe."

"Did you guys get hit by their weapon?"

Chloe keyed the ICS. "Just you."

"Why just *me*?"

Chloe laughed. "Because we three are what you might call 'invisible.' That's why Bob chose us to help."

"Invisible?"

Amy keyed the ICS. "We were CABESA Projects in middle school and high school. Experiments used for weapons testing and development for six years near Peaksville Defense and Space and Peaksville Institutes of Health. President Walker was our Congresswoman."

I nodded. "In 2020, we finally learned how to become invisible. That's why Bob had me learn how to fly."

"Wait, so Bob knew I'd be knocked out?"

I smiled. "More or less."

Kelly rubbed her forehead again as she orbited in the Gulfstream 650 ER. "Where is Bob?'

I pointed at the Sharjah Blue on MFD-3.

"No."

I nodded. "Five are onboard. You slept through a lot."

Kelly sighed.

.   .   .

B ob rested with Jack in a secluded, port side deck storage room on the Sharjah Blue. "I don't know if we can find Aaron, Ruby and Vic."

Jack pointed. "Up there."

Bob whispered. "Where?"

"In the bridge window. That's Tony from Peaksville. The Idaho person who helped us."

Bob looked at Jack. "You trust him? Tony may have been compromised since our last meeting."

"Tony might know where to look."

Bob checked his backpack. "What's your charge?"

Jack looked at his MEDWEAP gauge. "I'm at eighty percent."

Bob looked around for an outlet. "I'm at forty." Bob unraveled his power cord, fiddled with his adapters and plugged into the Middle Eastern poolside yacht power.

Jack looked at Bob's backpack. "You're green and blinking. It's flowing. How long will it take?"

Bob shrugged. "Maybe one hour. Maybe five hours. Not sure. We never carried this MEDWEAP stuff on my SEAL Team."

Jack leaned back and wiped the sweat from his forehead. "Charlie's waiting."

Bob sighed. "Dangerous, huh? All by herself."

Jack nodded.

"Think we should cut her loose?"

"She's a sitting duck, Bob."

Bob keyed his mic. "Charlie?"

"Yes."

Bob rested in the darkness, sighed and whispered. "Head back to Star Ferry. This isn't going to be resolved anytime soon."

Charlotte held on tightly as rogue waves continued to rock her tactical boat. "I don't want to leave you guys alone."

Jack whispered into his SATCOM radio. "Get home, Charlie. Check on Gloria."

Charlie could vaguely see a faint glow of Hong Kong city lights twenty miles north. "Call me if you need me. I'll turn around."

"Okay."

Charlotte checked her digital compass and Multi-Function Display, added power and departed towards Hong Kong in the darkness.

. . .

B urner talked to himself as he erratically hovered over the Signature Flight Support FBO flightline in Hong Kong International. "Nice and easy, Burner. Just a walk in the park."

He descended through fifty feet and whispered. "Easy."

Twenty-five feet. "Almost down."

Brianna calmly encouraged him. "You can do this."

The fixed-wing, Super Hornet pilot worriedly confirmed wheels down one last time before touchdown.

Wham!

Burner accidentally got airborne again.

Wham!

"Ah!" HIRF woke up and screamed as the Airbus main mount strut oleos screamed in pain over the sound of the rotors.

"What?" Spooner bounced and opened his eyes. "Where are we?"

Washington smiled at Brianna and tended to his two Seahawk pilots. "It's okay, now. We're on deck in Hong Kong."

HIRF looked around the Super Puma, rubbed his eyes and panicked. "We lost Burner!"

Washington smiled at pointed to the flight deck. "Burner's flying."

"Burner's what!"

Brianna smiled. "It's okay, HIRF. We're okay, now."

Lurch slept through the landing.

"In case you haven't noticed." Burner shut down the engine, laughed and keyed the cabin PA. "We're on the ground."

Spooner yelled "We noticed! Nice landings. Both of them."

Brianna walked forward and smiled. "First helicopter landing, Commander Burner?"

"And last."

Burner keyed his SATCOM as the ambulance crew approached the Airbus H225 Super Puma. "Gettysburg, our Airbus is safe on deck in Hong Kong. Tell SMO ambulance is here. We'll get HIRF to the hospital."

The Hornet and Seahawk pilots in the dark CATCC situation room laughed and cheered. "Burner did it!"

Captain Smart keyed his mic. "Nice job, Burner. We're steaming home. Take good care of HIRF, Spooner and Washington. You're the SRO."

" A mber Jack One, this is Stingray Two."

"Charlie!" Madison replied on SATCOM.

"Maddie, I'm one mile behind you. I watched the whole rescue from my

ESOC. The Sharjah Blue is twenty miles to our southwest. We still have five on board that yacht. Bob told me to go to Hong Kong. They're steaming southwest too quickly and my fuel range became an issue."

Ryan got on the SATCOM. "Charlie, are they captured?"

"Bob and Jack are apparently looking for Aaron, Ruby and Vic. I don't think I can help anymore. Neither did Bob. Can I follow you to Star Ferry?"

Ryan saw Charlotte's boat. "Shine your flashlight at me."

Charlotte complied.

Ryan returned a few blinks from his searchlight.

"We see you. Follow us home, Charlie."

Chloe checked her scope from the Gulfstream. "The Sharjah Blue is doing thirty knots towards Singapore and the Straits of Malacca. If we don't rescue them soon from Hong Kong, we'll have to wait until tomorrow. Then operate from somewhere else."

Bob keyed his SATCOM mic from the Sharjah Blue and whispered in the night breeze. "Concur from Sharjah Blue. This boat is steaming fast."

Charlotte keyed her mic. "What about Ruby, Vic and Aaron?"

I looked at Kelly in the Gulfstream 650 cockpit.

Kelly looked at our gas and shook her head no. "We need to regroup."

Chloe keyed her SATCOM mic in the Gulfstream weapon bay. "Jack, we're coming for you guys tomorrow."

Jack keyed his mic. "I hear you, Chloe. We're recharging our batteries, literally and figuratively. We still haven't found the other three."

Amy keyed her mic for parting words with her little brother. "Jack, this is Amy. Your favorite sister."

Jack whispered in the man-made breeze hiding on the Sharjah Blue deck. "Love you, Amy."

"Don't get taken."

Kelly and I laughed in the cockpit. "How touching."

Jack double-clicked.

Bob laughed. "Was your sister joking?"

"Half-joking. That was the sentimental side of Amy."

President Walker answered her cell phone and simultaneously closed the divider in her Presidential limousine. "Bud."

Mr. Light stepped outside the Sharjah Blue Officer's Lounge to improve satellite phone reception. "Mrs. President, I have an update."

"Go."

"We have three intruders in custody. Two of them are CABESA Projects. We have two other intruders roaming the Sharjah Blue. Ivan fought with them but they escaped."

President Walker's vehicle rounded the bend at the Lincoln Memorial. "What else?"

"The Sharjah Blue is southwest of Hong Kong steaming for the Indian Ocean. Taking on water but the pump system is keeping up. Nuke and Ben are recovering from the Weapon Control Center EMP blast. Tony expects to be through the Straits of Malacca and into the IO in one day."

"Tony Murdstone. The young Peacekeeper from Idaho with ship-driving experience told you that."

"Yes, Ma'am."

President Walker fiddled with her limousine minibar latch. She opened it. She looked at a bottle of bourbon. Then she closed it. "What has Mustafa Muscat said?"

"Ivan Smirnov and I are scouring the ship for the two wandering intruders. We haven't notified Mustafa."

"What about Omar Muscat?"

"He's too drunk and scared to call his father. I try to avoid that imbecile."

No response.

Mr. Light checked his satellite phone screen. "Abby, are you still there?"

President Walker paused. "I assume you want me to call Mustafa."

"I believe he's golfing with Web and Dr. Braun."

"I better call him, Bud."

"Copy that."

President Walker face-palmed and sighed. "Bud, I want you to ride the ship all the way to Dubai."

"That reminds me. I have more to pass. Do you want the good news or bad news first?"

The limousine approached the White House. "Oh dear. The good news first."

"One of the so-called Projects is merely a Peaksville High School friend of the Projects. He's not really a CABESA Project."

"Was that good or bad news?"

"That was my good news."

"The bad news?"

"His name is Aaron Webster. He's Web's son."

"Is Web compromised or untrustworthy?"

"Web is good. They haven't spoken since Aaron's graduation."

President Walker's sighed as the limousine door opened. "I'll notify Mustafa."

CHAPTER FORTY-TWO

A my hosted us in her JW Marriott Hotel Hong Kong suite on the twenty-fifth floor.

Knock! Knock! Knock!

Chloe stood up and answered the door as Kelly and I rested. "The pizza is here!"

Charlotte sipped a Diet Coke. "What now?"

I grabbed my SATCOM radio, keyed the mic and whispered. "Gigi?"

Gigi, Thomas and Casper rested in a small jungle cave. "Hey, Gracie."

"You guys okay to sleep on Proboscis tonight?"

"You guys sleep." Gigi smiled. "We'll sleep. Tomorrow we'll all get our five friends off the yacht."

I looked at Kelly.

Kelly nodded with her eyes closed on the bed. "Good plan."

"Kelly said good plan, sis.' Love you. Turn off your radio to save the batteries. Say good night to Casper and Tommy Boy for us."

Gigi whispered. "Love you, Gracie."

Bob called and whispered. "We found them. We can hear them through ducting. I need to get Vic some explosives to escape. But we can't fit in the ventilation ducting."

Kelly groggily keyed her mic with her eyes closed. "Bob, confirm you're too fat. Repeat. Confirm Bob too fat."

Bob whispered. "Hardy-har-har. Even Jack, our Muay Thai fighter, isn't skinny enough."

Charlotte looked at her sister and called the Sharjah Blue operators. "Jack, could Chloe or Gigi get through the ducting?"

Jack keyed the mic. "Negative."

I keyed my mic. "Copy all, Bob. Expect a rescue tomorrow. HICSON said you're heading for the straits below Singapore and above Indonesia."

Bob double-clicked.

Amy sighed. "I'm worried about little Jack."

Chloe selected her second piece of veggie pizza from the JW Marriott. "Jack is a Muay Thai instructor."

Amy took a bite of her triple-meat pizza slice and purposely talked with her mouth full. "I can shtill kick hish ash."

Captain Smart initiated a SATCOM call. "Any HICSON, this is Gettysburg looking to speak with any Airwing FIVE pilot."

Amy threw her SATCOM radio to Spooner. "Maverick. It's Goose."

"Go, Sir! This is Spooner!"

"Spooner! Where are the others?"

"Washington, HIRF and Burner are meeting us in the Marriott in twenty minutes. HIRF's neck x-Rays were negative. Everyone's okay."

"Good. Air Ops arranged an early six o'clock C-12 from Hong Kong Signature FBO to Okinawa. Then expect a COD ride to the Lincoln from Kadena Air Base.

Spooner nodded. "C-12 to Okinawa at six o'clock. Copy all, Sir."

Captain Smart paused. "This message is for *all* of you from the USS Abraham Lincoln. Thanks! You're great Americans!"

Amy joked. "Homelanders. Right?"

Captain Smart paused. "Americans! You all be careful tomorrow."

"Bye, Sir!" I un-keyed my SATCOM mic and looked at Lurch. "I think you're in charge, here. What's our plan?"

Lurch grabbed a Marriott pen and pad of paper. "Kelly, how early can we get the Gulfstream airborne for Proboscis?"

Kelly sat up. "Maybe six." Kelly leaned back and closed her eyes. "I'm so tired. Yes, let's go for six o'clock launch. Taxi at five a.m."

Amy slammed her body back on the bed. "Brutal."

Lurch opened a large, paper map of southeast Asia. "Okay, Kelly. After Proboscis, we have several intercept options as they transit past Indonesia, Thailand, Malaysia, and Singapore. We have Kuala Lumpur International. Phattaya Beach has U-Tapao airport. Singapore has Paya Lebar military airport with the crappy duck and rice dish that always gets me sick."

Chloe stopped eating pizza. "Bob and Jack need a small person to deliver explosives to Vic, Aaron and Ruby. Right?"

Charlotte laughed. "My little sister about to suggest Phuket International Airport."

Kelly checked the map. "Phuket works *awesome* for an intercept after its Straits passage."

Lurch, undeniably the largest person in Hong Kong and perhaps Southeast Asia, smirked. "You know a small person in Thailand?"

Chloe nodded. "Amy will like this plan the most."

Amy sat up quickly and flashed a devilish smile. "I forgot."

I laughed. "No way."

Amy nodded. "Yes way."

Lurch folded the map. "Phuket to get the little person?"

Kelly agreed. "Phuket."

Knock! Knock! Knock!

Chloe grabbed a third piece of pizza and answered the door. "Gloria!"

Luke and Emma helped my exhausted and slow sister into the suite.

I got up to hug her. "You look good!"

Gloria sat on a couch. "So tired!"

Emma nodded. "She did well. She's going to be okay."

I smiled. "I know she is."

Ryan looked at Gloria. "Did that Dr. hands guy ever return?"

Emma shook her head negatively.

Luke looked around. "Ruby isn't back yet?"

Charlotte explained. "We're going to pick her up tomorrow. She's on the yacht."

"The bad yacht?"

Charlotte nodded. "She's okay, Luke. Don't worry. We'll get her."

Madison pointed at the Navy pilot. "Spooner, you need rides in the morning for commercial flights?"

"Please."

Amy looked at Spooner. "Why do they call you Spooner?"

"Fall asleep and you'll find out."

Brianna sighed.

Amy rolled onto her side, tucked into a fetal position, closed her eyes and snored loudly.

Emma laughed. "Spooner?"

"Yeah?"

"Never, ever mistake me for my twin sister."

Spooner laughed. "Roger that."

"Quick!" Kelly lifted an open pizza box. "Eat before Spooner and Amy ruin your appetite."

. . .

I van Smirnov entered the Sharjah Blue brig and studied Vic, Ruby and Aaron.
Aaron was on the floor nestled between Vic and Ruby. "Could we have some water?"

Ivan left and returned with three plastic bottles. "Who sent you?"

Ruby and Vic sipped their water.

Aaron addressed the mysterious, old Russian. "We sent ourselves."

"Nobody ever sends themselves. Everybody has a handler." Ivan smiled patiently. "Why did you board the ship?"

Aaron shrugged.

"I am very old. I have seen people comply and be tortured and killed. I have seen people *not* comply and be tortured and killed. Ninety-five percent of the people sent to the gulags in my country between 1919 and 1990 committed no crime. Only *thought crimes* as Mr. Orwell called it. But it wasn't fiction. It was very, very real. Real pain. Real loss." Ivan looked directly at Aaron. "My father was taken from me for being a dissident, or malcontent, when I was young. Your story is quite opposite. Isn't it young man from Idaho?"

Vic and Ruby looked at Aaron.

Aaron shrugged.

Ivan looked at Vic's titanium legs. "Army?"

Vic shook her head. "Navy."

"Navy." Ivan knelt down and studied Vic's face. "Your expression is much too confident for surface or subsurface Navy."

Vic looked away.

"However, unlike a Navy pilot, you harness your emotions."

Ivan gently held her wrists. "Your knuckles are scarred up. You have been in hand to hand combat. You are a SEAL." The Russian touched her titanium legs. "Or, you *were* a SEAL."

Vic shrugged.

"Name?"

"Vic."

"I was Soviet SPETSNAZ. Do you know SPETSNAZ, Vic?"

Vic shook her head.

"Of course not. You are just a child. How old are you?"

"Twenty-four."

"I am seventy-eight." Ivan laughed. "I was born before Sputnik beat the Americans into space."

Ruby cried on Aaron's shoulder. "What is your name, sweet girl?"

"Ruby."

Ivan smiled and touched her cheek. "Ruby, you are not military. Why are you here? Even *after* your night swim?"

Ruby shrugged.

"You are Aaron."

Vic and Ruby quickly looked at Aaron and gasped.

"Your father is a much better golfer than me, Aaron. Your golf courses in Idaho are better than Russian golf courses."

Ruby wiped her eyes and shook her head. "You have the wrong Aaron."

Vic subtly observed the conversation.

"Aaron Webster. Your father engineered the modern MEDWEAP when he worked at Peaksville Defense and Space. Much progress compared to the junk electronics Uncle Joe Stalin used on your Moscow American embassy personnel before his death in 1953." The Russian smiled. "I do have the correct Aaron Webster. No?"

Aaron shrugged.

"Don't worry. I will not torture you. I will not kill you." Ivan walked towards the door. "But I will require information before you are released. Your assault on our ship was well-funded. And your President did *not* approve this funding. Of this, I am quite certain. Welcome to the Amazing, Sinking Sharjah Blue. You are my guests."

Ivan secured the brig door and looked through the metal bars.

Click!

"Get some sleep, Homelanders." Ivan winked and left.

K elly completed her pre-sunrise walk-around of the Gulfstream 650 ER at Signature Flight Support FBO in Hong Kong International and checked my work. "Let's see what you got."

I fumbled through my paperwork. "Here's weather. Proboscis Island doesn't have a forecast so I used Brunei. Weather at Phuket. I filed us at forty-thousand to save gas. And I signed your name for the Jet A fuel. Kelly Gross, right?"

"It's Cross."

I winked. "Just kidding."

Kelly laughed and grabbed the fuel chit. "Don't be messing with me at six o'clock in the morning, *Beaker*."

I waved to Burner, Spooner and Washington as they helped HIRF board the Navy C-12 Beechcraft King Air.

"Ryan!" Burner ran to our Gulfstream. "Where's Ryan?"

Kelly pointed at the cabin door. "Probably already asleep."

Burner ran inside the cabin and gently woke him. "Ryan."

"Yeah?"

"You saved our FNG twice in two weeks." Burner extended his hand for a strong handshake. "I wanted to thank you again for helping Tater!"

Ryan smiled.

"Woah!" Amy grabbed a fistful of Burner's green Navy flight suit, pulled him close and held her nose. "This thing is ripe!"

Emma slapped her leg. "He crashed in that flight suit."

Chloe laughed. "Twice!"

"You need a big hug, Amy." Burner squeezed Amy and rubbed his body on her. "Enjoy your new perfume, *Essence of Flight Suit.*"

Amy squirmed. "Stop!"

Emma smiled. "She likes it."

Burner left with a smile. "Good luck, today."

I watched Lurch and Brianna start the Airbus H225 Super Puma engine. "Kelly, what's their route?"

"Lurch needs to refuel in U-Tapao near Phattaya and Bangkok. He doesn't have our speed or legs. They'll meet us in Phuket. You ready?"

"Grace!" Luke ran from the FBO lounge to the flight line. "Madison said she'll help Gloria to hospital visits. I want to get Ruby back!"

I looked at Kelly. "Do we have room?"

"Room for Luke?" Kelly paused, snapped repetitively and showed her open palm. "Pay up, Bucko. One thousand dollars."

"A thousand?" Luke patted his pockets. "What?"

"One thousand dollars. Did I stutter?"

I smiled. "Kelly's kidding, Luke. You're sure you want to go?"

Luke nodded. "Ruby's a hostage. I want to help."

I hugged him. "Saddle up, partner!"

"Shadow two-two, this is HICSON base."

I keyed the mic on our secure SATCOM frequency at forty-thousand feet. "Go ahead."

"Shadow, we see you and Harbor Watch taking separate routes. Be advised, the Sharjah Blue will begin passage through the Straits of Malacca in two hours."

Amy keyed her mic from the Gulfstream weapons bay. "Copy, Gus. We see them on our big board. We thought Destiny was working the radios, today."

Betsy keyed her mic after a ten second pause. "Destiny's parents died in a house fire last night."

Amy looked at Chloe and gasped.

Chloe keyed her mic. "We're so sorry."

"Thanks, Shadow. Phuket and U-Tapao fuel is covered in advance. Call me if you need anything. We'll be watching from the Capitol."

I keyed the mic. "Thanks Gus and Betsy."

Amy went on ICS. "Poor Destiny."

Chloe pointed to her scope. "Casper, Thomas and Gigi just reactivated their homing beacon. They moved from Point Delta to the Proboscis Island runway."

"Good." Kelly pressed some navigation buttons on Multi-Function Display #2. "That'll save almost an hour on deck."

Gus keyed the HICSON base SATCOM mic again. "Kelly?"

"Yes, Gus."

"The Sharjah Blue just took on a new bridge crew from Singapore Changi International via helicopter."

Kelly paused. "How many?"

"Three."

"Copy."

CHAPTER FORTY-THREE

Captain Smart wandered around the hull repair efforts after the CVN-72 Department Head meeting in his cabin.

A sailor saw the approaching Commanding Officer and yelled to the Repair Locker Team. "Attention on deck!"

Before each worker dropped all tools to stand and brace against the bulkhead, Captain Smart interrupted the 250-year-old U.S. Navy ritual. "At ease, at ease. Carry on, shipmates."

Captain Smart went straight to the Jordan brothers.

"Petty Officer Jordan?"

Antoine raised his metal welding visor. "Captain."

"Antoine, your wife Brianna got some helicopter stick time last night. Her pilot got knocked out. She flew the Airbus until the VFA-195 Operations Officer took over."

Antoine smiled. "My wife and Burner flew a helicopter?"

The Navy O-6 laughed. "It's not a helicopter trip I would want to be in. Total goat rope. But yes, they did well. And they carried the downed 615 crew to Hong Kong. Make sure you thank your wife for me."

Antoine beamed with pride and nodded.

"Anyhow, just wanted to pass the word. Brianna was a real hero up there in the Airbus helicopter. I'll let you get back to work."

"Thanks, Captain."

. . .

O mar Muscat stood in the Sharjah Blue passageway and looked through the brig bars at Aaron, Vic and Ruby. "You damaged my ship."

The three hostages didn't respond.

"You." Omar pointed at Aaron. "Apparently your father is my father's golfing buddy."

Aaron shrugged.

"Ivan's dad was a loser dissident. He deserved to go to the gulags."

Ruby and Vic slid closer to Aaron and held his hands.

"Not you. Your father is a Global Patriot. A great manufacturer and engineer and Champion of World Peace. You threw everything away by hanging out with the wrong crowd. You're a family embarrassment."

Aaron stayed silent.

Omar opened a bag. "Do you know what this is?"

The three hostages didn't flinch.

Omar smiled at the high-tech weapon and flipped a few switches. "This is the latest PDS MEDWEAP engineered by your genius father. Your father is very disappointed in you, Aaron Webster."

I flew manually for an hour at forty thousand feet then set the Gulfstream autopilot. "That was a fast stop on Proboscis."

Kelly nodded. "Not hiking through the jungle to find Point Delta was a Godsend."

Gigi poked her head in the cockpit and smiled. "Thanks for picking us up!"

I laughed. "How was Thor last night? Did he eat any monkeys?"

"He slept between us and kept us all warm in the cave, like a one-hundred-pound space heater." Gigi shrugged. "Thor misses Vic, this morning. He found Vic's luggage and won't stop smelling it."

"Poor thing."

Kelly checked MFD-3. "The Sharjah Blue just passed Sentosa Island in Singapore. We're going to be descending into Phuket in ten minutes. Did Chloe call her Thai contacts?"

Gigi yelled into the cabin. "Chloe!"

Chloe joined Gigi in our cockpit doorway. "At your service."

Kelly looked at Chloe. "Tell us about the little person you are getting from Thailand."

I smiled at Chloe and subtly shook my head no.

Chloe winked. "Oh, he's cool. It'll take about forty-five minutes to jump on a baht bus to get him. And Mr. Bali will be standing by in his ski boat at the pier."

Kelly smiled. "I can't wait to see our small person."

I winked at Gigi and Chloe. "You'll like him, Kelly."

"Can we trust him?"

Chloe nodded. "He'll never say a word about this operation."

Gigi agreed. "He's smart. Just like you, Kelly."

Kelly nodded. "Okay. You all know something that I don't. Just remember that playing with fire can get you burned."

"Mercedes?"

"Yes."

Krissy Moriarty winked at President Walker in the Oval Office. "Are you okay?"

Mercedes paused as the COD from Okinawa caught the two-wire and rattled the Lincoln with Burner, HIRF, and Spooner onboard. "Who is this?"

"It's Krissy."

"Hi, Krissy. Why are you calling?"

"I heard you ejected last night."

Mercedes waited five seconds before responding. "Who told you that I ejected?"

President Walker listened quietly to the speaker phone and shook her head negatively.

"Someone told me at FXH News. I can't remember. I assumed there was a leak from the Pentagon. Did you eject?"

"My skipper told me not to talk about anything. They have to do a safety investigation, first."

"Mercedes, it's me Krissy. Your old friend from Coeur d'Alene. You can tell me why you ejected."

Mercedes watched the CVN-72 PLAT Camera as HIRF exited the COD in a neck brace. "I didn't eject. Maybe you got bad information."

Krissy looked at President Walker and shrugged. "Are you sure?"

Mercedes laughed. "Ejecting is probably something that I would remember."

"Okay, then."

"Yep. Okay, then. Hey Krissy, my Operations Officer is calling me into a meeting. Thanks for calling."

"See you, Mercedes."

"Bye."

Click!

President Walker looked at Krissy. "My daughter is lying."

Krissy Moriarty stood attentively at the Resolute Desk. "Do you want me to run the Mercedes ejection story anyway?"

President Walker shook her head. "Let's wait until Mr. Muscat's yacht makes it back to Dubai."

Krissy hugged the President before leaving the Oval Office. "I wish you were my mom."

Bob and Jack managed to intercept Tony Murdstone and pull him aside into an obscure Sharjah Blue ladderwell.

Jack whispered to Tony. "Is it safe here?"

Tony nodded.

Bob whispered. "What's happening, now?"

Tony looked around. "It's not good."

"What's not good?"

"Omar Muscat is torturing Aaron, Ruby and the girl with titanium legs."

"Vic."

Tony pointed at Bob. "Yeah, Vic. I forgot."

"You saw the torture?"

Tony nodded. "Omar is a jerk. He is sneaking the torture with a NEXTGEN MEDWEAP. Ivan and Bud don't know what he's doing. And my dad is afraid to get involved."

"Damn," Bob replied.

"Ivan and Mr. Light are looking for you guys. Be careful."

Jack whispered. "Yeah, we've seen them snooping around. Bob, we need to let Tony go. Do you have any more questions for him?"

Bob shook Tony's hand. "Thanks, Tony."

Dr. Hands walked into Gloria's chemo room with charts in his hand. "Good morning, Gloria. How is my favorite patient from Idaho?"

Gloria acted tired.

Madison looked at Dr. Hands. "How long have you worked at this hospital?"

He smiled. "I freelance."

Madison squeezed Gloria's hand.

Dr. Hands checked Gloria's chemo ports and smiled at Madison. "I used to live in Peaksville, you know."

Gloria whispered. "I remember your name."

"You both went to Peaksville High School, didn't you?"

Madison wiped Gloria's forehead with a damp cloth. "Gloria was homeschooled for most of her childhood."

Dr. Hands smiled. "Your name is Madison."

Madison Goodwell gasped.

"Your father worked in the nanotech field. PsytoSCOPE, right?"

Madison looked away.

"It's okay, Madison. I was a friend of your father. Before he went into hiding."

Madison's eyes welled with tears.

"Where is your husband today, Gloria?"

Gloria closed her eyes.

Madison defended her friend. "She's tired."

"You're afraid of me. It's okay. I understand."

Madison sat closer to Gloria. "Where's the real doctor?"

Dr. Hands changed the subject. "You both rescued Mercedes after the Navy collision two weeks ago."

Madison subtly nodded.

He continued. "Madison, you and Ryan rescued her last night after her ejection. Second time. Quite impressive."

Gloria feigned fatigue and kept her eyes closed.

"I was her golf and tennis coach."

Gloria opened her eyes.

"While Mrs. Walker campaigned for Congress and bundled millions of dollars through the CABESA Initiative, I basically raised Mercedes in Coeur d'Alene. Or 'Tater' as she is known on the Lincoln."

Gloria struggled to speak. "We like Tater."

"I noticed." Dr. Hands smiled. "Tater likes you guys."

Madison and Gloria smiled.

"I'm supposed to call President Walker and turn you in to the secret police."

The girls lost their smiles.

"But we never spoke. Right?"

They nodded.

"Anyhow. Thanks for saving Mercedes. Gloria, your chemotherapy here at the Hong Kong Cancer Center is officially covered through a secret line of accounting." Dr. Hands left his business card. "Call my secretary if you have any problems with billing or service."

Madison read the card and smiled. "Homeland Minister of Comfort."

Gloria cried. "Thanks."

Madison hugged Dr. Hands. "You're like an angel."

"Call me if you need anything. Thanks again for rescuing Mercedes." Dr. Hands smiled and left the chemotherapy booth.

CHAPTER FORTY-FOUR

The westbound, damaged Sharjah Blue cleared the Straits of Malacca and cruised into the Indian Ocean towards Southwest Asia.

Amy and Charlotte studied the scope in the back of our Gulfstream 650 ER. "Harbor Watch, this is Shadow. I'm seeing three personnel on the bridge. Two have their hearts and heads lit up with Imaging Probes. The third one holding the hot cup of coffee is strangely clean. We'll have to go manual and use thermal on that guy holding the hot drink."

Lurch studied the new bridge personnel from four miles. "Shadow, Harbor Watch. I'll neutralize the third guy using our Airbus thermal interrogation system. You take the two with Imaging Probes." Lurch helped Brianna configure her MFD for thermal targeting and MEDWEAP attack.

Ryan looked around the cabin of the H225 helicopter and yelled. "Are we all ready?"

Luke, Emma and Casper nodded.

Ryan noticed Luke's pale color. "You good, buddy?"

Luke nodded again. "I'm good."

Ryan checked their gear for SATCOM radios, MEDWEAP's, EMP grenades, and emergency beacons. "Okay, we're all above ninety percent."

"Casper, you're exiting first and breaking off, right?"

Casper smiled.

Ryan continued to review the plan over the helicopter noise. "And you're okay with going down to the nuclear reactor by yourself?"

Casper nodded and smiled at Emma.

"Emma, you'll hold Jerome, right?"

"Got him." Emma smiled and comforted their little friend. "Do you think he remembers us?"

The spider monkey planted a kiss on Emma's cheek.

Ryan laughed. "What do *you* think?"

Emma yelled over the engine and rotor noise. "I'm so glad Jack and Chloe brought him to Phuket." Emma whispered to Jerome. "We'll have you back in the Phuket Wildlife Reserve with your little friends by dinnertime, buddy."

Jerome hugged Emma.

Amy called Lurch and Brianna. "Harbor Watch, this is Shadow. You are cleared inbound."

Lurch transmitted inside the Airbus on PA. "The bridge trio is down. Insertion in twenty seconds."

Luke shivered in fear.

Ryan patted him on the back. "Let's get Ruby. We go in. We go out. Don't worry."

Brianna transmitted on the PA. "Ten seconds until landing."

Charlotte looked at the Sharjah Blue on the scope. "What's that?"

Amy called the Airbus on SATCOM. "Brianna, two people on the Sharjah Blue deck appear to be firing at you and Lurch."

Brianna looked at Lurch. "You good?"

Lurch lowered the helicopter towards the landing pad on the stern. "Getting hit."

Just ten feet over the deck, Lurch lost control of the Airbus H225.

Casper jumped onto the deck, tumbled, found a nearby hatch, and disappeared into the belly of the ship.

Ivan Smirnov and Mr. Light set their MEDWEAP to EMP and fired at the cockpit of the flailing Airbus H225.

Lurch and Brianna went unconscious. The Airbus helicopter tilted and rolled from the Sharjah Blue deck into the Indian Ocean under the bright, morning sun.

Crash! Splash!

I watched the cockpit video feed from twenty thousand feet with Kelly. "They're down! Harbor Watch is down! Chloe, where are you?"

Casper stealthily crept from hatch to hatch, scuttle to scuttle, ladderwell to ladderwell with a full backpack.

A hand suddenly grabbed Casper's elbow and violently pulled him into a ventilation room.

Casper struggled to fire his MEDWEAP but was subdued.

"It's us."

Casper sighed.

Bob looked at Casper. "Where are the others?"

Casper typed into his iPhone and pointed to a direction he believed was aft of the ship from the small dark room. "*Airbus Crashed. Swimming in IO now.*"

Jack gasped and whispered. "Who was in the Airbus?"

Casper typed. "*Lurch, Bree, Ryan, Luke, Emma.*"

Jack looked at Bob. "Emma is my sister."

Bob nodded.

Casper typed again. "*And Jerome.*"

"Who is Jerome?" Bob asked.

"He was the little guy who was going to navigate the ventilation ducting to the brig."

"Thai?"

Jack shook his head. "Spider monkey."

"A monkey. Naturally." Bob keyed his SATCOM radio. "Shadow, this is Stingray One."

Amy replied. "Go!"

"Shadow, we have five swimmers in the IO. Six including Jerome. Casper is on the yacht. Requesting rescue for the swimmers."

Charlotte transmitted from the Gulfstream weapon bay. "They aren't swimming anymore. Chloe and her Phuket equestrian boss were standing by with a ski boat."

Bob whispered into his SATCOM radio. "Verify you found five swimmers and one spider monkey."

Kelly got on the radio. "Dear Gorilla, this is Kelly. The spider monkey was rescued along with five dissimilar, evolved homo erectus, opposing-thumb-bearing humans. We are reattempting Sharjah Blue insertion. Click your tongue twice if you copy, Gorilla?"

Bob rolled his eyes and double-clicked.

Amy called our cockpit from the Gulfstream cabin. "Kelly, I like your style."

I face-palmed. "Charlie, don't you wish you were down there in a boat?"

Charlotte looked at her scope. "Not really."

Casper typed into his iPhone and showed Bob. "*Where is nuclear propulsion deck?*"

Bob pointed. "Forward thirty frames. Down six decks. Look for signs labelled NPP or Nuclear Propulsion Plant in the Red Tile area."

. . .

O mar Muscat fiddled with the MEDWEAP and continued to torture Aaron, Vic and Ruby in their holding cell through the brig door. "How are we feeling, intruders?"

Ruby cried in pain and periodically lost consciousness.

Vic rested her head on Aaron's shoulder with her eyes closed and tried to take the pain without displaying discomfort.

Aaron sat between Vic and Ruby with his arms around them as his heart raced at one-fifty BPM.

Omar laughed, studied the MEDWEAP, and repeatedly fired on the three hostages. "What is your favorite setting? Or should I ask what is your least favorite setting?"

Aaron got directly in front of Ruby and Vic.

Omar laughed. "Let's see. We've tried AFIB. We enjoyed the PAIN setting. The NAUSEA setting was fun but messy. FLATLINE. What does that word mean? Shall we find out?"

Ruby and Vic wept as Aaron tried to hide them.

Omar pointed the weapon and flashed a wide smile.

Bang! Bang!

Omar dropped to the ground.

Thud!

Aaron yelled down the hallway. "Bob? Jack?"

Ivan Smirnov appeared in the locked doorway and looked through the bars. "Bob and Jack. Let me guess. Bob is the Navy SEAL. Jack is the skinny Muay Thai fighter. Or do I have that backwards, Comrade Webster?"

Omar lay bleeding to death on the floor.

Ivan shrugged. "I told you I had seen too much torture and death in my life. Besides, I like you guys."

Aaron squeezed the hands of Vic and Ruby.

Ivan pointed at Omar and theatrically gasped. "Oh, God. What happened? Did you witness this suicide? Nod your heads."

Aaron, Vic and Ruby nodded their heads.

Ivan placed a small, backup handgun in Omar's limp right hand. "Omar was distraught about his father's expensive, damaged yacht. He thought he was going to be blamed. He took his own life. Sadly, Omar shot himself. Twice." Ivan smiled.

"Thanks," Ruby whispered.

"You probably don't want to stare at Omar as you wait to be rescued." Ivan pulled Omar from the doorway.

Aaron, Vic and Ruby didn't answer.

"You are waiting for a rescue from my *Fight Club* friends, right?"

Ruby nodded.

Ivan smiled and pushed a twelve-pack of water bottles into the cell. "I know you are, Ruby." Ivan walked away.

M r. Bali sped towards the Sharjah Blue in the ski boat.
Chloe yelled in the wind. "Mr. Bali, I'm glad you had a life vest that could fit a spider monkey!"

Mr. Bali agreed as he approached the starboard side. "Jerome seems to be enjoying this."

Luke nodded. "Probably *too* much."

Emma pointed upwards. "Someone dropped a rope ladder."

Ryan stood up and began to reach for the ladder. "Probably Bob."

Ryan yelled over the speedboat noise. "Emma, ladies first."

"Jerome followed Emma and quickly passed her on the back side of the rope ladder."

Ryan looked at Luke. "You're next."

Luke hesitated. "Is it safe?"

Ryan yelled as a wave crashed between the ship and small boat. "No! But Ruby's in the yacht! Climb!"

Luke grabbed the rope and followed Emma.

Wham!

A rogue wave suddenly slammed against the small, ski boat's outboard engine.

"No!" Mr. Bali screamed as his engine failed.

Ryan instinctively dove for the rope ladder but missed, crashing into the Indian Ocean between the vessels.

Chloe screamed.

Lurch dove in after Ryan.

Luke turned around from the rope ladder as Emma and Jerome summited. "Do we wait?"

Brianna watched Mr. Bali's futile attempts to restart his outboard engine. "Climb, Luke! Climb!"

A my spoke into our Gulfstream ICS to Kelly, Charlotte and me. "Are you watching this? The speedboat totally stopped moving."

Charlotte agreed. "Better call them."

Amy transmitted. "Chloe? This is Shadow. What's up?"

The Sharjah Blue sped away from the inoperative speed boat.

Chloe looked at Lurch and handed him the SATCOM. "Shadow, this is Lurch.

We're dead in the water. Engine failure. Emma, Luke and Jerome made it onboard. Casper got onboard ten minutes ago. That makes eight HICSON operators plus one spider monkey with no viable egress."

I sighed and looked at Kelly. "Suggestions?"

Kelly shook her head negatively.

I looked at the expansive Indian Ocean as the ship steamed westward. "By the time we got a boat, it would be out of range, right?"

Kelly checked the MFD-2 and MFD-3. "The yacht is doing thirty knots. Quickly running out of options."

Amy keyed the microphone. "If we depart, you'll lose air support."

"All HICSON assets, this is Gettysburg."

Amy paused. "The Lincoln Skipper has been listening?"

I transmitted on SATCOM from the cockpit. "Go ahead, Sir."

"You arrange egress. Tater arranged air power."

Kelly looked at me and replied. "Copy, Sir! Thanks!"

I didn't understand. "We depart to get egress?"

Chloe transmitted on SATCOM. "Kelly?"

"Yes?"

"Mr. Bali said to go to Phuket International Airport. Taxi the Gulfstream to the River Kwai Tour Company. They will be waiting for you."

"River Kwai Tours?"

Chloe bounced between Lurch, Ryan and Brianna as the disabled ski boat nearly capsized in the Indian Ocean. "Yes, find Mr. Bali's cousin. Same last name. He will be waiting for you."

Kelly rolled into a steep turn and added power towards Phuket. "Copy."

CHAPTER FORTY-FIVE

M r Light intercepted the Murdstone boy near the Officer's Lounge. "Tony!"

"Yes, Sir."

"You look nervous."

Tony shrugged and attempted to smile. "We're taking on water and got attacked last night. I guess it's normal to be nervous."

"Have you seen any intruders?"

Tony shook his head.

"There was a small boat that pulled alongside. Did you see it?"

"No, Sir."

"You aren't lying, are you?"

"No, Sir."

Mr. Light put his arm around Tony and walked him to the deck railing. "You understand about loyalty, right Tony?"

"Yes, Sir."

Mr. Light picked up the long, stowed rope ladder and theatrically gasped. "This is soaking wet. How did that happen?"

"Rain?"

Mr. Light looked at the blue skies. "It hasn't rained all day. Try again."

Tony shrugged.

Mr. Light placed his arm around Tony Murdstone's shoulders and pointed. "Do you see that window up there?"

Tony nodded.

"That's my TSC Office. From that window, I can see about eighty percent of the deck. I saw you reeling in the rope ladder. Now, do you want to tell me why the rope is wet?"

J ack and Bob quickly found Luke and Emma with Jerome.

Bob smiled. "This is the little person?"

Jerome jumped off Emma's back and hugged Jack.

Emma whispered. "He's trained. We knew him in Idaho. Jack and Chloe brought him to Thailand years ago."

Luke carefully handed Bob explosives and sighed. "Lurch wanted you to have these. This small one is for the brig door. This large package is for the ship."

Bob nodded and accepted the package. "You look relieved."

Luke smiled. "Made me nervous carrying that package."

Jack looked around. "How did you get up to the deck from the speedboat?"

Emma whispered. "Tony Murdstone."

Bob nodded. "Tony helped us, too."

Jack looked at Bob, Luke and Emma. "Ready for some monkey business?"

Bob led the tactical primates to a dead end and explained the situation to Luke and Emma. "The passageway to the brig is continuously guarded by the Russian, Mr. Light, or Tony's dad. This ventilation ducting right here leads to their holding cell. Will Jerome go to the brig through this ducting?"

Luke shrugged. "Is there a chance Jerome could get lost? How does he actually navigate and find them?"

"He'll be a voice-guided monkey." Bob strapped explosive devices to Jerome's back. "Vic, Ruby and Aaron can hear us. We just can't see them. Are we ready to send the spider monkey?"

Luke checked his rig. "He's good. Ask Vic to call Jerome."

Bob yelled down the passageway. "Vic!"

Her faint reply echoed. "Yes?"

"Call Jerome!"

"Who?"

Aaron smiled. "Jerome's our friend."

Vic looked at Ruby. "Really?"

Ruby smiled then winced in pain. "Jerome's a good little boy. Call him."

Vic whispered into the ducting. "Jerome, come here. Come on, Jerome. Come here, boy!"

"Ooh, ooh, ooh! Ah, ah, ah!"

Jerome followed Vic's voice.

"Oh, God. This is too much. Jerome is a monkey?" Vic laughed. "I hear him coming."

"Keep calling."

"Here, Jerome. Come on, little buddy."

"Look up there at the little fingers." Vic laughed as Jerome opened the ceiling diffuser and joined the three hostages. "He's got some goodies for us."

Jerome didn't pass the explosives.

Vic begged. "Come on Jerome, give me the package."

Ruby opened her eyes and whispered. "He only barters. Give him a water bottle."

Vic smiled. "Here, buddy."

"Ooh, ooh, ooh. Ah, ah, ah."

Aaron smirked. "Plastic water bottle in exchange for the plastic explosives and detonators. God, I missed you all these years, Jerome."

"Ruby, you hold Jerome. I'm going to blow open the door latch."

Aaron covered Ruby and Jerome.

Vic set the explosive on the door lock mechanism and ran to Aaron and Ruby.

Bang!

Vic opened the door and Jerome celebrated. Vic whispered through the ducting. "Bob, we opened the door."

Bob replied. "Watch out for the Russian."

"Come on." Vic led the way. "One more gate." Vic set another explosive device. "Get down."

Bang!

Vic, Aaron and Ruby climbed a vertical ladder and opened a scuttle to find Luke, Emma, Bob and Jack waiting.

Emma smiled and gave Jerome a treat. "Nice job, Jerome."

Ruby laughed. "We're hungry, too."

Emma opened the bag of Phuket Wildlife Reserve snacks. "Help yourself."

Ruby looked inside. "Actually, I'm good."

Bob pointed aft. "There's an obscure exit at the stern. This way."

Mr. Bali repeatedly tried to unflood his ski boat engine in the high swells of the Indian Ocean. "Too much salt water. How do you say in English? *Car-Bray-Tor?*"

"Correct." Ryan nodded. "Carburetor."

"Look!" Lurch pointed to the westbound Sharjah Blue many miles away. "Something's happening."

Bang!

A limp body dropped into the sea.

Splash!

Brianna gasped. "What was that?"

"Gunshot," Lurch said.

"That was a body?" Brianna asked.

Lurch nodded.

Chloe cried. "Oh, God."

Ryan watched. "The falling person was wearing a yellow shirt. It wasn't one of us."

"Are you sure?" Chloe asked as the small ski boat rocked.

Ryan nodded. "I saw yellow."

Lurch borrowed Chloe's dry SATCOM radio. "Shadow, this is Lurch."

Amy replied from our Gulfstream. "Go ahead!"

"Did you watch the person fall into the Indian Ocean from the Sharjah Blue deck?"

I keyed the internal ICS. "Oh, God."

Charlotte looked at Amy and replied. "Negative. Kelly is on final approach into Phuket."

"No cameras watching?"

"We're sorry." Charlotte sighed in the Gulfstream weapon bay cabin. "We're too far. Too low."

Kelly finished her landing rollout into Phuket, sped down a parallel taxiway to River Kwai Tours and keyed her SATCOM radio. "We're hurrying."

"Red tile area. NPP Room." Casper tried the door latch. "Locked."

Casper continued to whisper to himself and looked in his backpack. "Explosives."

He stuck a small pack of explosives to the door latch of the Nuclear Power Propulsion Room. "Mixing nuclear power with plastic explosives. Real genius, Casper."

He ran to find shelter after triggering his ten-second timer. "Twenty feet away should be far enough."

Bang!

"I hope." Casper kept his eyes closed then felt his torso, arms and legs. "Okay, I'm still alive."

Casper ran to the Sharjah Blue NPP control terminal and attempted pre-briefed shutdown codes from House Intelligence. "1-2-3-4-5-6-7-8-9. You've *got* to be kidding me. What second-grader came up with that code?"

Casper smiled. "Nuclear core shutdown. Please confirm."

He selected *YES*.

The ship's nuclear-powered engine and screws immediately made an audible, decelerating shutdown sound.

Casper placed his second small explosive package on the control keypad, set the device for a ten-second delay, and ran from the Nuclear Power Propulsion Room.

Casper exited the room and crouched down.

Bang!

CHAPTER FORTY-SIX

"I knew my two *Fight Club* friends would come back for you. And I knew you would all choose this dark ladderwell to escape." Ivan Smirnov laughed and held his Makarov on Aaron. "I simply didn't expect a monkey."

Bob pointed his MEDWEAP at Ivan.

"If you zap me, my right index finger will constrict. My handgun will fire. No?"

Bob removed his finger from the MEDWEAP trigger and nodded.

"No more fighting, Bob." Ivan holstered his small Russian Makarov. "You and Jack are good fighters. Jack, I think you broke my jaw with that last kick."

Bob and Jack lowered their MEDWEAP's.

"There is a man named Bud Light who just killed your friend, Tony. Do not underestimate him. Bud is looking for you. Tony's father is here, but he is hiding from you. Apparently, many of you know Bud and Nuke from Idaho?"

Aaron nodded.

Jerome made a funny monkey noise.

"Ooh, ooh, ooh. Ah, ah, ah."

"It sounds like your monkey friend knows them, too." Ivan smiled. "While Russia was sending Sputnik into space with Cosmonaut Gagarin, your country was sending monkeys in the Gemini spaceships. Little monkey, your name is probably Able, no?"

Emma petted the spider monkey as it sat on Jack's shoulders. "His name is Jerome."

Ivan smiled.

Jack stood his ground. "And America *beat* Russia to the moon."

"True." Ivan nodded. "Very impressive knowledge of history, young Muay Thai fighter, with a monkey on your back. Aaron, I have a tee-time with your father in three days in Dubai. You are all very brave and loyal. You returned for the hostages. You all earned your freedom. Now, quickly go. God Speed. But don't get caught."

Bob shook Ivan's hand. "Good bye. And thank you."

The Russian smiled.

Bob continued the EVAC. Jack carried Jerome. Ruby, Vic and Aaron required the help of Luke and Emma after their painful episode with Omar Mustafa.

Emma smiled as they reached a port, aft catwalk reserved for maintenance. "Daylight."

Jack looked around. "Where's Casper?"

Ben Light tapped his father's shoulder in the Sharjah Blue TSC Office and pointed. "Dad, there's a small aircraft approaching. Ten miles out."

Mr. Light checked the radar scope. "Damn. What's our weapon status?"

"Not good. Our nuclear rods are halfway through a cool-down. The Nuclear Power Propulsion Room has been sabotaged. The Weapon Control Center room is destroyed."

Mr. Light looked at his son. "What do we have, Ben?"

"All we have are handheld MEDWEAP's and a box of EMP Grenades."

Mr. Light sighed and looked at his satellite phone. "Abby is going to kill me."

Ben watched the radar scope. "The airplane is at five miles. What should we do, Dad?"

"We'll shoot it down." Mr. Light stepped outside with his son onto a starboard platform adjacent to the bridge and TSC office.

"Dad. It's approaching! And it's a seaplane!"

Mr. Light checked his power. "What's your percentage?"

"Seventy-five."

"I'm at ninety-five. Set your weapon to FLATLINE."

"It's getting close, Dad. Probably one mile."

"Wait for your weapon to go green on Imaging Probes."

"Locked on. Now, Dad?"

Mr. Light got his green light and nodded. "Fire!"

The two generations of TSC Officers fired upon the seaplane.

Ben analyzed the flight path and smiled. "We got him."

Mr. Light fired again. "Make sure."

"Save your battery, Dad. He's going down."

Splash!

The small, two-engine seaplane smacked face-first into a rising swell and exploded on impact.

Bud and Ben high-fived.

"Good shooting, Son."

"Let's go call it in." Mr. Light's phone rang. "Speak of the devil. Abby's calling right now."

"No!" Emma Kernan cried on the port, aft catwalk of the crippled, eight-hundred-foot, luxury yacht. "Oh, God!"

Jack held his older sister. "Don't look."

"Should we swim to them?" Ruby asked while holding Jerome.

Luke wiped a tear. "I don't think it was survivable."

Bob agreed. "There's no way it was survivable. Unfortunately."

Jack watched the high swells and crashing waves gradually sink the twisted seaplane parts.

Vic cried. "What do we do now?"

Casper arrived to the catwalk, pointed at the airplane crash site and non-verbally inquired with open hands.

Bob explained to his computer-whiz operator. "They got shot down."

Casper sighed, pointed to his watch, and signaled number three with his fingers.

Jack watched. "Three what?"

Bob's eyes widened. "Three minutes."

Casper nodded and simulated a dive.

Bob looked at the Indian Ocean below. "The Sharjah Blue will explode in three minutes."

"No way." Luke looked down to the Indian Ocean from the catwalk. "I'm not jumping."

President Walker spun her seat to watch appreciative Homelanders dance and celebrate on Pennsylvania Avenue in front of the White House. "Bud, are you there?"

Bud found a suitable place to stand on the Sharjah Blue deck for a satellite phone call. "Yes, Mrs. President."

"Tell me you have good news, Bud."

No response.

"Okay, pass the bad news."

Mr. Light sighed. "The Sharjah Blue is badly damaged. We've lost propulsion, Ma'am."

"How?"

"Sabotage."

"Who's on the ship right now?"

Mr. Light paused to think. "Ben, Ivan, Nuke and myself."

President Walker paused. "Where's Tony?"

"I had to let Tony go."

"And Omar Muscat?"

"Ivan found him with a handgun in his hand. Suicide."

"The new bridge team from Singapore?"

"Dead."

"Mustafa's not going to be happy."

"Concur."

President Walker smiled. "I have good news for you, Bud. There is a twin-engine seaplane that took off one hour ago from a small Seaplane base in Singapore. I've sent the top nuclear propulsion expert from Norfolk Navy Shipyards, TSC reinforcements, and the finest civilian shipboard bridge and repair team in the world to navigate and shore up the Sharjah Blue."

Mr. Light froze.

"Bud?"

No response.

"Bud, did you copy the information about the inbound crew?"

Mr. Light watched the remaining seaplane wreckage surf the violent swells of the Indian Ocean. "I'll keep my eyes peeled for them."

"Thanks, Bud. It looks like we may get the Sharjah Blue home in time for the Muscat girl's Sweet Sixteen Birthday Party after all."

"Goodbye, Ma'am."

Click!

Mr. Light sighed and stowed his satellite phone in his TSC jacket and stared out to sea. "President Walker said the twin-engine seaplane was a repair crew."

No response.

"Ben, did you hear me?"

Mr. Light turned around. "Murdstone! I mean Nuke! Where have you been?"

Mr. Murdstone shrugged.

Mr. Light wiped his brow. "Have you seen Tony?"

No response.

"Nuke, have you been with your son, Tony?"

"You let him go. That's what you told Abby on the phone, right?"

"Did I say that? You misunderstood."

Mr. Murdstone charged at his old CABESA Initiative Idaho cohort and leaned him back over the railing. "You killed my son. Now, I'm going to kill you, Bud!"

Mr. Light was pushed backwards and struggled to breathe. "Stop it. I didn't kill Tony. Stop imagining things." Mr. Light gasped for air. "That's a conspiracy theory! Stop it, Nuke!"

Mr. Murdstone squeezed Mr. Light's neck and pushed. Harder and harder.

"You're choking me, Nuke."

CHAPTER FORTY-SEVEN

Ruby held Luke's hand. "Sixty feet is survivable, Luke. This is only forty. Don't worry."

Bob agreed. "Seventy is bad. Forty is easy. Strong, crossed straight legs, hands over your neck and face, piece of cake!"

Jack stepped to the edge holding Jerome. "I'm going with Jerome. I don't feel comfortable throwing him in. If I try to shed him on the way down, he won't shed."

Ruby nodded. "Tough to shed a spider monkey. Just hold him all the way down."

Luke visibly trembled.

Vic looked at the water and approached the edge with her titanium legs. "I'm going first." Vic looked at Casper and held his hand. "Ready to jump with me?"

Casper nodded.

They leapt.

Splash!

Vic looked up. "It's easy. Hurts for a second! Cover your face! Not bad!"

Jack jumped with Jerome.

Splash!

Jerome made monkey noises floating on the Indian Ocean surface.

"He didn't bite me!" Jack laughed. "But he pulled out some of my hair!"

Bob looked at Aaron. "Ready dude?"

Aaron nodded and they quickly jumped.

Splash!

Bob yelled. "Luke! It's a cakewalk!"

Luke's hands and legs trembled. His teeth chattered.

Ruby held Emma's hand. "Ready Emma?"

Emma nodded. Ruby held Luke's hand. "The three of us are jumping, buddy."

Bang!

A gunshot rang out from the Sharjah Blue deck.

Ruby squeezed Emma and Luke's hands. "That gunshot means it's time to jump, Luke."

Luke's fear took over. "No."

Emma yelled. "Luke, we're jumping!"

Aaron swam towards Vic, Bob and Casper. "Gunshot?"

Bob nodded. "Luke, someone is shooting! The ship is going to explode! Jump!"

"You both go." Luke trembled. "I'm staying."

Ruby whispered calmly. "We all jump. Now!"

Luke stepped back and tried to release Ruby's grip. "Go."

Vic yelled. "Come one, Luke! The water is warm!"

"Warm?" Luke's lips trembled. "Shh-sha-sharks."

Casper pointed at his watch, splashed and let out a terrifying scream. "Luke! Jump!"

Casper's extremely rare verbalization startled Luke.

Kaboom!

Ruby and Emma grabbed Luke's hands firmly and forcefully jumped with him as the ship's entire forward hull exploded.

The three entered the sea together foot-first.

Splash!

A aron, Casper, Bob and Jack removed their tactical floatation vests and helped Vic, Emma, Luke and Ruby.

Luke handed one of the vests back to Jack. "I can swim."

Jack insisted. "Take it, Luke. Your hands are still shaking, buddy."

Luke declined. "I can swim fine. I just can't jump. You have a Jerome on your shoulders. You need it."

Bob instructed the group to form a circle. "Alternate vest wearers with non-vest wearers. Arms over shoulders. Feet in the center of our circle. Any sharks get kicked in the face and we all stick together."

Luke got into position. "Sharks are in the Indian Ocean?"

Bob nodded.

"Great whites?"

Bob shook his head. "Mostly just tiger sharks."

"Okay." Luke treaded water. "Just tiger sharks. Those are small. Under four feet. Like a nurse shark. Or like a sand shark. Right?"

Bob smiled. "Luke, don't think about it. If you get bumped, close your eyes and start kicking."

Luke nodded and spit out some salt water.

Ruby and Emma started to cry as the Sharjah Blue quickly sank.

Vic comforted them. "You guys did good. We saved an American aircraft carrier. Don't cry."

Ruby cried. "The crash! That was the replacement airplane. Those were our friends."

"You're right! I lost my sister. I lost Amy!" Emma began to scream and sob loudly. "My twin sister was probably on that seaplane. Poor Amy! poor Grace!" Emma began to slur her words. "Poor Kelly! And little Chloe. Or was Charlotte on the plane? Oh, God! Who was on the seaplane? Who? Who was on the seaplane? Tell me now! I need to know who was on the plane! Tell me!"

Bob swam behind Emma and held her. "She's going into shock."

Emma began to hyperventilate.

Bob kept the high seas from disrupting her breath.

Jack looked around. "What's that noise?"

Aaron swam in silence. "A boat?"

Luke smiled. "A ski boat."

Ruby listened carefully. "Mr. Bali probably got his boat engine unflooded."

Jack heard a familiar voice. "Over there."

"Not good." Bob looked at Jack. "The Russian."

Ivan Smirnov, Mr. Light, and Ben Light drove up to the swimmers in a $3.8 million Cigarette 59 Tirranna speed boat and retarded the throttle to idle. "Comrades!"

Ben saw his Peaksville High School 2020 alumni. "Is Emma in shock?"

Bob nodded and kept her stable.

"Dad, we should help." Ben threw some plastic water bottles into the circle.

"Help?" Mr. Light stood and pointed a MEDWEAP at the swimmers as Mustafa Muscat's multi-billion dollar Sharjah Blue yacht sank. "I have a better idea."

Ivan placed his hand on the MEDWEAP. "Bud. Let's just leave. We survive with dignity."

Mr. Light pointed the MEDWEAP at Jerome on Jack's back. "Is that Jerome?"

Ivan laughed. "Bud, that's just a monkey. This is unnecessary, my friend. Ben, take us to Kuala Lumpur. If they survive the sharks, they deserve to live."

Mr. Light pointed the MEDWEAP at his son. "Don't add power, Ben."

"Woah!" Ben raised his hands from the jet boat controls. "Chill, Dad."

Suddenly, Mr. Light collapsed on the Tirranna deck.

"Dad?"

The old Russian instinctively scanned the sky as the Sharjah Blue's stern dramatically submerged in the distance.

Jack pointed. "A jet!"

Ivan strapped Mr. Light's limp body into a seat and nodded to Ben. "Malaysia, Ben. Quickly." Ben added fuel as the six outboard engines roared.

Bob held Emma's ears as the jet approached. "Cover your ears everyone!"

Zoom!

The silently-approaching USAF F-35 Lightning II overflew the Cigarette 59 Tirranna at fifty feet and eight hundred miles per hour. It was enclosed in a vapor sphere from exceeding the sound barrier.

BOOM!

The delayed-reaction sonic boom trailing the jet broke the windscreen of the Tirranna and gave everyone a healthy dose of temporary tinnitus followed by man-made sea spray.

Ruby removed her hands from her ears. "What was that?"

"*Who* was that?" Luke asked.

Aaron looked up. "Tater?"

"That was an F-35." Bob held Emma tightly in the high swells. "Tater flies Hornets."

Vic agreed. "That was USAF paint."

Still trembling from the trauma, Emma looked up at the airplane as it initiated a celebratory zoom climb to twenty-thousand feet and whispered in Bob's ear. "F-35? USAF? Was that Max Burns?" Emma began to yell frantically. "Max! Come back! I know it's you, Max! Help us, Max!"

"Who is Max Burns?" Bob asked holding Emma tightly.

Ruby whispered. "Emma's ex-boyfriend."

Luke shook his head. "Why would Max save us?"

Emma's face trembled as she squeezed Bob's shoulders tightly. "Max changed. He helped. Max came back to help. Max Burns helped."

Ruby stroked Emma's hair. "It's okay now, Emma. Everything is okay."

CHAPTER FORTY-EIGHT

B ob looked at his watch as Emma snored on his torso with rapid breaths. "It's been thirty minutes. I'm worried about Emma. Do we have any water left?"

No response.

Ruby whispered. "Emma spilled the last one before she fell asleep."

"Not good," Bob said.

Jack managed to get Jerome to finally relax. "It feels like three hours. This spider monkey is definitely not a sea-worthy animal."

Vic studied the sky. "The F-35 is still circling. Way up there. I can hear it."

Bob nodded. "That's a good sign."

Luke treaded water in the circle. "Ruby, stop kicking me."

Ruby looked at Casper with wide eyes.

Casper looked down and spoke. "Kick."

Aaron didn't understand. "We *are* kicking. To swim."

Vic looked down. "Casper means *kick*! A striped shark!"

The circle of shipwreck survivors began to connect their heels onto the heads of large tiger sharks.

"What!" Emma woke up and clawed Bob's face and neck. "No! No! No! No!"

Bob unsheathed his SEAL Pup knife and eyed one of the tiger sharks.

Vic grabbed Bob's elbow. "Bob, the shark blood might make it worse." Vic removed a titanium leg and handed it to Bob. "Try this."

Aaron held Emma while Bob's Navy SEAL training went into action.

Jack pointed as he kicked the apex-level predators. "Look!"

A seaplane approached from the east.

Emma opened her eyes and panicked. "Not again! Not again! Don't crash! Don't crash!"

Jack looked at his sister. "Hold her tight, Aaron."

Bob continued to fight the sharks with Vic's leg. "Everyone stay in the circle."

The seaplane set up for a moderate wind, moderate swell landing parallel to the swells. The pilot expertly plow-taxied to the swimmers utilizing high power and maximum up elevator to avoid digging the nose in the ocean.

Ruby watched the approaching twin-engine tour plane from Phuket. "Please be our friends."

The cabin door opened and Kelly yelled. "I have room for seven humans, one spider monkey, and one gorilla!"

The sharks dispersed.

"Thanks." Bob handed Vic her leg back and quickly began pulling Emma to the airplane's large port float.

I poked my head outside with Amy and Charlotte and threw them a rope. "Sorry we're late!"

"I'm so happy!" Ruby cried and paddled.

"Alive." Emma trembled and slurred her speech. "Amy's alive. You're alive. Alive."

Amy helped her twin board the plane. "Come on, Emma. We're okay, now."

Bob explained to the seaplane crew. "A different seaplane was shot down before the Sharjah Blue sunk. Amy, hold your sister. She needs rest and love."

Jerome climbed inside and found food intended for the swimmers.

"Ooh, ooh, ooh! Ah, ah, ah!"

I laughed. "Jerome, manners!"

Jack boarded the seaplane. "Mr. Bali, Chloe, Ryan, Lurch and Bree are in the ski boat somewhere."

"Enroute to Phuket!" Charlotte said. "Help just arrived for them."

I pulled Aaron into the airplane and hugged him tightly. "We did it, Aaron."

Aaron kissed me and smiled. "Yes, we did, Gracie."

Kelly did a walk-around on the floats then climbed inside. "We got everyone, right? Humans? Spider monkeys?" Kelly looked at Bob. "Gorillas?"

"I missed you in the ocean, Kelly." Bob smiled. "As a matter of fact, I wished you were with us when the tiger sharks attacked."

"Ha!" Kelly walked to the cockpit for takeoff. "Good one, Gorilla."

I slapped Bob's knee. "Are we finished?"

"Not yet, Gracie." Bob smiled. "Not yet."

EPILOGUE

Dear Reader,
     I hope you enjoyed reading
EXILE - Book #2 of FLATLINE FREQUENCY.
Please leave a POSITIVE REVIEW on AMAZON!

Please don't miss
     the other episodes in the
FLATLINE FREQUENCY series:
EPIPHANY - Book #1
EXOSPHERE - Book #3
Epiphany was Local!
Exile was Global!
Exosphere will be Out of this World!
Expected Release Date: June 2020.

Thank you,
     K.D. Buster